# EARTHKEEPER
## Awakening at Spider Rock

### Ethan Foxx

KNOWING
OWL

**Knowing Owl Publications**
**Glendale, AZ**

www.EthanFoxx.com

www.Facebook.com/Earthkeeper

**ISBN** SBN-13:978-0-9893455-1-4

To Mom and Dad,

Thank you for your encouragement and for always reassuring me how loved and valued I am. I am thankful to have been born to such loving parents and blessed to have been bestowed with the best traits and talents of you both combined.

A very special thanks and acknowledgment to my best friend and brother, Matt, and to my children, Jonny, Korey, Courtney, Christian, Kai, and Kiran. My appreciation also to Indio and Chris Cheisl for the openness and guidance that contributed to my vision for this book.

And to our Mother Earth, I know beyond any doubt you are a living being. You deserve much better from us.

# Chapter One

A thunderstorm had formed over the Arizona plateau by the time Eric Demeter turned north at Winslow and entered the vast desert of the Navajo reservation. A creepy ghost highway surrounded the reach of the headlights. There was blackness ahead, and the faint glow of the small town rapidly faded behind him. Into the darkness he drove for nearly an hour without seeing the lights of any other car or dwelling.

The storm increased. Eric tensed in an effort to hold the truck straight against the wind. With each branching flash of lightning, he could make out oddly shaped mountains silhouetted against the turbulent sky. Their monstrous shapes stood tall and close to the road, threatening to plunge down at any moment to grab hold of him as he drove past. The mountains gave way and the winding road straightened and led him into an expansive valley. The flickering reflectors and dashed lines of paint that divided the razor-straight road hypnotized him as they blurred by.

Startled by movement in the corner of his eye, Eric jerked his awareness to his driver-side window. There was nothing; just his faint reflection on the glass, cast by the dimly lit controls on his dashboard. He returned his gaze to the road ahead. Confused, he snapped his head to look right at what he thought was a man running along the passenger side of the truck in the darkness beyond the glass. He glanced at the speedometer. "Sixty-five...? Who could run...?" He looked back at the window and saw no one. "Phew! I gotta get some sleep," he mumbled.

Somewhere around 3:00 AM a few drops of precipitation splashed against the windshield. Seconds later, a sudden sheet of rain fell and distorted his view of the road ahead. Eric engaged the wipers, but they were nearly useless, having rotted for so long in neglect in the hot Phoenix sun. He leaned forward, close against the steering wheel, and stared ahead wide-eyed as he cautiously pressed on.

Warily searching the road ahead, he screeched to a panicked stop, just short of colliding with an unkempt horse that had wandered onto the road. The horse didn't jolt, as if this sort of thing happened to him all the time. It just turned and looked at Eric seeming to say, *Hey, I'm walkin' here*!

If only Eric had been able to remain so calm. He sighed heavily then began to giggle as he maneuvered around the steadfast equine. His heart pounded against his chest for a long while after the near miss.

Exhausted, he wondered if he had better stop and get a room as he drove through the small town of Chinle; but by then the rain had stopped, and the outpost disappeared behind him faster than he could decide. He continued north for another forty minutes.

Carefully counting the mile markers, Eric anticipated his turnoff for the dirt road that would take him west. His headlights reflected off of a gleaming circular shape. Stopping in the middle of the lonely road, Eric dug a large metal flashlight from the pack in the seat next to him. There it was, just as Mike had described, a paper plate marked with a black arrow and the word "glyphs" tacked to the fence post.

He turned onto the rough trail and the truck began to bounce and shake. Not too far from the paved highway, the trail forked. Using his flashlight, Eric carefully reviewed the directions Mike had scrawled out for him, but they made no mention of the split. "Now what?" he mumbled to no one. He stuck his head out the window and looked around, flashing his light in all directions.

Off the road to his right was a ramshackle old hogan: an octagonal, traditional Navajo home. The east-facing door was boarded shut and the dilapidated roof had partially caved in. Eric got out of the truck, inexplicably drawn to investigate the old dwelling.

Small rocks crunched under his clumsy feet. As he neared the hogan, he heard the faint sound of growling. He nervously swung the beam of his flashlight from left to right to locate the source of the sound. The blackness beyond his torch's reach formed an impenetrable wall that the light seemed to bounce off of. He slowed and his body tensed in an effort to silence his steps. He puffed quiet, shallow breaths and could feel his pulse throbbing in his ears. He located the growling coming from within the old structure. The noise intensified into moaning and shrieking that sounded unlike any animal he had ever heard. Shining his light through the spaces between the cedar logs, he could make out something thrashing around on the floor inside. Terror washed over him.

Eric sprinted back to his truck and raced down the road that forked right. The hogan vanished in a cloud of dust behind him. His camping gear slammed around violently in the back of his truck as it bounced over the rough road. He looked down from the rearview mirror to the road. Something suddenly appeared in the middle of the road ahead. He hurried to smash down the brake pedal.

He was unsure what blocked the road in front of him, a coyote or a wolf; but it was huge, and he was certain there was no way he could stop in time. The unyielding beast stared directly at Eric as the truck skidded closer. Eric cranked the steering wheel. Spinning nearly 180 degrees, the truck slid over the animal with a resounding thud that could be felt through the floorboard.

Idling forward, Eric watched his mirrors for any sign of the animal, but it appeared to have vanished.

"Forget this," he muttered. "This can't be happening." He made a hasty decision to head back to Chinle, get a motel room, and put this crazy night to bed. He focused intently as he drove cautiously back to the main road.

"Good God!" he exclaimed, as something slammed heavily into the back of his truck. The cab window behind him was forced open and something, or someone, grabbed him around the throat.

He struggled to pry the hand from his neck while negotiating the trail as it dipped into a boulder riddled arroyo.

On the steep climb out of the wash, Eric floored the gas pedal. As his truck shot forward his attacker was thrown from the truck bed. He blazed as fast as he could down the washboard trail, past the eerie hogan. He watched it pass by his left, when from the corner of his eye, he spied a man running up behind him and gaining. Eric looked at the speedometer; he was pushing thirty-five miles per hour. He looked back out the window. It was a dead heat; the man was right with him.

He wore no clothes, only a loin cloth; his visage fierce and terrifying. Empty, black eyes gleamed from deep settings in his white-painted face. His raven hair was long and matted. The many heavy necklaces and charms around his neck jostled wildly as he ran. A tattered teddy bear was strapped tightly to the man's back with sinuous cordage that had worn deep into the blistered skin around his ribs and chest.

Eric smashed the accelerator to the floor. His truck rattled down the rough road, pitching and sliding in the loose patches of rock and sand. His speed gradually increased: forty, forty-five miles per hour. The ghoulish man stayed with him, inching closer to the driver's side window as he ran.

Eric spun the wheel hard right, then left, sliding sideways onto the main highway. His speed gained dramatically on the asphalt: fifty, fifty-five, now sixty. The sinister man was still there, keeping pace with the accelerating truck. Suddenly he plunged his hands through the open window and grabbed the wheel. Tires squealing, Eric fought to keep the truck from pitching and rolling over.

His pursuer snarled and growled, teeth gnashing. Less than an arms' length away now, Eric could see him more clearly. He was ghastly and seemed barely human. Eric noticed a strange necklace hanging from the man's neck. Its charms were several small fingers and a woman's shriveled breast strung on a cord of sinew. They wrestled for the wheel until Eric reached desperately for his Maglite and smashed the specter's hands.

Eric watched the tumbling man shrink away in his mirror as the truck sped away toward town. Hands trembling and sapped of

4

strength, Eric's fingers loosely controlled the wheel. To still his fluttering heart, he focused on controlling his breathing.

The first signs of the sun teased the sky from deep below the horizon. Eric shivered as the bitter wind thundered throughout the cab, the low resounding hum pounding in his ears. Weakened by the event, he struggled with the stiff crank to close the window. He never eased off the gas as he raced down the highway as fast as he could manage, continuously checking his mirrors—and not for the Highway Patrol. If only there was a cop around to slap a heaping dose of reality across his face.

It was nearly daybreak when Eric pulled into the Best Western in Chinle. The huge parking lot was mostly empty. Still shaken, he bolted from his truck to the office and flung the door open. Heavy bells clanged against the glass door as it opened and closed.

Waiting to be helped, he fidgeted nervously, tapping quick rhythms on the counter. Shivering, he spun through the squeaky postcard display to distract his thoughts. Among the postcards, he spied one that pictured a towering spire of red rock and felt curiously comforted. From a solid base at the floor of a deep canyon, it forked midway into two rising columns. One seemed to be a couple of hundred feet taller than the other. Reading the reverse of the card he learned the awesome 800-foot monolith was Spider Rock, a sacred landmark linked with the creation mythologies of both the Navajo and Hopi peoples.

Finally, a round-faced Navajo woman peered out from a small room behind the counter and lumbered out to greet him. She seemed leery. It was straight business, no small talk. She suspiciously took in all of Eric's nervous behaviors, paying particular attention to his trembling hand as she gave him the key to his room. She then used a map to direct him to his room.

Outside, Eric watched over his shoulder cautiously as he leaned in to retrieve his pack from the truck. He hurried to the stairs and gripped the cold steel rail to hoist his exhausted body upward. At the top he surveyed his surroundings. He glanced across the parking lot, noting a restaurant and pool in the center of the grounds. The complex was framed by three two-story buildings arranged in the shape of a U. His room was in the middle of the first building, just feet from the stairs.

Immediately upon entering the room, Eric turned on the light and hurried to shut and bolt and chain the door. He slid the heavy drapes closed, ensuring through several attempts to leave no gap to be seen through. He switched on the TV before turning out the light and falling onto the stiff bed.

By the pale light of the television, Eric stared at the phone for several minutes. He labored with whether or not to report to the police what had happened. But who would believe him? He could hardly believe it himself. For the last hour he had fought to convince himself that the whole episode was a delusion brought on by lack of sleep, and though deep down he knew the explanation was incorrect, it was logically the most plausible.

His body was starved for rest. He convinced himself that if he called the authorities now, he would be up for hours answering questions and he needed to get some sleep. He went to the bathroom and dug out his toothbrush to prepare for bed. Leaning over the sink in the darkened room, he scrubbed his teeth. He consciously avoided looking into the mirror, mere inches from his face. He had always avoided mirrors in the dark, preferring not to acknowledge them, the same as he had always denied the dreadful feelings they aroused.

Exhausted, Eric slid under the covers where he only tossed and turned. It was more like a concrete slab than a bed. He kicked his feet wildly in an attempt to free his lower half from the sheets that were tucked snuggly under the mattress, binding him to the bed. He struggled hard to find comfort, and even harder to settle down for sleep.

The TV was no help in distracting his thoughts. The program was a documentary on schizophrenia with a young man explaining his disorder. "You can say it's all just happening in my mind, but when a sixty-foot tall demon is stomping up the street towards you, it's real—as real as anything you've ever seen."

Eric wondered if he, too, was losing control of his mind. "What the hell am I doing here?" he grumbled aloud as he scanned the details of his hotel room, overdone with Southwest decor. He wasn't one for adventure. He hated surprises. He feared change.

He maintained a strict system of consistency in his attempt to control his experiences.

He thought back to how, just two nights earlier, he was home spending his evening as always in front of the TV, blinking through each channel until some image or word caught his attention as useful information. He often excused his odd quirk as passive research, but the truth was that he found more amusement in the way random snippets of dialogue seemed to stream together. Sometimes it even seemed as though messages found their way to him in this way, but he could see through his narcissism enough to know that that was as absurd a notion as his sometimes thinking songs on the radio were being played just for him.

That night at home, he had scoffed at a program where paranormal researchers investigated demonic possessions, and then resumed flashing through the channels, paying keen attention to the audio fragments that blipped with each press of the button. Click: *"Were you or a loved one exposed to..."* Click: *"Another day of violence between opposing religious factions..."* Click: *"Open your eyes..."* Click: *"It's hurt people that hurt people..."* Click: *The ancients knew..."* Click: *"One hero would unlock the power to change the world..."* Click: Eric finally landed on a documentary about the tepuis of Venezuela: incredibly steep mesas rising high above the clouds like islands in the sky, each with its own unique ecosystem.

*What a coincidence*, he thought, having just learned about the tepuis from an acquaintance, an anthropologist who had recently departed on a trip to South America to study the spiritual cosmology and shamanic practices of various Indian communities. Eric leaned back comfortably, and within minutes was dozing off, lulled by the droning commentary.

Eric had always found it difficult to be at ease with the eeriness of nighttime. He thought often how the blue glow of his television and the sounds blaring out were his modern-day equivalent of the fire and drums once used to ward off beasts in the night. Additionally, he had become habituated to exhausting himself this way each night as a method to delay and shorten the nagging chatter in his mind that kept him from rest the second his head hit the pillow.

He remembered turning off the TV and tiredly tossing the remote onto the couch that night. He had just shut off the lights when suddenly terror gripped him. In the dark, his mind conjured up shadowy figures with gnashing teeth. His heart had pounded painfully as a sense of presence surrounded him. His knees buckled under the weight of what felt like a ravenous predator leaping onto his back and burrowing into his neck at the base of his skull. *It's all in your mind*, he assured himself as he had hurried toward his room.

Each night he would race down the hall in the dark, closing the door quickly behind him. Perhaps it was being alone, or the vacuum of his sparsely furnished house that caused such feelings of dread, but the anxiety always seemed to cease the second he enclosed himself in his small, square bedroom. Somehow, in the smaller space, he found it easier to shut out the fearsome thoughts. But this night it had been different. As he lay there he continued to see flashes of gnashing teeth. His chest grew tight and ached, and his breathing became difficult.

He recalled a memory or a dream he had buried away many years earlier of waking late one night as a young boy, unable to move. Lying on his side, facing the window, he had gazed into the large, reflective eyes of a luminous figure peering in through the part in the curtains.

His awareness snapped back to his uncomfortable motel bed and his tired, sore body. He lay on his back staring at the ceiling. Spattered lumps of plaster had been left by the builders long ago, which began to resemble scowling faces. "I've gone mad," Eric moaned. "I've really done it."

He shrugged it off, convincing himself that crazy people don't know they are crazy. Shutting his eyes tightly, Eric forced his concentration on a smaller universe and happier thoughts and places.

Eric had finally begun to drift toward sleep when a sudden, tremendous pounding on the door jolted him from the bed. Staying low he crept to the window and parted the drapes enough to peek out. There was no one there.

He remained still, his ears twitching as they reached to connect to any sound. Just then, he was startled by a rhythmic stomping on the roof. Eric jerked his head toward the ceiling as the heavy footsteps raced away, then he cautiously peered back out the window.

Eric's tired eyes almost missed the movement, but he was startled at what he saw. Racing across the rooftop of the adjacent second building was the ghoulish man. Without pause, he leapt gracefully from the second building to the roof of the third and stopped directly across from Eric's room. He crouched low as if preparing to pounce. Perched on the very edge of the roof, he glared at Eric from across the parking lot.

Eric felt as though the curtains were transparent, that the man could see right through them. He felt that if the man chose, nothing could stop him from flying across the parking lot, crashing through the window, and taking him down in an instant. He held his breath in awed silence. People in numerous rooms had obviously heard the noise on the roof and peeked out their windows; some poked their heads out their doors, but no one saw the man on the roof.

Just as the sun's blinding light popped above the horizon, the man shot up to his feet and ran the rest of the way across the roof. Defying gravity, he ran straight down the vertical wall and disappeared around the curve in the street. Eric fell across the bed and was almost instantly asleep.

# Chapter Two

"*Beep Beep.*"

Eric slowly awoke to the classic sounds of a Roadrunner cartoon. He strained to open one eye in time to watch the adversarial coyote guzzle down an entire jar of muscle-building supplements. The coyote instantly grew enormous leg muscles and began to chase the roadrunner. Their legs were like blurred wheels as they sped down the highway.

That familiar, panicked feeling consumed him. The skeptic in him wanted to insist, as it had in every uncomfortable event in his life, that all of this, even the coincidental cartoon, was some horrible dream. But he just could not wrap his intellect around what had happened. He reviewed it in his mind. He remembered every detail, and was particularly disturbed by the little fingers on the necklace.

The fingers were small and curved, just like baby Evan's were. Eric flashed back and remembered the way his son would fall asleep curled into a ball against his chest; the way his moist breath would wet his shirt as he slept. Mostly he remembered the way the baby's fingers, with their tiny fingernails, would wrap securely around his finger and not let go.

Tiny…everything in his memories of Evan seemed so tiny and delicate; even his cries; even his casket. Eric lay motionless in the bed, staring at the ceiling. A cold, single tear rolled sideways down his cheek and into his ear.

Funny how one thought leads to another. A picture of the grizzly necklace he had seen around the neck of the eerie specter from the night before formed in his mind, and he was appalled. Who would do such a thing, and why? Who were the victims? He revisited the thought of calling the police, but again wavered. He didn't know what to do. The only thing he knew for sure was that he was terrified.

"What have I gotten myself into?" he asked aloud. "What the hell am I even doing here?"

It must have all been a matter of wrong place, at the wrong time. He tried to reassure himself that it was a unique occurrence, and the last of its kind, but deep inside, he feared it all might be connected with the fearful visions of gnashing teeth and shadowy figures he had been experiencing for the past few nights.

The clock read 10:13 AM. Eric rose from the bed and stumbled about like a wobbly, newborn foal. He staggered into the bathroom, rubbing the crust from his eyes, and went about his morning routine, beginning with a hot shower.

Through the small bathroom window above the shower he could see the towering light poles of a sports field, and assumed it was the local high school. Ravens glided gracefully over the field, dipping and diving in perfectly synchronized pairs. Throughout his shower he watched them soar against the bright blue sky. It was an appreciated distraction. He closed his eyes and tilted his head to feel the soothing hot water pulsing against his scalp before running down his back. Startled by a loud thud on the window, Eric's eyes shot opened to see a large, iridescent raven that had slammed into the glass. Fluttering against the pane, the bird's cold black eyes looked menacingly through the window at him for a moment before it flew away.

Eric dressed himself in faded jeans and a thin black tee shirt with cracked white lettering that read, *Oh no, not another learning experience*. He packed his bag and poked his head out his motel-room door. Cautiously he looked around the full parking lot and across the rooftops before heading out to load his truck.

Until he caught scent of the busy restaurant, he hadn't realized he was hungry. He walked to his truck and circled it, inspecting for damage. There was no sign of blood or fur from the animal he had hit; no dents or scrapes. Everything checked out.

The motel desk clerk was busy. Eric took the time to wander the lobby. He hadn't really noticed when he had checked in, but there was a good-sized gift shop attached to the office. There were all sorts of Navajo goods for sale: silver and turquoise jewelry, rugs, baskets, sand paintings, dreamcatchers, and lots of photographic prints of the world-renowned, majestic landscapes of the high Arizona desert.

A nasally, guttural voice announced, "I can help you, sir."

Eric stepped toward the counter.

The short, barrel-chested Navajo clerk was friendly but reserved and avoided prolonged eye contact. His thick, graying hair was cut short in a way that lent a square shape to his large head. He wore square, wire-framed glasses and a silver, turquoise-laden watch.

Handing over the room keys, Eric asked, "Where is Spider Rock?"

The clerk casually pointed, "Oh it's right down the road there, not far." He continued, "Canyon de Chelly, it's just right there."

"Is the food over there any good?" Eric asked, nodding toward the restaurant.

"Mmm-hmm," the clerk answered, handing Eric a pen and sliding over the paperwork for a signature. "It's that or the Burger King."

Eric wanted badly to talk to somebody about what he had experienced, but didn't know quite how to begin. "Did anybody complain about anything strange around here early this morning; some loud banging or anything?"

Shaking his head, the clerk looked away. "Hmm-mmm."

"Alright then, thanks," Eric said, turning for the door.

Near the exit was a revolving display rack of paperback books, most of them by Louis L'Amour. There were also several books set around the Navajo Nation, by Tony Hillerman. One title caught Eric's eye. "*Skinwalkers?*" he called out to the clerk, holding up the book. "What's that about?"

The twisted expression on the clerk's face was as if Eric had uttered an obscenity. He shook his head and replied, "I wouldn't know."

Eric walked across the lot to the restaurant and was seated right away, even though the place was busy. Most of the patrons were Navajos, residents of Chinle and outlying areas. They were in good spirits, greeting one another and sharing stories and laughs in both English and their native language.

He felt out of place and alone. It was surely all in his head, but he felt judged and guilty, strangely taking on personal feelings of remorse for the historical plight of American Indians, something he had never really had any thoughts or opinions on. The guilt made him feel awkward and exposed. For fear of meeting eyes with anyone, he avoided looking around the restaurant too much, as he would have done ordinarily.

Eric's unintentional glance caught the waitress's attention. Coffee pot in hand, she hurried over to him. She was beautiful, young and slender, with a shiny, black braid dangling the full length of her back. "How you doin'?" she asked. "Ready to order?"

His voice jumped up in pitch, and with a strained overfriendliness he answered, "Um, yes, thanks…you. Eh-hem, thank you." Pointing at a simple bacon, egg, and toast morning special combination on the menu he squeaked, "I'll just have this, please. And a coke, thanks."

"Pepsi okay?"

"Even better," Eric smiled.

"Sounds good," she said smiling, and walked away.

Above the clatter of plates and silverware and conversations in English and Navajo, Eric heard a raucous group of European tourists. Amused, he thought to himself, *Just my luck; all these people and the only other whites aren't even American.*

It was funny, Eric thought, how he was the one feeling so out of sorts. By the looks of them, they weren't even from this time period, or reality. The tourists were dressed in hokey, western clothes, looking like extras in an old Gene Autry film: ridiculously

13

large cowboy hats, colorful scarves knotted around their necks, and all of them wearing cowboy boots.

Although he didn't understand their language, he listened intently to their conversation where intermittently he could decipher words like *cowboy* and *John Wayne*. He couldn't help chuckling at the way they emphatically said it, "*John Wayne.*" It was strange that no one but Eric really seemed to give them a second thought; that was until he caught the glance of a large Indian fellow sitting just beyond them.

He caught Eric's eye and he flashed a sly smirk. He was different from the other Navajos in both the way he looked and carried himself. Although the man was seated, Eric concluded just by the size of his head and hands that he was gigantic. He had large, strong facial features: chiseled nose and cheekbones, and a jaw that looked like it could withstand a solid whack with a two-by-four. He wore his dark, slightly graying hair unbound, but shorter on the sides, just covering his ears. A thick, bone choker necklace was tied tightly around his neck, and silver charms dangled from multiple holes in both ears. Over a gray, sleeveless tee shirt he wore an unbuttoned denim shirt with frayed, torn off sleeves. He wore his shirt like a vest to show off the tattoos of armbands with eagle feathers, buffalo skulls, and medicine wheels that adorned his massive, but not defined arms.

Eric looked away and began fidgeting with sugar packets. The view from the restaurant window didn't seem like much, just a narrow two-lane road with its occasional driver passing by, and across the way, a small housing area partly obscured by gnarled trees. Further up the road on the left was another motel, which, at least from here, seemed a bit nicer.

Most of the morning breakfast crowd had cleared out by the time Eric's food arrived. He snatched up a piece of bacon and bit into it.

"Do you need anything else?" asked the waitress, her energy level much less now than when she first helped him.

"Mmm, no thank you," replied Eric, stretching the rubbery bacon from his teeth until it snapped.

As she turned to walk away, she said, "Have a good meal."

"You too." Eric replied, somehow thinking she was going to tell him to have a good day. He shook his head, embarrassed.

He devoured his breakfast. The quality was mediocre, but it satisfied his aching hunger. Surveying the empty restaurant as he paid to leave, he caught eyes again with the large, smirking Indian. The mysterious man sipped coffee from a plain, white mug that looked like a dainty teacup in his enormous, crushing hand. His meal had been long since eaten and the plates cleared. He was taking his time.

With a slight, tightlipped smile, Eric acknowledged the man with a nod. He nodded back with a big toothy grin and raised his coffee cup in a toast. With the gesture, Eric noticed the man's left-hand ring and pinky fingers were missing. He nervously finished his transaction and left.

As Eric walked toward his truck he scanned the businesses and buildings further down the road. Eric scowled at the Kingdom Hall of Jehovah's Witnesses he spotted a few lots away. He thought back to the morning of the day before, when he had awakened tired and very sore.

His shoulders were pinched and the back of his head throbbed. *I've got to get a new pillow*, he had thought. His air mattress bulged and swayed as he climbed out of bed. He glanced at the alarm clock on the floor.

"Aw great," he whined, realizing he had overslept. With a groan, he bent over to pick up the phone from the floor and dialed the office. "Julie, it's me. Listen I'm running late," he said. "I'll be in as soon as I can get there."

"Better hurry," Julie replied. "Mike is back from the rez. He's been waiting around to talk to you about something before he has to leave for a story in Wyoming."

"The *rez*? Like you're from there, or something." Eric quipped. "What, are you playing Indian now?"

Frustrated, Julie snarled back, "Res-er-va-tion. He went up to the Four Corners area over the weekend. Just hurry up and get here. He can tell you all about it," she snapped, and hung up before Eric could respond.

"Julie," Eric called out, but the line was dead. "Wyoming? How much does that cost? There's nothing happening in Wyoming," he complained aloud as he tossed the phone on the floor.

Skipping a shower, Eric smoothed his shaggy, brown hair with his hands, dressed, and hurried for the door. He was angered at the sight of a thin, crinkled pamphlet on the floor in the entryway of his home. He stopped to snatch it up. It was a copy of *Awake*, a religious tract distributed door to door. The cover story was about the effort to convert American Indians on the reservation lands of northern Arizona.

Eric's attention was drawn to a long shaft of sunlight gleaming through the space between the door and the jamb, where the weather stripping had been damaged by the unsolicited pamphlet being forced into his home. He held his hand to the gap, feeling the heat seeping in from outside. He crumpled the magazine and stormed into the kitchen to toss it in the garbage.

Looking down the eroded road to Canyon de Chelly, his annoyance rekindled, Eric stared at the worship hall across the street with a disdainful glare. He shook his head and spat on the ground.

Further down the road was a large cottonwood tree, its leaves sparkling on the breeze. Hoping to gauge the distance to the park entrance, his eyes followed the road but could see no further than where it bent to the left. His heart sank, replaying the image of the ghoulish man running down the side of the motel and disappearing down this road.

"It's all in your mind," he assured himself. He felt a definite compulsion to see Spider Rock.

# Chapter Three

It took only a few minutes to drive from the motel to the entrance of Canyon de Chelly. Immediately upon entering the park, the road split. Eric followed it to the right, past the horse tours, and decided to make a brief stop at the visitors' center.

A couple of tribal cops leaned against a four-wheel-drive police cruiser, chatting away in the bright sunlight. Eric parked several spots away from them and climbed down from his truck. He thought hard about approaching the cops with his story from early that morning, but became hesitant, and felt urged to just get into the building. The cops stopped talking to watch him walk by.

Eric gave himself a cursory tour of the displays and bookstore, taking all the free brochures he could find. He stopped a moment to watch an elderly Navajo silversmith who was demonstrating traditional jewelry making techniques. Eric stuffed two crumpled dollar bills into the narrow slit in the clear, acrylic donation box and hurried out.

A loud flapping called Eric's attention to three flags waving high on their poles. They were taking a beating in the wind. The stars and stripes and the Arizona state flag were flying, as well as the flag of the Navajo nation.

Eric flipped through one of his brochures to learn that the flag of the Navajo Nation depicted differently colored mountains placed in the cardinal directions. Surrounded by a guardian rainbow, they were the four sacred mountains that defined the land of the Navajo, or Dinè as they call themselves. Within the mountains was an outline of the boundaries of their reservation.

Marked in two shades of brown, the smaller, darker area indicated the original reservation, and the lighter, larger area was the present expanded boundary. Eric was impressed to learn that they—as well as the Hopi, situated within Navajo land—were among the few tribes in the U.S. that were allowed to keep their traditional sacred lands. He scoffed, thinking that had anyone found gold or any other equally valuable reason to settle here, these people would surely have been pushed off their land for good like all the others.

His surroundings dimmed as a high, wispy cloud wandered over him. Eric glanced up and was awed by an unusual halo around the sun. It was a perfectly circular rainbow, a phenomenon that Eric had never seen, let alone heard of. It was beautiful. An intensely powerful feeling overwhelmed him.

He searched the parking lot, hoping to find someone to marvel the event with; but there were only the two cops staring at him as if they suspected him of being high on something. For several minutes, Eric enjoyed the glorious manifestation until the thin cloud dissipated and the rainbow vanished. He felt warmed and reassured, protected.

He climbed into his truck and followed the signs toward Spider Rock at the furthest end of the park. The road climbed steadily in elevation, rapidly changing the scenery from red, rocky earth and sagebrush to thick patches of juniper and piñon. Eric had left 115-degree weather back in Phoenix. He rolled his window down to enjoy the cooler 90-degree breeze and fragrant pine.

Alongside the road, midway through the park, he noticed another abandoned hogan. It was in shambles like the one he had encountered the night before and boarded up. But there was a wire fence around this structure. Eric slowed to read a sign that warned passers by not to disturb the house out of respect for Navajo custom.

Pulling over at the first possible spot, he poured through his brochures looking for more information. He learned that when someone died in a hogan, the body would either be buried in it or carried out through a hole cut in the west-facing section of the home. Either way, the door was sealed shut and the structure was permanently abandoned, and sometimes burned.

*Who or what was inside that hogan last night?* he wondered. *How long had it been there decaying?* He found it reasonable to think that what he had encountered was a coyote or perhaps a stray dog. After all, in the last half-hour from the motel to here, he had seen at least six strays wandering around.

He imagined that a coyote or a dog had somehow gotten in through the opened roof of the hogan and was digging at the body buried inside. He wanted so badly to believe his theory, but he didn't. What about the mysterious man with his inexplicable powers? A shuddering groan escaped as a jitter shot through him. He shook it off and continued toward Spider Rock.

Narrow roads snaked along the edge of the canyon. There were numerous pullouts and overlooks scraped into the roadside, but he let them pass, lured on by Spider Rock. He figured if there were time, he would stop to check out some of the other sights on the way back.

All along the sidewalk that lined the parking lot at Spider Rock were Navajo people: men, women, children; all of them selling goods from blankets they'd laid out on the ground. Eric looked over the items as he walked past. He was drawn to a flat, half-inch thick, rectangular piece of reddish-brown shale that had been painted to depict various glyphs.

"That's all designs from the walls of the canyon," a young woman spoke up in her broken Navajo accent. Her voice inflection was such that each phrase sounded like a question. "I see those and paint them."

"They're beautiful. You do very nice work," Eric smiled. "What are they?"

She pointed to the designs, explaining, "Sun, antelope, deer, hunter, rain, mountains—that's a bear track. And this one here?" She pointed.

"The spiral?" Eric asked.

"Mmm-hmm I think that means a journey?"

"What's this one?" Eric asked, pointing to one of the black designs. It was a wide-based triangular shape with four white dots painted on each side, the bottom curved in a shallow, off-center arch, giving an appearance very similar to a boomerang.

"Hmm, I don't know. I seen it over there, in that canyon there. That rock there," she said, pointing at the piece of shale in Eric's hand. "That's from the canyon. It falls right off the walls," she continued. "I paint them myself. They're fifteen dollars, or two for twenty."

"Well, I really like this one; but for just another five bucks…" He paused, scanning her other paintings. "Oh, this one's nice too," he said, bending over to pick up another piece.

"Kokopelli," She smiled, taking Eric's twenty-dollar bill.

Uninterested, he moseyed past the other vendors, not even looking at their goods, until he saw two of the cutest little girls he had ever seen. They were sisters, one about five, and the other seven or so, he guessed. Their many silver necklaces with turquoise and abalone charms were laid out neatly on a red, white, and black woven blanket.

"The necklaces are two for twenty," the younger of the two Navajo girls called out.

"How much for one?" he asked her.

"Ten dollars," the older sister blurted.

He bent down smiling. "So, what kind of deal would I get, then, if I bought more than two? How much for four?" he asked.

The younger girl whispered to the other. Her big sister grabbed a small calculator and started crunching numbers, speaking softly to herself, "Ten plus ten, plus ten, plus ten, equals…" After a significant amount of button pressing she nodded in self-assurance. She looked up and announced surely, "Forty dollars."

"Well, that is some deal," Eric chuckled. "Let's see. How about these?" He picked up two identical silver necklaces that were generously decorated with turquoise beads. The hanging charms were cast-silver dreamcatchers—hoops with web-like netting and tiny, silver feathers dangling from them.

He tried to plan what he would do with the four necklaces as he chose them. The only women even remotely connected to his life were his mother, to whom he hadn't spoken in years, and Julie, who worked for him at the office. For his receptionist, he snatched up a silver necklace with an inlaid abalone charm shaped like a dolphin.

Lastly, he selected a necklace with shiny, gray hematite beads and a cross. He thought he'd mail it to his mother for her birthday, along with one of the dream catchers, which she would surely see as an impious, pagan icon. It was against her religion to celebrate holidays or birthdays. Nevertheless, resentful of missing out on celebratory occasions as a child, Eric would go out of his way to send her something every year at Christmas and on the day of her birth just to spite her.

Eric strolled past the other vendors, avoiding eye contact. Just then a white passenger van from the Spider Rock campground pulled up, letting out two Navajo guides and a small group of scruffy college-aged kids wearing retro, hippy clothes and long, dreadlocked hair. Signs everywhere instructed tourists to stay within designated areas, the land around Spider Rock being regarded as very sacred to the Navajo. He and the other tourists were soon herded between waist-high railings that flanked both sides of a concrete path leading closer toward the first of two Spider Rock overlooks.

Eric stopped to marvel at the view of the canyon and the breathtaking red rock spire, letting the gaggle of young tourists pass. He honed in on a conversation behind him, where the two Navajo guides had settled on a rock. As they lit a small wooden pipe and began to smoke, one of the gangly hippies from the group wandered back, hoping to be included.

"So, whatcha doin'?" he asked in a grating voice.

Irritated by the disturbance, the Navajos silently continued smoking, trying to ignore him. Watching the scene unfold, Eric smirked in amusement.

"Nah, I'm cool," the kid stammered. "You guys don't need to worry about..."

"We're praying," one of the Navajos rasped.

"Yeah, praying," he chuckled, unfazed. "It's cool. I get it," he said, oblivious to his unwelcome intrusion.

"Leave us!" the Navajo barked. "It's tobacco. We're praying."

Embarrassed for the ignorant kid, Eric continued down the trail. The path soon opened into a large viewing area on the brink of a cliff that offered a 280-degree view of three narrow legs of the canyon, branching right, far ahead, and extending far back to the left, the direction from which he had come. Eric could see no end to any of the three winding channels.

The place was teaming with life. From all directions he could hear the calls of birds and the rustling of trees in the wind. The rocky ground all around the area was filled with flecks of quartz that sparkled brilliantly when the light and eye caught it just right. Everyone on the ledge was awestruck and silent.

A shadow passed over him. Then the piercing, raspy call of a red-tailed hawk, called Eric's attention skyward. "Kree-eee-ar." The hawk had swooped down to within ten feet above his head.

"My God, you are beautiful!" he said excitedly as it glided directly over him.

Having always had an affinity for birds, Eric often read birding guides but never did any watching in the field. He had never seen a hawk so close up before. The bird was near enough that he could clearly see all the details: its light morph coloration, pale chest with a dark band across its belly, and dark bars along each of its under-wing feathers. Its yellow feet were enormous with shiny, razor-sharp talons tucked in tightly near its rust-colored tail feathers. It cocked its head and focused its penetrating eye directly on Eric. In that moment, Eric felt as if time had snapped still.

The hawk glided off eastwardly to the right, over the edge of the canyon, never once flapping its wings. Eric watched it soar gracefully over the deep chasm, toward the prodigious tower of rock that stood across the canyon at the intersection of the three channels. From this vantage, Eric was actually above and looking down slightly at the 800-foot rocky steeple. He realized that Spider Rock did not simply rise from the canyon; rather it was a sturdy column of sandstone that had refused to be worn down by the forces of nature and time. It stood as a proud testament to its own resilience in a world of impermanence.

He watched in silent reverence as the hawk circled the monument, gently touching down on one of the two small pines that crowned Spider Rock. He thought about what luck had put them there, for the seeds to be carried onto the peak by wind or a bird to sprout and take root on the rocky surface. Indeed, it did seem a mighty gift for them to even exist under such precarious circumstances, not unlike the way life took hold on our small planet in its vast corner of the universe.

From the corner of his eye, Eric caught a slight movement on the ground at the base of the short block wall that lined the overlook. At first he thought it was a mouse, but upon closer inspection he realized there were downy feathers that had curled into slight balls and rolled around on the breeze. By their barred pattern and coloration, he guessed they were breast feathers from an owl.

His eyes drifted from the feathers, caught by graffiti written in bright red fingernail polish onto one of the bricks. Neatly written, it read, "Anna Redman," followed by "LIFE WASN'T WORTH SHIT," angrily scrawled in capital letters. Eric had overheard the tribal cops at the visitor's center talking about a young woman who had jumped to her death just two days earlier. He felt tremendous grief as he read her last earthly communication. Often cynical and judgmental of others as he was, her self-deprecating message tugged at his heart. "Your *whole* life worthless?" he questioned with delicate sincerity.

He leaned over the wall to view the sage-dotted canyon floor far below. A thin, winding stream reflected the gleaming sky. He thought about what a frightening fall it must have been for Anna; all that time to regret such a hasty and irreversible decision.

Eric fought to suppress the memories flooding his mind of all the times he had recently pondered ending his own life and was ashamed. He sat cross-legged on a large, flat rock and looked out over the canyon, contemplating how his sadness for Anna Redman far exceeded his own. He wished for her to be at peace and wondered if she ever would be.

He soaked in the all the beauty that surrounded him: the panoramic views, the gently whispering breezes, and the ambrosial scent of pine. The sky above was deep blue with thick, puffy clouds that distorted and morphed with the wind, their volume revealed by their bulging, gray-shaded bellies. The birds sang as if to rejoice their being in the presence of such beauty and in just being alive. Basking in the power of the canyon, Eric was filled with a notion of the preciousness of life. He wished Anna had sat and waited long enough to have felt it too.

# Chapter Four

Noticing the lengthening shadows on the ground, Eric realized that he had been caught up in his thoughts well into the mid-afternoon. He left Spider Rock and hurried back to his truck. Turning the key, he was startled by his radio, which he had left on too loud. He sped down the road listening to Afterlife: *"The tree that falls still makes a sound, and you wouldn't have to ask if you'd take the time to be around."*

He was zoning out as he drove along, until his eye caught something glistening off the right side of the road ahead. By the way it reflected the light and beamed a shiny blue color he thought at first that it was an anodized, metallic sculpture of a bird. He slowed and carefully watched the strange object as he approached. The bird's color shifted to black and Eric could see it was a raven whose iridescence had manipulated the sunlight in a way he had never seen. With a few forceful flaps of its wings it left the ground and perched on a sign pointing the way to the Sliding House ruins. Built and occupied by the Anasazi around 900AD, the aptly named ruins, filled with many circular ceremonial structures called kivas, had long ago begun sliding off its steep perch high on the canyon wall.

He and the raven watched each other as he drove past. Remembering that he was interested in seeing the ruins, he jerked the wheel and pulled off the road with squealing tires into the overlook area. He parked and left his truck, and headed straight for the trail at the far end of the parking lot.

Eric took advantage of the absence of guard railings and paved pathways to wander out to a weathered, rocky ledge. He leaned over for a look. It was a 700-foot dead drop. The incredible height caused his stomach to shrink. His knees wobbled, and vertigo overtook him.

A bee buzzed past his ear and captured his attention. It circled him several times, causing him to step back from the edge. Still somewhat dizzy, Eric swatted at the bee each time it flew in close, but it persisted as if intentionally trying to drive him away from the canyon rim. Eric walked back toward the path, swatting wildly, but the bee stayed right on him. After a few more seconds the bee finally buzzed away.

Eric took a few more steps up the trail where he was startled by an intently approaching native dressed all in black and wearing an open-crown hat. The dust-covered, wide brim was pulled low, obscuring his face. He was hunched over and walked with a decrepit gait. Around his shoulders he wore a ratty looking, woven blanket that seemed out of place on such a hot day and only lent an escalating sense of foreboding to his appearance. Eric's heart thundered against his chest. The daylight seemed to dim.

"I have protection potion for sale," the man muttered.

"No thanks," said Eric through the lump in his throat. "I already spent my money on necklaces and stuff." He attempted to sidestep the eerie fellow, but anticipating his move, the man blocked his way.

"Then you can have it for free," he hissed as he parted the blanket and thrust a small, leather pouch in Eric's face. Eric noticed the old man's bruised and crooked fingers wrapped together with a dirty, blood-soaked cloth. Was this the ghoulish hand he had smashed with his flashlight earlier that morning? He began to feel faint, his hearing hollow and reverberant. His spotty vision faded as he sank into darkness, collapsing hard on the ground.

Just then, the sunlight brightened and through a misty veil of unconsciousness he heard a deep, resonant voice that broke the spell, "He doesn't need your twisted medicine."

It could have been only a few seconds later when Eric fully revived and took the large hand that extended to help him up. There, smiling, was the big Indian man from the diner. "You okay?" he asked.

Eric grunted, "Yeah, I think so. What happened?"

"You fainted."

"I've got a splitting headache," Eric moaned, rubbing the back of his head and neck. "Did I hit my head?"

"You'll be okay now," he assured.

"Where'd he go, that guy?" asked Eric, scanning the area.

"He split."

"What was up with that dusty pouch he stuck in my face?" Eric asked, trying to make sense of things.

"It's called *Ánt'į,*" said the gigantic Indian. "Corpse powder."

"What?" Taken aback, Eric searched for the mysterious man's eyes, hidden behind dark, reflective sunglasses, and asked, "Corpse powder?"

"It's a cursing potion made from dead bodies; mostly from ground fingertips and bits of the back of the skull. The strongest potions are made from the bodies of children."

Eric was aghast. "And who are you?" he asked nervously.

"Call me Ocho."

"Ocho?"

The man grinned, holding up both hands and wiggling his eight fingers. "You've seen that man before," he stated as a certainty.

"Yeah, early this morning," Eric answered, "about fifty miles northwest of here. I came up late last night from Phoenix to research a story about some odd petroglyphs. I'm not sure what happened, really. Someone attacked me and chased me out of there—tried to wreck my truck. I think it was him."

"Well, I don't know why he's after you, but you better watch out," Ocho warned. "That guy has a whole lot of trouble inside him."

Confused, Eric wondered what the mysterious Indian meant.

"Are you really going back? He obviously doesn't want you there."

"I don't know. Man, I wanna go home," Eric whined. "I have a friend coming to meet up with me there tomorrow. I think I'll feel safer waiting around here again tonight, and go in the morning."

"If you say so."

Eric was beginning to feel better. He looked up and said, "Well, thanks for coming to the rescue, Ocho."

"Yep."

Eric had almost gotten back to his truck before feeling alone and afraid. He looked back at Ocho, who was now standing at the very edge of the cliff, head back and arms splayed to catch the sunlight on his palms. Eric turned and headed back toward the ledge. He got to within ten feet of him when Ocho whirled around.

"I thought you were leaving."

Eric replied, "I was kinda hoping to get to know you better and maybe ask you a few questions."

"You buy me supper?"

"Um. Yeah, sure," said Eric. "Do you wanna follow me back into town?"

"I'm walking, can I hitch a ride?" Ocho asked.

Eric fidgeted hesitantly. "Uh, okay," he answered, pointing to his truck. "I'm right over here."

Eric climbed into the truck and leaned over to unlock the passenger door. Ocho pulled his way in, rocking the truck on its suspension. As they wound their way down the road along the canyon rim, Ocho kept looking cautiously out the window. "Whoa, stop real quick at that sign up there, alright?" he asked.

Eric pulled over just past a sign that advertised horse tours.

"I'll be right back," Ocho announced as he hopped out of the truck. He trotted into a patch of trees and disappeared. A few minutes later, he emerged toting a large duffle bag over his shoulder. He dropped the heavy bag into the back of the truck and climbed into the cab.

As they drove, Eric tried to make small talk about how beautiful the reservation is or how nice the Navajo people were. To every comment, Ocho simply responded, "Yep."

28

"Have you lived here all your life?" Eric asked.

"Oh no, I'm a tourist, man, same as you."

"You're not Navajo?"

"Grandfather says I'm Cherokee," Ocho said. "I never knew my family or their name. People I knew always called me Ocho, but Grandfather calls me Whitewolf."

"No family? You just said you knew your grandfather, right? He said your name is Whitewolf, you said."

Gesturing to the sky, Ocho replied, "Grandfather."

Eric was puzzled. Ocho continued to tell his story: how he didn't remember much about his early childhood, only that he was held captive in a shack where he was horribly and violently abused until he ran away at thirteen. He went on to tell how he had been on his own for sometime, living off the land on the outskirts of small towns until he was taken in by an old woman in western New Mexico. He would do chores around her land, taking care of her animals, building carpentry skills, and doing repairs.

"She's the only thing like family I ever had," said Ocho. "I lived and worked on her ranch for twenty-eight years until she died almost two years ago. She tried to leave the land to me, but couldn't. I guess 'cause there's no legal record of my existence."

Eric glanced dubiously at Ocho.

Ocho went on to explain how she left the property to her daughter in San Diego with instructions to let him stay there. But jealous of having to share the ranch, she promptly evicted him. He said he had wandered ever since, following his instincts and the guidance of his mysterious grandfather.

Ocho looked at Eric and asked, "So what's your story?"

"Not much, really," he shrugged. "My name is Eric. My friend and I write an alternative newspaper called *The Searcher*. It's just a small rag that no one takes seriously."

"Like in the checkout line at the supermarket?" asked Ocho.

"Ha!" Eric laughed. "I'd like to think we're a bit more reputable than that. No aliens in the White House, or Indian doomsday prophesies for us," he chortled.

After a silent lull, Ocho asked, "That's it?"

"Yeah, pretty much," Eric nodded. "I'm a pretty simple guy."

But Ocho Whitewolf wasn't the kind to skim the surface. Clutching his chest, he asked Eric, "Simple, huh? What about the heavy heart you carry around? To me, it feels far from simple."

Eric looked away, his brow wrinkled in consternation. "Huh? No, I guess I'm just a little tense. It's all this weird stuff going on. I just don't know what to make of it."

Ocho nodded. "Yeah, I guess a run-in with a skinwalker like that back there would stress a dude out, but you're beating yourself up about something else. I can feel a dark hole through you. He sees it and so do I."

"I don't much like talking about myself," Eric said distantly, focusing more intently on the road.

"Grandfather taught me that it's not good to keep your wounds quiet inside. They don't heal if you ignore them. The dark ones burrow into your head and feed on it," Ocho said, touching Eric's temple.

Difficult memories broke through Eric's defenses and flooded his mind. He tucked the thoughts back into their abandoned places and shook it off. Realizing that he had almost missed his turn, he jerked the wheel hard left into the motel parking lot. The truck bounced heavily as it bounded up the drive. He parked along the side of the diner.

Eric twisted in his seat to better face his companion. "You called that guy back there a skinwalker. I saw that word earlier on a book cover and was intrigued. What is a skinwalker?"

Ocho grinned. "It's like a witch; bad medicine. They call them skinwalkers because it's said that they can shape-shift into animals or birds. They kill those closest to them as sacrifice to the spirits that will teach them the songs and spells that give them their powers."

Eric simpered, "The way you were smiling when you said it, I'd have thought you were joking. I don't even buy into this stuff, but I saw it myself. If I'm not losing my mind, that guy was running almost 70 miles-an-hour when he chased me last night..."

"Or was slowing time so he could keep up," Ocho suggested.

Eric was shivering, his body flushed and goose bumps popping up on his arms. "He had a baby's fingers and a woman's breast on a necklace," he continued. "Man, he was creepy. His eyes were black—nothing there."

"Yep," Ocho grinned. "The fingers were maybe his baby brother, or even his own child. The boob was probably his mother's; the one that fed him and gave him life. That's huge energy to feed the demons."

"Demons and witchcraft," Eric sneered. "Reminds me of how my mom always ranted about everything being of the devil and corrupted with evil." He laughed dismissively. "Religious bullshit."

"Maybe so, but it's for real, dude. Spirits are everywhere; in the trees and animals, in the earth and water, the clouds and wind, all around us. Most fulfill their purpose and are good—our relatives. But there are lots that are evil. They feed on the energy released by destruction. They whisper dark thoughts to us, but we don't think it's them we hear."

"Where I come from, that's called schizophrenia," Eric scoffed. "Maybe that's why I think I saw what I saw," he joked, fearful of the possible actuality of his retort.

"Whatever, dude. They're not worried if you don't believe in them. But you better be, 'cause they sure believe in you." Ocho warned.

"So these evil spirits, they give the power to these skinwalkers?" Eric asked.

"At first." Ocho explained, "These witches break the most sacred laws and taboos in order to feed the demons, hoping to get the powers to do their own will. But they don't realize that they are being tricked into letting the dark ones get inside. They give their will over to them, like slaves—flesh puppets. That's the real reason they're called skinwalkers. Dark spirits are made manifest in the world, walking in the skins of others."

"What? Like possession?" Eric asked incredulously.

"No, possession happens so often it's almost normal. The spirits are all around us. We're being influenced all the time by good and bad. But we still have our greatest power—choice. A skinwalker is different. A demon is literally born into our world

31

when it is invited in and overpowers a soul completely and takes its body. There's no exorcism; you have to kill them." Ocho grinned. "You hungry? Let's eat."

Ocho opened the door and climbed out.

"You're not scared of them?" Eric called after him.

"I'm careful, but no, I'm not scared." He leaned into the truck and said, "I have powers, and so do you. We have the freedom of our spirits." He closed the door and walked up onto the sidewalk. Stretching like a cat, he waited there for Eric.

After locking the truck's doors, Eric joined him on the sidewalk.

Puzzled, Ocho glanced at all of Eric's supplies left unsecured in the truck bed.

"Oh, right. Think it'll be alright?" Eric asked.

"Trust issues, huh?" Ocho ribbed. "We'll sit by the window."

They walked into the diner. It was early still. They practically had the place to themselves.

"You ever have a Navajo taco?" Ocho asked.

"No, are they good?"

Ocho grinned, rubbing his hands together. "Man, they are so good!"

They were seated right away and each ordered without needing to see the menu. They sat silent for a while. Then Eric spoke up, resuming the conversation from where it had ended outside. "I have a hard time with the whole spirit thing. It's just hard to get my head around it, you know? My mom was always going on about the rapture and the end times and all. It all seems so foolish, always worrying about the end when living day to day is hard enough."

"Yep," Ocho replied. He sat silent for a good while, soaking in what Eric had said and crafting a response. "Being in the moment is where we need to live today, or we miss the whole point of life; so you're right on there. And if you're living the best life you can in the time you have, why worry about the end that comes to us all, right?"

Ocho's eyes scanned the air above him. He leaned forward, grinning. "But spirit? Come on, dude. Why is that so hard to accept? It's just another form of energy. We accept that the atoms in all things are held together with invisible energy, right? Just 'cause you don't believe in spirit, doesn't mean it's not there. It means you choose not to experience it. You narrow your own scope of what is possible and you miss it, like a horse with blinders on. It's like, just 'cause you're only watching one channel, doesn't mean there aren't hundreds more playing out at the same time beyond your awareness. And even if you got a hundred TVs and tuned them all to different channels, you'd still only be able to process the info from one or two at a time." Ocho paused for a moment, seeming to be listening intently.

"But spirit isn't easily understood," he continued. "Because it happens behind the scenes, you dig? You have to learn to perceive it. You know how dogs can hear things we can't? Those sounds are real, even if our ears aren't designed to pick up those frequencies, right? But what if you could learn to stretch your perception to hear them too? It's like that. But the things I'm talking about, humans can't tune into with their brains. Spirit energy occurs at wavelengths humans can't easily detect with the usual limited senses. You can only perceive spirit with spirit, and to do that you have to tune out the brain and be in the moment. The spirit world is all around us. Look, right now there are things in the atmosphere: sounds we can hear, scents we can smell, life-giving oxygen we breathe. But it's all as invisible as the air. You can believe in air, right?"

Eric shrugged, "Well, yeah, but I can feel the air."

"And you could feel spirit too," Ocho replied, "if you opened up to it."

"But we can scientifically measure and prove the existence of the air around us," Eric argued. "There's not one shred of empirical evidence of a spirit."

"Look, you can go on not believing in anything for as long as you want; that's the great power of choice I've been talking about. But I believe that all things happen first in spirit, in invisible worlds." He grabbed his glass of water and put a straw in it. "Here, check this out," Ocho said. "Let's say the air all around us is the spirit world, and I blow some air through the straw into the water. I get a bunch of bubbles, right? Each of those bubbles is like a living thing manifested in a material world; spirit, in this case air contained in a thin—what's the word? Membrane…in a material world, lasting only as long as it can before it rises up, pops, and again becomes part of the air it came from. You wanna get really out there? Each bubble could be an entire dimension or universe. Hey, check it out, Big Bang!"

Ocho blew heavily through the straw causing an eruption of bubbles in his glass. The water spilled over the top of the glass, dripping all over the table. He roared with laughter.

Eric chuckled, embarrassedly scanning the restaurant to see if anyone was bothered. "That's pretty deep, Ocho. You have quite a way with words for someone with your story. Growing up alone in the wild that is."

"Thank you very much, Eric." He grinned, aware of Eric's skepticism. "I just pull the words from here," he said swirling the air above his head with his hand, "and they come out of my mouth when I speak."

"Hey, how do you know so much about the skinwalkers and what not?" Eric inquired.

"Some things you just know, you know?" he said coyly.

Their food arrived: grilled cubes of meat with lettuce, tomato and cheese, wrapped in warm frybread. Ocho seized it from the plate and took nearly half of it in one enormous bite. "Mmm," he grunted, cheeks fat like a chipmunk. Eric joined in. They chatted and joked for a good while, enjoying each other's company. It was the best meal he'd had in a long time and their evening together was over all too soon.

# Chapter Five

In his darkened motel room, Eric was out cold on his still made bed. Mouth agape, he was fully clothed with shoes on. A dark figure slowly and quietly crept closer to him. The shadowy man dug a handful of crushed, organic material from a leather pouch and forced it into Eric's mouth.

Eric's eyes popped open. He tried to rise from the bed, but the intruder shoved him back, muzzling his mouth with his hand. Eric kicked and squirmed, trying desperately to wriggle free. Suddenly he no longer felt restrained. He sprang from the bed and looked around in the dark. There was no one there.

He looked under the bed and around the furniture. He checked the door but it was locked. He peered into the empty closet and cautiously proceeded to check the bathroom where he peeled back the shower curtain. Still no one.

There was a foul, bitter taste in his mouth. Eric loaded his toothbrush with mint-flavored paste and bent over the running faucet, scrubbing his teeth. He glanced up and caught his reflection in the darkened mirror. It stared back at him coldly. It looked like him, but in the dark, it morphed and changed into faces that were not quite familiar. It was his, but strange. His reflection sneered at Eric and spoke into his mind.

*You killed him. You wished to be released. Are you free now? You wished him dead. You did it. You killed your son. You sacrificed your son for that freedom, that power.*

"Shut up!" Eric growled, pressing his hand against the mirror to cover his reflection's face. Skin and muscle stretched, and tendons popped as his reflection slithered head first through the mirror into Eric's hand and up his arm. Screaming and writhing in pain, he struggled to pull his hand from the mirror, but it was stuck firmly. The stretching and crunching continued through Eric's arm and into his chest. He grimaced in agony as it invaded throughout his body. He summoned all of his strength, and with his free hand, wrenched the towel bar off the wall and smashed the mirror.

The shattering glass cascaded around him. The ceiling and walls, too, splintered and rained down. The entire bathroom disintegrated, transforming his surroundings completely from a darkened room to desert.

It was day, but eerily dim. The surreal sky above him swirled with dancing bands of aurora in colors of green, purple, blue, and pink. Heavily eroded, red, monolithic sandstone mountains and sagebrush dotted the high Arizona landscape.

Without a sound, a delta-shaped light as bright as the sun streaked across the sky directly over him. It stopped abruptly over a nearby mesa and hovered. It pulsated in the distance like a beacon and ensnared Eric's curiosity.

Eric walked across the plain toward the mesa to investigate the glowing object. He was soon in a sandy wash at the base of the escarpment. The augural howling of a wolf called his attention to a thicket of shrubs and cottonwood trees so close against the cliff they seemed to sprout from the wall. Just above the trees Eric noticed a thin opening in the rocks, a fissure in the stone from the top of the mesa extending down to the cliff floor.

The wolf called again, its howl echoing through a passageway hidden behind the thick vegetation. Eric searched for a way through the impenetrable brush. In the soft, red dirt at his feet were canid tracks. He followed the trail of paw prints through a tight opening in the shrubbery. Thin, wild branches scratched at his arms and face as he crawled through, crouching low to the ground.

The tracks continued into a slot canyon that water and time had sliced through the rock, exiting here. Carved by millennia of flash floods, the undulating trail was extremely narrow, averaging only three to four feet in width. It was so tight in some places that it became necessary for Eric to twist his shoulders and squeeze his way through the hundred-foot-tall rippling, sandstone walls. The powdery, reddish-brown sand on the ground was thick and deep. It was like walking on dustless, finely ground flour, several inches deep. The way the light and shadow played on the wavy, striated walls gave the illusion of being surrounded and watched by stoic faces.

The wolf tracks led several-hundred yards through the labyrinth and mysteriously stopped in the center of a large, vaulted cavern. Eric wondered where the wolf had gone. The only way out was to turn back the way he had come or go up the high, steep walls that curled in at the top, almost touching. But one would have to walk upside-down to get out through that opening.

A brilliant shaft of light beamed down from the slit in the natural ceiling, lending an air of sacredness to the chamber. High on the walls above were twelve handprints that seemed impossible for anyone to have placed there without flying. Lower down the surrounding walls were petroglyphs unlike any Eric had ever seen. They began to glow, as if by turquoise-blue light emanating from within. One of the glyphs caught Eric's eye above all others: a several-armed spiral with two intertwined lines going diagonally through it.

Eric stared into the glowing design until he was transported far out into space where he looked down on the Milky Way as it cartwheeled through the void. In the vast blackness, the spiraled disc of blue, gaseous cloud and starlight drifted toward a vortex of faint, reflected light that stretched across the infinite universe. Its shape was a double helix, like a DNA strand, its luminosity similar to a strand of hair against black velvet, visible only when the light hits it just right.

As the galaxy's inner arms spun closer to the vortex, Eric was whisked into the star system, the light of the cosmos streaking past. In an instant, he was stopped in orbit high above the Earth. From here he watched our distant sun enter the mysterious whorl.

The star shook and violently erupted. Bands of plasma stretched and snapped like cracking whips, hurling massive globs of ionized gas at Earth with incredible speed, demolishing the entire network of artificial satellites that circled the earth. Completely enshrouding our planet, the smoky plasma swirled in earth's magnetic field. The lights that emanated from the technologically civilized regions on the surface of the planet's darkened hemisphere switched off. Eric watched in awe as the familiar geography of his home planet transformed before his very eyes.

North America divided in two, splitting the continent from Hudson's Bay to the Gulf of Mexico. Much of the Midwestern and Southern states became the bottom of a vast inland sea. The geological forces and changing sea levels made coastlines worldwide unrecognizable. The west coast of the United States was submerged, leaving the Cascade Mountains as a chain of islands. Volcanic eruptions around the planet darkened the atmosphere. Wobbling unsteadily on its axis, the earth trembled and shook as it carried its inhabitants along its orbit, flying at great speed toward the anomalous coil of energy.

Eric was teleported around the earth and shown the aftermath of the global cataclysm. Whole cities and their suburbs were laid waste by the devastating geological forces of earthquakes, hurricanes, tornados, wildfires, and floods. He searched desperately for survivors, but his visions showed him only mountains of debris, and scorched or flooded earth.

With a resounding thud, Eric fell hard on the ground. A reflection in a small puddle of murky water, inches from his face, caught his eye. The ever-changing shape was difficult to read as it danced and transmuted on the rippling surface. He strained to read what appeared to be red digital numbers. Slowly coming into focus for a quick moment, they shuffled and morphed unintelligibly. Eric slowly became cognizant that he was standing between the two beds in his motel room, staring at the clock. The confusing numbers continued to move illegibly as his eyes came into focus, streaming random, mutating patterns of twos, zeros, and ones. Finally coming into view, the clock read twenty minutes after midnight, changing as he watched to 12:21 AM.

Eric found it nearly impossible to sleep after his disturbing nightmare. Flipping the pillow every few moments to capture its fleeting comfort, he tossed and turned, tired and achy. His mind raced for hours at a time, punctuated with the short relief of shallow sleep, from which he awoke sharply at every sound and checked the clock.

Around 6:00 AM, Eric gave up on sleep and dug through his pack for a change of clothes. They were hardly different from what he wore everyday, like a uniform: worn, baggy, jeans and a dark tee shirt. He laid the clothes across the chair and walked to the bathroom. As he neared the door, his bare feet slowed to avoid glass shards. Fearing what it would cost to replace the smashed mirror, he poked his head around the door. The mirror was fine. "What a weird week!" he muttered to himself. "What am I even doing here? I don't believe in any of this shit. Mike can shove it."

Getting ready to go, Eric recalled his conversation with Mike the morning before last.

*"Shocking evidence links Johnson to Kennedy Assassination by Eric Demeter,"* Mike read aloud as Eric had entered the office. "Oh Eric, where do you come up with this stuff?" he asked caustically as he looked over Eric's article submission. "You know, for the resident skeptic you sure buy into a lot of conspiracy crap."

"It takes controversial headlines to sell a rag like ours, Mike—not more of that tired UFO and ghost stuff you're always doing."

Eric scooted around him and sat at his desk as Mike replied, "That's what makes us such a good team: you're grounded, inside the box, asking penetrating questions to understand the past from the narrow frame of the here and now. I'm looking to the future. And, you know, *my* headlines are the ones selling the papers. If you could stay on a channel for more than two seconds, you'd see that just about every network out there is running some kind of paranormal investigative show now. People are waking up, dude. They're starting to believe in a bigger universe with greater possibilities."

"Because there just isn't enough to worry about here in the real world," Eric muttered as if condemning Mike's viewpoint. He winced as he leaned back in his chair, rubbing his neck. He threw his feet up on the desk. Much to Mike's astonishment, he had somehow managed to plop his feet down amidst the layer of books and empty cola cans without sending anything flying. His worn, black Chuck Taylor canvas high-tops were sewn to the top with frayed, dingy-white laces. They were tied tightly, making his feet look abnormally long, like a clown's.

"Is there really any *shocking new evidence* in this Johnson-Kennedy thing, or are your suspicions getting the better of you again?" Mike razzed.

"There are some things that I found very suspicious, yes," Eric affirmed. "Read it, you'll see. Although," he admitted, his lips curving into a sly smile, "it is entirely possible that some of my beliefs may have crept onto the page, cleverly disguised as factual insights." He rested his hands on his belly, with his fingers interlocked. "You know how it is, Mr. UFO," he jeered. "Beliefs can easily become truth to the believer."

Despite their differences and bickering, Mike was Eric's only real friend—one of the rare few who could tolerate him. Eric was stubbornly resistant to change, incredulous and narrow-minded. Often offensive, the bumptious Eric seemed to blurt every critical thought that entered his mind, while Mike was generally more reserved and thoughtful, and much more labile.

"So, Mike, Julie said you have some news for me?"

Mike's gray eyes gleamed. Anticipating Eric's sarcasm he blushed, saying, "I went to one of those UFO conferences last week."

"Oh man, what a nerd," Eric chaffed. "I betcha there were some real crackpots there, huh? Anyone wearing Spock ears?"

"A few. Uh, crackpots that is," Mike chuckled. "Here, I brought you a souvenir. It just kinda jumped out and made me think of you," he said, handing him a postcard which featured an artist's rendering of a fleet of flying saucers hovering over a Mayan temple, set against a fiery sunset. In the sky, the giant, ghostly image of an alien face with spiraled galaxies reflected in its abysmal, black eyes loomed over the scene like an omnipotent architect overseeing some grand design.

"Yeah, that is so me," Eric laughed and slid it into his back pocket.

"Seriously, though," Mike continued, "this wasn't one of those crazy sci-fi conventions, like that one time."

Eric remembered the occasion he was referring to, when Mike had arranged a booth for them to represent their alternative news publication. The convention had taken place in one of the conference halls at the Phoenix Civic Center on the same day as a gun show, a tattoo convention, and a tropical bird show. Eric smirked, remembering the absurdity of bird and gun enthusiasts and heavily tattooed people intermingling in the common areas with sci-fi fans dressed in homemade Klingon regalia, made up in wigs and knobby facial prosthetics.

"Some of the speakers at the conference were accredited scholars," Mike continued. "One of them was a retired astronaut talking about how, while in orbit, he'd encountered objects with unusual flight characteristics that suggested intelligence."

"Intelligence, indeed," Eric jeered. "You'd think NASA would do a better job screening their astronauts."

"Anyway," Mike continued, "I ran into a guy I know from an outfit in L.A. He told me about this Navajo guy who found some interesting petroglyphs near his house where some other strange stuff has been happening."

Eric raised his eyebrow, and shot Mike a dubious smirk.

"He's been taking people to see them, and I was asked to go along," Mike added.

"So that's what you were doing in red rock country all weekend, huh?"

"Yeah, and you wouldn't believe these rock drawings, man. Some crazy stuff."

"Like what?" Eric asked.

"You know me, Eric, and the stuff I believe in. But I don't want to jump to any conclusions about anything I saw based on what I *want* to believe. That's why you have to go so we can get the skeptic's take on this."

"Are you gonna tell me there's pictures of aliens and UFOs? 'Cause that stuff's all been done."

"Well, yeah, of course," Mike said matter-of-factly. He looked Eric in the eye. His tone softened. "I suppose there could be other explanations, but it would be too easy if that's all it was. I

41

mean, there are some odd drawings of mythological beings they call the *ant people*; and some designs could be interpreted as spacecraft. Others seem to depict star systems that were only recently discovered, and even planets of our solar system. Most of the drawings are similar to the typical esoteric petroglyphs of the region. You know, swirls and stick figures and what not. But some seem to represent elements of cultures that arose much further away…even on other continents. It's the mystery of what some of these other drawings might symbolize that make them stand out. I figured someone who took a bunch of anthropology courses just for fun would appreciate this kind of thing."

Interested now, Eric quickly lifted and swung his legs over the corner of his desk, situating his feet and legs squarely under it. He straightened himself in his seat, leaned toward a mug full of pens, chose one at random, and put it to paper. It dragged across the pad leaving nothing more than a deep indentation where he had pushed it into the page. He firmly scribbled a small, counterclockwise spiral on the top left corner of the paper, trying to coax it to write. But still nothing.

Mike watched Eric's frustration rise and climax as he jabbed the worn out pen back into the mug and chose another. His quiet amusement gave way to a smirk that caught the corner of Eric's eye.

"I suppose that is a little strange, isn't it," Eric asked, embarrassed. "I always do that, I don't know why. That mug is full of dried up pens. I never grab a good one on the first try, and for some reason I always put it back."

"Perhaps it's time to rid yourself of some things you no longer need to hold on to," Mike immediately suggested.

"But isn't that what makes us who we are? Aren't we equal to the accumulation of our possessions?" Eric asked sarcastically, pointing at Mike and scoffing at his increasingly fashionable, brand name attire.

"If your worth is the equivalent of a mug full of spent pens and your empty house, then God help you," Mike chuckled.

"I wouldn't say it's empty. I've got a TV, a couch, and something to sleep on. What more do you need?"

Mike needled him, saying, "And you're lucky she didn't take that too."

"It wasn't luck. She didn't want them."

Eric's second choice in pens at first seemed to be no better; but after a bit of scribbling, the ink began to flow.

"Who is this guy? What's his number?"

Mike blankly stared back at Eric. "He doesn't have a phone, you have to go there."

"Are you kidding me? Who doesn't have a phone?"

"He lives far out there, miles from any paved road. Believe it or not, Eric, there *are* people who don't have a phone."

Eric paused momentarily. "Electricity?"

"Nope."

"Arrgghh!!! You've got to be kidding! How can anyone live like that?" Eric demanded.

Mike pulled a folded piece of paper from his shirt pocket and tossed it onto Eric's desk. "Directions. I told Oliver you'd be coming today or tomorrow. Oliver Begay. That's his name." Mike caught Eric's smirk. "Uh-huh, try to make a joke out of that," Mike quipped. "Really, though, that's a very common Navajo name. Please try to be polite. And you're gonna want to take camping stuff with you."

"No way," Eric protested. "What about a hotel?"

"You have no idea how big the rez is, man." Mike explained. "The nearest hotel is in Chinle. You'd have to drive over two hours each way on dirt roads. You can deal with it for a few days."

"Dude, you know I'm not a camper. I need my creature comforts. How do people live this way? What about hygiene?" Eric demanded.

Mike ribbed him, "By the looks of you, Eric, it seems that would be your last concern. People lived for thousands of years without TV, plumbing, and antibacterial soap."

"They also died by the thousands of plague," Eric snapped back. "What's with this Wyoming thing? Is there any way you can scrap it and come with me?"

Mike shook his head, "Sorry, bro. There are some strange cattle deaths happening at this guy's ranch. I'm gonna get up there and look into it."

"No, not more of that nonsense," Eric sneered. "Cattle mutilation? I'm telling you, it's occultists—friggin' devil worshipers."

"Well, you'll be the first one I'll call if you're right; but there's more to it on this one." Mike rose from his chair and started for the door. "I'll tell you what: I'm coming back tomorrow night. I'll drive up to the reservation on Wednesday and meet up with you there."

Eric smiled. "Cool. All right then, I'll see you in a couple of days. I'm gonna head out too—go shopping for a tent and everything. Maybe an RV," Eric quipped. "Oh, and Mike..." Eric called out.

Mike stopped and turned.

"Try not to step in any bullshit in those fancy new shoes."

"See ya," laughed Mike as he left the room.

Eric snapped back to the present and glanced around his lonely hotel room. He sat on the edge of the bed and surfed through the television channels for a few minutes. Then he laid back and almost instantly fell deeply asleep. It seemed only seconds later that the buzzing alarm nudged him from his exhausted slumber. He woke slowly and crawled sluggishly from the bed. It was 7:30 AM. Eric flopped back onto the bed and slapped the snooze button every time it sounded, finally getting up shortly after 9:00. He rounded up his things and carried them out to his truck.

Sitting on the tailgate wearing his trademark ear-to-ear grin, Ocho was waiting for Eric. Ocho blurted, "Hey dude," in a contrived, gravelly voice that sounded a bit like Cheech Marin.

"Hola, Señor Ocho," Eric replied, smiling.

Ocho jittered, "Man, that language drives me nuts!"

"What?" Eric chuckled.

"Anyway," Ocho said, "Last night you were talking about heading back to Phoenix today. I was thinking, why quit now?

Why not find out what's up there that someone doesn't want you to see?"

"I've been thinking the same thing." Eric paused a moment. "Hey, you wanna go with me, or are you having fun enough camping at the canyon?"

Ocho pointed at his big duffel, neatly tucked in with Eric's supplies, and smiled, "I'm glad you asked before I had to tell you what it was gonna be. Hey, I owe you. Wanna get some grub before we go?"

"Cool. Alright then," Eric laughed. "I just gotta check out real quick. I'll meet you over there."

Eric exited the motel office a few minutes later and paused to watch a hawk gliding on a thermal. He crossed the lot to the diner and scanned the room for Ocho, who by this time was flirting with the waitress. She didn't seem to mind.

Waving Eric over, Ocho called, "Hey, c'mon. Over here, dude."

Taking a seat across from Ocho, he immediately ordered a Pepsi. Ocho looked at Eric, his eyes inspecting the air around him. "You got a different color around you today," he said. "C'mon, let's do this," he continued, nudging Eric's menu. "Let's get this adventure underway!"

# Chapter Six

Ocho and Eric were soon on the road north, leaving Chinle. Eric hadn't seen this part of town in the daylight before. Ocho observed Eric's taking notice of the broken-down cars and appliances that littered many of the homes and yards. The small reservation town quickly disappeared behind them. Many places along the roadside were strewn with empty bottles and shattered glass.

Ocho nudged Eric's arm, chuckling, "You look like that guy—the crying Indian on that litter commercial."

"What?" Eric didn't know what to make of Ocho's irreverent sense of humor. "You're such a trip," he said.

They had continued in silence for several miles when Eric asked, "Remember that guy I told you about, that chased me outta here the other night?"

"That was no ordinary *guy*, but yeah," replied Ocho.

"Well, windstalker, or skinwalker, whatever...I mean, as if he wasn't strange enough, he had a ratty teddy bear tied to his back. What's that about?"

"I'm guessing he killed his own baby, like I said yesterday about the fingers. I'm guessing the bear was his baby's too. He wears it to keep the spirit tied to him. The dark ones love to feed on the ghosts that haunt us."

Eric thought about Evan.

Ocho watched him and the air around him intently. "You keep a spirit close to you, too."

"I know," Eric nodded.

"You gotta heal it and let it go, my man," Ocho said caringly.

Eric drew in a deep breath and said, "I had a dream last night, kind of about that, I think. A voice taunted me, telling me how I killed my son; that I wished for him to die. It was a spooky dream and all, but it really only repeated what I've told myself since he died."

"That's the way they do it. They use what haunts you against you," Ocho insisted.

Eric thought quietly about Evan. How he missed him. Looking back, his son was the only real sense of purpose his life had ever offered. He felt ashamed, wondering how different his life would have been if he had understood then the meaning that fatherhood and family gave him.

Ocho read the troubled look on Eric's face and sensed his pain. "What is it?" he asked. "What's eating you?"

Uncharacteristically, Eric opened up, explaining, "I was dating this girl, you know. I found out pretty fast that she just wasn't for me. I just couldn't figure out how to break it off without her getting all crazy. I've never been one to initiate change; you know what I mean?"

Ocho grinned and shook his head, "No. I ran away at thirteen, remember?"

Eric smiled and loosened up a bit, continuing, "…and my mom is this crazy religious fanatic, you know, Jehovah's Witness. That's why I have such a hard time with the concept of spirits and whatnot—because I was always told that when you die, that's it. You just blink out of existence…until resurrection anyway; that is if—and only if—you're a good Witness," he scoffed. "Ceasing to exist seems reasonable enough to me. They should've left it at that. I don't know; the whole religion—every religion for that matter— is contradictory and filled with confusing circular logic. But anyway, I'm off track. My dad had a lot of questions about it, too, I guess. So he left the church when I was a baby, and my mom shunned him, like the church said to." Eric laughed, "He was probably relieved to be free of her, you know, like, 'There is a God!' But I never got to know him. I don't know where he is. But, back to the point, before I could stand up and make a move, I knocked her up."

"Who, your mom?" Ocho asked, disgusted.

"No, yuck! My girlfriend!" Eric laughed. "I know, I'm all over the place, here."

Concentrating hard on arranging his thoughts in a way that would be more easily followed, he continued, "I mentioned my dad because I didn't want my kid to be without a dad like I was, you know? And with all the pressure from my mom and her parents to get married and make the baby legit, I did it. I married her. And, man, was she a nut! You know how they always say you marry your mom?"

"Again with the mom stuff. You're sick, dude," Ocho joked.

"Aw, forget it."

"I'm just playing, dude. Lighten up."

"Anyway," Eric continued, "I figured they'd have gotten along better, both being crazy and all, but she wasn't a Witness. In fact, she and I were atheists."

"I bet that went over like a fart in church," Ocho laughed.

"Yeah, but that and the fact we had a child together were all we had in common. She and I just never got along, you know?" After a short pause, his voice cracked, saying, "But I sure loved my baby boy."

Eric fidgeted and looked around blinking, trying to choke back the tears. "Anyway," he continued, "It's true, I did wish for something to happen to get me out of that mess. I wished it all the time. I never would have left her, and she never would have left me. She was obsessive, codependent, and jealous. And, like I said, I've just never been one to initiate change. We'd have killed each other before either would leave it."

Eric's tone became more serious and difficult. "And then one night, I put the baby to bed. I was tired and had some writing to do before a deadline. I heard the baby cry a bit, but he stopped. And I thought of checking on him, but I didn't." He explained. "I convinced myself everything was alright and just kept working. Evan just stopped breathing sometime in the night after that, and never woke up again."

48

Ocho put his hand on Eric's shoulder and consoled, "Wow, I'm sorry, dude."

Eric shrugged, trying desperately to maintain his composure. "Well, you know, through the whole pregnancy I kept hoping she'd miscarry so there'd be no more reason to stay. I just blame myself, you know, like somehow I cursed him. Although I know that's impossible."

"Well, I don't know, the universe has its mysteries," Ocho said. "But it seems just as good a guess that maybe he left willingly for both your sakes; to free you both from an unhappy lifetime, and his mother too. Don't keep him tied to you like that teddy bear, man. Let him go and be at peace. Let yourself be at peace. Everything happens for a reason. Maybe you got a lot of important things to do in this life that you never would have been able to do if you were tied down with family."

"Important things to do?" Eric scoffed. "Nah, I'm just drifting through space on a big rock," he said, watching the white paper plate with the black arrow nailed to the fencepost streak pass from the corner of his eye. "Whoa! Pay attention, Eric!" he exclaimed as he pulled off the road and slid to an abrupt halt on the rough dirt shoulder. The cloud of dust from his tuck continued north as he flipped a U-turn and took the dirt road west. "I almost missed it."

"That old hogan on the right," Eric pointed. "There was some kind of animal thrashing around in there when I came up the night before last."

"Hmm," Ocho acknowledged, watching it from his window.

"My directions don't really say what to do here at the fork."

"Let's get out and look around a bit," suggested Ocho, climbing down from the truck. Eric got out and followed him down the trail on the right.

Ocho squatted, looking at the path. "No one ever goes this way, not for a long time, except for you. Here's your tire tracks in," he pointed. "Here's where you came out, and…wow! that skinwalker was booking, huh? Look at that stride."

"What are these tracks?" Eric asked. "Dog? Coyote?"

"Hmm-mmm," Ocho shook his head. "Wolf."

"I don't understand. There aren't supposed to be wolves here. They were reintroduced far south and to the east from here, closer to New Mexico."

"What's not to understand?" Ocho teased. "There's the tracks right there. What is this, a Bigfoot investigation? What more proof do you need?"

"Bite me," Eric jeered. The Bigfoot comment touched a nerve, triggering Eric's deep-seated need to argue and debunk such paranormal conjectures. "Tracks are evidence, not proof," he said pragmatically.

"Well, guess what? These skinwalker tracks here prove your story, don't they," Ocho grinned.

"Practically speaking, I wish I could say yes, but I can't," Eric said. "Seeing, as they say, may be believing, but belief is not necessarily truth. Sure, I believe I saw something frightening here, but I still can't say conclusively what it was. As unusual as it was, there are still rational explanations to explore."

"Sleeping with the light on, huh?"

With a haughty smirk and raised eyebrow, Eric asked, "What's that supposed to mean?"

"It was a—whatdya call it? A megaform."

Eric laughed smugly. "You mean metaphor?"

"You know what I mean," Ocho snapped impatiently.

"Whatever. Sleeping with the lights on...I don't get it, sorry."

"I mean, people aren't afraid of the dark. They're afraid of what they can't see—of what could possibly be there, lurking in the unknown. If you sleep with the light on, then every time you feel scared, all you have to do is peek around and find comfort in seeing the things you know, and all that stuff you're afraid to see just goes away. Or does it?"

Avoiding the question, Eric steered clear of Ocho's eyes, glancing around at the time-sculpted sandstone mountains that dotted the landscape.

Ocho grinned, his face contorted in a rictus of delightful validation. "Look, mister thickhead," he chuckled, "you're doing it right now." He sauntered over to the trail that forked to the left.

"Look at all these signs, the wear over here. There's been people in and out of here for weeks. This is the way."

They climbed back in the truck and proceeded to the left. The road was rough, rocking the truck unevenly. Eric and Ocho swayed casually in their seats like horseback riders moving along at a plodding gait. It was a beautiful day with high spotty clouds. The late morning air was crisp and fresh.

The road sliced through a vast siltstone valley surrounded by mesas and a long plateau to the west. It dipped in and out of arroyos and across the occasional running brook. Other than a small flock of sheep they had spotted on a hill, and some branching trails, there was no real sign of human habitation.

"Look at that," said Ocho, pointing to a group of circling buzzards about a half-mile to the north.

"What's that all about?" Eric asked.

"Looks like they found something to eat," Ocho grinned sheepishly. "Or someone."

"Yeah, right," Eric laughed.

Finally, the long drive brought them to their destination where at the foot of a mesa they found two differently constructed hogans. One was the octagonal design Eric had become familiar with; the other was narrow and covered with a mound of dirt. Eric remembered reading about the two traditional styled hogans representing the feminine and masculine. Glancing at the directions, Eric said, "We're here. Now we look for a singlewide trailer."

The dirt road narrowed as it wound through a shady thicket. The tips of spindly branches squeaked as they raked down the sides of the truck.

"Whoa, now that's one creepy dude," Eric muttered, spying an old, wrinkled Navajo man hiding behind a nearby tree, watching them pass.

"Stop the truck," Ocho said sharply. He opened the door and climbed out before Eric could completely stop.

"*Ya'at' eeh*," Ocho called out. The old man slowly stepped out and stood in the shadow of the big tree, silhouetted against the shafts of sunlight that streamed in behind him. Closely watching the old man, Ocho removed his sunglasses and strained to make out any details. "We're looking for Oliver Begay," he said. The old man raised his left hand and, with its only finger, pointed further down the road, then disappeared into the trees.

"You're right," Ocho said, climbing back into the truck. "That is one creepy dude."

Further up the trail was a singlewide trailer home, propped up on cinderblocks. Nearby stood a few tents, and there were a number of vehicles parked in the shade of the steep mesa several hundred yards away. Eric spotted a familiar white Land Rover, covered in red dust.

"Awesome, Mike is already here. He must have come up overnight." Eric parked among the other trucks and vans and climbed out to stretch. "So, I guess we should set up camp with the others?"

Ocho and Eric carried their gear into the encampment, but there was no one there. "They're all probably at the glyphs," Eric said.

Within minutes, Ocho had his small, dome tent pitched. He dug a large bowie knife from his bag and strapped it onto his belt, then tossed his duffel into his tent and zipped it shut.

Eric, on the other hand, was still digging through the box in search of the assembly directions. Amused, Ocho watched him fumble for a bit, and then offered his help. "This tent will sleep, like, five. What, are you planning a slumber party?" Ocho jabbed. "What'd you need such a big tent for?"

"It was only ten bucks more than the little one," Eric reasoned.

"You got enough room to sleepwalk in there," Ocho joked.

"I just might," said Eric.

They finished setting up and sat on the ground for several minutes before Ocho got restless and suggested, "You wanna go find them?"

"I've never been here before. I wouldn't know where to begin to look."

"Duh," Ocho mocked, shaking his head and pointing at tracks on the ground. "Follow the signs, dude."

Ocho guided Eric through the rocky terrain around to the north side of the mesa. After an approximate forty-minute hike, they came to a ledge overlooking a steep ravine. The group was exploring the rocks below. Eric spotted Mike huddled in discussion with several other people. They cautiously descended the steep wall of the ravine, Ocho leading the way.

"Oh, thank God," Mike rejoiced, upon seeing Eric. "They told me you never showed up yesterday. We were just wondering what might have happened to you."

"I'm okay, Mike. I stayed the last two nights in Chinle…and made a friend, too." Eric motioned, "Michael Mathews, this is Ocho Whitewolf." Ocho greeted Mike with a smile and a nod.

Mike made introductions. "Eric Demeter, Ocho Whitewolf, this is Oliver Begay, who's been kind enough to show us around and let us camp out here."

"*Ya'at' eeh*," said Oliver.

"Over here," Mike continued, "we have Truman Krieger, Chad Shelton, and Sean Phillips, from UFORIA, the Unidentified Flying Object Research and Investigation Association; and this is Charlie Moreth. He got here a couple hours ago from Tuba City to write a piece for the *Watchtower*."

"Um-hmm," Eric muttered snidely. He recognized the Jehovah's Witness magazine known for its fervent preaching of the trials and tribulations of the end times. It was the companion publication of the *Awake* magazine that was so rudely shoved through the doorjamb and into his home days earlier.

Mike glared disappointedly at Eric and continued, "There are some other people here too. I don't know most of them."

"The word got out," Oliver said. "There are some people who came up from the university in Flagstaff. Anthropology department, I think."

"So, then, let's see what's so fascinating about all this primitive graffiti," Eric said.

Offended, Oliver glanced at Mike. Sensing the tension, Mike gently squeezed Eric's shoulder, saying, "Early native people regarded the land with a sacredness that most today can't even know. If they left marks on this land, it was no doubt done with reverence, and we need to respect this region as sacred."

"A sacred dumping ground," Eric mocked. "Have you seen Chinle?"

Mike fired an icy glare.

"Right," Eric said. "Sorry."

"Would you lead the way, Oliver?" Mike asked.

Oliver led the group along the ravine, stopping at each marking. Most were very ordinary, similar to the markings that were painted on the piece of shale that Eric had bought from the Navajo woman at the canyon.

"Well, as far as UFORIA is concerned, this is the smoking gun," said Sean, pointing to a large rectangular rock. Etched into the surface, were twelve figures with oddly shaped horn and antlered heads, standing beside a large triangle with wavy lines extending from its base. "It depicts what just might be visitors exiting a triangular craft, like the one seen over Phoenix a few years ago," Sean continued. "These lines at the bottom represent the thrust from its propulsion system."

"Wow! That *is* very fascinating, Sean," Eric said sarcastically. "But what if it's just Kachina dancers outside a teepee?"

The portly man with long, kinky, blond hair stuttered nervously, "I…uh, well…I guess, maybe. But there's been a rash of triangular UFO sightings all over the world recently: Belgium, Israel, Jersey, Phoenix."

"I've seen them," Oliver insisted. "Right over there," he said, pointing to a nearby mountain. "They do look a bit like that drawing. No noise; they just float on the air, like a hawk on the wind. That's why I wanted to show these to you UFO people."

Ocho stood in the back of the group, watching quietly with a slight smirk. Eric moseyed over to him whispering, "Dude, is it just me or does Sean look like that Mikey guy from *American Chopper*?"

Ocho shrugged, "I don't know what you're talking about."

"Never mind," said Eric, turning his attention back to the group.

Following Oliver up the wall of the ravine to a large, flat boulder, Charlie Moreth pushed his way through the group, saying, "This piece I find very, very interesting!"

The pictograph depicted, from the left, a large stick figure and a horizontal line that continued across the length of the brown three-and-a-half-foot rock. Midway through the line, rose a short line that ascended several inches at a slight angle, then continued horizontally, parallel to the line below it. Nine smaller stick figures traveled all the way across the bottom line, with three figures diverting from them to travel the top road.

"It depicts the rapture," Charlie said. "These people up here," he continued, "are the righteous ones; the hundred and forty-four thousand who have been enraptured and taken to be with God. All the rest are doomed to await the apocalypse."

"Oh, c'mon, man!" Eric sneered. "A hundred and forty-four thousand? Look, you nit-wit, there's only three."

"We'll see who mocks when you're left below," Charlie fired back. With a raised, flustered voice, he began quoting scripture and hell fire.

Shouting over him, Eric yelled, "If there's only enough room for a hundred and forty-four thousand of you boneheads, why do you go door to door recruiting more? Haven't you hit maximum occupancy yet?"

Mike stepped in between them saying, "We're all entitled to our different opinions here. None of us really knows what these pictures mean; that's why we're here." Mike grabbed Eric's arm firmly, asking, "You gonna be cool?"

"Yeah," Eric agreed. "It's just that, to me, this looks really simple—perhaps a migration depiction, which is a very common theme found in the pictographs of the ancient cultures of the Southwest. The largest stick figure on the left probably represents the whole of the people who were here at this spot when they broke up into two groups, one quarter of the tribe leaving and moving on in a different direction." He leered at Charlie, muttering, "I don't know, maybe they got sick of all the dogmatic bullshit and left to be free to find a simpler truth."

"Why do we assume that it reads left to right, anyway?" Truman chimed in. "How do we know it doesn't read right to left?"

"A good point," Eric replied, the others nodding in agreement. Charlie, however, shook his head defiantly. Eric teased,

"Yeah, reading right to left, maybe it means all the people of different faiths and persuasions make it to be with God, here on the left, despite their theological differences."

"No, no, no, it doesn't work that way," Charlie argued. "There's only one way; our scriptures tell us."

"Well, you must feel really privileged knowing that out of six and a half billion people on the planet, God is on your side," Eric jabbed.

"No, he's on my side," Truman chimed in, joking. "And death to all who oppose."

"You nailed it," Eric said. "That is how history brought us here, isn't it?"

Amused, Ocho watched the scene with a big grin.

Mike stepped in to end the bickering. "All right, all right, that's enough. This one is definitely open to many interpretations, but like Charlie said, it *is* very interesting; though, I think, for its similarity to the glyph on Prophecy Rock on the Hopi rez."

Wearing a brown bomber jacket and an Australian hat with a crocodile tooth band, Chad jumped in, "They also have rock art and a prophecy about *Blue Corn Kachina* appearing in the sky and bringing what they call the *Day of Purification*. It's supposed to bring about what they call the *Fifth World*, similar to the *Fifth World Age of Enlightenment* the Mayans speak of."

"I'm sorry, I just can't take you serious in that hat," Eric jeered.

Chad was confused and offended.

Embarrassed, Mike excused his friend's rude behavior. "Eric was never properly socialized for human interaction as a child..."

Agitated, Eric raised his voice to speak over him, "No, really, I mean, come on—I'm sure the UFO community really appreciates all you're doing; but the rest of us in the real world might take you more seriously if you weren't running around dressed like Indiana Jones."

Trying his best to ignore Eric, Chad spoke loudly for the benefit of making his point to the others, "There are also petroglyphs showing a maiden in a domed spaceship."

Eric rolled his eyes and wandered off on his own to look at some of the other petroglyphs in the area. To him, they were all quite impressive examples of prehistoric art: bear tracks, spirals, antelope, hunters with arrows, but nothing really out of the ordinary. The group from the university seemed to share his opinion. After a cursory inspection, they packed up and left in the late afternoon.

Catching up with Eric, Oliver recommended to his guests that they start back for camp. Mike shepherded Eric away from the group, asking, "Dude, what's up with you? Why do you have to be so rude like that?"

"What do you mean?" Eric asked, defiantly. "That Charlie Moreth guy is a twerp. 'Moreth!' What an annoying name. It makes it sound like I have a speech impediment. *Yeth, I'd like to thpeak with mithter Moreth.*"

Not amused, Mike sat on a rock, saying, "You weren't just rude to him; what about Chad? Not to mention how rude that was to me."

"Really Mike, you didn't see what I was talking about?" Eric insisted. "Chad, with that big mustache? And that hat!" He said, laughing, "He looks like Higgins from Magnum PI as Indiana Jones."

Mike smirked, trying not to laugh at Eric's snarky comment. He was too angry to be appeased. "You really embarrassed me back there, acting like that," he said sternly. "You've been acting so strange lately."

"What? Please, Mike," Eric protested. "When have I ever not been vocal about how I feel about all that UFO nonsense?"

"I'm not just talking about you being rude and offensive," Mike argued. "That's the only thing normal about you right now. Look, for starters, you blow off a whole day sightseeing. You barely know that tattooed giant, and yet you drive him up here with you. Did you see that huge knife of his? I mean, c'mon, that's not strange to you? I figure you of all people would be afraid to wind up dead with your head in a duffel bag. I mean, really, you're the most distrusting and skeptical guy on the planet!"

Eric nodded. "Yeah, I know."

"And you're lost inside your head way more than usual," Mike continued.

"I know."

"You're acting very strangely," Mike repeated.

"I know."

"So what's going on, then?" Mike demanded.

Shrugging his shoulders, Eric said, "I don't know."

Mike snapped, "Are you gonna tell me about it or what?" he shouted.

Eric hung his head, saying, "I haven't been able to get my head around it yet, do you understand?"

"No, I don't!" Mike argued. "You haven't given me a damn thing to understand."

"I'm just not ready to talk about it," Eric sighed. "The truth is I don't know how to describe what's been happening the last few days, without sounding like one of these numbskulls. Religious or paranormal believers, they're all zealots, you know. They all invest so strongly in what they want to believe that they make pieces fit without scrutiny or reason."

Offended and frustrated, Mike ranted, "But why do you have to be the guy who rips off Santa's beard in front of the kids? You're so doubtful about everything! You have to go out of your way to shoot holes in other peoples' beliefs all the time. Why? What's that about?" Mike demanded. "Are you not zealous in your atheism, with that stupid evolving fish with legs sticker on your car? You have to promote and share your belief in nothing with others? You might as well get on a bike and go canvassing door to door like a missionary. And, what, am I one of *those numbskulls*, too, because I believe in something otherworldly going on here? Am I a kook?"

"I'm sorry I upset you, Mike," Eric said calmly.

"I asked you here because I knew you would remain coldly analytical; that's what we need here," Mike said. "Just, please, try not to be such an asshole. We're here; let's have some fun with it."

"You're right," Eric replied. "I don't know what's eating me. I can't explain it, but I've been talking with Ocho about my mom and dad, and that whole thing with the church. It's just bad timing for that *Watchtower* guy to be here. I've been thinking a lot about Evan, too. My emotions are about to bubble over; all my rage, all my despair."

"Despair? Whatdya mean despair?"

"I can't talk about it right now, Mike. It's just too hard. You know me, I've always been the kind to bottle it up to deal with by myself, later, when I can," he said.

"But you've been talking to Ocho, a complete stranger. It's so unlike you to talk about stuff like that with anyone—let alone someone you just met," Mike said. "That's the most you've even talked about it with me, and we've been best friends since we were kids."

"I know," Eric nodded. But it's weird. Ocho has a way of pulling it out of me.

"Where'd he come from anyway?" Mike asked.

"I met him in Chinle. He's got a crazy story. He doesn't really know what all happened when he was a kid, but he was taken from Oklahoma when he was really little."

"What do you mean, 'taken?'" Mike gestured to the sky, asking, "Abducted, or kidnapped?"

"Please," Eric scoffed. "Actually, I really wouldn't know what to believe either way, it's so outlandish. He says he was held captive in a hole under a shed near the Texas Mexico border where he was ritually tortured until he ran away at thirteen."

Enthralled, Mike asked, "Ritually tortured? Sounds like by a brujo?"

"A what?" Eric asked.

Mike explained, "A brujo is a wizard or sorcerer; like a shaman but enabled by dark spirits—black magic, real ugly stuff."

A shiver shot through Eric. "Whoa, that's really too much." He stuttered as his body quivered.

"What? Tell me," Mike begged.

"I was attacked near that old hogan at that fork in the dirt road early Tuesday morning when I first got here. I was chased out of here by what Ocho called a skinwalker. I know, it sounds funny."

"Not at all," Mike assured him. "You know me. I need no convincing of the supernatural. I believe."

"Well, it followed me into town, and found me again at Canyon de Chelly. Ocho chased it away."

"What a fortunate coincidence," said Mike.

"I said the same thing; to which Ocho said there's no such thing. He said 'Grandfather' brought him to me," Eric explained. "I don't know what he means by that, the ghost of an ancestor or what. I think he thinks he talks to God. But whatever, delusional or not, I feel safe with him."

"Already I thought he was a pretty interesting guy, although intimidating looking," said Mike. "But wow! And hey, Mr. Skeptic," Mike chaffed, "how come you're not shooting holes in *his* story?"

"Have you seen the size of that guy?" Eric joked. "Of course I have doubts; that's my nature. And sometimes I want to call him on it, but he intrigues me. The truth is he's got a clever way of explaining otherworldly matters in a way that interests me and actually makes some kind of sense."

"What? Who are you?"

Eric shrugged. "I know, right?"

"Well, I must admit it's a lot of fun watching you get yours, the way he joshes you," Mike said. "And, man, he really is a trip— a really funny guy. He's had everyone laughing since you all got here. It's just what we needed," Mike said, climbing to his feet. He slapped Eric on the back, shouting, "So, you're here, you're safe, let's have some fun then, right?"

"Right," Eric smiled.

Walking back to camp Mike said, "So, guess what I listened to the whole way up?"

"Hmm, what?" Eric asked.

"Scatterbrain!" Mike answered excitedly.

Eric smiled, "Scamboogery?"

"Scam-boog-er-ree!"

"That's not too lowbrow for you these days?" Eric teased.

"Are you kidding? That's a classic album. I don't know why I dug it out, though. I hadn't listened to it in years. It just jumped out at me when I was loading up CDs for the road."

Eric smiled, singing, "Down the road, on a quest!"

60

Mike joined in, "Down the road, that's where we're at our best!"

"What a fun band. That's the soundtrack of good times, man," Eric chuckled. "Remember that day, our road trip up Highway 89? That perfect day? We listened to that disc the whole way up and back. No worries, no cares; it seemed like the skies just opened up and everything was right with the world."

Mike nodded, "I thought about it the whole way up."

"Life was so much easier then, and fun, you know?"

"Yeah, I know," Mike said. "Life still is fun," he insisted, playfully tripping Eric.

Eric stumbled, regaining his stride within several quickened steps. "Dude, you gotta let me borrow that CD for the drive home," Eric said.

By the time Mike and Eric caught up with the others at camp they had a roaring fire going. Ocho, Truman, and Sean were joking and laughing, roasting hotdogs over the fire. Chad was frustrated, pacing the area, trying to get a signal on his Blackberry so he could check his email.

"If you can't get that thing to work, you can always do smoke signals," Ocho joked. "What's so important that you can't unhook yourself from that electronic leash for a couple days anyway?"

Before Chad could respond, Truman jumped in, "He's a tech junkie. He can't live without his text messaging and emails for a minute. He goes through withdrawals. That damn Blackberry is always in his hand."

"More like *crackberry*," Sean laughed. "Watch him. He fiddles with it like every thirty seconds."

"He's so caught up in text-speak, he doesn't even remember how to spell complete words any more," Truman jabbed. "He'd hardwire his brain to that thing if the technology were there."

"It seems like evolution intended something else for us," Ocho mused. "Hey Chad!" he shouted. "When do you ever find time for silent introspection?"

Chad was absorbed in what he was doing, stroking his dark mustache and reading the email in his PDA. He looked up, muttering, "Huh? Hey you guys, I got a message that there is a new UFO flap happening in Mexico."

"A new flap? Since that eclipse in 1991, it's always been a hot spot," Mike said, digging around in the cooler for the hot dogs.

Zipping up his jacket, Chad said, "Dr. Martain says it's heating up since Monday."

"Who is Dr. Martain?" Eric asked.

"He's one of the best known UFO researchers in the world," Mike answered. "Most famous for his research of the Roswell incident."

"Uh-huh, Roswell," Eric sneered, "Say no more."

"He's also a well respected physicist," Chad said, in defense of his mentor. "He's in Mexico right now, investigating the recent sightings around Popocatepetl." Chad pulled his hat off and scratched his head, saying, "He's heading over to Chichen Itza tomorrow, where it's going off big time. I'm going to leave here tomorrow and meet up with him there."

"What's Popo-ca-whatchamacallit?" Eric asked.

"It's the most active volcano in Mexico," Mike explained.

Eric's memory flashed a scene from his apocalyptic dream, seeing central Mexico reduced to rubble and covered with pyroclastic ash and lava flows. "Well, stay away from Mexico City," he warned.

Finding his comment odd, Chad asked, "Why?"

Shying away, Eric said, "There's just too many damned people there."

"You got that right," Mike said, handing Eric the package of hot dogs. "That place is a madhouse."

"Hey, what ever happened to that Charlie Moreth guy?" Eric asked.

Pointing at a maroon minivan parked about a hundred yards away, Truman said, "He went right to his car. I don't know why he didn't leave. I can't imagine why he's so interested in these glyphs, but he'll probably be seething there all night. I don't think he likes you."

"No, probably not, 'cause I'm beyond saving," Eric jeered.

Ocho forcefully slammed a log onto the fire, sending a huge plume of glowing cinders into the air. Having been closest to the fire, Eric swiftly jumped away to avoid being burned.

"Because you have the wits to save yourself," Ocho said.

# Chapter Seven

Unable to achieve any deep level of sleep, Eric tossed and turned in his sleeping bag. The uncomfortable ground beneath him was hard and sharp rocks dug into his back. The last of the others had finally gone to bed, leaving behind the smoldering embers crackling quietly. Above the din of the pulsing chirps of crickets, a deep, monotonous snoring rumbled from Ocho's tent twenty yards away. His snoring sounded like an idling tractor. Eric opened his eyes and gazed at the stars through the netted canopy.

Not wanting to dress or brave the dark and cold, he tried with restless legs to belay the urge to relieve his bladder until morning. But knowing he'd never get any sleep if he ignored it any longer, Eric finally succumbed to his nagging bodily impulse. From a lying position, he slid into his pants then sat up to put on his shoes and jacket.

Quietly zipping the tent closed behind him, Eric stepped cautiously into the dark and began searching for a private place among the few nearby junipers. He moved discerningly from place to place, feeling that no matter where he went he could still be seen. He knew everyone was asleep, yet he felt watched, as if the stars themselves were peering down at him. He became frightened at how far he had wandered from the camp, and settled on a spot surrounded by three large juniper shrubs. He looked skyward as he relieved himself, and his eyes were soon fixed on the full moon, high in the eastern sky.

Eric's eyes had quickly adjusted and he could see rather well by the reflected moonlight, but still he felt uneasy. He felt like there were eyes all around watching him. For the first time in his life, the moon's topography revealed to Eric's eyes the semblance of a human face: the fabled man in the moon. Eerily, he felt as though it were looking back. The feeling of being watched was so unnerving that Eric quickened his business and, zipping his fly on the go, walked briskly back to his tent.

After a few moments to catch his breath, he was soon soundly asleep, dreaming that he was still outside. The moon was huge in the sky and seemed to be within his reach. Cartoonish eyes seemed to appear on the glowing orb and winked at him. The moon sank rapidly below the horizon and was replaced by a quick-rising sun that gave light to a cartoon world. Greeting him in an animated voice, Mr. Sun said, "Hi, Eric!"

"I'm a cartoon!" Eric said excitedly. He seemed to be drawn with a lanky body and large head. Just like a cartoon for preschoolers, the entire world was anthropomorphous and sublime. Rolling green hills filled with frolicking doe-eyed critters and fluttering birds all enthusiastically greeted him, "Hi, Eric!" They all rejoiced and sang together harmoniously. The rocks and trees and flowers, too, were all alive with happy faces. Everywhere he went, they all greeted him, "Hi, Eric!" The mountains and clouds watched over him, smiling as he explored the dream world.

Astonished, Eric noticed a network of thin, barely visible cords of light interconnecting all things in this whimsical world. Animated Asian dragons dipped and dived, flying along rivers of energy that flowed through the sky. In the ground at his feet was a crystalline vein that pulsated and glowed with power. He followed it up and over a hill to a pristine, Edenic valley. At its heart was a massive mother tree that fruited large crystal prisms, and whose roots fed the energy veins that extended out of sight in all directions.

Primitive people inhabited the valley. They were all connected in the harmony of this world, rejoicing and singing, and frolicking with the animals, great and small. Eric watched a curious woman approach the tree, reaching for one of the crystals that hung from a low branch. All of the characters of this fanciful world grew concerned, shouting frantically, "No, no, don't touch it!"

Plucking the crystal from the mother tree caused it to tremble and shake. It dropped its remaining crystals onto the ground where they were swallowed by the earth. The tree sank into itself, disappearing inverted below the ground. In the hole where it had once stood, swirled a fluidic, rippling whirlpool, a portal from a mysterious dimension that suddenly burst forth with hideous creatures.

The once blissful world of his dream was horribly transformed by the arrival of these malevolent, ghoulish beings. The sky darkened and erupted thunderously as the animals and people ran screaming from the malign intruders. The ghouls flooded through the landscape, pillaging and laughing balefully as they pounced on the people and rode on their backs, burrowing and disappearing into the backs of their heads.

No longer aware of the wicked beings or their diabolical influence, the people began hurting the animals and each other, and with axes felled whole forests. The living Earth screamed and cried as they clawed at her. Digging deep into her, they ripped out her shimmering, life-giving veins to fuel their recklessly expanding industries.

The helpless sun closed his tearful eyes rather than watch the raping of his loved ones below. Acrid smoke belched high into the sky, nearly choking the life out of the inhabitants of the world, who all had now changed in appearance from the once adorable, jovial characters to gaunt, sunken-eyed drones with expressionless faces. The cords that connected the people to the energetic network dimmed, causing them to lose almost completely their once harmonious connection to their world. The animals ran and hid from the people as they carried out their greedy work with no emotional connection or reverence at all.

The sinister, raucous laughter of the ghouls reverberated in Eric's ears, and overwhelmed his awareness. Choking on the thick smoke, he tossed and turned in his sleeping bag. The laughter continued. He abruptly awoke and shot up surprised to find himself sitting in his tent.

Eric rubbed his eyes in an effort to bring himself completely out of his dream. The laughing outside continued coming from the men gathered around the fire as the smoke carried directly into his tent on the breeze. Eric recognized Ocho's infectious, boisterous laugh above the others. He could hear Mike out there as well.

Eric shook off the unusual dream and dressed to join the guys by the fire. They were all laughing with amusement at Sean who, having forgotten to pack any tool capable of safely retrieving his coffee urn from the fire, was trying to fish it out with a brittle, charred stick of wood. His jacket sleeve was pushed up around his elbow, and all of the hair on his hand and arm had been singed. The boiling coffee spilled over the pour spout into the coals, sending out plumes of ashy steam.

Frustrated, Sean stomped away from the fire. "Unless any of you guys has any other idea, I'm spent," he said.

Ocho laughed as they all looked to each other for suggestions and came up short.

"Move," he grunted, playfully pushing Sean aside. Pulling his sweatshirt sleeve over his hand like an oven mitt, Ocho plunged into the flame and pulled out the kettle. "Coffee, anyone?" he roared.

"Duh," growled Sean, smacking himself on the forehead.

It was a cool, crisp morning with a low, gray overcast. The dark mammatus clouds that blanketed the sky bubbled downward with ominous, saggy pouches. The shrill, squeaking call of a bird rang out. Catching everyone's attention, the bird flew from shrub to shrub encircling the camp, calling from each cardinal direction beginning in the east.

"That was weird," said Eric.

"It's a flicker; a woodpecker," Ocho explained. "It's an omen. It signals huge leaps in spiritual growth," he said, looking at Eric. "They are drummers too, the way they tap Earth rhythms on the trees. Drumming heals and can shift awareness."

"Hmm, cool," Eric smiled, incredulously.

"It *is* cool," Ocho insisted. "That bird is big Medicine."

"How do you know so much about Indian spirituality and stuff anyway, if you never lived with your people?" Eric asked.

"Spirituality?" Ocho grinned coyly. "Seems it should come from your spirit, not your people, huh? Some things you just know, you know?"

"So, what? Do you just make it up on the fly, then?" Eric asked, cynically. The other guys became tense, looking away and fidgeting.

"Well, I'm gonna go pack up, so I can get to Albuquerque in time for my flight to Cancun," Chad said, scurrying off.

Ocho smiled at Eric, saying, "I spent many years of my life listening to my teachers: the animals, trees and rocks, the wind and fire, water and earth, and of course, Grandfather. When you really know something, you don't need to explain it. You don't need to struggle to understand it. It just becomes clear and easy, like breathing. You don't need to think about it, you just do it. I have a personal connection with the things I've learned and know; a direct connection to the source. No middle man; no restrictions; no filtering anyone else's interpretations; no need to shed any bad-fitting skin that someone else squeezed me into."

"That must be so nice," Eric said. "I've been struggling half my life to recover from all the conditioning my mom and school and society has forced on me—all the doctrines and dogmatic traditions. You're right, it is like shedding skin."

"Well, we all have to recover and heal," Ocho said. "Just being born into this world is painful enough. It's like waking up in a strange place with amnesia, and you have to trust that people are going to be honest and treat you right. But they don't know any better than anyone else. You really have to find your own way if you're going to accept responsibility for your life."

"But what about laws and rules?" Mike asked. "How would people know right from wrong without institutions to tell them?"

Ocho nodded, taking a moment to craft a response. "We all build on the knowledge and wisdom of our ancestors. And that is good," Ocho said. "Deep inside, we all know right from wrong, good from evil. We can feel it. No matter what rules or laws anyone lays out, it's still up to each of us to choose right from wrong. We have to listen to our spirit's connection to the Great Mystery to find ultimate truth. It can't be found in people."

They sat quietly for a while, pondering Ocho's words. Mike took several gulps of his coffee and dumped the rest over the coals, sending a billowing cloud of ash and smoke into the air. He jumped up from the cooler he had been sitting on. "So, who wants to go see what we can find in the ravine today?"

# Chapter Eight

"Whoa! Eric, look at this," Mike shouted. Eric hurried to climb a narrow, rocky ledge where Mike stood examining a large flat wall of rock. The rock was carved to depict people standing around an elliptical spiral, drawn on a flat horizontal plane. Under the spiral was an inverted tree.

"No way!" Eric exclaimed.

Startled, Mike asked, "What?"

"I had the strangest dream last night about this tree," he explained. "Ocho!" Eric called. Ocho bounded up to the ledge and looked at the ancient glyph.

"Cool," he said. "I've seen that tree in a vision. There were a bunch of crystals growing on it."

"Really?" Eric asked. "I had this crazy dream last night. I was a cartoon." Grabbing Mike's arm, Eric affirmed, "Mike, I swear. I've had so many weird dreams lately. I've just tried to ignore them; but this one was such a trip. The whole world was cartoonish, like animated shows for preschoolers, where even the trees and rocks are alive and able to interact with the people."

"It's cool how easy it is for the little ones to accept the world that way, huh?" Ocho announced. "And, then, somehow we forget that spirit moves through all things."

Eric rolled his eyes and shook his head dismissively, then continued recounting his dream. "I saw a little cartoon lady try to pick a crystal from the tree, and it collapsed into itself, growing upside-down in some other dimension."

"What could it mean, Ocho?" Mike asked.

"Hmm," grunted Ocho. "Don't know yet."

Impatiently, Eric asked, "Well, how does it fit your vision?"

"How does it fit with yours?" Ocho volleyed.

Eric stared at him blankly.

"You see, that's the thing with visions, you only see little bits of the picture at a time. But your vision, and mine, means something, I guarantee you that. And we'll keep having 'em until we figure out why."

The three split up to wander the ravine in search of more interesting pictographs. About a half mile from where Oliver had taken them, Mike found a place that was filled with rock carvings. He went to work taking digital photos and drawing copies of each significant find.

A couple of hours had passed before Eric found Mike. "Why do you waste your time drawing them out like that if you're taking pictures?" he asked.

"In case the real wasted time was in taking the pictures," Mike answered.

Eric looked at him quizzically.

"You know I don't trust putting all my stock in digital information," he continued. "It's weird, I know, but even when I write now, I do it all with pen and paper and have Julie type it up."

"That's right," Eric chuckled. "I forgot about your growing fear of some worldwide technology crash. For such an ordinary dude, you're pretty weird."

"Yeah, ever since I learned about that big solar flare that hit Canada back in '89. It overloaded the power grid and left like six million people without power. It just got me thinking."

"Big deal, they got it back up and running. Right?" Eric shrugged.

"But that was '89, dude. Think of how much has changed with technology since then. We've placed our entire communications infrastructure in the hands of satellites. They'll be the first to go in another big geomagnetic storm. It would be chaos, and that's just a start."

Eric's memory flashed his dream about the erupting sun, only half-listening as Mike rambled on about the risks of losing our historical record now that news and film archives are being transferred to space-saving digital storage media, while discarding hard copies. "We should be marking our existence in stone like these people did," said Mike, "or the archeologists of the future aren't gonna be able to find any legible trace of us."

Feeling anxious, Eric asked, "Where'd Ocho go?"

"Oh, check it out," Mike said, flipping through his sketchbook. "Look," he said, pointing at a copy he had made of a rock carving that depicted a mountain divided by a jagged line. "Ocho found this drawn on a rock over there. He thinks the jagged line suggests a river or spring."

"Why does that look familiar?" Eric mused.

"That's what Ocho said. Then he made the connection. Look," Mike said, pointing to a mountain a few miles to the North. "He went to go check it out."

"Whoa, I had a dream about that mountain the other night!" Eric said excitedly. "If it means anything, that line is a slot canyon. It goes through the mesa for, like, half a mile, then opens up into a cavern with a bunch of really interesting petroglyphs."

"You actually think your dream might be some kind of prophetic vision?" Mike asked, taken aback by Eric's opening mind. "Who the hell are you?"

"I know, right? I'm gonna go catch up with him."

"We should get Oliver to guide us," Mike said. "I wonder what's up? I haven't seen him all day."

Eric was antsy. "I can't wait," he said. "I gotta get up there."

"Alright," Mike said. "I'll double back and find Oliver and the rest of the guys."

"Cool, I'll see ya over there," Eric said, immediately scanning the ground ahead for the best way out of the ravine.

Before long, Eric was impressed with his ability to find Ocho's trail. He laughed, replaying Ocho's deep voice in his head, *"Follow the signs, dude."*

Ocho's tracks led Eric for over three miles, through winding, rocky paths and several arroyos. Finally the footprints stepped out into a sandy creek bed. The mesa was very close now. Eric trudged through the deep, pebbly sand, negotiating algae-filled puddles and mosquito swarms as he followed the wash that wound around the mesa.

He soon came upon the shrubs and cottonwoods just as he had seen in his dream. The ground between the sandy bed and the thicket was full of large, rounded rocks that caused him to lose Ocho's trail.

In a tree up ahead Eric caught sight of a gleaming, white object, placed at eye level. The tree forked into a perfect Y-shape about five feet up the trunk. Balanced in the cleft was a wolf skull, its menacing canine teeth protruding downward. The skull was brittle and bleached white from sun and age, and the jaw was broken in half. The mandible was connected only by the left hinge. The right half was snapped off and balanced between the tree limbs underneath the skull.

For a moment, Eric thought Ocho had placed it there as a sign to anyone who might have followed, but there were no tracks near the tree but his own, and the skull appeared to have been wedged into the fork of the tree for some time. Eric was momentarily overcome with anxiety, imagining the object was cursed. "Oh, that's just nonsense," he hissed, snatching the skull from its perch.

A loud fluttering of wings startled him, causing him to drop the skull as birds fled from the tree branches overhead. Watching the skull shatter into pieces on the ground, he instantly began feeling dizzy. The ground seemed to crawl. Eric blinked several times in an attempt to straighten his vision and looked around to see who or what might have frightened him and the birds. But he saw nothing.

Suddenly there was a whooshing sound. He whirled around 180 degrees to face the sound as it seemed to race up behind him. An invisible, ominous energy tore at his nerves. The leaves of the tree rustled above him, and the huge branches eerily twisted and creaked on a stiff, swirling wind.

"Ocho?" Eric called. No response. "O-cho!" Still nothing. His vision darkened into a narrow tunnel as his skipping heart seemed to tumble end over end in his chest. His hands trembled, and his feet grew cold and numb. Eric felt that he was losing control. He found it increasingly difficult to distinguish whether this was really happening or another dream.

Staggering toward the impenetrable undergrowth before him, he searched desperately for a path through the gnarled spinney. He crashed through the thorny brush. The cracking branches snapped under him as he fell to the ground at the base of the shrub. Not ten feet away, he spotted a narrow passage through the bramble. He jumped to his feet and forced his way through the thick twigs, finally arriving at a trail.

Ocho had been this way; his boot tracks were fresh in the dirt. Crouching low, Eric followed the footsteps through the thick undergrowth, which led into an opening in the rock ahead.

The slot canyon was exactly as it had appeared in his dream. Once inside, he felt immediately calm and unafraid. As the waves of adrenaline receded, painful stinging called his awareness to his many cuts and scrapes. He traversed the undulating gorge easily, as though he had passed this way a hundred times before. Eric soon found himself in the vaulted cavern, the many petroglyphs and handprints high on the wall precisely as he had foreseen. Just as in his vision, the tracks he had followed came to an abrupt halt in the center of the cavern. There was no other sign of Ocho Whitewolf.

Eric scanned the sandy floor and walls for any clue that could help him divine where Ocho might have gone. His attention became fixed on a comforting, familiar shape carved into the wall; a place that touched him more deeply that any other place he had ever been—Spider Rock. Transfixed, he stared unblinkingly at the image until he was aware of nothing else. Not the world around him; not his stinging scratches; not his breathing; not the swelling, thunderous, sound that reverberated through the narrow canyon. Not even his own existence. He stared until his trembling vision was overtaken by a brilliant, white light.

# Chapter Nine

By the time Oliver, Mike, Truman, and Sean arrived, the creek was swollen with swift-moving water. A deluge gushed from the slot canyon. "Where is all that water coming from?" Sean asked.

"Rain," Oliver simply replied.

"Rain?" asked Sean. "It's been cloudy all day, but I never felt a drop."

"You always get flash floods this time of year in Arizona," Truman explained. "It could be raining miles away, and the only warning you get before getting slammed with a wall of water is the rumble of rolling boulders and debris."

"God, I sure hope they weren't in there when it hit," Mike said, nervously.

"What do we do?" Sean asked. "I wish we had Chad and his phone now."

"I've got mine," Truman said, digging it from his pocket. "Uh, scratch that. I'm out of range."

"Chad had service back at Oliver's place," Sean said. "Shouldn't we go back and try there? Or we could even drive into town for help if we have to."

"I'm not leaving here without Eric," Mike said adamantly. He thought back to when he met Eric on the first day of kindergarten. He was scared and shy, and wanted so badly to just run home in tears, until Eric approached him and asked if he wanted to play. They played all recess, pushing Eric's Star Wars land speeder toy up and down the concrete walkways. From that moment Eric had always been like a brother.

Pacing nervously, Mike announced, "Eric said there was a slot canyon here that he was dying to explore, and there it is. If it wasn't flooded when he got here, I guarantee he went in there."

Scanning the area, Oliver suggested, "Well, let's look around and see if we can find any sign of them. Maybe they found another way back to camp. Truman, if we could take your phone, Sean and I will check there, just in case, while you and Mike look downstream. If they aren't at camp, we'll call for help and meet you back here."

For hours, Mike and Truman tirelessly walked the water's edge, carefully inspecting every bush and tree for any sign that they might have clung to them if they had been washed along by the water. The hopeful friends searched until dark, before Oliver and Sean arrived with a dispatch of tribal police and several fire and rescue workers.

The star-filled sky was cloudless and clear. By this time, the water that rushed from the canyon was reduced to a mere trickle. The rescuers waded across the now slow-moving creek and ventured into the narrow canyon. Mike listened intently to the conversations of the police and other rescue workers for any news or word. Mike called Oliver over. "What's a *Hatałii*?" he asked.

"It's a traditional Navajo medicine man. Why?" Oliver asked.

"One of those cops told the other that he was really close to here yesterday with the feds, investigating a murder. They found the mutilated body of a *Hatałii*. He said the buzzards had been at him."

"Are you sure?" Oliver asked. "This area is really remote. Nobody has lived anywhere near here forever. Why would a *Hatałii* come up here? There's no one out here to heal. And who would have found him?"

"He could have been dumped here," Mike suggested.

"Yeah, maybe so," Oliver agreed. "Is there any word on your friend?"

"No, not yet," Mike replied, sadly. "I overheard the searchers on the radio saying it's just too dark in there to find anything. They said there are areas where water has pooled, where someone could get pinned underneath; but they can't find anything until it recedes. What a nightmare!"

"I'm sorry I wasn't here," Oliver said.

"It's not your fault, man," Mike assured him. "It's not like anyone of us could have known this would happen."

The swift water rescue team spent several hours searching the thicket and banks of the creek bed, but came up empty-handed. They abandoned the search and left around midnight.

Oliver placed his hand on Mike's shoulder saying, "C'mon, my friend, let's go back and get some food and rest."

"I'm alright, thanks," Mike said, forcing a smile. "You guys go ahead. I'm gonna stay here in case Eric shows up."

Truman and Sean looked at each other, silently expressing their doubt that Eric or Ocho would be seen alive again. "Do you want me to stay with you?" Truman asked.

"No, no, you guys go ahead, I'm cool," Mike answered.

Sean stepped forward, asking, "Are you sure, man?"

"No, really, go back."

Sean was actually relived to be dismissed. "Okay, then, if you're sure," he said.

"I'd feel better if you came back with us," Oliver said. "This place can be very dark at night."

"I'll build a fire and camp out right here in the sand," Mike said. "Don't worry, I'm alright."

"Okay," Oliver agreed. "We'll bring you something to eat in the morning. Then we'll get into that slot canyon and see if there is any sign of them. Will you wait for us?"

Mike nodded and said his goodbyes to the guys after they had helped him gather wood to burn. The enormous, red moon rose late in the northeastern sky, magnified by the atmosphere that curved along the horizon. He kept a fire going long into the night. For hours he prayed earnestly for his friend to be safe from harm; but if he were truly lost, he prayed for a sign, and for the strength to accept it.

Moments after each prayer, he nodded off and then shook himself awake and looked at the moon. It was a night of a long moon for Mike. Each time he checked, it had made little progress in its westerly trek across the sky. It was finally beginning to sink in the West, when eight lights in a V-formation approached quietly from the Northwest.

The object eclipsed the moon, revealing to Mike that the lights, four on either side, were attached to a solid triangular object. From the base of the mesa, Mike's view was obscured as the mysterious object disappeared behind the large mountain. Mike was exhilarated by the sighting, but after another hour, exhaustion overtook him, and he fell heavily asleep.

Aroused by the nearby sound of tinkling bells, Mike opened his eyes to see a column of approaching figures, dimly illuminated by the small flame and faint glowing embers. Frightened, he closed his eyes, pretending to be asleep. To his surprise, they appeared within his mind as luminous apparitions. Awestruck, Mike tried to blink them away, attempting to hold visions of other, mundane things in his mind. Lying motionless, Mike kept his eyes tightly closed.

Sensing his fright and wonderment, the twelve figures attempted to put him at ease by arranging themselves in a wide semicircle around him, so as to not surround him completely. They were each different in appearance, each of them wearing clothing and masks evocative of kachinas, the various ancestral spirits deified by the Hopi and impersonated in religious rituals by masked dancers.

"What do you want?" Mike blurted.

They made no sound but communicated directly into his mind. "A time of great upheaval is coming to the Earth. The people of this world have been misled and have forgotten ancient wisdoms. They have been corrupted and now they live against Earth, not with her. Earth will soon be purified to bring an end to this age of separation."

Mike wasn't sure if he was awake. It seemed that he was shown visions of global cataclysms: geomagnetic storms, massive unprecedented earthquakes, volcanoes, tornadoes, hurricanes, tsunamis, and floods.

Horrified, Mike asked the mysterious strangers, "You mean the end of the world?"

"The end of separation," Mike heard telepathically. "The end of this world." The voice in Mike's head continued, "From a crack in the universe, all things flow like water bubbling from an underground spring. Everything in existence spills forth from this source of creation: the Earth, the sun, this and every galaxy, all traveling through the universe like bubbles on the stream. This galaxy has been floating through the creative source for millions of years. The people were placed here by the Creator to be her caretakers." The strange entities continued, "But the people have become greedy and have not fulfilled their divine purpose. Earth was to have been readied to pass safely through the void, but places of Earth's power have been abandoned and forgotten. Soon the Earth Mother will need those who still remember their obligation to restore her to health. In the process, they will heal themselves. Piercing the illusion of separation, the people will remove the veils that have blinded them to their connection to all things. You will soon see again, and so will your missing friends. Mourn no more, they are not lost; but now, sleep."

# Chapter Ten

Mike awoke to Oliver, Sean, Truman, and Charlie Moreth standing over him. Silhouetted against the morning sun, Charlie said, "Sorry about your friend, Michael; such a loss."

Uncertain about Charlie's sincerity, Mike said nothing. He sat up rubbing his eyes. The guys sat around him. Oliver handed Mike some warm food bundled in a cloth. "I hope you like mutton," he said, quickly getting the fire going.

"Mmm, it's great, thanks." Mike tore off a piece of the fatty meat with his teeth. "You guys, I had the most amazing experience last night," he said with his mouth full. "I saw a huge, delta-shaped object in the sky. It drifted silently, right over me and disappeared behind the mesa," he said, pointing.

Oliver nodded, "This is the mountain. I've seen them here from my house."

"Amazing," Truman said excitedly. "There has to be a connection. This has to be a place of great significance."

"God damn it!" Sean cursed. "Why didn't I stay here last night?"

"Hey! Watch your mouth," Charlie demanded.

"Sorry Charlie," Sean said. "I'm just disappointed. I've waited my whole life for something like that."

"I understand your being upset," Charlie replied. "I've waited my life, too. Not for a UFO sighting, but for a theophany."

"Speaking of divine manifestation, I think I was actually visited last night. I was given a vision, a warning of a turbulent future," Mike said.

Sean asked excitedly, "Did you have a close encounter of the third kind?"

Charlie skeptically interposed, "Close encounter of the third kind? You watch too many movies."

"There is sometimes truth in fiction, Charlie," Truman jumped in. "It's a technical term. The third kind of close encounter classifies an observation of or interaction with animate beings associated with a UFO."

"Is that what you saw, Mike? Aliens coming out of a flying saucer?" Charlie asked.

"No, not exactly," Mike answered. "I did see this unusual flying object. I don't know what it was. But I couldn't say if the beings I saw were from the craft because they came later from out of the darkness on foot. Whatever they were, they looked more like kachinas then anything else I could associate them with."

"What do you mean?" asked Charlie.

"They looked a lot like the kachina dolls that the Hopi carve."

Charlie looked confused.

"What, you've never seen one?" Mike asked impatiently. "They spoke telepathically, directly into my mind. There were twelve of them in strange masks. No—they were more like helmets, some shaped like animals, and others were unlike anything I have ever seen. They wore elaborate shirts or cloaks, and kilts and boots made from shimmering fabrics unlike any I have ever seen. They wore jingling bells, and three of them had feathered wings."

"Feathered wings?" Charlie interrupted excitedly. "Like angels of the Lord?"

"Hold on now, I didn't say anything like that," Mike said. "The three wore feathered wings, connected to their arms somehow. Their masks and clothing represented an eagle, an owl, and a hawk, I think."

Perplexed, Sean asked, "Why would interstellar travelers wear animal costumes? Are you sure you didn't dream it all?"

"I am positive that I didn't," Mike insisted. "But I can't say who or what they are, or where they come from, and I don't care if it fits with what any of you is able to believe."

"Well, it sure fits with what I believe," Charlie said. "They had wings; spoke to your soul; prophesized of future tribulations. They were agents of Jehovah! And how's this for animal and eagle faces? Straight from the Bible, Ezekiel 1:10:

> And there were the hands of a man under their wings on their four sides, and the four of them had their faces and their wings. And as for the likeness of their faces, the four of them had a man's face with a lion's face to the right, and the four of them had a bull's face on the left; the four of them also had an eagle's face. That is the way their faces were. And their wings were spreading out upward.

"Is that not what you saw?" Charlie asked.

"I see where you're going with this, Charlie," Mike said calmly, "but I'm not ready to jump to any conclusions. You want to see them as angels; they want to see them as aliens. A Hopi would see them as benevolent spirits. All I know is that they were here and they were real. They told me the Earth is about to go through some cataclysmic changes."

"Tribulations," Charlie interrupted.

Glaring at Charlie, Mike continued, "They knew I was here, worried for Eric and Ocho. They assured me that my friends are alright, that we will find them alive and well."

"Then let's quit all the blah, blah, blah, and get into that slot canyon," said Truman.

As they crossed the creek, Sean approached Mike saying, "When we get some time later, I'd like to take an official report of your sighting."

"Sure, of course," Mike said. "After we find Eric."

Oliver stepped into the passage through the rock. His feet sank deep into the thick, sandy mud, his foot slipping out of his shoe with his next step. He dug through the cold mud until he found it, and stumbled back out and sat on the rocks. "You're gonna want to take off your shoes," he said. "But bring 'em with you."

"I want to find Eric too and all," Charlie wheedled, "but we don't all need to go tromping through there, do we?"

"Stay if you want," Mike said, taking off his shoes and rolling up his pant legs.

"I'll hang back here with Charlie," Sean said.

Truman kicked off his shoes. "What a couple of pansies," he scoffed.

"You going then?" Mike asked.

"I ain't skeered. They don't call me Tru-man for nothing," he quipped.

Trudging through the mud and wading through the sporadic pools, the three slowly squeezed through the narrow channel. After an arduous trek, they spilled into the cavern, covered in mud.

"Whoa, look at this place," Truman said. "You never knew this was here, Oliver?"

"No, no one ever comes this way," he answered.

A brilliant shaft of light beamed down from above as Mike scanned the ceiling and walls. "Amazing," he said. "It's just like Eric said it would be."

"Hmm?" Oliver questioned, looking strangely at Mike.

"Eric saw it in a dream the night before he got here," Mike explained.

Investigating the many glyphs that lined the walls, Truman said, "Look how precise the carvings are. They look brand new."

"Yeah, you're right," Mike agreed. "And with all the flash floods that have ripped through here shaping these walls, these carvings might barely exist at all if they were ancient."

"Are you saying they are fakes?" Oliver asked.

"It's not at all what I expected," said Mike. "I wouldn't want to guess what they are without significant scrutiny. But look. These designs are sites from around the world, aren't they? Doesn't that one look like the peak above Machu Pichu?"

"It does," Truman answered. "And there's a Mayan-looking pyramid over here; and Serpent Mound over there."

"Weird. I'd like to try to date these. Maybe we can get that team back up from Flagstaff. It looks like we'll be here for a few more days, if it's okay with you."

"Fine with me," Oliver said. "But what about Eric?"

"You know, it's strange," Mike pondered, "but somehow I know he and Ocho are okay. They'll turn up soon enough. I can feel it."

# Chapter Eleven

Chad's plane landed in Cancun shortly after 10:00 AM. As they taxied slowly to the terminal, he retrieved his Blackberry from his jacket pocket and checked his messages. A text message from Dr. Martain read: "*Meet me at Chichen Itza as soon as you get in*".

The second the plane rolled to a stop at the gate, all the passengers shot to their feet. Chad stood hunched under the overhead cargo bin, his neck wrenched uncomfortably and his hat knocked crookedly on his head. The passengers glanced nosily around the plane, no one formerly acknowledging one another and shying away from any lasting eye contact.

Chad pushed his way into the crowded aisle behind an attractive young woman, a haughty belle here to whoop it up in Cancun with a couple of her girlfriends. The throng of passengers surged forward, pressing Chad tightly against her. She looked over her shoulder at him snobbishly, to which the socially inept Chad joked, "Don't worry, I brought protection."

"Eew," she said as she shuddered in disgust.

Amused with himself, he smirked proudly, not even remotely aware of the offensive inappropriateness of his joke. The crowd surged again. "Come on people, you can only go as fast as the person in front of you," Chad muttered over his shoulder.

After exiting the plane, he worked his way through the crowded terminal and immediately boarded a tour bus headed for the Mayan ruins. As the bus wound through the crowded road leaving the airport, Chad watched a 747 as it barreled down the runway gathering speed for takeoff. He watched it climb higher and higher until it was a silhouette against a peculiarly quivering sun.

"Can I take your trash?" the stewardess said, smiling in a contrived sort of way.

From being lost in his thoughts, a business traveler snapped to attention. "Mmm, yes, thank you," he said, handing her a condensation-spotted, plastic cup of melted ice, stuffed with a wadded napkin. The low drone of the engine outside his window was hypnotic, as the plane cruised on at 38,000 ft above northern Arizona, on its way from San Antonio to Salt Lake City. He sank deeply back into his thoughts. Weighing heavily on his mind was the way his small children had clung to him, not wanting him to leave. "This is really important. I'm really close to wrapping up this deal," he had tried to explain to the kids, but it did not change the way they felt. "I'll be back soon, and we'll have all the time in the world. We'll do something fun," he promised. But he had lost the sale anyway. He felt horrible. If he had only known the trip would be pointless, he would have stayed home with his family, he thought. But the truth is he would surely have found something else to keep him busy because downtime had always made him feel idle and unimportant in the world.

He stared through his reflection in the window. His view from near the tail was almost completely obstructed by the enormous, cylindrical engine on the other side of the glass. The sky suddenly exploded with color. The overhead reading lights and movie screens went black. The low hum of the engines fell silent. The plane tipped nose down and hurtled toward the ground.

Apart from a few wailing and panicked passengers, the majority were quiet, resolute, and introspective. Many softly recited prayers. The businessman tightly gripped the armrests. He closed his eyes and pictured his family, realizing now that he had never been more important to anyone in the world than he was to them.

Miles away, in the farthest corner of northwestern Arizona, just outside of Kingman proper, a boy had raced home from school to play the used Nintendo videogame system his sister had bought him for his birthday. Playing *Mario 64*, Aaron maneuvered the title character to access inter-dimensional worlds through paintings hung on the walls, where he searched for magic stars that would allow further access to other hidden realms. Playing happily, he sat on the floor, absorbed in the game. Without warning the screen suddenly went black.

"No!" shouted Aaron, angrily yanking the game cartridge from the slot and blowing forcefully across the circuit card hoping to clean away any dust. He set the cartridge back in the slot and pounded it down with his fist. Rapidly he flicked the on/off switch back and forth. He got up and stomped around the room, grumbling. He stomped over to the TV to check the connections. Repeatedly he unplugged the units and plugged them back in.

"Mom!" Aaron shouted as he threw his bedroom door open and thundered down the hall. "There's something wrong with my game system!"

"The power just went out," she answered from the kitchen.

"Didn't you pay the bill?" Aaron huffed condemningly.

His mother looked up from her Hollywood gossip magazine and glared at him over the half wall that separated the kitchen from the living room. "Of course I paid the bill. Sometimes power just goes out," she said impatiently. "Deal with it."

"Can you fix it?"

She shook her head. "We'll just have to wait 'til it comes back on."

"Dad could fix it," he grumbled.

Angrily, his mother asked, "What?"

"Nothing."

"Why don't you go outside and play?" she suggested.

Still grumbling, Aaron stormed outside, slamming the door behind him. Seconds later he rushed back inside shouting excitedly, "Mom, come take a look at this!"

"What is it?"

"There's something wrong with the sky," he called. "You gotta see it!"

Annoyed, she sighed and laid her magazine on the table, splayed open to keep her page, and rose from her chair. "What is it, a storm?" she asked as she stepped out onto the front porch. She froze mid-stride, staring dumbfounded at the violently swirling, multicolored sky.

Aaron asked his mother, "What is it?"

She just shook her head. "I've never seen anything like it." Frightened, she moved toward the door. "Let's go back inside and call Dad," she said.

For a moment, Aaron got excited. Then he realized she intended to call his step dad. Following after her, he mumbled, "What's Jerry gonna do?"

She picked up the phone and put it to her ear. "Phone's out too," she said with obvious concern. "Where's you're sister?"

Aaron shrugged his shoulders. "At Laura's house?"

"Go get her, quick," she commanded. "And come straight home."

Curiously, the tour bus had stalled and ground to a halt. Chad looked out the windows at the congested streets of Cancun. Traffic was frozen. Inoperable cars were crumpled into each other as their befuddled drivers and passengers poured into the streets, pointing in awe at the rainbow burst of colors rippling across the sky.

Chad gaped in horror at the plane he had watched climb gracefully into the sky, now cartwheeling nose over tail as it plummeted toward the crowded street. He jumped from the bus and pushed through the scattering crowd, running as fast as he could into the lobby of one of the resorts just off the main strip.

The plane slammed forcefully into the jammed street, sending debris and a spreading wave of bulging fire in all directions. Amidst the chaos and panicked screams, Chad pushed his way into a darkened stairwell and tumbled down the steps and over a mass of fallen people as the surge of broiling heat and fire ripped through the lobby behind him, blasting through the wall and covering him with a cascade of bricks and debris.

Mike, Truman, and Oliver emerged from within the mountain amazed to find the turbulent sky filled with a rippling aurora of pink, green, blue and purple. "Whoa, that can't be the northern lights," Truman exclaimed.

"I think it is," answered Mike.

"But we're way south," Truman argued.

"I know. And it's broad daylight," Mike agreed, "but what else could it be?"

Everywhere the sky swirled with electromagnetic activity. From all directions, over the horizons rose high columns of smoke.

"What's going on?" Truman asked, nervously. "And where's Sean and Charlie?"

Oliver pointed at their tracks leading away. "It looks like they went back to camp," he said.

"Well, let's go ahead and get back, too," Mike said. He took a few quick steps before stumbling on an ant hill. The coarse dirt scattered over several feet. Within seconds, hundreds of ants stormed out of the ground, running frantically in all directions. Watching the chaotic scene, Mike began to feel sorry for the panicked creatures. He couldn't quite understand why he felt so incredibly sad, but somehow he knew that it had to do with much more than the destroyed ant colony.

Shortly they arrived at the camp to find Sean and Charlie terribly shaken. "What's going on?" Truman asked.

"Oh my God, guys, I think we're under attack from terrorists!" Sean exclaimed.

"What? Why? What happened?" Truman asked.

"Me and Charlie got bored and hungry, and decided to come back to camp. We were halfway back when, all a sudden, the sky got all psychedelic and a plane just dropped from the sky!"

Charlie jumped in, explaining, "It was high in the sky; just a dot with a long vapor trail. The trail just stopped right there," he said, pointing to the southwestern sky, "and it just dropped, falling in the direction of Flagstaff; falling, falling, falling, boom! See the smoke? Look, it's been burning for over two hours, like no one has even tried to put it out."

"Look, there, and there, and there, and there," Sean said, pointing out several other distant plumes of black smoke. "We think those are planes too. It's got to be a coordinated attack, like 9-11."

"I think they were brought down by EMP," Mike suggested.

"You think they got their hands on a weaponized electromagnetic pulse?" Sean asked anxiously.

"No, no, the technology for that is way off," Truman answered.

"Unbelievable," Mike said. "I was just talking about this with Eric yesterday."

"What?" asked Sean.

"Solar flares. Usually the particles ejected from the sun are deflected by the earth's magnetic field, with some of it swirling around a bit in the north and south magnetic poles, causing aurora phenomena. But look at the sky. It would take an unimaginably massive solar storm to put enough electromagnetic particles into the atmosphere to cover the sky with aurora borealis like this. This far south; and in broad daylight. A sun storm of that size would surely knock out satellites, the power grid, planes, even the cars. It could even affect weather worldwide."

Skeptically, Charlie argued, "Come on. Really? Even the cars?"

"Oh yeah, everything." Mike explained, "We learned through all the atomic testing in the '40s and '50s that an EMP would stop a car engine. It interrupts the spark and shuts the motor right down. The fluctuating polarities can make any electrical item inoperable." He walked over to his Land Rover, inserted the key in the ignition and turned it. Nothing happened. No radio, no start. "Hey guys," Mike called out. "Try to start your vehicles."

None of the vehicles worked. Charlie shouted from his minivan, "My flashlight doesn't even work. The batteries are brand new!"

"No, an EMP wouldn't affect a flashlight," Truman argued. "I don't think."

"Mine's out," Sean responded.

"Mine too," Mike added as he shook the batteries inside the plastic casing. "Oliver, do you have power?"

Oliver shook his head. "Never did."

"You've lived all your life without electricity?" Sean asked, astonished.

"Well, no. When I was away at school, I had it. Also when I lived in Phoenix for a few years, until I started feeling dependent on it, like I could never go back to living without it. It was then I started to remember what my grandfather always said, and I came back to live here."

"Why's that?" Sean asked. "What did your grandfather say?"

"He taught me how, for thousands of years, our ancestors passed down their knowledge from generation to generation. We built on that knowledge and made few improvements. Not because we were inferior, but because we never needed much more than we had always used. Because it had always sustained us. We lived content and in balance, provided by the Earth with all we needed, until Kit Carson took us on the long walk to the first reservation, and made us needy of the white man and what they gave us. Many fled to Canyon de Chelly and jumped to their deaths rather than be forced to live that way. Out of desperation, some broke taboos and turned to the *Witchery Way* to survive on the run. Most others gave in, having no other choice. The elders and traditionalists since then are still afraid that we have become too reliant on new technologies. They've seen how fast white people have made new advancements and abandoned the knowledge that they had previously built on without passing it down to younger generations."

"It's true," Mike added. "Look how much we've forgotten in just three generations. Everything is mechanized, and the production of each part is specialized. There's practically nobody who knows how to produce something from raw material to finished product. We'd be screwed if some cataclysm wiped away our technology."

"And our elders always said it," Oliver continued. "They warned that the people of the world would become so dependent on their inventions that they would soon forget how to survive without them. They said that when that day came the people would seek the help of indigenous peoples to teach them how to survive off of what Mother Earth provides. But that's what scares me. How will we be able to help? More and more Navajo live like modern people and have no interest in learning the old ways; it's too much hard work. So many Navajo don't even remember what it means to be Diné. The missionaries have been up here trying to *save* us for hundreds of years, but there is no saving here. If you ask me, it's been the death of our culture. Now most Navajos are Mormons and Baptists and Catholics; and now the Jehovah's Witnesses are spreading like wildfire, too."

"Hey!" Charlie shouted, offended. "We *are* teaching you how to be saved. You think that when final judgment comes you'll be able to get by with a bow and arrow and beef jerky? The only salvation is in Jesus."

Wrestling with his urge to clobber Charlie, Oliver clenched his fist tightly until his knuckles turned white. As much as Mike felt that Charlie deserved a good rap in the mouth, he stepped in between them saying, "Well, if the solar flares are big enough to bring down planes and shut off all our technology, Jesus better hurry up and do something; because you know the towns and cities will have fallen into chaos."

"You think so?" Truman asked. "You've got to give the American people more credit than that. Moments like these bring out the heroes in us. It's moments like these that we shine."

Mike thought of the frantic ants fleeing in panic from their scattered earthen mound. "I wish I had that kind of faith," he said. "Sadly, I have to disagree about the fortitude of the American people—the whole human race for that matter. Right now, I'm sure they're working together to do what they can to help one another. But with a worldwide power outage, the food will rot on the shelves, and it'll be some time before transportation and communication lines are up and running again. Too few are prepared for something like this. No one out there knows how to go about getting food anymore. And I'm one of them. As far as most of us know, food comes in cans and boxes, and neat cuts of meat from a Styrofoam tray, wrapped in plastic. People will do what they must to get by, and soon they will turn to taking from one another. It'll be survival of the ruthless—the rise of marauding bands of takers."

"No, I don't think it'll get all *Mad Max*, like that." Truman argued. "The government can declare martial law and dispense rations. We trained for that in the National Guard."

"They prepared to move it by horse and buggy?" Mike argued.

Truman responded defensively, "By whatever means necessary!"

Charlie jumped in, raving, "These are the trials and tribulations. The end times. Billions will die; and when the wicked are all destroyed, millions will be resurrected to live in an earthly paradise with the righteous survivors, where we'll be ruled by a heavenly government. It's even written on the rocks right here."

Frustrated, Oliver walked away, muttering, "You're not the only one with prophecies, dumb ass."

"So, Mike," Truman said, leading him away from the others, "if this is all because of an EMP from solar flares, they should be able to get things up and running again soon, right?"

Mike pulled the wheeled cooler over to the fire pit, the icy water sloshing violently inside. He sat on the cooler and said, "I don't know. It seems like what's going on is a continuous electromagnetic disturbance, not just a single pulse. It stands to reason that once the sun storm subsides, anything that's not fried might work again." Mike looked cautiously over his shoulder at the others. Charlie was chewing Sean's ear with end times prophecies. He said quietly to Truman, "But I don't think we're going to get a chance to find out. This is just the beginning. It's all happening just like the vision those strange kachina-like beings showed me last night. They specifically showed me geomagnetic storms like this, and, judging from that, the worst is definitely yet to come: worldwide earthquakes and volcanic eruptions; unprecedented hurricanes, tornadoes, tsunamis, and unchecked wildfires. We're talking global devastation on a biblical scale. Part of me feels really glad to be out here, away from the cities. But I'm really worried for my friends and family."

"Yeah, family," Truman said, thinking deeply. "The worst part is, out here, we'll get no word about what's happening with the rest of the world, whether your vision comes true or not. And what makes you so sure we'll be safer out here anyway? Did they tell you that?"

"Well, er, no. I just have a strong feeling about it, like we're all supposed to be here right now for some reason.

Somehow, it just makes sense to me. And, of course we'll be safer camping up here in the high deserts. I mean, would you really want to be back in your office in L.A. as it hits the fan? After all, it's not earthquakes that kill people, it's the collapsing buildings and falling debris."

Truman agreed, nodding. "So what do we do? Sit around here for weeks trying to wait out something that may or not really be happening? Some event we have no way of confirming?"

"I don't know what to do," Mike sighed, irritated that Truman expected him to have the answers. "I was told that all of this would happen as a result of a rare cosmic event. The sun passing through some kind of anomalous region of space is what caused these solar eruptions. If I understand it correctly, it'll really go off when the Earth passes through it. And I can only guess when that will be. It could happen tomorrow. I think maybe we ought to just focus all our attention on that mountain. That's where we'll find our answers."

# Chapter Twelve

Exhausted and dehydrated, Eric crouched to sit in the shade of a rocky overhang to rest. He didn't know where he was or how he got here. All he knew was that he had awakened in a shallow cavity high on a steep canyon wall. Unlike the red siltstone of the slot canyon, the walls here were tan and streaked with long, vertical swaths of dark brown where the mineral reactions with rain runoff had left their artistic mark. For hours he had treaded back and forth along a narrow ledge, searching for a way either up or down. The path extended for twenty yards or so in either direction of the cave, each narrowing trail tapering to mere inches before terminating flush with the cliff face.

Leading up near the end of the ledge to his right were hand and footholds carved into the glittering, sandstone wall. Over time, however, they had eroded and become far too shallow for Eric to risk. There were hand and footholds to the left as well, leading down. But even if he were not mildly afraid of heights, Eric would have had to be truly desperate to try them. His only option, he decided, was to wait for help.

He sat watching the dancing lights ripple across the afternoon sky, each wave appearing to reach closer and closer to the ground. The gorgeous iridescent sky and the beauty of the canyon, juxtaposed against his helpless situation, made Eric wonder if it was another one of his strange dreams. He wondered where he was. He wished Ocho were here. The air was motionless, hot and heavy. Wearily hopeless, Eric hung his head, a bead of sweat hanging from the tip of his nose. He jiggled his head, trying to shake the droplet loose, when he was startled by a quick movement near his foot.

Instinctively, he kicked at the intrusive, fist-sized object, sending it tumbling end over end. It came to a rest just short of tumbling over the ledge. Curled in a ball, it sat still for a moment before unfurling to reveal its arachnid form. The tarantula crawled purposefully toward Eric. Repulsed and frightened, he jumped up and backed away toward the rear wall of the cave, where he stood compulsively scratching the head-to-toe itch he suffered every time he saw a spider. Curiously, his body pulsed and tingled against the sandstone wall. Afraid to turn his back on the hairy spider, he wrenched his neck to look over his shoulder and inspect the wall. There was a faint carving of Spider Rock. The corner of his eye caught the tarantula advancing.

"Leave me alone and I'll let you live," he bargained with the giant spider. It stopped, remaining motionless for a long moment. Eric relaxed and stepped away from the wall. Without warning, the tarantula bolted toward Eric at top speed, driving him back. With no place to retreat, he kicked again, sending it several feet across the cave's narrow floor. Upon settling, it instantly unfurled and determinedly charged again. Frightened, Eric shouted, "What do you want?" He kicked the relentless spider harder, this time sending it over the edge.

For the rest of the afternoon and all through the night, Eric sat doubled over with painful hunger. The night was terribly cold. Getting little sleep, he watched the dazzling aerial light show to pass the time and distract his thoughts. By morning, he was so hungry he thought of the tarantula, wishing he hadn't so hastily evicted his companion and only potential food source.

He spent the day watching the canyon rim across the gulf for any possible rescue, but aside from the occasional, swiftly darting cliff swallow or echoing raven caw, there was no sign of life. Watching the sky, he hoped to see a helicopter or plane, but there was nothing. Not even a high vapor trail.

Early morning on the third day, Eric thought he must surely be hallucinating as he watched a black object float silently above the canyon. Silhouetted against the aurora phenomenon, the enormous black triangle blocked the stars. Eric wondered where he had seen the familiar shape.

One by one, four lights appeared on the left side. Wrapping around the object, four lights continued to appear on the right. He recognized it as the black boomerang-shaped object with eight white dots that was painted on the piece of shale he had bought from the Navajo woman several days earlier at Canyon de Chelly. He remembered her saying, "I don't know what it is. I seen it over there, in that canyon there."

He looked out in the dark, wondering if he had somehow wandered back to Canyon de Chelly, or if he had ever really left. He chuckled to himself at the thought of seeing an unusual object in the sky, and wished Mike were here to validate the experience, to try and convince him it was real.

By daybreak, his stomach pangs had subsided, but his throat was dry with an incredible thirst. Weakened and dizzy, he decided to try to climb up using the worn hand and footholds before the sun warmed and deprived him further of strength. He shuffled along the ledge, grabbed the wall, and tried to stick his foot into one of the shallow holes; but his shoe was too big. Unable to get any traction, he decided to try again barefooted. He stuffed his socks into his shoes and tied the Chuck Taylors together by their laces, and draped them around his neck.

His arms trembling and hands fatigued, Eric inched slowly toward the top. His blistered and bleeding fingers throbbed with pain as he climbed, coaching himself to keep going and not look down. *I'm gonna make it*, he thought, until he got stuck at the top, unsure how to pull himself onto the ledge. He wiggled his toes deeper into their holds and stretched to reach over the rim. Feeling for anything anchored firmly enough to climb out with, his hand soon found a craggily juniper root. Digging away the dirt underneath it, Eric struggled to get his hand wrapped firmly around. He threw his other hand over the edge, securing a two-handed grip. With a forceful push of his legs, he scooted his belly onto the ledge. The effort had sapped his energy. With all his remaining strength, he forced his body to roll over until he lay on his back, staring up into the strange looking morning sky.

His strength slowly returned until he felt able to get to his feet and start exploring. Unsure of which direction he was going, he wandered along the rim of the canyon well into the afternoon. His black shirt absorbed the glaring sun. His arms and face were badly burned, his lips dry and peeling.

He staggered along, eyes barely open, wearily tripping over rocks and shrubs until he collapsed hard to the ground. His muscles ached as he lay there a while gathering his strength for another try. Slowly he pulled himself up and stood on wobbly legs. Glancing across the canyon, Eric noticed an old, white-haired Indian man standing on the opposite rim waving him over.

Cupping his hands around his mouth, Eric's dry throat cracked as he shouted, "Hey! How do you get to the other side?"

The old man, still waving, answered, "You *are* on the other side."

Exhausted, Eric's sight faded to black and he dropped to the ground.

He had no way of knowing how long he had been out. His breathing was the only sound he heard. Eric's wide eyes strained, clawing for any sliver of light in the pitch black. A faint glow emanating from his hands caught his attention. Waving them in front of his face, he was amazed to visually perceive his fingers in the dark, but their luminosity cast no light on his surroundings.

The more he focused his eyes to inspect his unusual glow, the more difficult it became to maintain sight of it. He soon learned to relax his stare to maintain his perception of the luminescence that shone from within him. Once able to control his extrasensory awareness, he could perceive the aura radiating from his whole being.

Eric watched the waves of pervasive energy that emanated from him, soon realizing that they actually recycled through him. Bands of energy forming a spherical lattice around him funneled down through the top of his head, through his body and out his feet, flowing out into the circular stream, and cycling again down through his head. The energy that surrounded him and fed him was his, yet he was also simultaneously pulling in the ubiquitous energy from the boundless space that surrounded him.

As his awareness expanded, Eric became conscious of an immense network of energetic connections. It was structured similar to a web, but constructing cells like a honeycomb, extended infinitely in all directions: behind him, in front of him, to each side of him, above and below him. Residing within each of the billions of cell-like spheres were other beings: human and animal, even plants and trees, all appearing as luminous apparitions. Like the energy that cycled through Eric, every entity connected to the infinite web was encapsulated and comprised of a common energy shared throughout the entire interconnected network.

He thought of how Ocho had told him of the power available when calling upon the spirits of all his relations in the invisible world. How spirit was energy. Instantly, upon thinking of Ocho, Eric noticed him in a cell nearby. He was walking, seemingly unaware. Then he stopped and suspiciously looked over his shoulder, directly at Eric, as if his senses had somehow told him he was being watched. Not sensing Eric, however, Ocho continued walking, but remained on a strand of the web close by for as long as Eric kept him in his thoughts.

Shifting his thoughts to Mike, the same thing happened. In a nearby cell, he envisioned Mike sitting on an ice chest, warming himself near a fire. He seemed to be deeply troubled, his energy cycling slowly through him. He was speaking to someone apparently seated next to him, but Eric could not see who it was.

Eric's attention was pulled toward the cell closest to him on his left. In it was a hawk, wings outstretched, soaring motionless on an invisible updraft. To his right was perched a white and tawny barn owl, its piercing eyes looking straight ahead. Below him was a large grizzly bear, and above him was a black jaguar that seemed acutely aware of him. It looked through Eric, beyond him, its keen perception indicating that something was happening behind him.

Eric spun around, surprised at the sight of an enormous bioluminescent spider crawling down the energy web toward him. The giant spider dwarfed everything, each leg appearing to be over a hundred feet long. It was coursing with energy, a flowing band of pulsing current that formed a figure eight that made up the abdomen and the fused head and thorax of its arachnidan body. As the huge spider turned to move across the web, Eric noticed the similarity of its body to the infinity symbol.

Having always been terrified of spiders, Eric felt incredibly uneasy as the spider approached, but being part of the web he was unable to flee. There was nothing he could do but watch the spider come closer and closer. He thought of all the spiders he had crushed under his feet, and what they must have thought looking up at him, so gigantic and full of ignorant malice. He felt strange at the reversal. Eric looked into its eight shiny eyes. Seeing himself reflected in the deep, black mirrors of its enormous eyes was unsettling. The spider hovered over him for a moment, then suddenly snatched him up and wrapped him tightly in a glistening silken shroud.

In the dark womb of his cocoon, memories flooded Eric's mind. He recalled the paralysis of fear as he stared into the black, mirror-like eyes of a luminous being outside his window when he was a child. He remembered the intrusive dark presence in his hallway; the hideous skinwalker attack; the visions of tumultuous Earth changes; being transported by the unusual glyphs in the slot canyon to the cave high on the canyon wall. He had vague memories of collapsing unconscious of heatstroke on the canyon rim, and of an old Indian man with his white hair and craggy, sun-weathered face.

Groggy from his ordeal, Eric slowly sat up, adjusting his eyes to the dark. The earthen floor was cold and moist. There were dimly glowing embers in a pit in the floor, and a deep, empty shaft. In the center of the circular room was a ladder crafted of round limbs leading up through a small covered hatch in the ceiling.

From his anthropology courses, he recognized this chamber as a kiva, an underground structure constructed by Pueblo peoples and used for ceremonial purposes. Who brought him here, Eric wondered? How long had he been here? He waited a good while for someone to return, but no one came. Bored and curious, he climbed up the ladder and out of the kiva.

Eric emerged, overwhelmed by the glaring sunlit world. He stood squinting tightly as he looked around, trying to gain some sense of where he was. The kiva was built at the foot of a sheer tower of red sandstone, just above the floor of a wide section of canyon. The kiva entrance was carefully concealed, nestled within a small outcropping of water-eroded rock. Lifting his head, Eric's eyes followed the rocky spire to the dancing, multicolored sky overhead. He was staring upward at Spider Rock.

He explored the surrounding area for a couple of hours, hoping to find some easy way out of the canyon; but the rapidly setting sun made it clear he would be here yet another night. He made his way back to the kiva. Feeling uncomfortable about whether or not he should be found in the kiva, he chose to camp outside in a nearby circular clearing amongst a stand of junipers. He spent a long, uneasy night under the stars where he was easily spooked by the nocturnal sounds and barely slept.

Just before dawn, Eric was startled awake by the snapping of a twig. The crickets had all fallen eerily silent. There was no breeze in the trees. His ears tightened as he strained to detect any sound in the hollow silence, but all he could hear was the pulsing of blood with each heartbeat in his ears. He rubbed his eyes and peeled the lids wide open with his fingers, scanning the area. "What is that?" he whispered to himself as he stared out into the darkness. His eyes caught the faint reflected glint of what seemed to be a white, disembodied face floating in the blackness between two large junipers about twenty feet away.

He stared into the apparition, his vision fading and distorting unreliably as he strained to make out the face in the dark. "Is that someone?" he whispered. "No. There's no one there. Is that a face?" The apparition stared back blankly.

Eric wanted so badly to dismiss what he was seeing as an illusion or a hallucination, but the sense of presence grew increasingly unnerving. He felt surrounded and watched on all sides. He held his breath, occasionally taking small, quiet, shallow gasps. The piercing shriek of an owl drew his attention to his right. He snapped his head to look, seeing the quick whoosh of a dark figure darting behind a bush. Looking back, he shrank with fear. The face was gone, and now there was no doubt. He was not alone.

# Chapter Thirteen

Frantically wrestling to free himself from his sleeping bag, Truman jolted up from his slumber, alerted by the commotion in a nearby tent. Mike was under attack, fighting furiously against what sounded like a ravenous animal. The nylon tent shook and bulged with the thrashing of the combatants inside.

"What's going on in there?" Truman shouted as he struggled with the zipper of Mike's tent. Finally, in frustration, he ripped the flap open, shocked to see his friend pinned to the floor of his tent, straddled by a ghoulish man.

It was a skinwalker, different than the one who had attacked Eric. He wore the matted skin of a black wolf, its face worn over his head, and the body draped down his back. The skin's limp tail swung wildly as the witch fought to keep Mike pinned to the ground. The body and face of the skinwalker were painted black. The snarling wolf snout that jutted over his face cast a deep shadow, behind which gleaming eyes flashed a greenish glint as do an animal's in the dark.

With both hands wrapped tightly around the skinwalker's wrist, Mike struggled to keep it from plunging into his chest a sharpened human bone with a small, tawny brown-spotted feather adhered to the tip.

With Sean and Charlie running up to see what was happening, Truman raced into the tent and grabbed the skinwalker around the neck in a chokehold. The demon spun around, breaking free, and thrust the bone dagger deep into Truman's shoulder. There was an audible snap as the tip broke off in the muscle. With blurring speed, the ghoul bolted from the tent and charged at the others.

"Help me, God," Charlie shrieked as he wrestled Sean in front to shield himself from the fiend. Before Sean knew what hit him, the ghoul tore into his belly, ripping out his intestines. A guttural breath had barely passed Sean's lips before the witch tied the tangled entrails tightly around his throat and used them to drag him by the neck into the void of night.

Mike and Truman stumbled from the tent searching the darkness while Charlie dropped to his knees shouting, "Oh mighty Jehovah! Praise you, God, for sparing me!" Without a word, Truman raced over and kicked him in the mouth, snapping his head back and knocking him to the ground.

Truman staggered around in the dark calling, "Sean! Sean!" He looked at Mike with weary crossed eyes. "Where's Oliver?" he asked and collapsed unconscious to the ground.

Wasting no time, Mike found a dense branch, the length of a baseball bat, to use as a weapon against any further attack. For the next half hour, he stood guard over Truman and Charlie.

Suddenly a voice thundered, "What the hell happened here?"

Startled, Mike jumped and spun around. Relieved, he fairly rejoiced as he recognized Ocho. "Ocho!" Mike shouted as he ran at him and threw his arms around Ocho's enormous torso.

"Whoa," Ocho said, uncomfortably patting Mike's back. "What's going on? What the…What happened to Charlie? He's bleeding like somebody finally punched him in the mouth?"

"Truman hauled off and kicked him in the face."

"Ho man!" Ocho laughed boomingly. "I wish I was here to see that!"

"I do too," Mike said, sadly. "We could have used you. We were attacked by a brujo."

Ocho shuddered, "God, that language. It's like fingernails on a chalkboard."

"What? Well, what do you call it? A skinwalker, then," Mike fumbled. "It got Sean. It took him."

Ocho sprang into action. "Which way did it go?" he asked.

"Over there. It dragged him away into the dark, that way."

"Was he alive?"

Mike shook his head, "I don't know. It all happened so fast."

Ocho jerked his bowie knife from its sheath. "Follow me," he ordered as he swiftly set off to follow the bloody trail.

"What about them?" Mike called.

"Leave 'em. It won't come back here tonight. It's too busy with Sean."

Tightly clutching his makeshift club, Mike hurried after Ocho. "What do you mean?" he asked. His voice jarred with each step.

"It'll spend the whole night doing more gruesome things to Sean than you would ever want to imagine," Ocho replied. "How long of a head-start does it have on us?"

"I don't know," Mike shrugged. "It's hard to say, 'cause my sense of time is like really distorted right now. Maybe between twenty minutes and an hour, I guess."

Following the blood and tracks, Ocho led Mike along the creek, staying near the riparian trees that lined the rocky ground furthest from the water. It was twenty-some minutes until Mike's eyes finally adjusted fully to the pitch darkness.

"Ocho," Mike whispered, "Where is Eric?"

"I don't know."

"Where have you been all this time?"

"Shhhh," Ocho hissed, frustrated. His pace slowed, and his footsteps became more controlled and cautious. His giant knife gleamed in his ready hand. Mike tightened his grip on the branch, quietly crunching the dry, curled bark.

Suddenly a shadowy wolf leapt from the darkness at Mike, knocking him to the ground. Pinned, Mike blocked the wildly snapping jaws with the branch. Bits of bark and dirt fell into Mike's stinging eyes, temporarily blinding him as the snarling canine's slobbery teeth ground away at the branch. With a mighty roar, Ocho jumped onto the wolf, jabbing the bowie knife deep into its side several times. Knife in hand, Ocho pried its mouth open, snapping its lower jaw from its hinges. He kicked the weakened animal off of Mike, sending it tumbling across the gravel. The wolf rebounded and leapt at Ocho. Again Ocho's knife glinted as he thrust the blade deep into the wolf's chest and threw the animal back to the ground. He straddled the beast, plunged his knife into its throat and sawed off its head.

Without a word, Ocho walked directly to a patch of cottonwoods and wedged the wolf's matted and bloody head between the trunk and a branch of a nearby tree. Its jaw hung open and offset, and its pink tongue dangled over its snarled lips and teeth.

"Why did you put the head in the tree?" Mike panted.

"This body was an evil spirit's doorway into our world. Its power will spill out and haunt this area. Take the head off, the power gets trapped inside. The tree keeps it rooted to one spot until it completely decomposes. Once that happens, the demon falls back into the lower world."

"What if someone comes along and takes the skull out of there before then?"

"Duh." Ocho jeered. "Aren't you listening?"

"So, was that animal working for that brujo, like a witch's familiar?" Mike asked.

Ocho looked confused.

"A familiar. You know, like a witch's black cat," Mike explained.

Ocho shook his head and pointed to the wolf's headless body. "Look."

Horrified, Mike watched the wolf's steaming body slowly morph into human form. It was the black-painted-body of the man he had fought earlier in his tent. "Man, this is just insane!" Mike said. "You spend your whole life believing in this sort of thing, and when you see it for yourself you just don't want to believe it anymore."

"Until you've seen so much, you can't just keep explaining or denying it away," Ocho insisted.

Closely examining the decapitated remains, Ocho noted missing fingers on the elderly man's left hand. "Me and Eric saw this guy when we first got here. This is him. The creepy old guy that was hanging out in the woods near Oliver's house who pointed us which way to the camp."

"Creepy old guy?" Mike asked. "My God, that's Oliver's uncle!"

"Yeah," Ocho said suspiciously. "And where is Oliver, anyway?"

"I don't know," Mike answered, looking down and thinking deeply. As he stared down at the corpse's fingerless hand, his heart sank and he began to tremble with fear. He jumped away from Ocho. Nervously clutching his club in a threatening posture, he shouted at Ocho, demanding, "What did you do to Eric?"

Ocho remained calm. "Nothing. What's your problem?" he said.

Nodding toward the black-painted body, Mike quickly answered, "Black wolf. Missing fingers on left hand? You're my problem, *White Wolf!*" he shouted and nodded toward Ocho's missing fingers.

"C'mon, Mike, settle down," Ocho insisted. "You know I'd kick your ass before you even swung that stick."

*Whack!* The brittle branch broke into pieces against Ocho's head.

"Ouch," Ocho whined, virtually unfazed. "Damn, dude."

Mike hurriedly backed several feet away. He bent down and scooped up a large, heavy river rock with both hands. "Don't move, Ocho," Mike threatened, poised to heave the massive stone.

"What's in your head, Mike? Talk to me."

"It all makes sense. Eric told me you were raised by a witch! He was grooming you to be what you are, Brujo!"

"Again with the Spanish?" Ocho jittered. He slowly sat on the ground, teasing, "Why don't you put that rock down before you drop it on your foot?"

Mike cautiously backed further away, lowering the rock as he moved.

"It's true. That evil man made me what I am today," Ocho said. "But it's not what you think. I don't know how I even came to be with him. I was just a baby. I want to believe he stole me from a loving family, but that awful Mexican liked to torture me with the story of how my mother sold me for a bottle of booze. He kept me in a hole dug in the dirt floor of a metal shed in Mexico somewhere, just across the border from Texas."

Ocho lifted his hand, revealing his nubs. Wiggling his remaining fingers, he continued, "He snipped off my fingers with pruning shears when I was like five or six. He laughed at me when I cried. He hung me from hooks and beat me unconscious."

"Why?" Mike asked, disgusted.

"To infect me with hatred. To steal my energy. To take my power and feed it to the demons." Ocho explained. "He fed on my energy, using pain and fear to milk it from me. When I was older, around thirteen I think, he marched me outside and handed me a shovel. He made me dig my own grave. He covered me up and left me there. I couldn't breathe. My mouth was filled with the gritty dirt. It was so dark. Then, all the sudden, it was bright, too bright to even see. Grandfather came to me, with his long, white hair. He told me I had important things to do. He said he'd tell me what to do; that he would walk me through it. The Mexican came back and dug me up. I remember he got really pissed off that I wasn't dead. He pulled out this knife," Ocho said, holding up his giant blade. "Grandfather told me, *'Quick! Throw dirt in his eyes!'* I did, and then I wrestled the knife from his hand and killed him. Grandfather told me to cut off his head and bury him in that hole, and I did."

"What did it feel like to kill him?" Mike asked.

"You mean, did it feel good?"

Mike shrugged.

"No," Ocho said, looking away. "I never wanted to kill anyone. And no kid should ever have to go through the things I did. But everything happens for a reason, I've learned. I was really scared then. I didn't know nothing. I followed Grandfather back across the border, and he taught me how to hunt and fish, and live off of the Earth, the way he said we were supposed to. In the Earth I had found my mother. For years I lived that way, wandering. But it was hard. Grandfather wanted things to be easier for me so he led me to Irma Coldwell. And she was like a mother to me too, but it was still scary, and I could only speak Spanish. But she could too, and she taught me English. I haven't spoken Spanish since. I can't stand to hear it."

"You said the witch fed on your power. Do you have magic power?" Mike asked.

Ocho nodded. "Don't we all?" he asked.

"What?" Mike asked, confused.

"And we have choice," Ocho continued. "That's the greatest power of all."

"No, not like that," Mike said. "I mean, do you have magic powers, or special abilities? You know, like him?" Mike asked, motioning to the body.

"None I would abuse," Ocho answered. "There's a lot I want to tell you, but we really need to find Sean and get back to the others."

Ocho and Mike cautiously followed the wolf tracks into a wooded area. Mike looked up when a drop of something wet fell on his forehead and ran down his nose. The spindly branches of the trees were silhouetted against a brilliant, starry sky. There wasn't a single cloud. Confused, he wiped the droplet off his nose with his finger. It was blood, dark like oil and sticky.

"Ocho?" he called, straining to scan the darkened canopy. Something caught his eye. "What is that up there?"

"It's Sean," Ocho said softly as he gently squeezed Mike's shoulder.

The mass suspended in the trees was barely recognizable. Ocho climbed the tree and carefully scooted across a long horizontal branch to cut it down. "Back up, Dude," he said before sending Sean's body to the rocky ground. It hit with a splattering thud, like a sopping wet sponge on tile.

"Oh my God," Mike groaned. His muscles violently contracted and he retched, spewing the sour contents of his stomach all over the ground near his feet.

Indeed, it was Sean. What was left of him. He was splayed open, sliced from chin to groin and turned inside out. None of his organs were anywhere to be found, along with most of his skeleton and flesh.

"He was skinned alive," said Ocho. "The skinwalker did a quick, sloppy job of it too."

Mike struggled to fight back tears. It was all so surreal, like a horrible dream. "Where's the rest of him?" he asked with a trembling voice.

"I don't know, and I doubt we'd ever find it."

Mike thought deeply for a while then sighed, "God, I hope Eric is okay."

# Chapter Fourteen

"Hello? Is there anybody out there?" Eric called. There was only silence. He struggled to maintain his courage but his heart rate increased with every beat. "I saw you jump behind those bushes. I know you're there."

Just then, the figure stepped into the open. He crept low, ready to spring forward. The white-painted face stared menacingly at Eric. It was him, the skinwalker who had attacked him that first night on the rez.

Eric backed up slowly, trying to widen the distance between them. His mind scrambled to find a plan, the best of which was to get inside the kiva. Perhaps the sacredness of the ceremonial site would ward off the demon. It was at least twenty yards uphill, across rocky, uneven terrain. Having witnessed this ghoul running at over eighty miles per hour, and the grace with which it jumped from building to building, Eric had little confidence he would make it to the kiva in time. But he knew he did not want to find out what this thing might do to him.

With a split decision, Eric turned and bolted toward the kiva. Almost instantly, he was knocked forcibly to the ground and grabbed around the ankle.

"What do you want?" he screamed, kicking wildly, and connecting a solid, lucky blow to the skinwalker's face. Breaking free, he followed up, smashing a large rock against its temple. He spun and continued his desperate dash to the sanctuary of the kiva.

Running faster than he'd ever moved, Eric soon made it to the base of Spider Rock. A shiny cord was suddenly let down from above. Instinctively, Eric lashed the viscid cord around his waist. Adrenaline surged through his body as he expected the skinwalker to catch up with him at any second. His stomach seemed to drop as he was suddenly and rapidly pulled from danger. He ascended higher and higher up the rocky tower.

Watching the ground shrink further below him, Eric's relief was shattered as his pursuer emerged from the darkness, reached the cliff face and, without slowing, ran straight up the vertical rock wall toward him. The creature ascended effortlessly, leaping from rock to rock as gracefully as if the steep spire were lying on its side. It lunged, barely missing Eric as he kicked off the wall and swung out of reach. As Eric swung back like a pendulum he extended his feet and landed a solid kick that knocked the skinwalker off the rock.

The demon fell nearly twenty feet before catching a finger hold on a rocky protrusion. He hung there a moment. Then, as if he were an astronaut in zero gravity, he pulled against the ledge and rocketed upward, grabbing Eric around the ankles.

Eric thrashed, trying desperately to shake free of the creature's grip. A streak of white swooped unexpectedly out of the darkness, its razor-sharp talons slashing into the skinwalker's wrists. As the figure turned to make another pass, Eric recognized his defender as a beautiful, white-faced barn owl. The raptor swooped in, slashing through the demon's grip. As he hurtled toward the ground below, the witch transformed into a shiny, black raven and flew away pursued by the owl.

As Eric was hoisted higher and higher, he could no longer see the ground, just the blackness below. Above him, the sky was alive with rippling, dancing bands of color, and beyond that, innumerable stars. Steadily rising, he watched in awe as the top of the spire came closer and closer into view.

Brimming with nervous anticipation and curiosity, Eric was excited to meet his savior who was, presumably, on the other end of the cord. He slid onto the pinnacle, and stood brushing himself off. Much to his surprise, there was no one here. The shiny cord that had transported him rapidly dissolved before his eyes.

Perplexed, Eric sat on a flat rock and watched the most beautiful sunrise he had ever witnessed.

Mike and Ocho staggered wearily into camp. Mike collapsed in an exhausted heap, his weary eyes fixed on the blazing, vermillion sky to the east.

"Where'd Truman and Charlie go?" Ocho asked. He crouched, examining the ground. "Here's Charlie's tracks. He walked outta here. That way, back toward Oliver's, looks like. And Truman was here; carried away by two people."

"Oh God, no. Who?"

"Don't know. Indians. Moccasins, this set. And those are sneakers." Ocho sprang from his crouched position and set off to follow the tracks. Over his shoulder he called, "You coming?"

"Yep," Mike answered, slowly rising to his feet. "It's not like they could've gotten that far carrying him."

They followed the tracks nearly a mile, to the top of the mesa where they found Truman lying unconscious under a tree with two Hopis kneeling over him. Ocho cupped Mike's mouth, hurriedly dragging him behind a bush. "Don't get in the way. They're not hurting him," he whispered.

"What's going on?" Mike asked quietly.

"Looks like the old guy is healing him."

The elderly man hovered over Truman shaking a gourd rattle above him from head to toe as he chanted Hopi phrases in repetitions of four. He was small in stature, his face heavily wrinkled. His grayed hair was bobbed, the bangs cut straight across, and he wore a red scarf wrapped around his head and tied in back. He wore a long-sleeved, denim shirt buttoned to the top and tucked into a pair of old, threadbare, faded blue jeans. His pants were too big, the waist folded under a tight belt to make them fit.

At first glance, the man with him looked younger, but was probably in his early forties. His thick, black hair was cut short, and he wore a dark blue tee shirt, dark track pants, and worn-out running shoes. He lit a bundle of herbs to smolder and blew the white smoke over Truman from head to foot.

Shaking his head, the old man spoke to the other. They stopped what they were doing and rose to leave.

"Truman!" Mike shouted, running out from behind the bush. Ocho chased after him. Mike knelt over Truman asking the Hopis, "Is he dead?"

They exchanged several words in their native tongue before the younger answered, speaking to Ocho, "No, not yet. He was stabbed by a *powaqa*—evil medicine."

"I know, I was there," Mike said. "He was stabbed trying to help me fight that thing off."

"We tracked the witch down and killed it," said Ocho, "but not before it killed one of our friends. What can we do to help heal him?"

Speaking in Hopi, the old man shook his head waving his hands to say it's over.

"He's cursed, inside," the younger man interpreted. "We can't carry him all the way back to our village in time to save him."

"Then we need to do it here," demanded Ocho. "But what do you mean cursed inside?"

Mike spoke up, "Ocho, the skinwalker was trying to stab me with a sharp bone. There was a feather on it. He stabbed Truman in the shoulder and snapped it off inside him."

Without hesitation, Ocho pulled out his knife, knelt over Truman and cut into the wound. Truman jolted awake, screaming and writhing in pain. Mike wrestled him, pinning him down while Ocho searched, digging his fingers into the wound. Frustrated, Ocho complained, "I can't get it out!"

Truman passed out, his head and body drenched with sweat.

"Here," Mike said, "I've got smaller fingers." He dug into the wound. "I can feel it. It's embedded in the shoulder bone. If I can just get a grip on the feather, maybe it will pull the bone fragment out with it."

"Wait," Ocho said, handing Mike the knife. You gotta pry it out with this."

With his left hand, Mike slowly worked the knife into the wound, using his fingers to guide it into place as he held the soggy feather. He pried the piece of bone out of place, and readjusted his grip around it and the feather and pulled. "I got it!"

The old man took off his headband and bandaged Truman's wound. He then spoke curtly to his companion, who immediately gathered wood and started a fire.

Truman slowly awoke nearly an hour later. "Where am I?"

"You're safe, buddy," Mike said.

"My arm is killing me."

"Hold on," Mike said, forcing him back down. "Do it!"

Ocho pulled his red hot knife from the coals and plunged the searing tip into Truman's wound, cauterizing it closed. Truman screamed, squirming away.

"Sorry, buddy," Mike said, holding him down. "We've got to." Truman's eyes crossed and closed, as he fell again from consciousness.

## Chapter Fifteen

The two Hopi men kept their distance from Truman as they debated back and forth in their native tongue. Ocho rose from the ground, where he had sat with Mike at Truman's side for the last hour. "What were you guys doing out here when you found Truman?" Ocho asked. "Isn't your reservation like eighty miles from here?"

The two conversed quietly in Hopi before the younger spoke up. "We were led here," the younger man said.

"By who?"

He smirked coyly at Ocho.

"Who are you?" Ocho asked.

"I am Kurt Lomawaima. This is Tuwa Kuwanlelenta."

"I'm Ocho Whitewolf and this is Mike…what was it?"

"Mike Mathews," Mike announced.

"What are you doing up here on Navajo land?" Kurt asked.

"We were led here," Ocho said smirking.

Mike chimed in, "We're kinda stuck here, now. We were investigating some interesting petroglyphs in the area before things got really weird. One of our friends is missing, and another was killed by a skinwalker. The solar storms have knocked out our vehicles and ccll phones."

Kurt spoke Hopi to explain things to his elderly companion. He nodded, not seeming too surprised.

"When you found our friend by the creek, was there no one with him?" Mike asked Kurt.

He shook his head. "He was alone. There were tracks leading away. We also saw the tracks of your heavy friend being dragged away, and yours chasing after."

"Sean," Mike announced. "We couldn't save him. He was dead when we found him."

"I am sorry," Kurt said.

"Well, thank you for helping Truman. I'm really not surprised Charlie left him there; that snake."

"What is so important about the rock carvings that brought you all here?" asked Kurt.

"I'm not too sure what they all mean. Some, we thought were similar to your Prophecy Rock at Oraibi. But what they really did was lead us to petroglyphs in a slot canyon not far from here. That's where the real mystery is."

"Old Man Tuwa is the expert in reading the symbols of the ancient ancestors," said Kurt. "Can you take us there?"

"Well, that's the thing. The drawings in the ravine that we came here to see are definitely old, presumably from the Anasazi, but the carvings in the slot canyon look brand new, unlike anything any of us has ever seen. Except for some designs that clearly depict mysterious places throughout North and South America."

Reading Mike's face, Kurt asked, "What do you make of them?"

"At first sight, I want to say they are fakes because they are so new, so perfect. But my gut tells me they are very important. They lie in the heart of a mountain over there," Mike said, pointing. "Where there have been recent sightings of something unusual in the sky, a huge flying triangular…something."

Kurt looked at Mike strangely.

"I know what you must be thinking," said Mike, "but I saw it myself three nights ago. And I was visited as I camped there, by a group of twelve mysterious people dressed like Kachinas. They spoke into my mind and showed me these really disturbing images. Very apocalyptic visions."

Kurt spoke to Tuwa in Hopi again. His tone sounded urgent. Looking intensely serious, Tuwa nodded.

116

"Take us there," Kurt said.

Alone on the top of Spider Rock, tired, hungry, and exposed to the sun, Eric squeezed under the shade of the small piñon that crowned the peak. He began to worry that he might starve to death up here. How did he get here anyway? he wondered. He replayed the whole event in his mind, but none of it made sense.

He remembered reading in one of his brochures about Spider Rock that Navajo mythology tells of a young brave who, while fleeing from a rival warrior, was rescued by Spider Woman, who spun a cord of web to rescue the young Navajo. Noticing the white rock that crowned the red spire, he also remembered reading that Navajo children were warned to behave, lest they be taken to the top of Spider Rock and eaten by the mysterious chthonian deity. The white rock was said to be what was left of their bones.

Eric convinced himself that he had merely taken these stories and grafted them into his waking consciousness. *But, then, where am I?* he wondered. *I must be hallucinating, or crazy. This is all a delusion*, he thought, convincing himself that he was probably in the throes of another lucid dream. He wandered to the edge of the peak and leaned over for a dizzying view of the canyon floor nearly a thousand feet below. Slipping on loose rocks, he fell, and was instantly seized by another silvery cord and hauled back away from the edge. He spun around, hoping to see where the mysterious line had come from, but there was no one there. The strand rapidly dissolved.

"Unreal," he said as he sat catching his breath. He had to try and get hold of himself. He closed his eyes and sank instantly into the underworld he had seen earlier, that infinite, interconnected web of energy. A picture, or vision, began to appear. The giant, luminescent spider he had seen before hovered over him. As he stared into the spider's many shiny, black eyes, the creature communicated directly into Eric's mind. He opened his eyes and found himself once again in the mundane world.

"Thank you," he said to no one in particular. "I understand what I have to do."

# Chapter Sixteen

"I can't remember the last time my feet hurt this bad," Mike complained. "What I wouldn't give to have my Land Rover."

"Ho yeah," Ocho agreed, trudging slowly along with Truman slung unconscious over his shoulder like a sack of potatoes.

"And to think, it looks like we'll be hoofing it from here out."

"We can handle it," Ocho huffed.

Mike stopped, looking around. "I'm so turned around. Is this it?" he asked.

"Not yet, the easier way through is just around the bend here."

Ocho led Mike and their new Hopi companions through the thorny scrub and into the slot canyon. They traversed the now dry, undulating trail that led them into the cavern at the heart of the mountain. Just inside the cavern, they saw someone standing there, examining the precisely etched images on the far wall.

"Eric!" Mike rejoiced. "Where have you been?"

"Where do I start?" Eric answered. "What's up with Truman, is he okay?"

Ocho laid Truman in the soft, red sand, and eased himself down to rest. Following his lead, they all sat comfortably to share the events of the past few days. "Truman got stabbed and cursed by a skinwalker," Ocho explained. "We all worked on him and, if his shoulder doesn't get infected, he should be fine."

"When did this happen? What'd the skinwalker look like?"

"Late last night," Mike explained. "He was an old man, painted black, wearing the skin of a wolf."

"It was that creepy, old man we saw near Oliver's place the day we got here," Ocho blurted.

"Oliver's uncle," Mike added.

Eric was shocked. "What? Really? I was attacked by one of those things last night too, the same one that chased my truck. I barely got away. Just how many of them are there?"

"Just one now, I hope," Ocho answered. "Yours. We killed the other one."

"Oliver's uncle?"

"Well, Ocho did, anyway," explained Mike. Then adding, "Without much help from me, unfortunately. But not before it killed Sean and mutilated his body."

Eric was horrified and saddened by the news. "My God, that's awful," he said. "He seemed like such a nice guy." He felt bad for the way he had heckled Sean and wished he had taken the chance to be friendlier. "It's good you killed that thing" he added.

Mike nodded in agreement. "It was originally after me," he said. "It would have killed me for sure, if hadn't been for Truman and Ocho. I've never seen anything like it, Eric. He shape-shifted into a wolf. Ocho fought it off, cut off its head and wedged it into a tree to trap the demon."

"No way," Eric said. "That's just too weird. The day I followed Ocho in here I pulled a wolf skull out of a tree."

"You did what?" shouted Kurt.

"This is Kurt and Tuwa," Ocho said, hurrying to introduce their new friends. He excused Eric's mistake, saying, "He didn't know. And for all we know, the demon he let out is the same one I put back."

"Let's hope so," Mike said. "I don't want to ever have to face another one of those things again."

"Well, I've had an incredible last three days," said Eric. "Like I said earlier, I don't really know where to begin. But, first things first, I'm friggin' starving. I haven't eaten since the last morning we were all together. Does anyone have anything to eat?"

Tuwa dug into his buckskin satchel and handed Eric a large piece of jerky.

"You understand us?" Mike asked.

Tuwa answered, "I understand hunger."

"Thank you," said Eric and hurriedly tore off a piece of the jerky with his teeth. "I feel weird enough telling you all about all this, especially not knowing you guys very well." He motioned to Kurt and Tuwa as he continued chewing. "Anyone who knows me knows I'm pretty grounded in reality."

"Downright narrow-minded," Mike razzed.

"After I pulled the skull out of the tree, it got really spooky," Eric continued. "I was scared, and felt compelled to get into this cavern as fast as possible. I'd had a dream about this place a couple of nights earlier. Once here, I noticed that glyph over there. It's Spider Rock."

Tuwa and Kurt nodded in agreement.

"The more I stared into it I just sort of zoned out, and found myself miles from here high on a cliff wall in a shallow cave."

"How do you know where you were or how far away it was?" Kurt asked.

"Let me finish and I'll tell you," Eric snapped. "I spent two days there, getting weaker and hungrier. Then I climbed out and fainted on the rim. There was an old man I had seen on the other side. I don't know if he moved me, or how I got there, but I woke up in an old, round kiva at the base of Spider Rock. That was yesterday."

"So you're saying that something about this cavern teleported you?" Mike asked.

"Yes, exactly."

Drawing a triangular shape in the sand, Mike said, "I saw this craft in the sky over this mountain the night you disappeared. Maybe they took you."

Ocho disagreed. "I got here before Eric did. I came in and noticed that drawing there," he said, pointing to a steep, Mayan-styled, stepped pyramid. "The next thing I knew I was on top of a tall, overgrown hill in the jungle. All a sudden, the ground shook me off my feet. I tumbled down the hill. I looked up through the trees, and the sky was going crazy with light, like we've been seeing.

"Then, all a sudden, the ground split open and a big crystal came up out of it. It was about four or five feet tall and a few feet around. I couldn't hardly lift it an inch. It had to be 800 pounds or more. No way I could move it. I covered it up with branches and walked around a bit to see if I could find a village or a town. I felt at one point like I was being watched or followed, but I didn't see anyone. I went back to the hill and climbed up to look around, but there was nothing for miles but jungle. Grandfather told me to be patient, to sit tight. Then all a sudden, I was back here. That's when I went back to camp and found you, Mike."

Intrigued, Mike said, "So, then, you were in fact teleported. But what activates it?"

"I don't know," said Eric. "But we need to find out. The big spider told me to bring her what she called an '*Earthkeeper.*' I saw that in my mind to be a big crystal, like the one Ocho just described."

"All right, hold on. What the hell are you talking about, a big spider?" Mike demanded. "You hadn't eaten or slept for days. You could have been hallucinating."

"I know. That's what I thought too. It's all so strange and fantastic. I know I shouldn't believe any of it, but I do. I was attacked again in the middle of the night by the white-faced skinwalker. I ran to Spider Rock, and the big spider saved me. Spider Woman saved me." Tuwa smiled at Kurt, then at Eric. "It's true," he insisted. She lowered a web and pulled me up all the way to the top of the rock."

"I'm sorry, Eric, I'm having a tough time with this," Mike said. "Is it a woman or a spider?"

"Both…and neither. She's infinitely more than we can understand. I saw her as a spider, huge, hundreds of feet tall, but understood her to be a woman."

"So you're saying there was a giant spider at the top?"

"Not like you'd think. Not that could be seen. It's hard to explain. It's like another dimension. She lives in a sort of boundless space under this world, on a web she created that interconnects all living things with each other and the Earth."

"So, then?" Mike asked, "If she's from some other dimensional reality, how did she physically pull you up and help you in this world?"

"The way I perceived it, there is a bigger, much more complex, unifying reality that we can't even come close to fully comprehending. We exist there in her world too. But this is the world we know to be real. It's illusionary, and she weaves it. Her living on the web means she's outside the web, not connected the way we are; and she can only physically affect our world through a portal at Spider Rock."

"I'm just having a hard time with this, Eric, I'm sorry. It's so hard for my mind to comprehend this underworld stuff. It's even harder to accept that this is really you talking like this, and believing yourself. The only thing I know for sure is that you'd be the last person I'd expect could even make something like this up."

"And you'd be the last person I'd expect to be such a damn doubting Thomas," Eric snapped.

Tuwa spoke a few words to Kurt. "You will come to understand," said Kurt. "That is why we were led here. For Tuwa to be your *álo;* your spiritual guide. Spider Woman is sacred to us Hopi, since long before the Navajo came to be here and know her. The creator, *Taiowa*, created *Sótuknang* to create the universes. *Sótuknang* made Spider Woman to weave the world and all people and animals and other living things to live upon her."

"Well, I don't know about all that," Eric said dismissively, "but I do know that we need to take some kind of special crystal, called an Earthkeeper, to Spider Rock. Apparently so that this region is kept safe when the Earth passes through some kind of rift in the universe, what the spider called the *Well of Creation*."

Mike sat up excitedly. "Now, that, I can understand! I told you about that triangular-shaped craft I saw? I was visited that night by twelve beings, dressed kinda like kachinas. They spoke into my mind and showed me a vision of what you're talking about. It's all starting to come together now. We were meant to be here for this reason."

"Yep, everything happens for a reason," said Ocho. "That crystal is like the dream me and you had, Eric, about the tree that dropped those crystals into the ground. Now we need to find out what makes this place work, so we can go back and get it."

"Count me out," Truman grunted unexpectedly, startling everyone.

# Chapter Seventeen

They examined the cavern glyphs late into the night, discussing their possible meanings. The flickering light of their small fire and torches sent shadows rippling across the walls.

"I'm worried about Truman," said Mike. "Has he said anything else?"

"Nope, not another word," Ocho said. "He's just been sitting over there with that empty look on his face."

Mike glanced over to where Ocho had indicated, but no one was there. "Where'd he go? Guys, where's Truman?"

Eric ran over excitedly. "Did he teleport?"

"He left tracks," said Ocho, pointing at the impressions in the deep sand. "He went that way." Ocho pointed in the direction of the entrance to the canyon.

"I better catch him," echoed Mike as he ran through the narrow corridor. He exited the slot canyon to find Truman sitting on a large, flat boulder beside the trickling creek, watching the sky. "No aurora tonight? Has it stopped?" Mike asked.

Truman shook his head. "Nah, it's cloudy."

Mike sat slowly on the rock next to him, catching his breath. Several moments passed in silence with Mike unable to find any suitable words.

"I'm okay, Mike," Truman offered, anticipating his concern.

"Are you sure?" There was another long silence. "You know, it may not be safe out here alone," Mike said, scanning the shadows cautiously. "There may be another one of those things that stabbed you—one of those skinwalker witches."

"I'm not afraid of that," Truman said surely. He paused for a moment, and then continued, "I'm afraid for my kids."

"I didn't know you were a father."

"I haven't been much of one for some time."

"What do you mean?" Mike asked.

"Ah, there's a lot to it," Truman sighed, wanting to avoid the explanation. "Long story."

"It's not like I have anywhere to go," Mike said, not wanting Truman to shut down again.

Truman took a deep breath and exhaled heavily. "I used to have a wife and two kids. A regular family—certainly not heaven, but not hell either. I mean, I guess, we were all as happy a family as anyone could hope for, with the usual ups and downs and day-to-day stress. Yeah, looking back we were happy—overall. But then overnight everything changed.

"About seven years ago, I was driving home from a weekend exercise with the National Guard. It was really late at night. I just sort of looked up and had an amazing sighting of a low-flying, saucer-shaped bogey. It came up from behind me and buzzed over my car. I followed it for forty minutes. It was just playing with me, staying just far enough ahead not to catch, like dangling a carrot in front of a donkey. Finally it stopped, just hovering there. I got close enough to get a good look, but its lights were too bright to make out any detail. Then it just shot straight up and out of sight, faster than anything I've ever seen, and disappeared against the stars. Although I couldn't see it, I could feel it up there, watching me.

"The whole experience was just incredible, and my whole life changed. It was like waking up from some dull hypnosis or amnesia. The world I was living in suddenly seemed so small and unimportant. People I knew joked about how I went from jock to nerd in one night, 'cause, up 'til then, I never really got too deep. I just sort of splashed around in the shallows of the mundane day-to-day. Aside from cutting up other people, sports and cars and hunting were all I ever really talked about. But after that night, that was it. I was obsessed. UFOs were all I thought about and all I talked about. That's when my real education began. I studied and researched everything I could get my hands on, no matter how irrelevant it seemed to UFO phenomena. Hoping to find undiscovered connections."

Mike nodded, smiling, completely able to relate.

Truman continued, "The whole thing really scared my wife. She started having nightmares about aliens coming into the house while we were asleep. She said my bringing it up all the time was causing her bad dreams. She told me to quit talking about it, afraid it would scare the kids too. Mostly, though, I think she was scared of what people were saying. They all thought I'd lost it—her family, mine. The whole damn town. I felt so alienated from everyone—pardon the pun—but I just couldn't let it go. I'd stay up all night staring at the sky, holding my camera ready. Hoping to see it again. Hoping to get proof so everyone would know it was real, and just how important it was. I founded UFORIA to devote my energy to the research. But it got in the way of everything. I got fired from my security job, and my wife divorced me.

"Three months later she married the stuffiest, most normal guy she could find in the town; a dude we both made fun of and picked on all through school. I think she was looking for someone who would never change on her. No surprises."

Truman's body grew more tense. Speaking through his teeth, he said, "Then she started making visits with my kids as awkward and difficult as she could. Even they started talking to me like I was a flake. They sounded just like their mother. Then they started complaining about being scared to be with me on weekends, so I just stopped trying. I moved to L.A., and I haven't seen them since. Not until last night."

"Last night?" Mike asked. "What do you mean? You were unconscious last night and most of today."

Truman's demeanor intensified. Covered in goose bumps, he fought to keep from shaking with chills. His eyes focused unblinking as if he were trying to burn a hole in the ground, and his lips and square jaw quivered as he continued, "The whole time I was out, I was really out. Like out of my body out. I was somehow just sort of lingering, hovering over my kids. I could see and hear them. Man, they've gotten so big. I didn't want to leave them. I fought to stay there. I was ready to die to stay there. But somehow, here I am.

"Mike, if the Earth is getting ready to scratch us off its back like you all are saying, I can't just leave them there. I'm going to get them and bring them here, where you and everyone else seem to think it'll be safe."

Not wanting him to go, Mike asked, "You really think you'd be able to convince them to come?"

Without hesitation, Truman answered, "Even if they won't, I'll be where I need to be."

"C'mon," Mike said, frustrated. "Think about it! Think about everything that's happened, the way everything is falling into place. Everything about your past happened for a reason. We were all brought here for a reason. Don't you see that you *are* where you need to be? This is important!"

Truman grabbed Mike angrily by the shirt and pulled him close, growling, "I am going to get my kids. There is nothing more important than that."

"Settle down, dude." Mike said, straightening his shirt. "I'm not gonna stop you. Where are they? How you gonna get there?"

"They still live in Kingman. It's about two hundred miles from here, give or take. I can walk it. I'm leaving at first light."

"Truman, honestly, I hate to see you go, but I understand. I don't know what got into me. I'd do the same thing if I had kids. Go get them, but get back here safely, and fast. I really do believe this is where it's all going down."

"Thanks Mike," Truman said, placing his hand on Mike's shoulder. "As much as I'd like to see if that UFO you saw comes back. Or better yet, if you can figure out how to activate the wormholes in that cave, I just really need to make sure my kids are going to be alright. You know me, once I set my mind on something it's hard to see me going anywhere else."

"That's it!" Mike shouted. "It didn't even dawn on me that the triangular craft *was* here when Ocho and Eric teleported. It has to be them activating it. And wormholes! Of course! The cave is connected to the locations depicted in the glyphs by a series of wormholes."

The distant flashing of lightning and low, slow rumbling of thunder caught Truman's attention. The whole scene made him feel strangely uneasy. "It looks like rain coming. We better get them out of that canyon in case it floods again."

The group was soon gathered around a fire at the edge of the creek and settling down for the night. Tuwa circled the camp spreading a ring of fine corn pollen and herbs while chanting prayers.

Mike sat down next to Eric. "Sorry we didn't get any of the camping stuff moved over," he said.

"No worries. I actually got kinda used to sleeping outdoors," Eric chuckled. "The first night, a little moth flew up and landed on my shoulder. I figured, if something so small could survive out here, I could too. You know, I really grew a lot out there the last few days. It was one hell of a learning experience."

Mike laughed. "They always seem to find you."

"It's hard to get any real sleep on the ground, but I really do like sleeping under the stars. At first you feel alone, small and vulnerable, but once you let go and give in to it, you feel part of something bigger. And the aurora is just gorgeous, isn't it? Sometimes it seems like it'll reach down and lift me up into the sky."

"Hmm," Mike chuckled. "Talk about a role reversal. The lights creeps me out, the way they almost seem to be alive. It's like they have an intelligence about them. You know, medieval Europeans believed the aurora were harbingers of apocalyptic doom. Who'd have thought, with all their silly superstitions, that they actually got something right? But with all the skinwalker stuff going on, I guess the auroral display should be the least of my worries, huh?"

Eric grew solemn and thought deeply for a moment. He grabbed Mike's arm tightly. "Tell me I'm not going crazy."

"No more than usual," Mike joked, trying to keep things light.

"No, I'm being serious," Eric sternly insisted. "I've experienced some serious shit here this week. I saw it. I heard it. I can feel it all over again when I replay it in my head. It's just more than I ever asked for, you know? I keep wanting to just explain it all away and have things go back to normal. But then I've never felt such a strong sense of purpose as I do now."

"It's hard to be believe," Mike said softly, "but as much as I have always believed in the paranormal, my thoughts have wrestled back and forth quite a bit. I guess it's just the human brain's natural tendency to reduce what we experience in each moment to only what is absolutely necessary to survive at the time. I think, subconsciously, we are constantly questioning the reality of our experiences, and are only aware of the process when something doesn't quite fit. It kinda makes you wonder how much more is happening beyond our awareness, and just how much of what we do experience is actually real. You know, with you, though, I always felt you fought so hard to debunk everything because deep inside, maybe even subconsciously, you knew there was something more going on than mundane reality. And it scared you. So you just, like, shut yourself off in a small room and closed the door on it, so to speak."

For a moment, Eric felt angered and defensive about Mike's comment, but he knew that he was right. Even his metaphor was spot on. Eric was surprised to acknowledge it, remembering how he would hurry down the hall night after night to the sanctuary of his bedroom. His mind flashed quick images: shadowy faces, gnashing teeth, his nightly flashes of terror. Fleeting images from his early childhood were conjured: standing alone in the backyard of his home in his footed pajamas watching what looked like constellations or star formations floating across the sky. Running through thick woods being chased by a bright spotlight that beamed down from above. Huge, penetrating black eyes.

Eric swallowed the lump in his throat. Hesitantly, he conceded, "You're more right than I want to admit."

He looked around the crackling fire at the others who were all fast asleep. Ocho lay on his back snoring intermittently, arms crossed over his chest as if he were dead and resting in a coffin.

129

Eric debated over telling Mike about some of his strange memories and fears, but he honestly didn't know if they were memories of real events or dreams.

After a quiet moment, Mike said, "You know, the more I think about it, I can't help being sad about what's going on around us."

"Which part?" Eric gibed.

Mike cracked a slight smile. "A little over a week ago I realized I had finally become satisfied enough with my life, as much as it was, to start looking for someone to share it with. I even set up a profile on one of those matchmaker sites, hoping to find the new Mrs. Matthews."

Confused, Eric said, "But I thought you were gay. No offense."

"What?" Mike cawed. "Are you kidding me?"

Eric scrambled to set it right, explaining, "Not that you look it, or act it. It's just that I've known you for almost thirty years, and in all that time, you've never dated. I've never seen you flirting. You've never even mentioned having an interest in girls."

"I can't believe you," Mike said angrily. "In all the years you've known me it never occurred to you that it might be something else? That, maybe, I was just more focused on intellectual pursuits? Or maybe, just maybe, I was focused on myself, learning exactly who I was before allowing anyone to get close enough to dilute my sense of self?"

"*Dilute your sense of self?* Wow, you see? That's what I'm talking about. You've been watching too much Oprah or something," Eric said laughing. "And you're surprised that people think you're gay?"

Flustered, Mike fidgeted and flashed Eric a dirty look. "What do you mean, 'people?'" he asked, embarrassed. "Who?"

"No one," Eric insisted, chuckling innocently. "It was a joke." Mike just scowled. "Oh, come on, Mike, calm down. I didn't really think you were gay, I was just kidding with you."

"No you weren't," Mike charged. He leaned back and said calmly, "But it says a lot about you, that you were always such a good friend, despite what you believed about me. I mean, what you *wrongly* believed."

Eric brushed off the compliment, saying, "You're the good friend, Mike. You were always watching out for me. You've always been there when I needed you. You're the brother I never had."

Deeply moved, Mike looked at the ground, saying softly, "I've never spoken about this to anyone, but I had a twin brother named Gabriel. Just before our fourth birthday, we were playing in the front yard. I don't know exactly what he was doing. I was watching a caterpillar munch on a leaf. My dad got in the truck to go to the store, and as he was backing out of the driveway, he accidentally ran over my brother and killed him."

"Oh, my God, that's awful!" Eric gasped.

Mike shrugged, taking in a deep breath. He looked away for a few seconds and then blew it out heavily. "I've struggled all my life, trying not to blame myself for it. I can't even explain how difficult it is to be a twinless twin. I always worked doubly hard to excel in everything I did for some reason. Like I had to somehow make up for the loss of what Gabriel might have contributed to the world. And how I tried to please my parents! They never even spoke of him again, as if he had just vanished. It made me wonder if I had made the whole thing up. It really messed with my head. Finally, I had to research it in the county records to make sure it really happened. You just can't imagine the void it leaves, losing a twin. I can't even look in the mirror some days."

Eric squeezed Mike's shoulder, "Well, there's one more thing we have in common. I have a problem looking into mirrors too."

"So, that's why you always look like a bum," Mike laughed.

Eric straightened his shirt and smoothed his hair. "So, if that happened right before your fourth birthday," Eric said, "that would be what? A year before we met?"

Mike nodded. "I felt so alone after my brother died. Starting school that day was terrifying. Thank God for you. I don't know where my life would have gone if not for you. You've always been the brother I needed." Mike smiled at Eric, "So, that's my sad story."

"Yeah, really sad," Eric said. He sat sullenly for a moment, taking it all in. Then he teased, "Especially that part about internet dating."

Mike chuckled through his nose. "And what about you?" he asked. "Did you ever think you might try it all again? Find the right girl and have a family?"

"Nope," Eric answered immediately, shaking his head. "I'm the type who was destined to live alone. Besides, I'm a pretty unlikable guy."

"Oh, I don't know about that," Mike said. "I saw the way that good-lookin' receptionist from the office next door was always flirting with you. She timed all her breaks to be out there when you were."

"Yeah, her," Eric smirked sheepishly. "No, a girl like that is fun for a day, maybe two, but any more than that, what could she offer? She's a vampire. That kind of energy draw would just make me want to drive a stake through her heart. I've been there and done that. And, have you ever talked to her? I'll take brains over body any day. Besides, she smokes."

"Wow, you *are* a pretty unlikable guy," Mike chuckled. "Yep, you're destined to be alone, alright."

Not letting it show, Eric was saddened by that thought. It was true, however. He had his chance at family and would never take another. He sat quietly, unsure just how to feel about that realization. "Hey, what ever happened with that cattle mutilation thing in Wyoming?" he asked, taking the attention off himself.

"Oh yeah, that's right," Mike said, enthusiastically. I don't know who coined the term *mutilation*. It's more like highly-precise dissection."

"I was right, though, wasn't I? Devil worshippers, right?"

Mike laughed. "Yeah, it's a really progressive cult," he chaffed. "Instead of a sacrificial knife they used a surgical laser. No, really. I really don't think so."

"Stranger things have happened."

"Well, I guess so, but these mutilations were in a very remote area. A surgical laser would require cumbersome equipment and a power supply, and there were no tracks in or out. It was like these cows were dropped from the sky."

Eric was only half listening as he began to think about the way Sean was killed and mutilated. It had weighed heavily on his mind since he heard the news. While being enormously relieved that he had once again escaped his attacker, he felt horrible for what Sean must have gone through. He was glad the guy was avenged when Ocho killed the skinwalker, but dreaded the moment they would have to tell Oliver about his uncle. He wondered about why no one had seen him in the last couple of days.

"...they were only partially dissected," Mike continued. "Eyes and tongue, and glands and sections from around the jaw and neck were removed. They were drained completely of blood, but not a drop was found anywhere near the scene. And recently, cattle from different stock and different areas just started dropping dead by the dozens—all across the region. I don't know if it's related to the mutilations, but it's strange. None of the lab results showed any known disease. None of the vets I talked to had an explanation for it."

Eric heard very little. "I hate to change the subject, Mike, but why do you think no one has seen anything of Oliver?"

Mike nodded. "Yeah, I've been wondering the same thing. Maybe we ought to walk that way with Truman when he leaves in the morning and check on him."

## Chapter Eighteen

At dawn the group was on their way to find Oliver. There was a cold breeze and the morning sky was overcast with ominous clouds, giving indications of imminent rain. Far in the distance, dark clouds moved toward them, stretched and sagging with moisture, a dark, gray wall of sky that smeared to the ground.

Ocho moved uncharacteristically slowly, wincing as he lumbered along. Noticing his difficulty, Eric slowed to walk with him.

"You alright, dude?"

"Mmm, I'm fine," Ocho muttered.

"You sure?" Eric asked, concerned. "We could stop and rest"

"Nah, it's cool. My body is just reminding me I got a bad back and knees. I guess these last couple-a-days caught up with me."

"Well, damn, dude! You carried Truman on your back for like three miles yesterday, and he's no creampuff."

"Yeah, he's a pretty stocky dude," Ocho agreed. "I wonder how that Charlie guy is recovering from his kick to the face."

"What?"

"Ho, yeah, man, Truman hauled off and kicked him full-throttle in the mouth."

Eric laughed. "It's got to be wrong of me to take so much joy in that, but I just can't help myself." Scanning the ground for a suitable place to sit, he said, "C'mon, Ocho, let's rest a bit. Hey guys," Eric shouted, "go on ahead. We're gonna rest here a bit."

Ocho eased himself to the ground, shuffling around until comfortable.

"What did Charlie do to deserve that anyway?" Eric asked, joining him on the ground.

Ocho chuckled. "So much has been going on, I never thought to ask. But I've been waiting for someone to thump that smug twerp ever since we got here. I thought all along it was gonna be you, though."

Eric looked around, taking in the sights. Across the long valley, rays of sunlight beamed through intermittent breaks in the cloud cover, illuminating the majestic landscape.

"Ocho," Eric asked, "what do you think is going on here?"

"I don't really know. I know we were all brought together here for a reason, though; something really important. You're the key. Grandfather brought me here to protect you."

Eric sighed uncomfortably, "Oh, I don't know about that."

"You don't need to," Ocho insisted. "I do."

"Well, I am glad you're here. I've got to admit, I'm pretty scared. That skinwalker almost got me the other night. I don't even want to know what he would have done to me." Eric paused in silence, waiting for a comment from Ocho. None was offered, but none was needed, Eric had been told what was done to Sean.

"Ocho, I just can't stop wondering about Oliver, and where he's been," Eric said seriously. "Do you think he knew about his uncle?"

"I've been wondering about that too."

"Do you think Oliver could be a skinwalker?"

Ocho shot to his feet, blurting, "Now, that, I didn't think of." He started hastily up the trail, calling back, "You coming?"

It was pouring rain by the time they arrived at their camp on Oliver's land. They hunkered down in the tents for shelter, all but Truman. Soaked to the bone, he braved the weather to roll his sleeping bag and pack his tent. He stuffed some chips, nuts, and granola bars, and a few water bottles into his pack.

Mike watched from his tent. "You're welcome to share my tent with me until the rain passes."

"No thanks. It's just water. I ain't gonna melt. I really gotta get going, it's a long way."

"Be safe," Eric called out.

"Hold up, Truman," Ocho shouted, digging through his duffel. Seconds later he emerged from his tent with a poncho and a large knife in a thick rawhide sheath which had been covered with fringed buckskin and adorned with beads. "Here, take these," he said.

"Ocho, thanks a lot." Truman immediately slid the poncho on and pulled the hood over his head. He pulled the powder coated black blade from the sheath. "Whoa, this is a KA-BAR! Were you a Marine?"

"No, I just love knives...and watches, in case you were wondering what to get me for Christmas," Ocho laughed. "That knife is made for war, dude—indestructible. It's a great all around tool, too. I hope it comes in handy for you."

"The way you've got it decorated looks really cool. Man, I don't know what to say."

"How 'bout, see you later," Ocho jested. "Get going."

Tuwa and Kurt approached.

"I don't know how to thank you both enough," Truman said. "Mike told me what you guys did for me. I can't believe I slept right through it. I wish I could have gotten to know you better."

Kurt smiled. "You'll get your chance. I'm going with you. I figure I'll take you cross-country. Fastest way off the rez."

"Oh, you don't have to do that. I was planning to just follow the same roads I came in on."

"I'm a cross-country runner," Kurt replied. "Been doing it since I was a kid. I know the trails that will save you a lot of miles and time. I've run across this land a million times."

Mike approached, urging, "Let him take you, Truman. We need you back here as soon as possible."

Truman nodded and smiled.

From the shelter of Eric's large tent, he, Ocho, Mike, and Tuwa watched until Kurt and Truman disappeared from view.

"Well, I certainly feel better with Kurt guiding him," Mike said. "Now, about Oliver, where do we start?"

Eric spoke up, "Mike, we need to consider the possibility that he may not want to be found."

Mike was confused. "What do you mean?"

"He might be one of them."

Mike shook his head. "No, not him, I just know it."

"How?" Ocho asked, abruptly. "How do you know?"

"I don't really know, I just believe. For some reason, I just feel really worried about him. I hope he's all right. But if you guys are right, we'll really need to keep our wits about us."

"Well, it's not going to help anyone if we get hit by lighting or catch pneumonia out there. We should dry out and see if this rain might die down a bit, plan our next move," Eric suggested.

The group hunkered down in Eric's tent, where Mike told Eric, Ocho, and Tuwa in greater detail about the skinwalker attack in his tent that led to Truman's injury and Sean's death. Over the next hour they spoke of happier things, chatting and joking over jerky and granola bars while waiting out the rain. Tuwa followed along pretty well, surprising the guys with his sense of humor and what a grasp of the English he really had. Ocho sat near the open flap whittling a long, thick branch, the curled shavings piling up just outside.

"What are you doing, anyway?" Eric asked.

"Making a bow. Those snacks won't last much longer. We're going to need some real food soon."

"Cool," said Eric, excitedly.

"Don't get too excited," Ocho warned. "There's probably not a whole lot around here in the way of big game like elk and deer, maybe some antelope and javelina. I'm getting ready to go set some snares, too. I hope you guys like rabbit and snake, 'cause that's probably what we'll be having a lot."

"Bring it on!" Eric growled.

Mike did a double take, looking at Eric strangely. He stood and leaned over Ocho to peer out at the sky. "It's slowed quite a bit, but I don't think this rain is gonna pass anytime soon," he said. "We've wasted enough time here. I'm gonna walk down to Oliver's trailer and see if he's home."

Eric promptly rose to his feet. "I'm coming with you."

137

Grabbing Eric around the ankle, Ocho said, "Not without me."

Old man Tuwa slowly rose as well, slinging his satchel over his shoulder. The four men trudged over the wet ground to Oliver's house. The rotted wooden steps creaked as Mike stepped up and knocked loudly on the trailer door. He silently waited a moment and knocked again. Eric and Ocho walked around the trailer. Eric hopped up and down, trying to see into the high windows.

"See anything?" Ocho asked.

"Nothing. Hey Mike," Eric called out. "When's the last time anyone saw him?"

Mike walked around the backside of the trailer, answering, "Four or five days ago? It was the day of the solar storm."

"I hate to even say it," Ocho remarked, "but I think we better let ourselves in and check it out.

"Agreed," said Mike. "Let's try the door." He once again pounded on the flimsy aluminum door. He waited, holding his breath as he listened. He peered through the door's small window, but through the dirty glass, could only see a small part of the living room beyond the narrow kitchen.

Eric curiously watched Tuwa, wandering further up the road, disappearing into the thicket that lay between the trailer and two hogans at the foot of the mesa.

Mike twisted the doorknob. "It's unlocked," he said, slowly opening the squeaking door. He poked his head in, looking around the vacant kitchen. "Oliver? Oliver, are you here?"

Mike ventured through the messy kitchen and into Oliver's living area, followed by Eric, and then Ocho. Eric looked around. The wobbly shelf unit against the living room wall was leaning far to the left, its laminated planks peeling to reveal crumbling particleboard underneath. On the warped, dusty shelves were a small, portable, mono radio-cassette player, several books and tapes, an oil lamp and matches, and various Indian-crafted knickknacks.

"Hmm, Bob Marley. Never would've pegged Oliver for a reggae man," Eric said, picking up one of the tapes to read the song list. He examined the room further, noticing the shaft of dull light that shone through the window illuminating millions of gently swirling dust particles. He noticed the dingy, matted carpet and the old stained and torn couch. "It's got a real Goodwill kinda' vibe, doesn't it?" Eric joked.

Mike was embarrassed, hoping Oliver wasn't there to hear Eric's insulting comments. "It's better furnished than your house," he whispered.

"Maybe, a little," Eric replied, smiling.

Creeping single-file down the narrow hallway, they moved on to investigate the rest of the trailer. Eric poked his head into the bathroom. The tub was half full of brown water. Seeing himself in the mirror, Eric was appalled at how dirty his face was. He turned the squeaky faucet knob. "Guys, there's no water."

"Yeah, he's not hooked up," Mike said, quietly. "He would drive fifteen or twenty miles every week and hand-pump from a well to fill up some barrels."

Astonished, Eric voiced, "What a drag to have a perfectly good toilet and shower and not be able to use them."

"I'm sure a lot of people everywhere are thinking that same thing right now," said Mike.

Having gone on ahead, Ocho came back from investigating the rest of the small trailer. "Well, the good news is that he's not dead in here, but he's not here."

"And just where he is and what he might be up to is what worries me," Eric said. "I just have a real creepy feeling." He started for the door, saying, "Let's catch up with Tuwa and check out the hogans." He slowed to examine the photos on the wall in the living room. "Hey guys, is this Oliver's uncle?"

Mike dragged his finger across the photos, carefully looking them over. "No, he's not in any of these pictures." Tapping on the glass, he said, "I'm guessing this is his grandfather, evidently the man who raised him after his parents died. He was an amazing looking man, wasn't he? Look at those eyes."

"So he's dead then?" Eric asked.

"Apparently," Mike answered. "I really don't know Oliver that well, but I remember him saying he'd be completely alone out here if his uncle hadn't returned."

The hair on Eric's arms stood on end, and a chill shot through him. "Let's get moving if we're going to catch Tuwa."

The rain had slowed to a soft drizzle by the time they emerged from the rundown trailer. They trudged along the soggy trail, moments later entering the thick stand of trees.

"Right here is where we saw Oliver's uncle that day." Ocho said.

Arriving at the hogans, Eric asked, "Where'd he go? Tuwa?" he called. He poked his head into the dark hogan. The eight angled walls were bare. A thick layer of fine, dustless sand, similar to that found in the slot canyon, insulated the floor. "Oliver?"

Eric was startled by an abrupt voice from behind him. "He's not here." Eric whirled around, his heart pounding in his chest.

"Charlie," said Mike, surprised. "I thought you left."

Charlie's striped polo shirt and tan Members Only jacket were stained with dirt and blood. His greasy hair was matted to his head and his bent wire-framed glasses sat crooked on his face. Through his swollen, split lips he answered, "I came back to see if I could get my van to start."

Eric and Ocho fought to keep from laughing at the way his tongue poked through the gaping hole where his teeth used to be as he spoke.

"Did it work?"

"Obviously I don't know yet, Mike. Do you think I'd be standing here talking to you guys if it did?" Charlie said sardonically through a feigned smile, an affectation of friendly, humorous banter.

"When was the last time you saw Oliver?" Mike asked.

"The day all the planes crashed. I left that night when I woke up, after that blankedy-blank Truman attacked me."

Amused, Eric smirked, whispering to Ocho, "*Blankedy-blank?*"

Ocho smiled wide.

Eric whispered to Ocho, "He doesn't even ask where Sean or Truman is, or if they're alright?"

Charlie continued, "I came here looking to see if Oliver had a phone I could use, but he wasn't anywhere to be found. I walked all the way out to the main road and part way to Chinle before the rain hit. I didn't see one car, not one person out there. I realized it was ridiculous to walk anywhere out here, the reservation is so darn big, so I headed back. I almost got lost where the road forks near that junky old hogan."

At that moment, Eric's mind flashed quick images of shadowy figures and gnashing teeth, and someone thrashing around on the ground inside the hogan.

"Do you hear that rattling?" Mike asked. "What is that?"

Immediately, Ocho headed in the direction of the sound, calling, "This way."

The group followed him into the chaparral. They crept cautiously closer to the sound, finding Tuwa sitting on the ground under the cover of the trees. In a trance-like state he sat, slowly and rhythmically shaking his gourd rattle. Spread out before him on a small woven blanket were some stones, herbs, animal fetishes carved from wood, and several strings of multi-colored beads.

"Oh, come on," Charlie scoffed.

Flashing him a dirty look, Ocho shushed him. Following Ocho's lead, they sat quietly nearby. Eric struggled to concentrate on other things, but his mind increasingly and uncontrollably flashed images of dark figures and someone writhing violently on the floor of the collapsing hogan. The rattling abruptly stopped. Eric opened his eyes. Tuwa was looking directly at him.

"You know he is there, Eric," Tuwa said. "with the *nukpana catori*."

Confused, Eric asked, "With the what?"

Tuwa searched for the right words, "Evil spirits—ghosts. We need to get him."

Ocho shot up, "What are we waiting for, then?"

Charlie rose slowly, asking, "Wait a minute, what's going on?"

"That abandoned hogan you saw at the fork in the road? Oliver is there," Eric explained. "He's a skinwalker like the one who killed Sean. Remember him? We're gonna get him before he gets us."

"Well, good luck with that," said Charlie.

"Hang on, Charlie," Mike pleaded. "It's really not safe to be out here alone."

"I have no intention of being out here alone. I'm leaving. I'll tell you what, I'll give you guys a ride when I get my van going."

"I'll tell you what," Mike countered, "Your van is fried from the solar storm and going nowhere. I am sure of it. If it starts, cool, I'm glad for you. But if I'm right, you have to come with us. There is safety in numbers."

# Chapter Nineteen

By late afternoon the group drew steadily closer to the crumbling, abandoned hogan. Tuwa and Ocho led the overland march, often leaving the dirt road to blaze faster trails across the vast desert landscape. Eric walked with them while Mike, following from further back, filled Charlie in on what had been happening. The sky was bubbling with rapidly morphing, gray clouds that seemed to hover low enough to be touched, but not a drop of rain had fallen for the last two hours. Nobody complained.

Eric veered off course toward a small rocky arroyo.

"Whoa, where are you going?" Ocho asked.

"To take a leak."

"Nope, not without me," Ocho said, trotting after him.

Uncomfortable, Eric protested. "C'mon, Ocho, I'm a big boy."

"No way dude, you don't leave my sight."

Curious, Charlie asked, "Mike, what's going on there with Ocho and Eric?"

"Ocho believes that Eric is the key to surviving the natural cataclysms those animal-masked people told me are coming."

"That's just nonsense," Charlie sneered. "The only one who could save us from these tribulations is Jesus."

"Well, whatever any of us believes, Ocho believes it is his purpose here to protect Eric and help guide him to fulfilling his destiny. You want to argue with him, go right ahead, but I won't.

Besides, I'm getting a lot of good laughs out of it. I think it's hilarious that Eric has to try and go to the bathroom with Ocho hovering over him like that. Eric is extremely bladder shy. We went to see the Stones one time, and he stood at the urinal for nearly ten minutes trying to go, while the impatient line grew longer behind him. He eventually gave up and tried to hold it 'til he got home, but he couldn't. The concert traffic jammed the roads, and he couldn't hold it anymore. So he had to get out of the car and piss on the side of the freeway while everyone yelled and honked and called him Peewee. Man, I nearly wet *my* pants I was laughing so hard," Mike roared. "Then the lanes started moving and he had to run to jump back in the car, and got the front of his pants and shoes all wet. That kind of stuff happens to him all the time."

"Yeah, Ocho's really on to something," Charlie railed. "Sounds like just the guy to save the world."

Miles away, Kurt and Truman's pace slowed from a fast jog to a walk. Breathing heavily, Truman adjusted his backpack strap, lifting it away from his sore shoulder. "Phew, I haven't had a good run like that in a long time."

"Could have fooled me," Kurt said, "I didn't think you'd be able to keep up half as long as you did."

"Well, it felt so good to be active, I didn't want to stop. Man, you can run though."

"Indian power," Kurt joked. "We're natural runners—it's in our blood."

Truman stopped to pull a bottle of water from his backpack. He twisted off the cap and handed it to Kurt, who took two large gulps from the bottle and gave it back. Too winded to drink, Truman clutched the bottle, struggling to slow his breathing.

"You alright?" Kurt asked.

Truman nodded and resumed walking. "It's just been a while."

Kurt pointed to Truman's arm, asking, "How's your shoulder?"

144

"It's sore," Truman answered, rubbing it as he scanned the area. "Man, all the scrub grass everywhere, this really doesn't look much like a trail."

"None of these old trails get used much at all, but they go back thousands of years, all the way back to the migrations of the ancient ones."

"Migrations?" Truman asked. "I thought the pueblo peoples were sedentary. At least that's what they taught us in school, anyway. I mean, isn't Oraibi one of the oldest continuously inhabited settlements in North America?"

Nodding, Kurt explained, "We were instructed that the migrations had to take place before the people could settle. We really don't talk too much about these things because the Hopi long ago faced so much persecution from the Christians. And because much of it is too sacred to share with outsiders. But I will tell you about the migrations because I believe you have true respect for my people."

"Oh, absolutely," Truman affirmed.

"When the people emerged into this fourth world, they were told by *Másaw*, the guardian spirit of this world, that they were not permitted to just wander until they found a nice place to settle, like they had in previous worlds. He told them that all the clans must migrate across the new land in all four directions, to the seas and back, before returning to the center. In the north they walked until they reached ice and could go no further. In the south they walked until the land came to an end at the cold waters, and then they returned. Each clan needed to complete the long migrations in each direction before they could settle here on this sacred land.

"The ancients settled many villages along the way before abandoning them to complete their journeys. Many journeyed into tropical lands far to the south where they found plentiful food and a comfortable climate. Life there came easy, so many stayed. There, they built temples and cities of stone and never finished their migrations. Many clans lost their way and settled in the lush lands because they did not remember that our life here on this fourth world was supposed to be difficult: so that we would always rely on the creator to provide. So that we would always evoke his

145

blessings through ritual and prayer. So we would not fall back into the wicked ways that caused the people to be cleansed from the first three worlds."

"You know," said Truman, "it's interesting that you talk about these previous worlds. I've read that the Mayan calendar depicts five worlds: three previous worlds, the fourth or present world, and the soon to come fifth world, or *Age of Enlightenment*. Could the clans you mentioned, the ones that stayed in the tropical regions of the south to build stone temples, be the Maya? "

"I've always thought so…and the Inca and Aztec too. All of the red clans. You gotta remember, this was thousands of years ago that the clans came to the fourth world and began their migrations."

Using a stick to draw a counter-clockwise rotating swastika in the dirt, Kurt explained, "Not all of them completed their migrations to return here to the *Túwanasavi*, Center of the Universe. Many settled all over the Americas."

"Well, it's certainly comforting to know that if your ancestors could traverse all of the Americas on foot, I can certainly make it to Kingman and back," said Truman, turning his attention to the turbulent gray sky ahead.

"That's right over where you're going," said Kurt. "It looks like you're in for some rough weather."

Kurt led Truman further up the gradually rising trail. At the top of the hill they could see revealed before them an immense, rocky plain that stretched as far as the eye could see.

"See the interstate out there?" Kurt asked, pointing.

Truman squinted to see the faint line that crossed the desert. Confused, he said, "That can't be I-40. There's no way we ran that far. Is there?"

"Yep, and way out there is Highway 89. Just beyond where they meet out there is Flagstaff. Once you get there, you've made it almost halfway. See, I told you I could save you a lot of time by cutting across on these trails," Kurt smiled proudly. Truman looked to the west, in the direction of Flagstaff. "You can't see it, the way those clouds are sagging down," Kurt said, "but there is a tall mountain there. Flagstaff is right below that."

146

Humphrey's Peak, Arizona's highest point, was completely obscured by dark clouds. Above the valley loomed a giant swirling storm, a supercell similar to those frequently seen over the Great Plains.

"Follow this trail to the interstate, then go west through Flag, and all the way to Kingman," Kurt suggested. "Be safe, and hurry back, alright?"

"I'll try," Truman said. He shook Kurt's hand, saying very sincerely, "I can't thank you enough."

Over the next several hours, Truman crossed the plain, progressing steadily closer to the interstate.

"Dear God," Truman exclaimed in disbelief, witnessing the aftermath of what he guessed must have been a powerful tornado. The unbelievable swath of devastation stretched for miles in each direction. Immobilized cars and trucks and bodies and debris littered the highway and surrounding ground. The destroyed vehicles, some upside down or on their sides, looked as if they had been wrecked in a massive high-speed pileup. Tractor trailers were picked up and slammed several times into the ground, some tossed hundreds of yards from the road. Some of the vehicles had erupted into flames. The twisted, charred wreckage was still smoldering.

The incredible power of the tornado was obvious, having completely scoured the asphalt from the road in places. Truman instantly began going from body to body, looking for survivors. There were none to be found. He came upon the wreckage of a cattle transport trailer that had been flipped over and ripped in two. The strength of the tornado had been so intense that the fur of some of the cows had been sucked off, leaving bald patches of pink skin, dotted with pinprick spots of blood.

Disheartened, he walked westward along the highway, weaving through the debris. The gun rack in the smashed rear window of an overturned pickup truck caught his attention. Truman grunted and glass crunched as he pried the warped driver-side door open. The driver, dressed in Mossy Oak apparel, was contorted like a rag doll tossed down to the roof of the inverted truck.

"I hate to do this, buddy," Truman said, taking the dead hunter's rifle and sidearm. He rooted through the man's belongings, pilfering anything useful for survival. He found the man's crumpled jacket wadded underneath his heavy body, and a bag of beef jerky and several boxes of shells in the glove box. "Sorry dude," Truman sighed. Crawling out of the truck, he spied the large antlers of the dead elk that spilled out of the truck when it was thrown. Infested with maggots, the reeking carcass was unsalvageable for meat. Disappointed, he continued west along the battered highway.

He jogged against high winds for nearly an hour. He was amazed how, within the distance of two or three miles, the topography rapidly transitioned from barren, rocky scrubland to tall, ponderosa pine. Against the dark clouds, the many dormant volcanoes surrounding the town of Flagstaff could be seen in the distance. Large trees were scattered along the roadway, having been ripped from the ground and thrown. Others stood ominously like giant tombstones, stripped of their needles and branches. Along the railway tracks that ran parallel to the highway was a derailed freight train, the wreckage stretching just under a mile.

"Hey! Stop!" a shrill voice cried out.

Truman stopped and looked around curiously.

"Over here!" It was a female voice. "The red Kia! Help me, please!"

The little two-door car was tossed from the road where a large freight car had smashed down on the hood before flipping onto its side, spilling pallets of used car battery cores all over the ground. Truman raced over to assess the situation. The windshield and rear window were smashed, and the remainder of the car was dimpled all over with dents the size of softballs. The young woman was pinned, the dash and steering column pressing down on her legs and wedging her into the seat.

Truman forced the door open. He dropped to his knees to get a better look. "Can you move your legs at all?" he asked.

"No, they've gone numb," she answered.

"How long have you been here like this?" Truman asked as he groaned and strained to pull the dash back.

"Three days. I'm sorry, I'm a mess," she said, embarrassed.

Truman realized, while stuck there, she had wet herself. He stopped struggling with the dash long enough to look directly into her face, and said, "Oh c'mon, you're beautiful."

Although his aim was to put her at ease, he wasn't just being compassionate. Despite her disheveled, light brown hair, and her smeared makeup and dirty face, she was very attractive and her dainty features only accentuated her beauty. Her hazel eyes enchanted Truman.

She smiled.

"Eh hem, anyway, back to work," Truman said shyly, wrestling the steering wheel back. "Three days, huh?"

"Yeah, well, three days since I broke down," she said. "Did your car break down too?"

Truman shook his head, "Not here on the highway. I came on foot from up on the reservation. What happened here?"

"I don't know," she said. "I was driving back to Tempe where I'm finishing my Master's at ASU. I had been visiting my mom and dad in Santa Fe. My car just died. Everyone's did. I don't know why. It was really bizarre. No one could get a signal on their phones, so we had to wait for help to come. We waited and waited, but there was no one. A lot of people finally left their cars and walked to Flagstaff, but my dad always told me to stay and wait for help. So I stayed with my car all night, while other people camped out along the side of the road. A lot of people were getting really irritable, arguing and freaking out and stuff, so I just waited in the car with the doors locked. I was really scared."

She started to cry. Tears rolled down her cheeks and dripped off her quivering chin. "I stayed here all day yesterday too," she continued. "It was so hot and sticky all afternoon, I thought I might broil to death. And then another huge storm rolled in. The clouds were almost black, and they lined up like a wall across the sky. It was really calm, almost no wind. And then, bang! All hell broke loose. The biggest hail I've ever seen came down. At one point, it was the size of grapefruit!"

Her tears broke through the floodgates and she sobbed, "One poor guy's head was smashed in. People were running and screaming, pushing each other out of their way and fighting to get into other people's cars. It was so chaotic.

149

"The wind really picked up, and was howling in a way I've never heard before. I had to look to see if the train was running again, it was so loud. It got louder and louder. It sounded like a cross between Niagara Falls and a jet plane. And then I saw them: tornadoes on all sides. I don't know how many. They tore up and down the interstate, weaving around each other, rarely moving from the roadways, and not very far when they did."

She sobbed, almost reliving the experience as she continued, "Stuff was flying all around when one of them passed really close, and I can't see, there's so much stuff flying around, smashing against the car and windows. And I'm screaming. I'm screaming for help, but there's no one who can help me. I'm completely out of control, you know. My car just floats up off the road and is set gently over here. The tornado looped around and tore through the train and threw that freight car right at me. I'm watching it flying towards me and I'm like, *this is it, I'm dead*. I'm terrified. I was sure I was going to die."

Truman gently and caringly squeezed and kneaded her arm. "But you made it," he said reassuringly. "You're okay."

Calmed somewhat, she continued, "I'd never even seen a tornado before. They're not even supposed to happen here. They seemed almost alive. Like they were attacking us on purpose. Like they were working hard not to miss anything. Then back there, they all met and came together. It looked almost like a giant monster walking away on two legs with two long arms reaching down, destroying everything in its path!"

"I just came from that way," Truman said. "For miles and miles everything is just destroyed. It must have been like an F5. It sucked the asphalt right off the road in places. You're a real lucky lady. You're the first person I've found alive."

The young woman sobbed heavily.

"It's okay," Truman said, holding her hand. "You're gonna be okay now, you hear?"

She nodded.

"What's your name, sweetheart?" he asked.

She struggled to regain her composure. She wiped her tears away with her hands and sniffed. Then in a delicate voice she answered, "Tabitha."

"I'm Truman. Listen, Tabitha," he said, softly. "I'm gonna get you out of here, but I need to go find some kind of tools and something to pry the dash back."

"No, don't leave me here," she pleaded.

Truman squeezed her hand promising, "I'll be back in a flash."

Tabitha nodded.

Truman ran off, sifting through the wreckage and searching through the surrounding vehicles.

"Jackpot!" he exclaimed, finding an abandoned work truck. The signs on its doors read, *Don Wright Garage Door Installation and Repair*. With the butt of his rifle, he smashed the small padlock open on the lid of the toolbox and dug through the tools. It looked like everything he needed: several wrenches and screw drivers, a pair of bolt cutters, and a pair of heavy, steel bars. He collected the booty and ran as fast as he could back to Tabitha.

"What'd I tell you?" he said reassuringly as he dropped to his knees to examine the assembly of the dash and driver's seat. "Well, it's gonna be tough getting to anything, with this tiny, little, clown car…"

"It was cute," Tabitha said, defensively.

"Yeah, I'm sure it was," Truman chuckled. He opened the rear hatch and crawled over the glass and into the back seat, squeezing himself upside down to the floor behind the driver's seat. "If I can get these bolts undone," Truman grunted, straining, "I might be able to just pull you backwards and away from the dash."

While the sun rapidly set, he worked tirelessly in that uncomfortable position for nearly an hour, struggling to keep the wrench on the bolts as he turned in the dark. Finally, he had the seat disconnected. "Okay, you ready?" he asked and started pulling the seat.

"Ouch! Stop! Stop! Stop!" she cried.

Truman looked her over once more. "Okay, hang on," he said. "I'm gonna try cutting that dash away a bit."

Determined, he worked, cutting piece after piece with the bolt cutters. Then using the steel bars he had found, he pried and wedged the dash and steering assembly up several inches. He climbed through the back and once again tugged at the seat. With that last effort Tabitha was freed.

"They don't call me Tru-Man for nothin'," Truman joked as he lifted her out the back of the car.

"Cheesy," Tabitha teased.

"Let's have a look at those legs," smiled Truman.

"I haven't shaved them in days," she excused, nervously.

"What? Really? Why not?" Truman mocked. "They don't look broken, but I'm no doctor. They do look like they hurt though. They're pretty swollen. Can you move 'em?"

Tabitha tried, but couldn't straighten them. "I can wiggle my toes."

"Alright. Rest here a bit," Truman grunted, setting her gently on the ground beside her car. "I'm going shopping. The RVs around here are bound to have some food and medicine in 'em. Maybe I can find some water and stuff too, so you can get cleaned up a bit."

"Oh, that'd be heavenly," she sighed.

Truman smiled, "Be right back."

A while later he returned pushing a wheelchair with a wobbly rear wheel. A five-gallon jug of water and two motorcycle helmets were nestled into its seat.

"What are the helmets for?" Tabitha asked with a hint of amusement in her voice.

"Hey, these things are fast and dangerous," Truman joked, shaking and erratically swerving the wheelchair. "Seriously, I saw them and thought it might be a good idea to have them in case we run into any more of that hail you saw. Things look pretty stormy ahead."

He dug into the large camping pack he had found in the wreckage, now overstuffed with all the other items he had found potentially useful. "I'm gonna need to organize all this stuff better," he said, finally finding the bottle of ibuprofen he was looking for. "Here," he said, handing Tabitha some of the pills, "this'll help take the swelling down."

Truman started a fire and set up camp next to her car. "We'll hunker down here for the night, and get set to head out first thing in the morning."

# Chapter Twenty

Staked spread-eagle, naked and face down on the ground, Oliver struggled to lift and hold his head above the thick sand so he could breathe. His wrists and ankles were tied tightly to four posts with thick braided cordage made from the fibers of yucca plants. The rough, dry ropes dug into his limbs, which were burned and bleeding after days of writhing and struggling to free himself. His mind was cloudy, unable to process and reason or filter the unrelenting waves of sensory information that flooded him.

Unsure how long he had been here or where exactly he was, he guessed it had been a few days, but his concept of time was skewed. He was, however, able to recognize the cycles of night to day to dark again. He knew only that when he awoke in this place days earlier, it was dark, pitch black, and his head ached.

When he had come to, he could sense that he was in a confined space as he called out for help. There was no response, no sound but the distant droning chirps of crickets. He knew he was utterly alone in this nightmare, yet an overwhelming sense of presence began almost immediately to creep up. The air around him grew steadily colder as the unnerving presence surrounded him, looking him over.

"Who's there?" Oliver cried out. There was no response. He cautiously held his breath, straining to listen in the darkness for any sound.

*Bang*! A sudden noise rang out.

"Who's there? What was that?" Oliver heard a faint whisper. It sounded female, and although it was mostly undecipherable, Oliver thought it had said, pleading, "Not my son."

*Bang*! The disheveled timbers of the collapsed ceiling above him knocked together, sending a small cloud of dust and gritty sand cascading down.

Oliver's stomach was queasy, a rising jittery feeling shooting through him. His mouth was fouled with a bitter, metallic taste. His mind and body were swept up in a frantic rush. His heart raced. His pupils dilated into large, black wheels that eclipsed all but a thin ring of his brown irises. Multicolored kaleidoscopic and geometric patterns swirled and morphed in his vision as the terrifying sense of a menacing presence grew all around him. He sensed several entities drawing nearer.

The sounds of footsteps and whispering made their presence known. Aggressive apparitions materialized in the dark, pulling his hair. His neck burned with scratches. Oliver shrieked in terror as entities swirled around him. Rapidly disintegrating into delirium, the overwhelming panic and helplessness culminated in a complete disassociation with reality, transporting him to some place else.

Still bound at the wrists and ankles, Oliver floated in a dark abyss surrounded by many grotesque demons. One by one they taunted him, relentlessly racing toward him at blurring speed, and then stopping mere inches from him. With gnashing teeth, they snarled in his face, opening their enormous, slobbering jaws wide, threatening to bite his face off.

Also present in the void were several people, although Oliver was prevented from seeing them clearly. They appeared as vapor, distorted and formless. The many demons coalesced into one large, hideous mass, writhing with monstrous entities and tortured faces.

For a brief moment, Oliver was comforted by a vision of his grandfather. But all too quickly his awareness phantasmagorically shifted, viewing the horrible abuse of a Navajo boy at the hand of his older brother. He watched the evil young man brutally murder a young mother and her baby and the baby's grandmother, mutilating their bodies. He saw a vision of his grandfather, years younger, running frantically through the desert, clutching a baby tightly against his chest.

For days, Oliver was haunted by horrific visions, enduring an onslaught of ghostly attacks, and suffering terrifying hallucinations of being covered in crawling insects. The intensity of his experience rose and fell in waves, but the sense of ghostly and demonic presences never abated. At times he would lose all consciousness then awaken on the floor of the hogan with the foul, metallic taste in his mouth renewed. Within minutes the intense visions would recur, each successive round more potent and frightening than the preceding one.

By the middle of the third day Oliver had been reduced to little more than a frightened, caged animal, every reaction primal and visceral. He snarled and growled at the slightest sounds.

"I can hear him in there, wolfing out or whatever," Eric whispered to Ocho, who crouched behind a juniper at the rear of the hogan. "It's just like that night. It was probably him I heard thrashing around in there."

"Well, what's the plan?" Mike asked. "We can't just barge in there. Shouldn't we try to lure him out into the open?"

Shaking his head, Ocho whispered, "No, he'll be too fast out here and have the advantage. We'll be better off taking him by surprise—kill him in there." He jerked his bowie knife from its sheath, gripping the hilt of the gleaming fifteen-inch blade tightly in his sweating hand. "I'll kick the door in and get him. You guys be ready in case he gets a hold of me."

"Wait," Tuwa said, grabbing Ocho's wrist. Ocho scowled at the old man, his fierce eyes demanding to know why.

Tuwa stammered, searching his memory for the English word. "Ghosts," he explained. Oliver's growling and thrashing intensified within the hogan.

"If it's a matter of superstition, or fear of ghosts, or whatever, I read somewhere that Navajos sometimes burn the abandoned hogans. Let's just burn him down in there." Eric suggested.

Ocho immediately made and ignited a torch. Tuwa obviously seemed unsure and increasingly uncomfortable as Ocho set the dilapidated hogan ablaze. He wandered into the surrounding shrubs to distance himself from the flames, trying in vain to ignore the shrieking and howling that blared from within the hogan.

155

Tuwa stopped suddenly. At his feet were signs of evil medicine. Dark, malevolent symbols were etched into the ground, at the center of which was a large pile of gathered plant material. Tuwa immediately recognized the large, white, trumpet-shaped blossoms and thorny, spherical seedpods as potent ingredients commonly used in a malign witch's brew to drive its victim crazy or, in higher doses, to kill an enemy.

The plant was *datura stramonium*, a highly toxic member of the deadly nightshade variety. More commonly known as jimson weed, the flower contained high levels of tropane alkaloids which, when ingested, caused terrifying auditory and visual hallucinations that could not be differentiated from reality.

"Stop!" screamed Tuwa, racing toward Ocho, frantically waiving a cluster of the flowering plants. "He's cursed, he's cursed."

Having once been a victim of the torturous hallucinogenic potion himself, Ocho instantly recognized the deceptively beautiful flower. He sprang into action, kicking through the barred, flaming door. Shielding his face with raised arms, Ocho charged through the invisible wall of searing heat and disappeared into the smoke.

"Ocho, what are you doing?" shouted Eric.

Flames spread rapidly through the old timbers as Oliver squirmed and contorted under a thick blanket of acrid, black smoke. The agitated demons were all around him, taunting him, provoking him. A large, fiery entity, covered head to toe with hundreds of eyes rushed up, slashing through the bindings on his feet and wrists with its long, razor-like claw. With great strength it seized him, grunting, "I got you." Oliver thrashed and bucked, freeing himself from the clutches of the frightening ghoul and dropped to the ground.

"Get back here!" the wraith shouted, grabbing Oliver in a full nelson and dragging him through the flames into a blinding white light.

Ocho and Oliver tumbled from the smoky doorway, both of them falling hard onto the ground outside. His mind awash with terrifying hallucinations and unable to recognize his companions, Oliver rapidly sprang to his feet and broke to run.

"Get him!" shouted Eric.

Mike rushed at Oliver, swinging a thick branch at his head. Seeing Mike as a thorn-covered demon with long, spindly, treelike limbs, Oliver ducked and took several steps to run before Eric tackled him to the ground, throwing up a cloud of dust. Eric appeared to Oliver as reptilian with scaly skin and large, lifeless, black eyes, whose body morphed into a serpent, coiling and constricting tightly around Oliver's legs.

Oliver hissed and growled, kicking wildly to free himself from Eric's tight grip. He broke free, growling, "You can't hurt me!"

"Wanna bet?" Mike shouted, taking another swing. Ocho threw himself between Oliver and Mike, his muscular arm taking the brunt of the blow.

"It's okay, he's not one of them!" shouted Ocho, just as Oliver blazed up behind him, jumping high to smash a large rock against Ocho's head, knocking him to the ground.

"My ass," Mike sneered.

Rock in hand, Oliver bolted toward Mike, who still appeared to him as a demon. Mike drew back his club to swing when Oliver unexpectedly stopped mesmerized, and dropped his rock.

Mike was confused by the look on Oliver's face. It was as if Oliver were looking through Mike as he said softly, "Grandfather?" Oliver began wandering in small circles, looking around, saying, "Where has my grandfather gone?"

Ocho got up, wiping the blood from his forehead with his arm. "He's not a skinwalker," Ocho explained. "He's under a spell, been hallucinating in there for days. It could be days more before he's back to normal. We have to find a way to convince him to head back with us, now. It's not safe here. The witch could come back any time."

"Then, shouldn't we wait and ambush him—get him before he comes for us?" Eric asked.

"There's no way we'll be able to keep him quiet," Ocho said, pointing to Oliver. "Besides, the skinwalker probably knows we're here. He could be watching us right now. We gotta move."

# Chapter Twenty-one

"Oh, dear Lord," Charlie gasped in disgust at the sight of Oliver's nakedness. "So, I take it you found him?"

Eric nodded, "Right where Tuwa said he'd be."

"So, he's still alive? He must not be one of those witch things after all. Lucky you all didn't kill him, huh?"

Eric nodded.

"Well, when I saw that smoke," Charlie said, "I almost went down there to help; but I figured I'd be of more service staying up here to pray for your success and safe return."

Eric scoffed.

"Anyway," Mike butted in, explaining, "Oliver is not in his right mind. He's under the spell of some kind of psychotropic drug that apparently produces terrifying visions. He really went after us back there, but he's pretty well subdued right now. He trusts Tuwa well enough, but he's still not too sure about us."

Oliver jumped excitedly, shouting, "Oh, of course! That's it, of course!"

"What?" asked Tuwa. "What is it?"

Everyone leaned in intently to hear Oliver's revelation, but he quickly settled down, his thoughts shifting randomly. Uncomfortable with everyone looking at him, Oliver stepped back and asked in obvious confusion, "What—?"

When he said no more the group moved on, disappointed that Oliver was unable to tell his story.

You know," Eric said to Mike, "I've had some pretty traumatic experiences these last few days, but none as terrible as having to wrestle a naked guy, out of his head on psychedelics."

"Yeah, I know," Mike laughed. "That was a bit awkward."

"Just a bit?" Charlie shrieked. "It's still awkward."

"Well, then, Charlie," Mike said. "Have you got anything in that backpack of yours that Oliver can wear?"

Charlie hastily dug through his pack, retrieving a pair of gray sweatpants and a white undershirt. He tossed the clothes to Tuwa.

Tuwa spoke softly to Oliver, handing him the pants. Oliver immediately put his arms through the pant legs and staggered around blindly, confused as to why he couldn't manage to find the opening to poke his head through. The guys chuckled. Watching Tuwa trying to help Oliver dress was like watching a frustrated parent wrangle a toddler.

"Pick it up guys," Ocho demanded, observing the sky. "We're gonna lose the light before we get back."

They walked steadily for hours making no stops. The light of the sun gleamed from its seat behind the mountains in the west, setting the clouds ablaze with hues of orange and red. Within several fleeting minutes it was dark.

Like a broken record Oliver repeated, "Where is my grandfather? Who will perform the *Blessing Way* for me? Who will take the *Chindi* from me?"

"Dear God," Charlie complained, "I beseech thee, make him stop talking."

Trudging onward, Eric blurted over his shoulder annoyed, "You're so quick to pray for something that suits you. Why not pray for Oliver's quick recovery?"

Following behind, Charlie glared at Eric, saying nothing.

"What is this *Blessing Way*, anyhow?" Eric asked.

After a long moment, Tuwa answered, "Sacred Navajo prayer chant. Restores harmony. *Chindi* is ghosts. They are all over him now."

Chanting rhythmically, Oliver repeated, "Where is my grandfather? Who will perform the *Blessing Way* for me? Who will take the *Chindi* from me?"

"Aw, I wish we'd left him there," Charlie groaned.

"Hey, stuff it, dude!" Ocho growled. "You don't know what he's been through, what he's still going through. So shut your pie hole, or you'll be picking up the rest of your teeth!"

Without another word, the group continued walking. An hour after sundown they made it back to camp.

"As much as I want to go to my tent and just crash," Ocho said, "Oliver can't be left alone. Tuwa, take him to his trailer," he instructed. "I'll be right behind you. Eric, you're coming with me. In fact, Mike and Charlie, you guys better come too. We'll all stay together."

They settled into Oliver's living room, hardly a word spoken between them. Within minutes all but Oliver were fast asleep. By the dim, flickering light of the oil lamp, he sat on the floor staring at the photos on the wall, muttering, "Where has my grandfather gone?"

After some time, quick movement caught the corner of Oliver's eye. He swiftly focused on the window in the trailer door. A partial face peering with one eye into the trailer receded from view, disappearing beyond the left frame. Oliver rose and cautiously crept toward the window to investigate. He labored to lighten his creaking footsteps on the warped kitchen floor as he inched closer to the door.

Oliver struggled to focus through his faint reflection in the dirty window. Unable to see more than a few feet into the darkness beyond the front steps, he pressed his forehead to the cold windowpane, his eyes now an inch from the glass.

Thud! Oliver gasped in surprise at the noise and fell backwards to the floor as a giant, gray moth slammed into the window and fluttered violently against the glass. No sooner than Oliver could catch his breath, heavy footsteps thundered across the roof, waking everyone in the house.

Ocho shot to his feet, jerking his bowie knife from its sheath and ran to Oliver. He wrapped his large hand around Oliver's arm and dragged him back to the huddled group in the living room. Everyone's eyes fixed on the ceiling, and senses heightened, they anxiously awaited any sign to tell them what was happening.

Heavy footsteps pounded up the kitchen wall, racing across the roof, and down the bedroom wall at the other end of the trailer. Seconds later, the footsteps pounded up the bedroom wall, across the roof, and down the kitchen wall. Tuwa dug a buckskin pouch from his satchel and raced through the trailer laying a thick line of corn pollen along every threshold and windowsill. Back and forth the footsteps pounded several times before stopping abruptly directly above them.

Everyone listened intently.

"Is it over?" Charlie asked.

"Shh!" Ocho hissed.

Twenty grueling minutes dragged by silently, without incident. Oliver was soon back to chanting for his grandfather. Exhausted, Eric sat on the floor. The others followed his lead, while Ocho remained standing, alert, knife in hand. The others were soon once again asleep.

For several hours, Ocho tenaciously stood guard. He knew that at any moment a skinwalker could crash through the window, or tear through the thin aluminum walls or roof and make quick work of the sleeping crew. Exhaustion was taking its toll on him. His eyelids heavy, he leaned against the wall, head bobbing and snapping back each time he dozed off.

Suddenly a brilliant light beamed through the windows, bleaching out all color and casting no shadows. The light shot away returning them to the dark of night. Oliver and Ocho raced to the window, each saying, "Grandfather?"

Mike and Eric shot up and ran over asking, "What was that?"

Ocho pointed. They stared dumbfounded out the window at a bright glow behind the plateau where the slot canyon lay a few miles to the west.

"We've got to get there fast!" exclaimed Mike.

Groggy and sluggish, Charlie slurred, "Are you crazy? What about the scary guy that was dancing on the roof?"

"I'll take my chances," Mike insisted. "We have to get there, don't you understand? They are the ones who activate the wormholes. This is our chance to get the crystal Ocho was taken to."

"I'm with you," Ocho said. "C'mon everybody, let's get moving."

They immediately set out, stopping briefly at the camp to grab their packs and what food they had left. The group split up to gather their essential belongings from their tents.

"Should we pack up the tents real quick?" Eric called out.

"No time," shouted Mike, "not if we're gonna get there before they leave."

Ocho grabbed his partially completed bow and slung his large duffel over his shoulder. Scanning the area he asked, "Tuwa, where's Oliver?"

Tuwa looked around worriedly. "I don't know. He was just right here next to me."

"Oh no," said Ocho, dropping to the darkened ground to better scan for tracks. "We gotta find him, fast. Here, this way. He went and wandered off."

They tracked Oliver to the thicket of trees near his trailer, where he was found kneeling in a clearing, arms raised to receive blessings.

"Good for you," Charlie said. "Receive Him and be saved."

"Shh," Ocho hissed in a whisper, "Show some respect. Let's give him some room."

The group backed off a bit, watching from the trees.

"Do you see that, Ocho?" Eric whispered.

"That smoky glow in front of him?" Ocho asked.

"I don't see anything," whispered Charlie.

"Me neither," Mike agreed.

Eric went back to Ocho. "You see a smoky glow?" he asked.

Ocho nodded, "Yeah, why? What do you see?" he asked, quietly.

"Oliver's grandfather. The guy from the photo, plain as day. You really don't see that?"

Ocho relaxed his focus. He crossed his eyes. He squinted, closed one eye, then the other. "I wish I did," he whispered, shaking his head. "What's he doing?"

"He's singing some kind of song. I guess in Navajo," Eric explained. "He's got some kind of shell or pot or something in his hand, I can't tell which. But something is smoldering in it. The smoke is just billowing out. I can even smell it. It's really sweet. He's, like, bathing Oliver with it, fanning him with feathers. He's just an amazing-looking dude: silver hair, penetrating eyes, wearing a humongous silver necklace."

Eric watched the ceremony unfold. "Whoa!" he exclaimed in a whisper.

"What?" asked Mike.

Tuwa nodded, smiling at Eric reassuringly. He motioned with his hands, enacting pulling something from his chest and releasing it into the air.

Astonished, Eric asked, "You saw that?"

"Saw what?" asked Mike.

Ocho listened intently.

"Oliver's grandfather was singing and bathing Oliver with that smoke," Eric explained. "Then he pulled a smoky mass from Oliver's chest. It was an old woman. She rose like smoke and just sort of dissipated into the air. Then he pulled out another woman, young and beautiful. And then he pulled out another smoky mass just like the others, but it was a baby. It morphed into a man that looked very much like Oliver. Then it floated up and disintegrated like the others. Phew, it was weird, man."

"Wait," Eric said. "His grandfather is placing his hands on Oliver's head now. Man, he and his grandfather are both shining with really bright, white light." Eric gasped, "He just, sort of, faded away."

Oliver folded over to rest his head on the ground. Eric began walking over before Ocho pulled him back, saying, "Give him a minute, dude."

Oliver remained motionless for some time before pulling himself slowly to his feet. Tears rolled down, washing his dirty cheeks. He stared at the guys for a moment, processing his thoughts, then walked over and hugged Tuwa warmly. Ocho gently squeezed Oliver's shoulder. Eric and Mike laid their hands on him, Mike saying, "Good to have you back, Oliver."

# Chapter Twenty-two

By the dim light of the moon, Ocho led the group through the ravine and to the creek. "Not much further from here," he said.

Eric had wanted to talk to Oliver for some time about what he saw, but didn't quite know how to bring it up. Finally he mustered his nerve, asking, "Are you okay, Oliver?"

Oliver nodded, "I'm still feeling a bit funny. Kinda jittery, but yeah, I'm okay."

As they walked, Eric continued, "I saw what happened back there. I don't know how or why, but I saw the whole thing."

Confused, Oliver asked, "What are you talking about?"

"I saw your grandfather performing the *Blessing Way* for you."

Oliver became agitated. He grabbed Eric by the shirt and growled in his face, "Don't ever make jokes about my grandfather."

"Settle down, Oliver," Eric said. "I swear to God, I mean no disrespect. I'm not joking, and I'm not lying. I saw him."

Tuwa gently pulled Oliver's hands from Eric, saying softly, "It's true, I saw too."

"But my grandfather has been gone for a long time."

Anxiously, Eric asked Tuwa, "How can he not remember?"

Tuwa squeezed Oliver's arms and stared into his eyes. Oliver's memories of the incident flooded back. "Grandfather," Oliver said. "It's true."

"I saw him," said Eric. "I watched him pull the, what are they called? *Chindi* from you."

"I remember. I guess deep down I just didn't want to. It was my mother, and my grandmother, and my twin brother," Oliver said in his guttural, staccato accent. "Growing up around here, I always had heard stories about that old, rotting hogan by the main road. The story was that the man that lived there was *Yeenaaldlooshii,* which means 'he goes on all fours'—a man that practices the *Witchery Way.*"

"A skinwalker," Eric interposed. "Believe me. I know more about them than I ever wanted to know."

"Well, then you know they have to kill someone in their family to learn the evil chants that give them powers, specifically the power to shapeshift. I always had thought the stories everyone told around here were just sort of urban legends. They said the family that lived there was slaughtered by a skinwalker. That he killed his mother and wife, even his own son. I always had figured it was just an abandoned hogan where someone died of old age or something, but grandfather came tonight to reveal the truth: that skinwalker was my father, Grandfather's son. He killed my twin brother and mother and grandmother. Grandfather saved me when I was just a baby and raised me here. He told me back then that my mother and father were killed in a car accident, and never mentioned I even had a twin."

Mike wrestled for a moment with sadness, remembering his lost twin, Gabriel. "Oliver," he asked, "do you have any idea how you came to be in that hogan?"

Oliver shook his head. "All I know is, I fell asleep on my couch that night, and woke up tied to the floor of the hogan. I don't really want to talk about it. It was too horrible."

"Well, some good did come of it—your family," Eric said. "You freed them, Oliver. You saved them."

Tuwa nodded in agreement.

Oliver took a moment to soak in the information and nodded. "Well, I have just one question, then: Where the hell are we going?"

The guys laughed.

"One of those triangular UFOs flew over your house and seems to have landed behind the mesa where that slot canyon is," Mike explained.

"Oh yeah," Oliver nodded, remembering. "Didn't I tell you? I see them there all the time from my house."

Mike told Oliver, "We've found that the designs carved into the walls in the cavern are somehow connected to the actual places around the world that they depict."

"What do you mean?" Oliver asked.

"I mean," Mike explained, "that it seems to be a transportation terminal, some kind of teleportation system. Eric and Ocho have both somehow been sent through and brought back. We're not sure how, but the best we can figure is that the UFO must have activated it, because it was seen in the area every time it happened."

"We're here," said Ocho, pulling the spindly branches back to reveal the trail.

Inside the narrow canyon, there was not a shred of light. They stumbled along, slowly working their way deeper into the mountain, feeling along the smooth sandstone walls.

"Let there be light," Charlie said, flicking a butane lighter he dug from his pocket.

"You've had that this whole time?" Eric asked, condemningly.

With his gap-toothed lisp Charlie unapologetically explained, "I didn't want to waste the fuel."

"What do you think you're doing now, you bonehead?" Eric shouted. "We could have made a torch or something!" Shaking his head in disdain, he muttered, "Fool."

Among the debris left by the recent flash flood, Ocho found a wide-spreading branch with many dry, curled leaves. "Settle down, dude, it's cool," Ocho said. "Charlie, how 'bout a light?"

Charlie flicked the lighter and the branch blazed in Ocho's hands. "Grab some more of these, guys. Whatever you can find that'll burn. All you can carry."

They settled into the circular cavity and built a fire. In the flickering light, Mike scanned the vaulted walls. "Did you guys notice?" Mike asked. "From what I can tell—I mean, some of these places are unfamiliar to me—but the sites depicted here all seem to be in the western hemisphere, the Americas mostly."

"Do you think there might be other hubs like this that lead to other continents?" Eric asked.

"Who knows?" Mike said. "For all we know, there may be portals to other worlds."

"C'mon you kooks," Charlie groaned, "we've been here for almost an hour now, and no one seems to be going anywhere."

Eric was angered by Charlie's comment. He pondered for a quick moment what roads brought him here, where the Jehovah's Witness, of all people, would lump him into the "kook" category. His feelings, however, soon turned to amusement. His lips curled into a slight smirk. He glanced over, catching Ocho's eye. As if he'd been reading his mind, Ocho flashed his toothy, sheepish grin. "He's right," Eric said.

"I wonder if we got here too late," said Mike, disappointedly.

"How can we be so sure that those things have anything to do with this place?" Eric asked.

"Those things?" Mike fussed. "You mean the UFOs. I can't believe you still won't call it as it is. You've seen them yourself! You really can't see that there is some otherworldly intervention happening here?"

"Chill out, Mike," Eric said. "Obviously there is intervention here. I spent the night with a giant spider, remember? I'm only saying that we can't be sure just what it is that activates this place. And those UFOs are just that: unidentified things that fly. All we really know about them is that they're still able to fly. Their technology seems to be unaffected by this continuous electromagnetic activity. That is if it is technology, as we understand it, that even makes them fly. But we don't know who or what they are, or if they have anything to do with what is going on here, or even what their motives are. How can we be sure they're here to help us in any way at all? Maybe they mean to hinder us, or just to sit back and watch. We just don't know. It's just that with all that's happened, and all that's on the line, we need to be cautious."

168

"You're right," Mike said. "I thought you were just naysaying my affinity for UFOs again. But I just can't help but feel like they're here to herald a new age. I guess we all tend to make sense of things based on our predetermined beliefs, not just Charlie there."

Charlie looked up, confused. "Well, whatever that's supposed to mean," he said, "I haven't seen anything unusual in the sky, and I haven't seen anything to make me believe that this place can do any of the things you've claimed it can. Maybe you all had some of Oliver's jimson weed. What we should really be doing is praying for a way back to civilization."

"Prayer is good," said Ocho, "but better with action." He rose from his seat near the fire and walked over to a glyph on the wall, a depiction of a Mesoamerican stepped pyramid with a long, horizontal line at the foundation. Beside the pyramid was a large tree rooted on the line and one inverted tree reflected identically below. Rising behind the pyramid was a spiral, its center eclipsed by a circle.

"I was here," said Ocho. "Standing here just like this. Then I was someplace else, in the jungle. I don't know how it happened," he explained.

From his seat in the sand next to the fire, Charlie scoffed and rolled his eyes as the others rose and huddled around Ocho to examine the glyph.

"Tree of Life," Tuwa said, pointing at the design on the wall. "And sun, there."

"I wonder if the spiral behind the circle has anything to do with the Mayan prophecies of the galactic alignment that happens every 26,000 years," Mike commented. "I heard or read somewhere that Mayan legend told of a rift or portal that opened, allowing evil to enter the Earth."

"Like my dream!" Eric blurted, "The one where I was in a cartoon! This design is similar to the one we saw on the rock in the ravine. The one with the trees above and below the spiral."

Mike was excited and speaking loudly. "It all fits!"

Transfixed, they stared at the glyph, in awe of their discovery. Suddenly the ground shook. A low hum rose from deep beneath them as bright light filled the cavern, bleaching everything to white. As instantly as the light and sound washed over them, it disappeared, returning the cave to flickering firelight.

"What the…" Charlie exclaimed. He looked around the empty chamber for any trace of his missing companions. Alone and afraid, he ran through the slot canyon as fast as he could, stumbling from the fissure into the gnarled thicket. The first rays of the morning sun pierced through the clouds in the east. The spindly branches raked Charlie's skin as he clumsily thrashed his way through. Exhausted, he collapsed on the cold, rocky ground next to the creek.

The sound of footsteps crunching in the rocks behind the nearby trees brought dreadful feelings that instantly washed over Charlie. He focused intently on the darkened grove of cottonwoods. From behind a large trunk, a white face peered at him. Without warning, the entity raced toward Charlie at blurring speed, stopping mere inches from him. Charlie gasped in fright, looking up into the horrible face of the one hovering over him. It was the ghost-faced skinwalker that had been terrorizing Eric.

# Chapter Twenty-three

Standing amidst the thick vegetation atop a steep hill, Ocho announced, "We're here."

"But, where is here?" Oliver asked.

"The drawing of the pyramid in the cave looked very similar to the structures at Tikal," Mike said. "Based on that, I'd guess we're probably somewhere in northern Guatemala; but maybe Belize, or even Mexico."

Oliver was confused. "So, then, if we were brought to the place in the drawing, where is the pyramid?" he asked. "All I can see is miles and miles of trees."

"Well, when I was transported to Spider Rock," Eric suggested, "I wound up in a cave on the canyon wall and had to walk the rest of the way. It's gotta be around here somewhere."

"Um, yeah," Mike announced, confidently. "We're standing on it."

Eric examined his surroundings more closely, seeing the basic shape of the pyramid underneath the plant growth. "How long must it have been here, forgotten like this?" Eric asked, amazed.

"Centuries," Mike answered.

The top of the pyramid rose fifty feet above the jungle canopy, and over two-hundred feet from the jungle floor. One tree, however, a giant ceiba much larger than the others, almost equaled the height of the structure.

"Look, there it is," Mike pointed to the tree. "That must be the tree in the glyph."

Sacred to the Maya, connecting the heavens, the terrestrial realm, and the planes of the underworld, the enormous ceiba tree had a widespread canopy, a tall, branchless trunk, and a sprawling buttress root system that intertwined with the roots of the nearby trees.

"When I was here before I went and stood between those roots there," Ocho said. "They're like giant walls, maybe fifteen feet tall." Ocho pointed at a large fissure in the ground near the giant tree. "That's where the big crystal came up," he said. "Follow me. Be careful going down, everybody, it's really steep."

Ocho led the group down the hill and cleared away the leaves and branches that concealed the milky crystal. "Beautiful, huh?" he grinned.

"I'll say," Eric agreed, laying his hand gently on one of the smooth, angled sides. The prism vibrated with energy, waves pulsing up his arm and throughout his body. His eyes grew heavy and he felt lightheaded. He closed his eyes and slumped forward, feeling as though he were tumbling through space. He removed his hand and the strange feelings left him just as suddenly. Eric opened his eyes and noticed something hiding in the nearby trees, watching them. He stared unblinking into the dark jungle.

"What are you looking at?" Ocho asked, readying his grip on the handle of his sheathed knife.

"Yeah, what do you see?" inquired Mike, anxiously.

Eric pointed, whispering, "That really dark area under that plant with the big leaves…do you see it?"

Awed, Mike exclaimed, "Whoa, is that a…"

Eric cut him off, "Yup, a jaguar."

The majestic cat watched them for a moment longer, then slowly slunk away. Eric looked to the top of the overgrown pyramid, and pointed. "The chamber at the top is a temple. We need to get in it."

"How do you know?" Mike asked.

Eric smiled at Ocho and said, "Some things you just know, you know?"

Ocho nodded, grinning.

"How long do you think it would take to clear away all that growth to get inside?" asked Eric.

"Oh, I don't think we'd need to clear it all away," Mike said, confidently. "The way it was depicted in the glyph was classic Mayan architecture. Straight up this way will be the stairs, and at the top, a door. We would only need to clear that part there."

Discouraged, Eric said, "Now, if only we had some tools."

"Fire," suggested Tuwa.

"Whoa, gees," Eric exclaimed, surprised. "You've been so quiet, I forgot you were here," he laughed.

Enduring a relentless downpour of rain, Truman wheeled Tabitha's wobbly chair along the interstate, weaving around the miles and miles of stalled, abandoned cars and trucks that lined the highway. They steadily drew closer to Flagstaff, crossing through the outskirts of town. Evidence of heavy storm damage was everywhere.

"All that stuff you told me about—do you really think it can get worse?" Tabitha asked, surveying the wreckage. "Do you really think there is no way this will all pass so things can go back to normal?"

"I would love to believe that, but I've just seen too much already," Truman answered, sadly. "I believe it will definitely get worse, and may have already. God knows what's happening everywhere else."

Little did Truman know that, in fact, Dallas and Oklahoma City had been virtually erased by mega storms, as were many other cities and towns throughout the Great Plains and Midwest. Severe flooding plagued cities and towns along the Mississippi River. Several rapidly moving, category five hurricanes were lined up to batter the Gulf States, while another had already plowed along the East Coast, resulting in extensive damage to cities along the eastern seaboard, including Washington D.C., and causing downed buildings and extreme flooding in New York City. Heavy rains overpowered the nation's aging infrastructure, causing bridge and dam failures across the states, the torrents scouring away entire cities within minutes. Wildfires had scorched the outlying areas of San Diego and Los Angeles, and without functioning firefighting equipment or coordinated efforts, were blazing out of control toward the metropolitan areas.

All around the world, similar episodes of extreme weather were unfolding, triggering an incomprehensible death toll. With vital communication networks inoperable, and given the overwhelming scale and extent of the ongoing disasters, there were no organized federal disaster relief efforts underway anywhere.

Upon entering Flagstaff proper, they were both relieved to find much of it still standing. Many buildings however, particularly the older brick buildings from the early 1900s, were reduced to rubble. People were working together in the heavy rain, sifting though the ruins in search of survivors. Small detachments of National Guard troops were maintaining order and leading search efforts. Using manual handsaws, they labored to clear the vital roadways of downed trees and debris.

After explaining to one of the guardsmen that he was transporting an injured girl, Truman was directed to a makeshift triage outside of the hospital downtown. The overwhelmed medical center was comprised of several large army tents and canopies where the injured were assessed and sorted for treatment. Truman wheeled Tabitha to the waiting area. "You good?" he asked.

Tabitha hesitantly nodded.

"Alright, then," Truman said, "It was really nice to meet you. I hope everything checks out alright."

Tabitha was upset. "You're leaving already?" she asked anxiously.

Truman nodded. "I gotta get to Kingman as fast as possible."

"Can't you wait with me a while?" Tabitha pleaded. "I don't want to be here alone. If things are pretty well under control here, chances are Kingman is fine too."

Truman shook his head. "I really don't know what's going on there. I just can't take any chances with my kids. Even if there haven't been any storms like what happened here, I'm sure there will be soon. I know it sounds crazy, but I really think civilization is about to be wiped out. I gotta get them outta there before it's too late."

174

"So, what if what you're saying is true?" she asked. "How are you going to convince your kids to just pack up and leave with you, after everything you told me about the way your ex bad mouthed you to them all the time? And where the hell do you think you're going to go? Where is safe?"

"The four corners area, up on the reservations," Truman snapped defiantly.

"Why?" Tabitha demanded to know. "Do you really know, for sure, you'll be safe there? What proof do you have?"

"Proof?!" Truman growled, frustrated. "I don't need it; I believe what I've seen. All I have, all I've ever had, really, is faith, and it's all I need!"

Tabitha relented, "Sorry, Truman, I know you need to do this. I'm just afraid for you to go." She looked him squarely in the eye, saying, "And you know, you really need to be better prepared for those tough questions when you show up looking like some kind of crazed doomsday prophet."

"Is doomsday prophet a step up or a step down from being a crazy UFO nut?" Truman chuckled.

Tabitha smiled, her eyes gleaming. "Good luck, and be careful," she said. She took Truman's hand and pulled him close. She hugged him warmly, pulling him down to her. She gave him a kiss on the cheek and said, "Thank you for saving me."

"It was my pleasure," he said, strapping on his pack. "Tabitha, if you don't think I'm crazy, head for Chinle."

Eric stretched his aching back and wiped the sweat from his forehead. The group had labored nonstop throughout the day, burning and clearing the hilltop of its undergrowth. With makeshift wooden shovels that Ocho had fashioned from log-split staves, they scraped away the nearly two feet of topsoil and leaf litter.

Glancing down near the roots of the giant ceiba tree, Eric was confused and shocked. "Mom?" he asked in disbelief. Unnoticed by the others, he scurried down the structure and gave chase. He pursued the vision of his mother behind one of the enormous lateral roots, where she turned to face him. Her lips curled into a slight smile as she rapidly evaporated, leaving only questions.

Eric sat between the roots in the shade of the ceiba to contemplate the strangeness of seeing his mother here, all these miles from Phoenix. He had not seen or spoken to her since Evan's funeral, and here she was wearing the same black dress. He thought it peculiar that his mother would be wearing the dreamcatcher necklace he bought for her at the Spider Rock overlook: the one she was sure to hate. The necklace was still carefully wrapped in tissue paper in his backpack. What could the vision possibly mean, he wondered.

Exhausted, he closed his eyes. The cacophony of birds and distant calls of monkeys soon faded to total silence as Eric slowly slid effortlessly into the ground, following the roots of the tree deeper and deeper underground. In the darkness, a faint glow revealed a cave entrance ahead. At the speed of thought, Eric transported himself to the heart of the cavern, skipping the entrance altogether.

The dank cave, with its striated stalactites and stalagmites of varying size and shape, was hollow and reverberant, the sounds of slowly dripping water echoing throughout the cavernous chamber. A thick fog hugged the ground. The soft glow of the cave grew steadily more intense, forming a spiraling smoky tunnel of brilliant white light. Emerging from the swirling portal, a dark, silhouetted figure moved sinuously toward him. Eric was cautious, but stood his ground as a black jaguar materialized before him. The glossy, black beast stared deliberately at Eric with its piercing, yellow-green eyes. As the cat gazed into him, a voice spoke into Eric's mind. "Be not afraid to look into the dark mirrors," it said. "Subdue the ferocious ones who look back at you, and see beyond sight."

The jaguar turned and moved away, disappearing into the smoky light. As it faded to darkness, Eric once again glimpsed his mother inside the rapidly closing tunnel of light, smiling as she held baby Evan. The vision disappeared. Eric didn't know how he knew, but he was instantly certain his mother had died.

Unsure what to feel, he was comforted by the thought that she and Evan were together. But his complete lack of grief confused him. Strangely, he was happy she had passed, though not for any malicious reason. Quite the contrary, he couldn't remember the last time he felt such love for her, if ever. Suddenly, he was rushed up through the ground, following the roots back to the surface where his journey had begun.

Mike hovered over him nervously. "Eric, are you okay?" he asked.

Eric was sprawled out, flat on his back. He was sluggish. His eyes were slow to focus, his mental faculties seeming out of sync.

"Eric," Mike repeated. "Eric, c'mon, wake up. Wake up, Eric!"

Ocho squeezed Mike's shoulder. "He's okay, Mike, just give him a second."

Through the tree canopy, Eric stared into the twilight sky, watching the bands of plasma as they swirled high above in the magnetosphere. The darkening jungle was alive, bustling with the sounds of its inhabitants.

Slowly, Eric sat up. "What's going on?" he asked.

"We're through," Mike exclaimed. "Everyone was so busy clearing the top of the hill, nobody noticed you were missing until Ocho found the opening. We were all excited and ran over to see the temple chamber, when we noticed you weren't there. What were you doing, napping?"

Eric was curious. He desperately wanted to know about the temple. "What's inside?" he asked.

"It's really very unusual," Mike proclaimed. "From everything I've ever studied, I expected the walls to be carved with elaborate motifs that would chronicle the history of this place; but the walls, floor and ceiling are black. We cleaned them up really well. They're clad with smooth, volcanic glass—obsidian—like a hall of mirrors, shiny, black mirrors."

"I had another vision," Eric said. "I sank into the Earth, into a cave, where I was met by a black jaguar who told me to look into the dark mirrors. It said that to look into the dark mirrors is to see beyond sight."

Ocho beamed. "You journeyed to the lower world and found one of your power animals," he said, grinning.

Tuwa nodded in agreement.

"I don't know about all that," Eric insisted reluctantly, struggling to cling to his outmoded skepticism.

"Yeah, you do," Ocho insisted confidently.

"Why do you do that, Eric?" Mike asked.

Confused, Eric asked impatiently, "Do what?"

"Go back and forth like that. You've had so many intense and profound experiences these past few days—hell, all your life really—and you still always revert to doubt."

"I don't really know why," Eric conceded. He thought silently for a moment, then voiced softly, "After Evan died, I laid in bed for days, crying. It felt like I'd cried every ounce of moisture from my body; I thought I'd shrivel into a raisin. I wanted so badly to believe he had gone to a better place, but having rejected religion, I also rejected God. I figured God was just made up to keep us all in line, like how we threaten kids that Santa can see them being bad or good.

"One night, I cried out to whatever higher power there may be, *let me feel you!* Instantly, I felt a gentle touch on my chest. A warm, radiant feeling of the purest love you could ever imagine rippled throughout my body, filling me from head to toe. I could even feel it in every individual hair on my head and body. I sobbed like never before, and the sadness and pain drained completely from me. I slept like a baby."

Eric hastily wiped a tear from his eye, hoping no one noticed, and continued, "By morning I had explained it away, convincing myself that the experience was little more than the effect of stress and grief on my body; and all that pain seeped back in. I really don't know why I do that. I mean, who wouldn't want an experience like that? But I feared a life transformed by such a testimony. That's why I go back and forth like that. Deep down, I guess I've always just been hoping for a normal, simple life, where I can ignore my conscience and make my own mistakes in defiance of what I know is right."

With a grunt, Eric tiredly climbed to his feet and brushed the leaves and dirt off of his clothes. Noting the rapidly darkening surroundings, he suggested, "We better get a fire going."

"I'll go find something to eat," Ocho said.

Within an hour, Ocho emerged from the darkened jungle lugging the limp, bloody carcass of a large boar.

"Whoa, that was fast," exclaimed Mike.

"No kidding," Eric gasped in agreement.

Ocho explained, "This place is full of game."

Mike looked more closely at Ocho. "What happened to your mouth?"

Surprised, Ocho wiped his mouth with his hand and looked at the blood smeared across his fingers. "Huh," he muttered. "It's not mine. I must have touched my face and got boar's blood on it."

Trying not to appear obvious, Mike suspiciously examined the boar's body as Ocho and Tuwa prepared it. The neck was mauled by powerful jaws, its jugular brutally severed. There were no other wounds.

"How'd you catch this one?" Mike asked.

Ocho turned to face Mike. "Why all the questions, dude?"

"I'm just impressed with how fast you hunted," Mike explained. "I'm curious about how you did it, that's all. I mean, this boar looks like it was brought down by a predatory animal. A big one, too."

"Ocho the *Whitewolf* does it again, huh Mike?" Ocho grinned slyly. "I was tracking the boar," he explained, "but a jaguar beat me to it. I scared it away and took the prize. What's the matter, you not hungry?" Ocho asked, sarcastically.

"I was just curious," Mike excused.

"Well, this is gonna take a while to cook," Ocho said, lighting a torch. "Grandfather says Eric should see the temple tonight."

The group followed Ocho to the foot of the overgrown pyramid. Eric's eyes followed the enormous hill up to the cleared temple chamber at the top, his heart pounding with trepidation.

"This place is kinda creepy at night, huh," said Eric.

"I guess so," Mike answered. "But I'm really excited for you to see it. And with your vision about the dark mirrors? What a coincidence."

Ocho grinned coyly at Eric. Eric smiled back, saying, "Yeah, big time coincidence. But someone I know says there's no such thing."

"That's right," Ocho affirmed. "What you call coincidence, I call a sign, a way to know we're on the right path. And this path," Ocho said, stopping and handing the torch to Eric, "This path is Eric's."

Eric took several hesitant steps up the hill.

"Wait," Tuwa called, digging in his satchel. Chanting Hopi phrases, Tuwa pulled out a small buckskin pouch and gently drew three yellow lines of corn pollen across Eric's forehead.

Cautiously, Eric climbed the hill, careful not to slip on leaf litter or stumble over the sprawling, twisted roots that anchored the trees and shrubs to the pyramid. By torchlight, having only one hand to stabilize himself as he climbed, the ascent was difficult and tiring. Eric groped along, plagued by the fleeting fears of encountering one of the region's many deadly snakes, or falling backwards down the steep hill to severe injury.

Finally, he reached the top. He sat just outside the temple entrance to catch his breath and gather his courage before entering the imposing and eerily dark room. Startled by the tickle across his leg, Eric jerked to his feet, brushing off a giant centipede, which fell writhing on the ground before righting itself and scurrying off into the vegetation.

"Okay, I'm going, I'm going," he growled, cautiously creeping toward the opening. He extended the torch through the doorway, carefully inspecting the room for any other creepy crawlers that might be lying in wait. All clear, he stepped inside.

The temple chamber crowning the pyramid was small, ten feet squared, with a narrow, east-facing pocket door. Eric ventured to the center of the murky room, his perception skewed by the infinite reflections of himself, receding indefinitely in all directions. With a resounding thump, the heavy obsidian-sheathed door was forcefully slid shut, as if by invisible hands.

Eric dropped the torch and scrambled for the door, straining to pry it open. Terrified, he looked into the eyes of his reflection, inches from his face as he struggled to slide the door back. His reflection transformed into a hideous insectile face with enormous, black, bulbous eyes. Eric screamed. He forced the door open with all his might and ran frightened down the hill and into camp.

Concerned, Mike begged, "What happened, Eric?" Ocho, Tuwa, and Oliver listened intently.

"I'm sorry, guys," Eric panted, collapsing near the fire. "I got really spooked."

Ocho stretched a sinew cord from one end of his newly completed bow to the other. "By what?" he asked, drawing back the string to check the tension before dry firing the bow.

Eric shook his head, denying to himself what he had seen. "The door slammed shut behind me. My reflection," he puffed, "turned into something like a mantis, a horrible face I didn't ever want to see again."

Mike perked up. "Interesting, very interesting," he said. "The praying mantis was named from *mantis*, the Greek word for prophet or seer. In your vision earlier, you were told to face the frightening images and see beyond sight. It's a seer's temple, used for divination. My interpretation of your vision is that if you face your fears, and persist in scrying into the black obsidian, very valuable information will be presented through you. Eric, you have to go back."

Shaking his head, Eric countered, "I can't."

"You have to, Eric," Mike insisted. "Everything that has happened seems to revolve around you. You're the key to all this. Wait a minute. Did you say the mantis was a face you did not or do not ever want to see again?"

His voice trembling, Eric struggled to speak. "I've never spoken to anyone about this before," he muttered. "I've fought hard all my life to stuff it away, trying to convince myself that it doesn't exist."

His lips quivered and teeth chattered slightly as a chill washed over him. "When I was little—four or five—I used to have all kinds of bad dreams, and I sleepwalked. I turned up in all kinds of places, mostly the back yard. My mom even took me to the doctor for it. He said it was Night Terrors, and had my mom put me on a special diet. Like that would help.

"For as long as I can remember, I've been haunted by a memory, or a dream; I don't really know what. But the pictures in my mind are really hard to blink away. When I was little, I woke up paralyzed, staring into the lifeless black eyes of a strange, luminescent being who watched me through my window. The next image I remember is standing in the cotton field across the street from the house I grew up in, staring up at the moon—a small, crescent moon; just a sliver of light, shaped like a fingernail clipping.

"I just watched the sliver of moonlight, staring into it so sharply that it appeared to be hovering over me, like I could reach out and touch it. Then it widened, this brilliant white light spreading downward, stretching to the ground, opening before me like a door from some invisible world. All a sudden, from the door, a bunch of those glowing, gooey, big-eyed things floated toward me. I don't know how many; six, maybe ten."

"What do you mean, gooey?" Mike asked, curiously.

"I don't know," Eric answered. "I can't explain it. Like they didn't have a skeleton, like they were made of goo or something. Like jellyfish. As scary as they seemed, they were nothing like what came next. The last image I remember before everything turns to black static is a tall, skinny, insect-looking thing. Like a praying mantis with a triangular head and huge, reflective-black, almost mirror-like, wraparound, bug eyes. Just like what was up there looking at me through the mirror. It's such a strange feeling to look into something so hideous, so frightening, and see yourself looking back, to see your familiar likeness reflecting back at you and yet feel so much terror. Yes, terror; terror personified. And to see yourself drowning in the abyss of those damned empty, black eyes, appearing so sentient and apart that you begin to question which of you is real and which is the reflection."

"Eric that is fascinating," Mike said, excitedly. "That really explains so much about you. You've gotta get back up there and find out what's next!"

"Did you hear me, Mike?" shouted Eric. "I can't!"

Ocho's voice boomed, impatiently, "You have to, Eric. No one else. It has to be you."

"Listen, Eric," Oliver chimed in. "I had to face things more terrifying than anything I ever had imagined: horrible demons; but they can't harm you, if you can keep from harming yourself."

Closing his eyes, Eric drew in a deep breath and exhaled heavily. He wondered what Oliver's advice possibly meant, imagining himself fleeing the temple in a panic, winding up with a broken neck at the foot of the steep hill.

"You can do this," Oliver encouraged.

Even with his eyes shut tightly, Eric noticed the subtle glow emanating from his hands and body, just as they did while in the darkened kiva at the base of Spider Rock. He remembered the web to which he and all things were connected. Hovering on either side were the hawk and owl, just as before. Eric felt warm and protected, yet he was still terrified at the thought of the mantis.

In his mind's eye, Eric retreated to the cave from his vision earlier that day. The glossy, black jaguar appeared again; but it was different than before. This time the jaguar growled menacingly, revealing its large, yellowed fangs. With blurring speed, it pounced, knocking Eric to the ground, sinking its teeth deep into Eric's neck.

Eric fought fiercely, kicking wildly and gouging at the cat's eyes. No match for the powerful beast, Eric was devoured completely. Alive inside the jaguar, Eric could feel its power coursing through him, and could see through its acutely focused eyes.

"Eric," Mike called, snapping his fingers several times. "Don't shut me out man. C'mon, we need to talk about this."

Calm and collected, Eric opened his eyes. He stood courageously, and without a word, walked directly to the pyramid and climbed the hill. Like the jaguar, his footsteps were silent and deliberate, his eyes keen in the dark. He entered the temple, sliding the heavy stone door shut behind him.

Eric stood confidently in the center of the chamber, the dying torch glowing faintly on the floor at his feet. Eyes watering, a tear rolling down his cheek, he gazed unblinkingly into the mirror. Eric saw in his repeating reflections the demons of his past: embarrassing moments; all his transgressions; the many ways he had wronged himself and others. He could feel the hurt he had caused and became aware of the way his offenses rippled outward, perpetually affecting others still.

The potential for evil that resided inside him manifested as his reflections coalesced into a multiple-headed, reptilian creature writhing in the air before him. The monster displayed tentacles with venomous barbs that Eric understood to be the way the demon propagated, each wrongdoing infecting others with an evil that grows inside, until ready to transmit again and again, spread from person to person.

"I will kill you!" Eric shouted, facing the demon headlong. The ghastly entity doubled in size, wrapping a tentacle tightly around Eric's neck, causing the base of his skull to throb with a familiar stinging pain. "I am more powerful than you in this world!" Eric gasped, struggling to uncoil the tentacle and break free from the creature's mighty grip. With an earsplitting hiss, the ghoul swelled and charged at Eric, gnashing its terrible teeth mere inches from his face. Like the hydra of ancient mythology, every act of aggression seemed to only strengthen the creature. Eric adapted a different strategy.

"You will never leave me, will you?" he asked, realizing that this evil was an inherent part of him. "I will never be free of you," Eric said as he came to understand. He remembered what Ocho had said about choice being our greatest power. The beast recoiled, moving erratically, hesitantly. "Then all I can do is accept responsibility for you and act accordingly, so that you never again see the light of day." With a resounding shriek, the demon shrank and vanished.

In the blackness, images flashed before him. Eric was shown a partially buried disk protruding from the ground. He soon recognized it as what was left of Seattle's Space Needle, buried under a massive mudflow that had been released by the ferocious eruption of Mt. Rainier and its subsequent glacial melt. The city was a wasteland, charred by pyroclastic flows and mostly concealed under ash and mud.

Eric was drenched in sweat with a sharp pain jabbing behind his eyes, radiating from deep within the frontal lobes of his brain. Yet Eric never blenched from the barrage of apocalyptic visions that battered his mind like waves eroding the shore. He stood steadfast to witness columns of black smoke and dust rising high above San Francisco, the mounds of rubble smoldering in the wake of record magnitude earthquakes and relentless aftershocks. Scattered amidst the haze, craggy walls loomed over the waste like giant tombstones.

The image of Eric's mother crumpled dead on the floor of her kitchen flittered across his vision. At the thought of his mother, he was shown a vision of a lifeless city, strewn with the bodies of its people and their pets. With no reason apparent to him for the tragedy, Eric pondered what could have happened to the sprawling suburbs west of Phoenix, and was instantly shown how the electro-magnetic activity and loss of power resulted in a catastrophic meltdown of the nuclear power plant fifty miles west of the city.

He saw himself standing with the Earthkeeper atop Spider Rock in the midst of an impressive lightning storm. Immediately, Eric understood that the placement and dedication of the large crystal atop Spider Rock was crucial in protecting the important landmark and surrounding area from nature's rampage.

Lastly, Eric was shown another buried city: a vast Mesoamerican temple and pyramid complex. A large group of people from many cultures and ethnicities labored to uncover and restore the buildings that surrounded the seer's temple, while building entirely new structures as well.

The front of his head throbbed with a pain he could no longer endure. Eric staggered across the room and, with what strength he had left, slid the heavy door open. "Ocho, I need you!" he cried with all the force he could muster before collapsing to the floor.

# Chapter Twenty-four

Morning broke as Truman entered Kingman, the rising sun behind him obscured by sagging, gray clouds. He had jogged and walked all night through heavy rain, taking only brief breaks, foregoing sleep. He was nervous about seeing his kids again, wondering what he might say to them. Unsure just how many years it had been, and his mind foggy from exhaustion, he strained to calculate how old they would be now.

Allison, he remembered, was the sweetest girl. He had spent many tender moments with her, sharing in her darling tea parties, and babysitting her dolls while she went shopping, pushing her toy grocery cart around the living room and filling it with plastic play food. She was a good big sister, always patient and helpful, almost motherly in the way she looked after her baby brother, Aaron. He was fearless, plowing through everything like a bulldozer. Always covered in bruises, he would never stay hurt for long. A quick kiss and he was ready to do it all again.

Kingman seemed quaint—a hick town, really, compared to Los Angeles. But for the first time in many years, it felt homey. Aside from some minor flooding, there didn't appear to be any major signs of catastrophe. Truman was relieved. Still, he wondered where everybody was, having not seen a soul as he passed through town. It's early yet, he thought.

Walking up the quiet street where he had once lived, he was awash with memories of good times spent with his family:

186

evening walks and bike rides with his children when they were little, wearing oversized helmets in ride-along bike seats. They were a truly happy family in those days before his unusual experience turned their world upside-down.

Truman paced nervously in front of the little, green, seventies era house, gathering his courage, rehearsing what he would say. Finally, he marched determinedly up the driveway and knocked firmly on the door. He waited and waited. No answer. He knocked again, louder. Hearing muffled shuffling beyond the door, he knocked again.

"What do you want?" a man's apprehensive voice demanded.

"It's Truman Krieger, I came to see my kids."

Several moments passed without response. Truman fidgeted on the stoop, shifting his weight nervously, straining to hear the indistinct voices inside the house. At last, the door creaked open slowly.

"Sheila, hi," Truman exhaled, through the lump in his throat. His heart raced. She stood just inside the door, staring at him coldly, awaiting his next move.

Feeling awkward, Truman internally processed how much her appearance had changed. Standing before him was a woman bearing a sense of age much more progressed than her actual early thirties. Her plucked and contrivedly curved eyebrows were shaped into thin symmetrical arches over her large, widely spaced brown eyes, making her appear even more smug and contemptuous than she wanted to show. To Truman, she appeared gawky in her tight denim shorts and white tank top, her short, abnormally large-breasted torso balanced precariously on thin, ungainly legs.

The long, nonverbal stalemate stretched on uncomfortably for some time, each awaiting the other's move. Then, in a grating voice she snapped sharply, demanding, "What are you doing here?"

Truman grappled with an unexpected anxiety. Sheila had a way of doing that to people. A domineering demeanor displayed at times throughout her life, it had become her defining characteristic in the months prior to their divorce. Trying his hardest to maintain eye contact and confidence, Truman said, "I really need to see the kids."

"I don't think that's such a good idea with all that's been going on," Shelia shook her head insistently. "They're already scared enough."

Maybe so, Truman thought, but he knew all too well how Shelia projected her fear onto them to defend against revealing what was really her weakness. He argued, "C'mon, Shelia, with all that's been going on; that's why I really have to see them."

"Dad?" called a boy's voice from inside the house.

"Hey, buddy," Truman replied, excited to see his son.

The boy pushed his way between his mother and the door jamb, poking his shaggy, dirty-blonde head out. Through his oversized teeth, his awkward, ripening voice muttered, "Did Mom call you to come fix the power? I've been telling Mom to call you, because you can fix anything."

Truman's eyes began to well up, relieved that his son hadn't forgotten him and was so happy to see him. Aaron was just five when Shelia filed for the divorce. Truman choked back his emotions and said, "I just came by to see you all, buddy." He smiled warmly at Aaron. "I like your hair, dude. You look like a rock star."

Aaron grimaced with a playful roll of his eyes, shaking his head nonchalantly. Taking Truman's hand, he pulled him through the door past his mother. "Dad, come in," he said excitedly. Truman followed him inside, stepping carefully over the blankets and pillows on the floor of the tiny living room. Shelia's gangly husband reluctantly rose from the couch to greet Truman.

"Pardon the mess; we've been camping out here each night to stay close together," he excused.

"Of course," Truman agreed. "Good idea." Truman extended his hand to greet him, saying confidently, "How you doing, Jerry?"

"Been better," he sighed.

Shelia started down the hall, explaining, "I'll go tell Allie you're here; she's in her room."

"Pouting, of course," Aaron added with a sneer. "She's pissed off 'cause Mom won't let us go anywhere. Not even the back yard."

"With good reason," insisted Jerry. He asked Truman, "How did you get here? Did you have any problems on the road?"

Truman shook his head, "I walked here from where I was researching incidents on the Navajo Nation, east of Flagstaff."

"So you got word, then, of what happened here?" Jerry asked.

Truman shook his head, answering with interest, "All communications have been knocked out along with the power. Why, what did happen here?"

Jerry explained solemnly, "It was a terror attack on Las Vegas. A big one. They even took out Hoover Dam and the hydroelectric plant there."

"What makes you say that?"

"That's just what people have been saying," Jerry responded, unsteadily. "A couple days ago some people wandered into town from just outside of Vegas. They had strange burns and were really sick by the time they got here. One of them was burned much worse than the others."

Intrigued, Truman listened intently as Jerry continued. "As she was dying, she kept raving about how God was in the sky, following her with a magnifying glass, but the consensus was that they had suffered radiation burns. From what people were saying as they passed through, I guess there were thousands of similar injuries and deaths all over the Vegas area. Some were really badly affected and others not at all. Best we could all figure, there was some kind of nuclear or dirty bomb attack. I don't know if that's what took out the dam. All I know is the power is out, and there's nothing else I can think of that would cause that. That's where we get all our power, you know."

Having been listening, Shelia came back into the room, adding, "Everybody has been hiding indoors since then, afraid the fallout will blow this way. That's why Jerry duct-taped around the widows there. A lot of people have left town already."

"And people were going crazy, Dad," Aaron interrupted, "running around with guns and everything."

189

"What do you mean?" Truman asked.

Shelia spoke over him, "It's all those survival nuts. You remember? The ones Timothy McVeigh was all tangled up with when he lived here back when? They looted the stores and disappeared into the desert."

"Now we're hearing about people being held up in their homes for whatever food they have," Jerry explained. "I don't know what we'll do if they show up around here. We've got nothing to defend ourselves with."

"You know how I feel about guns, Jerry, especially around the kids," Shelia snapped.

"Of course, dear," Jerry said apologetically. He turned his focus back to Truman and continued, "Almost everything we had spoiled without refrigeration. We had to really dig around the pantry for whatever odd things we could find, and we're down to the last of it."

"What are you doing for water?" asked Truman.

"We had a couple cases of bottled water from Costco, but it's almost gone. By the time I realized I'd better fill the bathtub, the water was out of order," Jerry lamented.

Allison entered the room and sat on the floor next to her mother, looking very upset. Her eyes swollen and red from crying, she stared at the floor and refused to look at her father.

"Hey Allie," Truman greeted. She smirked snobbishly. "I can't believe how much you've grown," he continued. "You're a young lady now. A beautiful young lady."

She rolled her eyes, moaning, "Oh Please, Dad, you have to say that 'cause I'm your daughter."

"Don't get her started, Dad," Aaron sneered. "If I have to hear her complain about not being able to shower one more time, I'm gonna stuff a sweaty sock in her mouth."

She jumped up, shouting, "Shut up, you little fag!"

Sheila jerked her daughter back, hissing, "Don't call your brother that word!"

"Look at his girlie hair," she jeered. "What other word is there?"

"Shut up, Smelly Allie!" Aaron shouted, throwing a sofa pillow across the room. It struck her in the face, knocking her head

190

into the wall. The room erupted into shouting as Allison sprang from the floor, charging at her brother. He leaned back on the couch, kicking his feet wildly to keep her at bay while Jerry and Shelia pulled her back. "Quit showing off for *him*," she screamed at Aaron, condemningly.

Truman became agitated, his demeanor becoming much more blunt and to the point. "Listen up!" he trumpeted. "I didn't expect coming here would be easy on any of us, but I came to tell you you're not safe here. I came to get my kids."

Shelia put her hands on her hips and cocked her eye defiantly. "What?" she demanded.

In a stern voice, punctuated with a rhythmic growl, Truman insisted, "They cannot stay here. I will not leave my kids here to die."

Sheila grew furious. "What makes you think they're going anywhere with you? No, *we're* staying right here."

Truman softened his voice to explain, "It wasn't a terror attack that knocked out the power and communications. It was a massive solar storm. I'm sure you guys must have noticed the northern lights.

"The flares have been bombarding the skies continuously for days, causing unusually strong and erratic weather. And, I'm willing to bet, the lady that was burned 'like a bug under God's magnifying glass,' was probably scorched by solar radiation leaking through wandering holes in the stratosphere. If you stay here you will starve. If you're not wiped out by a megastorm first, or killed in a raid on your house. And don't expect things to go back to normal anytime soon," Truman warned. "We're back in the wild west, people."

"Stop it, Truman. Just shut up," Shelia screamed. "You're scaring the kids."

"C'mon, Sheila, we both know that really means you're the one who's scared," Truman countered. "And you should be, goddammit! And so should they!" he insisted. "I'm not afraid to admit that I'm scared."

"Alright, you need to leave," Shelia commanded sternly.

Silently, Truman stood his ground, staring her in the eye.

"Go!" she screamed.

Truman dropped his head sullenly and turned for the door. He reached for the knob and stopped. He whirled around, thundering, "No, goddammit! I will not leave them again!"

"I wanna go with Dad," Aaron pleaded.

Shelia squeezed his arms tightly, scowling inches from his face. "You're not going anywhere," she bullied.

Truman set his heavy pack on the floor and sat inspecting his rifle, insisting, "Then, neither am I."

# Chapter Twenty-five

Silently crossing the trickling creek, Kurt watched the riparian trees cautiously, sensing that he was being watched. He hurried for the thicket outside the entrance to the slot canyon. Disappearing into the tangled branches, he hid low to the ground several feet from the trail that the others had tramped out on their previous visits.

Minutes later, clumsy footsteps approached, tromping through the narrow path. From his hiding place, Kurt watched the unusual man barge through the dense brush. At odds with his surroundings, his every move seemed a battle against nature. He disappeared into the narrow canyon with Kurt cautiously and stealthily in pursuit.

Agitated at the sight of the empty cavern at the end of the line, the man paced frantically around the vaulted chamber, inspecting the glyphs. Kurt watched from his hiding place behind a bend in the wall. Perplexed and frustrated, the man dropped to the floor, throwing a handful of sand at the wall and muttering unintelligibly.

Kurt stood perfectly still, breathing quiet, shallow breaths through barely parted lips. Leaning further out to better see the now sitting man, Kurt slipped, scuffing against the sandstone wall.

The man snapped to attention, and looking over his shoulder asked nervously, "Is that you? Are you there?"

Kurt was taken aback. He slowly stepped from the shadows, replying, "I'm here."

Startled, the man whirled around confusedly, inquiring, "Who are you?"

"My name is Kurt Lomawaima. I came here looking for my friends. Have you seen them? Two Indians and two whites?"

"Not for a few days," he answered. "I'm Charlie Moreth. I'm sorry; you have me at sort of a loss here. I thought you were someone else." He approached Kurt cautiously. "I never saw you at the camp at Oliver's. How do you know them?"

"Several days ago, my mentor and me came upon an injured man. A white guy, stabbed in the shoulder."

"Truman," Charlie grumbled.

Sensing Charlie's unusual disdain, Kurt was curious. "Yeah, right. Truman. My mentor and me, we helped treat his wound. I'm coming back from showing him the fast way off the reservation."

"What? Why? Where's he going?"

Kurt didn't know what to make of Charlie. His instincts warned not to trust him. "To find his family and bring them here," he answered reluctantly.

"Why on Earth would Truman want to bring his family to this godforsaken place?" Charlie denounced thoughtlessly.

Adamantly, Kurt replied, "We will be saved here on this sacred land."

In his mordant voice, Charlie mocked, "So I've been told."

Groggy and disoriented, Eric slowly awakened. The jungle was alive with the sounds of birds and monkeys all around. His eyes opened and came slowly into focus. Thin shafts of light shone down on him through the gaps in the thatched lean-to that sheltered him. Faintly, he could hear the others in the distance, laboring. Ocho shouted instructions and encouragement.

Smoke wafted into the shelter, carrying the smell of curing meat. His stomach ached with hunger. Stiff and sore, Eric rolled over and crawled to his feet. Encircling a central fire pit were four more lean-to shelters like his. Leaning against the rear wall of the shelter next to his, Eric recognized the bow Ocho had made along with a leather quiver filled with arrows. Over the fire pit, a large quantity of meat was being smoked on an A-frame constructed of sticks. An animal hide was stretched across a rectangular frame nearby to cure in the sun. None of this was here before. How long had he been unconscious, he wondered.

Tuwa sat in the shade of his lodge muttering prayer chants as he placed herbs, stones, small feathers, and various animal teeth and claws, into a small buckskin pouch strung on a braided cord. He glanced up at Eric's movement. He dropped what he was doing and, as fast as his old body could move, climbed to his feet. Smiling, he lumbered over to Eric, handing him a gourd full of water.

Sluggishly, Eric plopped to the ground and took a long drink. Gasping to catch his breath, he wiped his mouth with the back of his hand. "Oh, that's good," he puffed.

Tuwa hung the buckskin pouch around Eric's neck. Lifting it for a closer look, Eric asked, "What is this?"

"Medicine Bundle," answered Tuwa. "To keep you safe, and bring you power."

Eric nodded, "Thanks." His stomach rumbled loudly.

"I told you, I understand hunger," Tuwa smiled. He handed Eric a large piece of smoked meat and a couple of small, thorny fruits unlike any he had ever seen. The fruit had and unusual taste. Beneath its tough skin, it was mushy, and nowhere near as sweet as what he was used to, but it was agreeable and nourishing.

"What are these?" Eric asked, examining them.

Tuwa shrugged his shoulders. "I found them."

"How did you know they were safe to eat?"

"I asked."

"Asked who?"

"The plant they grew from," Tuwa answered matter-of-factly.

Eric smiled hesitantly. "Well, tell the plant I said 'thank you'. They were very good."

"You can tell it yourself, later. Come."

Eric followed Tuwa to the back side of the pyramid where they had cleared the vegetation and smoothed the dirt into a narrow, steep ramp to the top. Using cleverly positioned log poles as a sort of pulley and braking system, Ocho, Mike, and Oliver strained to hoist the large crystal up the ramp. From the level ground, they tugged at the rope to heave the giant stone, now two-thirds of the way there, further up the slope. Eric joined them, pulling with all his might. Within minutes, the Earthkeeper dropped into position at the top. They collapsed, winded. Eric's arms throbbed, pulsing into his fingertips.

"So the prince finally came to kiss you awake, huh, Sleeping Beauty?" Mike teased.

"Yeah, but he seemed more interested in finding out where you were," Eric bantered. "How long had I slept?"

"Three days," Mike informed him.

"Like Jesus, huh?" Eric joked. "Don't tell Charlie."

"Uh, Jesus came back from the dead, dude," Mike said.

"That's quite a bit different than sleeping like the dead," Ocho added. "And how do you feel after all that sleep?"

"Really run down," Eric panted. "I'm just sapped."

They joined Eric on the ground for a rest. "What happened the other night? In the seer's temple?" Mike asked.

"Part of it was really personal. But for the most part it was more of the same, really: more cataclysmic visions," Eric explained. "Except, with these I had the profound understanding that these events had already happened." He spoke compassionately, "Phoenix took a big hit Mike. There was some kind of meltdown at Palo Verde."

"The nuclear plant? How?"

"I don't know, Mike," Eric explained. "Because of the loss of power, I guess. Something to do with containment or cooling, or something. I know now that the meltdown is how my mom died. I don't know if your folks may have survived."

"They're summering in Minnesota," Mike announced, relieved. "I wonder if Julie is okay. Do you know how widespread the contamination is?"

"Most of the valley," said Eric. "Stuff is happening everywhere, guys, all over the world. I saw San Francisco and

Seattle too—what was left of them. Our job is to stop the four corners area from being hit. I don't know why, but everything tells me it's the jumping off place to something much bigger. Somehow we have to get that crystal to the top of Spider Rock. Why did you guys move it up there, anyway?" Eric asked, pointing to the large crystal at the top of the ramp.

"Grandfather told me to," said Ocho.

"Besides, it only made sense," Mike explained. "That's the portal, at the top."

Eric nodded. "Right. Good work guys. But that thing is really heavy. I have no idea how the hell we're supposed to hoist it eight-hundred feet to the top of Spider Rock."

"We'll blow that bridge up when we get to it," Mike said. "We still have to figure out how to teleport back."

"Right, then," said Eric. "Let's get ready to go."

The group worked together to gather their store of meat and dismantle their camp. From the corner of his eye, Eric noticed the movement of a single branch on a large shrub. It seemed to wave at him. He responded automatically with a reciprocal wave.

Ocho grinned, "What are you doing?"

Eric chuckled. Embarrassed, he excused himself, saying, "I'm just really tired. For some reason, I thought that bush waved at me, so naturally I waved back. I know, it's silly, huh? It all just happened so fast."

"Spirit moves in all things," Ocho smiled. He patted Eric on the back and walked away. Eric scoffed, looking at the surrounding plants and trees. They were perfectly still. Not even a slight breeze to move them. Thinking that perhaps a bird had lighted on the branch, he watched the plant more closely. The branch moved again.

Eric crept cautiously toward the shrub. There was no bird or snake or wind, or any other reason for movement that he could see. He recognized the plant's thorny fruit as what Tuwa had fed him. He lightly touched the branch, gently feeling the fruit, and spoke softly, "Thank you." The fruit detached from the branch and fell easily into his hand.

Eric glanced over his shoulders, catching eyes with Tuwa, who had watched the whole thing. Tuwa nodded, smiling, and went about his business. As he stooped to lift the heavy bundle of smoked meat, Eric ran up, taking it for him.

"I like watching you unfold," Tuwa said, warmly. "Like a squash blossom."

"Was that the plant you spoke with?"

Tuwa nodded.

"So you really talk with plants, then?"

"Of course I do."

Eric staggered at the thought of speaking with plants and other inanimate things. "I'm sorry, that's just too weird an idea for me," he said.

"Why?" Tuwa demanded to know.

"Baby steps," insisted Eric, "baby steps. I'm still freaking out about speaking with my power animal. Now, we're talking to plants?"

Tuwa smiled. "Where does medicine come from?" he asked.

"Pharmaceutical companies. You know, the great American drug cartels," Eric laughed.

Not amused, Tuwa looked blankly at him. "Plants," he said. "For countless generations we two-legged animals have benefited from cooperation with plants." He pointed to Ocho who was dismantling his lean-to, then continued, "For shelter, warmth, clothing, tools, food, and medicine."

Eric nodded, "Right, yeah. Where I come from, as an end consumer, it's really easy to take it for granted."

Tuwa asked, "How did our ancestors know which plants were poison and which would heal?"

Eric thought for a moment, "I never really thought about it, but I suppose, maybe, they watched what the animals ate."

Tuwa enjoyed watching Eric think. He nodded, smiling. "And?"

"There was probably quite a bit of trial and error. You know, someone would eat something that made them sick or die, or something that made them feel better."

Tuwa shook his head disappointedly. "The ancients used their power to talk with the spirits of the plants, like I did. We are related—children of the same greater mother and father. If we show them proper respect, and listen, they will tell us things. They offer their help to nourish and to heal us, to keep us alive for what we give the Earth in return."

"Why? What does the Earth get from us?" Eric asked, confused. "All we ever seem to do is take, take, take."

"Not always," Tuwa replied. "Not all people. Look all around you. Everything on this Earth has a reason. Every animal, every stone, every plant and tree.

"But, then, where does man fit in? We really don't seem to serve any purpose in the greater circle of life. We're outside of it, a dead end. We're at the top, consuming everything. What do we give back?"

"Energy," Tuwa answered, simply.

Puzzled, Eric shrieked, "What? Look, I'm the farthest thing from a tree hugger, but we've ravaged the planet's natural resources in the pursuit of energy." With his statement, he recalled the dream where the cartoon people were driven by the ghouls to mine all the precious metals from the Earth to feed the rise of industrialization.

The others in the group were astonished, having been accustomed to Tuwa rarely speaking. They had all assumed his silence was because he couldn't speak the language very well. They clumsily continued what they were doing, trying not to appear obvious as they listened in.

"Our Earth Mother is a living thing," Tuwa explained. "The life she sustains can only exist because she lives. All life on Earth lives in cooperation for the perpetual existence of life and recycling of energy."

Intrigued, Eric asked, "By recycling of energy, you mean how one living thing eats another?"

Tuwa nodded, "Partly."

"Well, I get that. But if all living things feed on the energy of another, if the Earth is alive, what does it eat?"

Tuwa explained, "Energy from endless space, and from Grandfather Sun."

"So, still, what are we needed for?" Eric asked.

"The energy that comes from out there flows through the air feeding the weather. Creator made us to be the caretakers of the

Earth, giving people power to call energy where it is needed. Through ceremony and prayer, we ask the spirits to bring rain and lightning. The lightning feeds the Earth."

"But wouldn't the lightning do its thing without us?" Eric asked.

"Yes, but it wouldn't always get to where it is needed."

Eric looked confused.

"How does energy flow through your body?" Tuwa asked.

Eric didn't understand how the question pertained to what Tuwa was teaching, but out of respect, he thought seriously before answering, "From the food I eat, I guess. So, I guess, then, it really came from the sun, if the sun fed the plants, and the animals fed on the plants, and I ate both."

Tuwa smiled, "Exchange of energy, yes. But there is more."

Eric thought a while. "Well, there are the veins that carry the oxygen throughout my body." Eric thought again of his dream. "Wait, the veins of ore that run through the Earth. Of course, the conductivity of metals. The veins of precious metals are literally the Earth's veins."

Pleased, Tuwa smiled. "And quartz, found throughout the Earth's crust, is an amplifier of electricity and other subtle energies. We call the lightning to feed our Earth Mother. Do you understand now the meaning of your crystal?"

Eric grew excited. "Of course, Tuwa, that's it! Thank you!" He explained, "Even with these visions, I only understand what's happening a little bit at a time. When I saw myself with the crystal on top of Spider Rock, there was a huge lightning storm. I thought it was just natural phenomena; rampaging weather like with all the cataclysms, but now it all makes sense."

"Not all," Tuwa advised. "There is much, much more to learn still. Be patient, it will come. You have many good teachers here, Eric: your friends Ocho and Mike, and me, and the spirits all around. But your greatest teacher is the crystal itself. Stones are the true historians, recording the events of the Earth over millions of years. Crystals are the best record keepers. And Earthkeepers, like that one there, have been absorbing information and power from the universe for billions of years. They have a power greater than you could ever imagine, and you will be changed forever."

Eric fidgeted nervously. "Changed? Oh, I don't know about all that. I don't know how much more change I can take."

For cultural reasons, Tuwa usually avoided prolonged eye contact, but he looked Eric squarely in the eye. "You will do fine," he said encouragingly, "or you would not have been chosen."

# Chapter Twenty-six

"Mom, I'm thirsty," Aaron yammered.

Frustrated, Sheila growled, "Aaron, I'm not gonna tell you again, we are saving the water for when we are really thirsty."

"Uh, yeah, I *am* really thirsty," he argued, "or I wouldn't have said anything."

Truman tossed a half-filled plastic bottle to his son, saying, "Drink mine."

"Whoa, sorry, Dad," Aaron said, "I ain't thirsty enough to drink water from the toilet."

Truman chuckled. "It's not from the toilet bowl, silly rabbit, it's from the reservoir—the big square tank on the back. It's fresh water, dude."

"Whatever you say, it's still toilet water," Aaron said, disgusted, and tossed the bottle back.

"You'll be drinking it soon enough," Truman insisted, "when you're *really* thirsty."

Jerry was worried. He asked, "How long do you suppose it'll last us?"

"Not more than another day or two," Truman announced. He glared for a moment at Shelia, saying, "There was only water in the one bathroom tank, after someone just had to flush the other."

"It was smelling up the whole house," she yelled.

Truman spoke sternly, "Look, we've done it your way the last few days, and we've wasted a lot of time. The food is almost gone. The water is almost gone. Everyone's patience is shot after being cooped up in this hot house all week. I think it's time to pack up and move out. We can stock up on water from the golf course water hazard on the way out of town.

"I looked in the storage shed out back and found the old bicycle trailer we used to pull Aaron in before he could ride in a bike seat. I tightened it up so we can use it to haul food and water and some blankets and clothes. I aired up the tires and got yours and the kids' bikes ready. I'll run alongside until I can find a bike or something on the way. The highways are littered with abandoned cars for hundreds of miles. We'll pick up all kinds of useful things on the way."

"No way!" Allison protested. "I'm not gonna be seen riding a bike."

Disappointed in his daughter's pettiness at such a critical time, Truman couldn't help the disapproving scowl on his face. Before he could say anything, Sheila sassed, "And where would we go? Four Corners? Leave the roof over our heads? All because a couple people you know said it would be safe there?"

"There's really more to it than that," Truman said.

"What else is there, huh, Truman?" she nagged. "What more aren't you telling us?"

"Alright, alright," Truman hissed. "Well, you know how I told you that my team and I were investigating what we thought might have been ancient Indian prophecies recorded on rocks near the Four Corners area? We were actually looking into a possible connection between some petroglyphs and recent UFO sightings."

Rolling her eyes, Sheila moaned, "Oh, here we go."

Truman yelled, "You wanted to know! Anyway, while we were there, one of the guys, a journalist from Phoenix, was visited by otherworldly beings that looked like the Kachina dolls you see in the roadside trading posts. They specifically told him about the dramatic weather changes that are happening, and said that we would be safe there in the high desert."

"Kachina dolls, Truman? Dolls?" Sheila jabbed. "Besides, we haven't had any crazy weather," she argued. "Just had a little rain."

"I told you all about those tornadoes," Truman snapped. "If you don't believe me, come see for yourself. And, Jerry, you saw the radiation burns on those people with your own eyes. Speak up, man. You know it's not safe to stay here."

Before he could speak, Sheila pointed her finger like a dagger, shouting, "You just shut up, Jerry!" The mousy man breathed out heavily, sinking into his chair like a deflating balloon.

Truman knew he was alone in this fight. Frustrated, he paced frantically as Sheila continued, "And you and all your stupid flying saucer shit! I will not let you come into my home to scare my kids like this, you fruitcake!"

Aaron shot to his feet screaming, "No, you shut up, Mom!"

Furiously, Sheila slapped the boy across the face with frightening speed. Before she could withdraw her hand, Truman had taken forceful control of her wrist, growling, "That is the last time you'll bully our son like this."

He promptly turned his attention to Aaron, commanding harshly, "And you will respect your mother; understand me?"

Sheila looked to her feckless husband, whose eyes darted around the room nervously, refusing to meet hers, as if they were oblivious to the unfolding scene.

Aaron stepped back, whining, "I just wanted to say something. No one ever listens to me," he complained.

"We're listening, son," Truman said apologetically. "Go ahead."

Hiding under his hair, Aaron mumbled, "I just wanted to say that…"

Shelia hastily interrupted him, criticizing, "If you want to be heard, you're gonna have to speak up."

"I know you're not a fruitcake, like Mom always says. I tried to tell her, but she says that it's just the ideas you put in my head."

"Tried to tell her what?" Truman asked.

"I've seen them, Dad."

"Seen what?"

"Them," Aaron professed. "UFOs, just like you."

Flustered, Shelia waved her hands as if she were swatting the very idea from the air around her. "I don't have to listen to this."

She paced nervously as Aaron continued, "I was five the first time I saw them, right before you left."

"Where, buddy?"

"In the back yard."

"Show me," Truman said excitedly, taking Aaron out back by the hand.

"I was standing right here, and it was right there," Aaron explained, pointing to the sky above the house, "really low, hovering over our house, not moving. It was invisible, like a shadow almost, blocking out the stars like a black hole in the sky. I could only see part of it, because the rest was behind the peak of the roof there, but it was really big. The part I could see came over the house to here, right over me."

"Was it a big triangle?" Truman asked.

Aaron shook his head, "Huh-uh, a circle. I don't know what I was doing out here. It was late. Everyone was asleep. I was scared, and I remember hearing Mom's voice like it was coming from a hidden speaker or something, telling me not to be scared. Next thing I know, I'm running through trees, like in the woods somewhere, being chased by lights, like when the helicopters are chasing the bad guys on TV. And I could hear Mom. For some reason, I always thought there were speakers in the trees with her voice telling me not to run, not to be afraid, that she wasn't a witch."

Sheila had been standing in the kitchen just inside the arcadia door, listening. "See how his story shifts around like that?" she called out. "What trees? We live in the desert. It's obviously a nightmare. And you remember how he used to sleepwalk, Truman. He had nightmares all the time back then. We all did, the way you were always talking about that stuff—putting ideas in our heads. Remember how he would scare the hell out of us, the way we would wake up with him next to the bed, just standing there watching us sleep?"

"I didn't just stand there," Aaron argued. "I shook you and shook you, and even screamed at the top of my lungs, but you would never wake up. So I would just sleep on the floor in your room."

"I have memories of you standing next to the bed, like your mother said. It really was very scary," Truman said. "It used to freak me out big time." Confused, he continued, "You really never did that?"

Aaron shook his head. "I'm telling the truth. I never just stood there. It was probably one of them."

Truman marched into the house, confronting Sheila, "What kind of nightmares did you have?"

She turned away. "I don't want to talk about this."

"No, you're going to tell me," Truman insisted. "If you're going to blame all of this on me for all these years, I want to know what was so horrible you would make me out to be some nutcase to my kids."

"I already told you. I told you back then that I dreamed about them being in the house."

"What did they look like?"

"Just like in the movies: big heads; bald; big black eyes. I dreamed them like that because of all those stupid books and videos you had everywhere. I told you to stop bringing that crap into our house, but you were obsessed. That's why I asked you to leave."

"Humph, *asked* me to leave," muttered Truman.

"What did you say?" Sheila hissed.

Truman demanded to know, "What nightmare was so bad that you decided you wanted me out of your lives?"

Sheila stood rigid with her arms crossed, her long nails scratching and picking nervously at her elbows and the backs of her arms. Cheeks flushed and short of breath, she recited her horrific dream. "There were six of those little, gray demons standing around our bed."

Truman corrected her. "You mean, Gray EBEs?"

Confused and irritated by the interruption, Shelia snapped, "Gray whats?"

"EBEs: Extraterrestrial Biological Entities," Truman explained. "Aliens."

"You can call them whatever you want, Tru," Shelia fussed, "But it was a nightmare, my nightmare, and I'm more inclined to call them demons."

Truman apologized, "I'm sorry. Whatever. Go on. Continue…please."

"Anyway, they lifted me out of bed and floated me down the hall like a birthday balloon on a string, and sat me on the couch. You were there, sitting in the chair with a blank look on your face. I kept waiting for you to get up and do something, but you just sat there watching and did nothing."

As Shelia recounted her dream, her words streamed monotonously with little pause to find the right words or for breath in between, as though she had told the story thousands of times. She seemed strangely emotionally removed, almost robotic.

"Then, three of them disappeared down the hall, and Allie cried out from her room. She cried for me, but I couldn't move," Sheila said, unaffectedly. "She stopped screaming, and then two of them came back down the hall with Aaron."

Finally showing some connection to her experience, her emotions manifested in two long tears rolling down her cheeks. She wiped her hands down her face, leaving red finger tracks on her pale complexion. Her lip quivered. "He was so little—just a little boy. I want you to get up and save your son. I want you to kill them. But you just sit there in your chair with that glazed look, with a big needle stuck through the top of your head. They just walk right out of the house with him, then come back for you. And you cooperate! You just…get up and go. And then I'm alone," she sobbed, collapsing into Truman, her head against his chest.

Truman was befuddled. He had never had even the slightest flash of memory of any of this. He found it hard to believe what he was hearing. As far as he knew, his obsession with the phenomenon stemmed from that one and only sighting all those years ago. He stood awkwardly, bracing his legs to counter her weight pressing against him, reluctantly patting her on the back. Uncomfortable and anxious, he looked over the half wall to the living room at Jerry, sitting in Truman's old chair. Jerry quickly looked away.

"Everything was pitch black, and I was all alone," she continued. "I couldn't move. I couldn't wake up. Finally, I was able to force one eye open and could see I was in our room, lying in bed. I tried so hard to move, to wake up. But I couldn't."

She regained her composure, swiftly stepping away from Truman, saying, "The doctor told me the whole thing was something called Sleep Paralysis, and agreed that my dreams were colored by the subjects you were constantly talking about. That's when I decided to file for the divorce. And the nightmares stopped when you left."

"Maybe for you," Aaron said.

"What do you mean?" Truman asked. "Does this kind of stuff still happen to you?"

Suddenly the house shook violently. The light hanging from the kitchen ceiling swung to and fro. The small table and chairs slid back and forth on the wood flooring, while pictures fell from the walls, the glass shattering on the floor.

"Quick, everyone, into the hallway!" shouted Truman.

They huddled low together in the narrow hall, hearing the smashing of dishes as they fell from the cabinets and crashed onto the kitchen floor. The TV wobbled forward from its seat in the entertainment center, its weight toppling the wall unit as it pitched over the lip of the shelf. Allison and Sheila held each other, screaming as the living room ceiling collapsed to the floor with a thunderous sound, sending a cloud of gypsum dust into the hall. Explosions rumbled in the distance. Then, as suddenly as it came, the shaking stopped.

Truman climbed over the sheet rock and broken furniture to the living room window, and pulled the curtains down. Outside, homes and buildings were collapsed and columns of rising smoke filled the sky.

"Watch for nails and splinters," Jerry warned, as he and Sheila worked their way over the debris for a look. Gaping in unblinking disbelief, Sheila's skin flushed with anxiety. Her heart pounded in irregular beats against her chest wall as she struggled for air. Unable to contain it any longer, she broke into tears.

Jerry opened his arms to receive and comfort his wife, but she unexpectedly turned, latching onto to Truman's arm. "Thank God, you're here," she praised.

Truman recoiled, stumbling over the mess as he stepped away from her. Sheila took a deep breath, instantly reassuming her stoic demeanor. "Okay, Tru" she said. "We'll follow you. Lead the way."

Truman nodded. "Hopefully the bikes are okay in the garage. I'll dig them out. I've already loaded the bike trailer with everything except whatever clothes you guys are bringing." He looked seriously at Allison, advising, "Don't get carried away. Bring only what you need—especially a jacket." She started down the hall with Truman yelling after her, "Sensible shoes for walking! One pair only!"

Sheila sucked in and blew out a deep breath and wiped her tears. "I'll help the kids pack," she said, disappearing down the hall.

Jerry hesitantly approached Truman saying, "Take good care of them."

"What do you mean?"

"I'm not going," he said. "I'm not needed any more."

"What? Of course, you are," Truman insisted. "She is *your* wife. That hasn't changed. Look, Jerry, you don't need to feel threatened by me. I'll be honest, I really didn't think this whole thing through when I came here for my kids. I was solely focused on them. I didn't really envision her coming along, but I should've realized that they would need their mother." Truman squeezed Jerry's shoulder, "Like she needs you. And those kids need you too, Jerry. Go on, get packed up."

# Chapter Twenty-seven

Mike stood over Eric as he slept in the soft sand of the vaulted cavern, deep within the slot canyon. Eric opened his eyes and looked around, both stating and questioning, "We're back?"

Mike nodded.

"What happened?" Eric asked. "The last thing I remember was all of us at the top of the pyramid, trying to figure out what to do to get back."

"I don't really know how it happened," Mike said. "We were all talking about it and throwing out ideas, when we realized you were gazing into the Earthkeeper in some kind of trance. Everything went black, and we woke up one by one back here."

"And the crystal?"

"Behind you," Mike pointed.

Eric looked at the crystal and glanced around the vacant chamber. "Where is everyone?"

"Tuwa went to fetch some water. Ocho and Oliver left to see if they can track down Charlie. I hope he's all right. That skinwalker is still out there somewhere."

Eric shuddered. "I had some kind of dream. I don't remember much about it, but I've got this anxious feeling, like a warning. I can hear an alarm going off in my head—not loud, just kinda there. I can only picture fragments of my dream, but there was a man…no, an animal—it kept shifting. I got a sense that I am in danger, like there is someone close to me who can't be trusted. Someone in our group."

Mike grew deeply worried. "How much do you know about Ocho?" he asked.

"Just what I've told you. But I know I trust him."

"Eric, he was raised by a brujo," Mike argued. "He was tortured and broken, and inculcated with the *Witchery Way*, just like Oliver's uncle was by his older brother, Oliver's father."

"And so was Oliver," Eric said. "Very recently, too," he added. Eric remembered the primordial evil he encountered in the temple and the way it propagated, infecting person to person. "But it can't be either of them. I'm sure of it."

Mike was growing frustrated. "But you can't know for sure. If either is a witch, you could very easily be deceived under some kind of a spell. There are just too many similarities between Ocho and the skinwalker he killed. He was a shapeshifter—a werewolf, Eric! I think your Ocho Whitewolf is, too. When I confronted him about it before, he told me that he did have magic powers, but he didn't say what kind. He just said that his grandfather taught him magic to help him hunt when he was alone in the wild. And you saw that peccary he brought down. It was mauled around the neck. Its jugular was severed."

"But he said it was a kill he took away from a jaguar," Eric explained.

"Yeah, think about that," Mike argued.

For a moment, Eric thought about the large wolf he had hit with his truck his first night on the reservation. Then he remembered all the times Ocho had been there to protect him. Ocho gave Eric a sense of security unlike any he had ever known. Eric shook his head defiantly, insisting, "No, not Ocho, I'm sure of it. I trust him completely."

"Well, I can't," grunted Mike. "Not when it comes to your safety. I have just as much at stake to protect you—more even. You're my brother."

Just then, Tuwa walked in with Kurt and Charlie. "Look who I found," he said happily.

"Hey guys," Mike said. He asked Kurt, "So you've met Charlie, then?"

Kurt nodded.

"And Truman got off alright?"

"I showed him the way cross country and saved him a couple of days. Then I stopped to check in at home for a couple of days at Hotevilla before coming back here." Kurt spoke to Tuwa in their native Hopi. Tuwa nodded, smiling. Kurt continued, "I thought Truman would be back by now. He had a really good pace going. I hope he hasn't had trouble."

"Hey Kurt!" Ocho blared boisterously as he entered the cavern. "What's up Charlie? Oh, hey, Kurt, this is Oliver."

Kurt greeted Oliver, "We know each other."

"We do?" Oliver asked.

"My father and your grandfather were friends. I was seventeen when they used to explore this area together. You were little then, and I came here a few times to watch you while they were out."

"Were you the gum-chewing guy?" Oliver asked, excitedly.

Kurt smiled, nodding. "You used to give me gum so you could laugh at the way my ears moved when I chewed."

Oliver laughed. "Yeah, they would wiggle like the wings of a butterfly. Man, I remember you were one fast runner too."

Ocho stood at the back of the group, grinning as he enjoyed the happy reunion. Smiling, he surveyed the faces of his companions, when he noticed Charlie scowling at Eric. His senses drew his attention to Mike, who looked away as Ocho's eyes fell upon him. Ocho was put off by the undercurrent of negative energy he felt in the room, but said nothing.

The group chattered amongst themselves for several minutes before Mike called out, "So, Ocho, Tuwa found Charlie and Kurt without even looking for them. Where did the tracks lead you?"

Irritated by Mike's attitude, Ocho walked toward him, stopping near the center of the cavern. "Oliver and me found out really fast that they were camped in the trees alongside the creek right outside the canyon there." He spoke sardonically, "We found them so fast because they were just right there! Outside the canyon there! But before we went over to say hello, we thought it might be more important to follow the barefoot tracks of someone else. The skinwalker that danced a curse on Oliver's roof has been coming around as recently as two or three days ago."

A chill fell over the now gloomy faces.

Frightened, Eric asked, "Are you sure?"

"We followed them to a place where many tracks have met, where dark ceremonies have taken place."

Oliver nodded in agreement. He spoke to Mike, "It was a recently investigated crime scene as well—yellow tape still tied off. The place where the *Hatałii* was murdered."

"The what?" asked Eric.

"A Navajo Medicine Man," Oliver explained.

"Remember all those circling buzzards we saw the day we got here?" asked Ocho.

"I've been thinking about what he was doing up here," Oliver said. "I wonder, if he hadn't been killed, if he might have become part of our group," he suggested.

Eric remembered the old Indian man who waved him on from the other side of Canyon de Chelly, bellowing, "You are on the other side."

In shock of the news, Kurt and Tuwa looked at each other, speaking excitedly in their Hopi tongue.

"The tracks you saw," Eric asked. "How many are there, Ocho? How many skinwalkers are we up against?"

"Yeah, how many?" Mike sneered.

Ocho's bellicose eyes pierced and deflated Mike's brazen manner. "Six," he answered sternly.

"And just seven of us," Eric sighed. "I've seen the way those things can move. How are we supposed to haul a thousand-some-odd pound crystal all the way up Spider Rock with even just one of those on our tail?"

"The same way we brought it here," Mike suggested. "We'll teleport it."

"Then we have to figure out how it works," Eric said, "because I still have no idea."

"It was them," Mike interjected, pointing to the sky. "Somehow, we need to make contact. They activate the wormholes."

Ocho spoke up, asking, "But, did anyone see any flying triangles back at the pyramid? I didn't. Eric, can you think of anything you maybe did to get back here from the seer's temple?"

Frustrated, Eric shook his head. "I don't remember anything about it."

Tuwa hesitantly rose to his feet. "Matter follows vision," he said.

"What's that supposed to mean?" asked Eric.

"When we do Medicine work, we first plant the seeds of what we need manifested in the other world—the world of spirit."

Eric looked confused.

Ocho spoke up, "Remember that day we met, in the diner? Remember how I told you that all things in this world are created first in the spirit world?"

"Yeah, but I still don't understand what either of you is trying to say."

Ocho continued, "Remember the glass of water?"

Eric laughed, "I remember the mess you made when you blew into that straw. Yeah, you told me that the water represented how the world of spirit is like an ocean of creative potential, and the bubbles of air were the temporary realms of physical manifestation. Like the created universe."

Charlie rolled his eyes.

"Exactly!" Ocho answered proudly.

"Well put," said Tuwa.

"So, matter follows vision," conceded Eric. "I still don't understand how that helps us move the crystal. What? Am I just supposed to think it there?"

"And maybe you can bend spoons with your mind too," Charlie scoffed.

"No, I don't think anyone could just move that huge stone with their thoughts, but that would be cool. I think I understand what Tuwa means," Ocho said. "All the times we moved through whatever this thing is, what were we doing?"

214

Eric shrugged his shoulders, "I don't know, looking at the glyphs on the wall?"

"Well, yeah, when we traveled from here. But every time we moved from here to there, or from there to here, we were focusing really hard on the destination—and we went."

"Matter follows vision," Tuwa said again.

"So," Mike interposed, "all we have to do is focus our intent?"

"Yes," answered Tuwa. "The same way we move between worlds." He looked at Eric, "The same way you journeyed to the lower world."

"Where I met my power animal," said Eric, remembering the shadowy jaguar. "Oddly, this all makes a lot of sense," he continued. "But we still have a big problem. For whatever reason, the junction from here to Spider Rock lets out in a shallow cave, two-thirds of the way up a sheer canyon wall, with hand and toe holds going up and down from the cave carved into the rock."

"I've got a hydraulic engine hoist back at my place," Oliver said, "and some chains and rope. If we can anchor it somehow and modify it a bit, we should be able to just lower the crystal down to the canyon floor."

"Great idea!" Ocho said, excitedly. "We could even lower each other down. Well, the last one of us will have to climb down."

"I'll climb down," Kurt offered. "I climb hand and toe holds everyday up and down the mesa where I live."

"Well, let's go get it," Oliver nudged. "If we go now, we can be back before dark."

"Alright," Kurt said. "You coming, Ocho?"

Conflicted about what to do, Ocho paced anxiously. "But what if we get held up? Those skinwalkers are out there. I can't leave Eric, and I don't think it's safe for him to go."

"That hoist is heavy," Oliver argued. "I mean, it's got wheels and all, but there are lots of places we'll have to lift and carry it. We can't move that thing all the way here without you."

"You must go," Tuwa insisted. "I will stay here with Eric." Digging his pouch of corn pollen from his satchel, he began chanting and singing prayers. He gathered a generous handful of the sacred material and spread a thick line to form a barrier between the narrow canyon and the opening to the vaulted cavern. "We will be safe here."

Ocho nodded. He trotted over to his duffel and dug around, pulling out a hard wooden stave with a large, egg-shaped river rock attached with rawhide at the end. "Here, keep this war club," he said, handing Eric the weapon.

"Cool, thanks," Eric exclaimed, tightly gripping the leather-wrapped handle and taking a few practice swings. "Is it broken?" he asked. "It feels like the rock came off."

"Nope," Ocho said shaking his head, "it's supposed to be that way. That rock ain't going nowhere. There's a gap of about an inch or two between the handle and the rock," Ocho explained, "but that rawhide holds it in place. It adds extra energy to the blow, the way the rock whips forward just before it connects."

"That's clever," said Eric.

With his concerns put to rest by his trust in Tuwa's Medicine, Ocho said, "I doubt you'll need to use it, but if you do, swing for the head, and keep swinging until whoever or whatever you're hitting stops moving."

Hesitantly, Eric nodded, sliding the weapon's handle through the belt loop on his hip.

"Okay everyone," Ocho said, strapping his bow and quiver of arrows over his shoulder, "let's go."

Mike moved indecisively, finally saying, "I'm not leaving Eric."

"Okay," Ocho nodded.

Charlie remained seated, saying firmly, "I'm staying here too."

"We need you, Charlie," coaxed Oliver.

"I don't even believe in all this mumbo jumbo," Charlie jeered. "It goes way against my beliefs."

"It's cool with me if he wants to stay," said Eric slyly. "We could probably use him more here anyway. In case we need to fight off those six demon witches who want to kill us."

Charlie shot to his feet and left with the others to help fetch the hoist.

# Chapter Twenty-eight

Camped a short distance from the highway, amidst the tall pines just west of Flagstaff, Truman and his kids huddled around a small, dwindling fire. Jerry and Sheila had retired for the night, sleeping soundly several feet away under a thick blanket.

Truman worried about his daughter. She sat motionless, staring blankly at the fire, and hadn't said more than a few words since they left Kingman. Having always been enormously empathetic and easily affected by the pain and sadness of others, she was very obviously troubled by the devastation and carnage they had witnessed on the roads out of town.

"Are you sure you won't eat, Allie?" Truman asked.

She glanced snobbishly at her father and shook her head.

Truman dug a can of ravioli from his pack. "What about this? You used to love this stuff."

Allison rolled her eyes, saying, "It's got meat in it."

"You really won't eat meat?"

Staring at the fire, she shook her head.

"Any meat?"

"She'll eat fish," Aaron said, "but only if she never sees its eyes."

Truman didn't get it. She would never see the eyes of the beef in the ravioli. Still, he shuffled around in his pack, looking for an alternative. "Look, I'll respect your choice to not eat meat," he said, "but it really limits your ability to survive under these circumstances. Our food will run out, and we'll need to hunt. It's likely that very soon the only choice you'll have will be eating meat or starving."

"Then I'll starve," she said. "Killing helpless animals is inhumane."

"You may have a point," Truman said softly. "But animals hunted in the wild are far from helpless. They have a fair chance. In fact, with their keen senses, they often have the advantage."

Allison stared at the glowing embers. Truman wondered if she was even listening, but he continued anyway. "I think whether or not taking a life for food is inhumane depends on the respect and gratitude we show, and how we honor their sacrifice. Remember, if humans didn't eat meat, we would never have survived the ice age."

She shot a fiery glance at Truman, and in a cold tone, said, "You need to respect my belief, and stop trying to convince me otherwise."

Truman chuckled.

"What's so funny?" Allie asked indignantly.

Truman shook his head. "It's just that—wow! You really are so much like your mother."

"Is that why you left us?" she asked. "Is that why you moved away and never even called to see how we were doing?"

Aaron stopped poking his stick into the fire to give his full attention to the answer to come.

Truman didn't know what to say. For all those years, he had blamed Sheila for driving him away. But deep down, he knew that rather than fight for his rights, he had run away from a reality too difficult to face. And once gone, he felt as though he had been freed.

Truman spoke softly in case Sheila and Jerry might hear him. "Your mother and I were high school sweethearts, and we loved each other very much. But neither of us were finished growing up when we had you guys. Hell, I'm still growing up. We grew apart through our different experiences and came to see the world—the whole universe—differently. We became totally different people—people who would never want anything to do with each other if they were meeting for the first time."

With a grunt, Truman got up and carefully stacked more wood on the fire. He sat back down, saying, "Look, kids, your mom and I split up for our own reasons. But it really was for the best, and I wouldn't change it. But if I could change anything, I would never have left you guys the way I did. It was all just so hard to take. I don't know if you guys remember, but your mother, you, and even the whole town looked at me as if I had gone crazy. Your mother told me that you were both afraid to be alone with me and didn't want to come for weekends anymore. Every time I called, she said you didn't want to talk to me. So eventually I quit calling."

Aaron was outraged. Through clenched teeth, he grumbled angrily, "She told us you were too busy chasing flying saucers to want to see us."

Pretending to sleep several feet away, tears rolled down Sheila's cheeks as she listened. Truman wanted to explode, but he bit his tongue. He looked at Allie. Her vacant eyes stared into the fire, stunned. Her lip quivered. Her eyes welled up with a flood of tears that she fought desperately to hold back. She gasped in shallow breaths as if a vacuum had sucked the air from around her.

"Kids, I'm sorry for everything," Truman said. "It's really all my fault. I shouldn't have given up so easily. I wish it were all different, but what's important is that we're together now."

Aaron scooted closer to his father, resting his head on his shoulder as Truman continued, "And I know times are scary, but I'm going to take care of you. I love you both very much. I always have." He put his arm around Allison and pulled her close.

She jerked free and climbed to her feet, saying, "Well, I'm really tired." She lifted her blanket from the ground next to Truman and spread it out to sleep several feet beyond the other side of the fire next to Sheila and Jerry.

"Hey buddy," Truman said quietly, nudging Aaron, "there's a little lake nearby. You wanna see if we can catch some fish for your sister in the morning?"

Aaron nodded excitedly.

"Cool," Truman said. "You better get some sleep too, then."

Tuwa tended the fire as Eric paced nervously across the deep sand, constantly looking down the narrow canyon for any sign of his friends. In the flickering firelight, their shadows danced twenty feet tall against the sheer sandstone walls. Glancing up at the stars visible through the opening in the vaulted ceiling above him, he said worriedly, "They should've been back a long time ago."

Mike leaned in whispering, "What if Ocho or Oliver sabotaged the trip and left us here like sitting ducks?"

Eric shook his head defiantly. "No, Mike, they just hit a snag of some kind."

"They just went a couple of miles to get the hoist. What could possibly have gone wrong? Unless, they were…"

"Shhh," Eric warned. He whirled around to look down the winding passage. He whispered, "I think I heard something."

"Did you see that shadow move on the wall?" Mike whispered.

Nervously, Eric nodded, taking out his war club, gripping it tightly in his trembling hand.

A shrieking wail bounced off the walls of the slot canyon, sending shivers down Eric's spine. Mike's hair stood on end. Trying to pinpoint where the sounds were coming from, Mike pulled Eric away from the rift. Another spine-tingling squawk rang out, followed by the fluttering of wings. In the darkness beyond the fire's glow, a small, shadowy shape flapped toward them. Stopping at the threshold of the cave, an iridescent raven swooped around and disappeared back into the darkness.

"What was that?" Mike asked.

Eric gave no response. His focus remained fixed on the winding channel, the only exit. His heart raced, adrenaline gushing through him. From behind a sharp bend in the chasm, the all too familiar ghostly, white-painted face peeked out at Eric and sneered. Eric's knees weakened. Frozen, he whispered to Mike from the side of his mouth, "That's the one that's been after me."

The skinwalker stepped into the open, chanting in what sounded like a thousand growling and shrieking voices. The cave rapidly darkened as the fire faded, being somehow choked of air. Tuwa raced into action, throwing a handful of herbs onto the embers, causing them to explode in an enormous fiery cloud that briefly illuminated the entire rocky cathedral.

In the reinvigorated firelight, Eric's eyes were caught by the unnatural movement of several human shapes, silently crawling headfirst like spiders down the impossibly vertical walls.

"Around the crystal, quick!" Tuwa shouted. Mike and Eric retreated to the Earthkeeper, while Tuwa chanted, scrambling to cast a small, protective circle around them. Senses frenzied and hearts pounding, the three huddled together shoulder to shoulder around the crystal. The ghouls crept steadily closer, surrounding them on the ground.

With subtle variations, they were similar in appearance: straggly, matted black hair; wet, glossy, black eyes; bodies adorned with many charms and necklaces made of human fingers, ears, and breasts, and parts of birds and bones and skulls of other small animals. Two of them wore the skins of coyotes. Their lanky bodies and long, rangy limbs were distorted and wrenched awkwardly. Their bare chests heaved as low growls rumbled with every breath in and out. The evil inside them boiled to the surface of their calloused, grayed skin, resulting in leprous blisters and festering sores scattered over their bodies.

One skinwalker, his face painted white, with five red slashes from forehead to chin, raced at lightning speed toward Eric. Stopping just outside the circle, he snarled and drooled over his gnashing yellow teeth. Eric tightened his grip on the club but wavered, cautiously remaining inside the circle.

Having been skeptical about the actual safety of the corn pollen circle, Eric was now convinced. Until now, Tuwa's Medicine seemed somewhat chimerical, almost like playing make-believe. But through his expanding vision, Eric could faintly see bluish, smoky apparitions standing guard over them. Forming a domed barrier around them were the ancient spirits of fearsome Indian braves, armed with rawhide shields and war clubs and lances. Standing within their ranks were animal spirits: a cougar, a bear, and several eagles patrolling the air above their heads.

With eyes tightly shut, Tuwa swayed on unsteady legs, shaking a gourd rattle and chanting his Medicine prayers. The ghouls countered with a chant of their own—a dark, hypnotic drone that pulsed like crickets in the night, but loud and shrill like the squeals of pigs. The cavern dimmed. Eric's eyes grew heavy. Struggling to maintain coherence, he shook himself alert in time to watch Mike fall unconscious to the ground outside the circle. Eric pounced, clutching Mike around the ankles, struggling to pull his friend back within the safety of the protected area. A hideous skinwalker with a skull-painted face quickly jerked Mike free from Eric's desperate grasp, dragging him across the cavern and several feet up the wall.

An enormous white wolf raced through the canyon and into the chamber. It bounded up the wall and leapt high into the air, biting through the skinwalker's wrist, severing his hand. The demon let out an earsplitting shriek as his prey fell heavily to the ground.

Mike's eyes blinked open to witness the large, white beast's jaws clamped around his treaded boot, dragging him across the sandy cavern floor. He fought, kicking at the wolf while Eric yelled, "Stop, Mike, stop!"

Despite the wolf's snarling and fearsome appearance, its glinting yellow eyes seemed somehow familiar and comforted Mike. He relaxed and was soon safe inside the circle. But the wolf was now in trouble, embroiled in frenzied combat with the demon witches.

They tumbled and thrashed around the cavern, the wolf's menacing growls nearly drowned out by the ghastly screams of the skinwalkers. The powerful wolf leapt onto one of the witches, knocking it to the ground and sinking its dagger-like canines deep into its neck. Yellow circles around the eyes of the black-painted face seemed to float in the darkness, as if its face were invisible behind the mop of coarse, black hair. Its head flopped backwards, barely connected by frayed strands of flesh and skin. A pool of steaming, goopy blood spread outward. As it jerked and flailed under the superior wolf, the other skinwalkers piled on, pounding the beast with heavy fists and slashing claws.

Eric paced worriedly inside the circle, watching the raging battle play out. Tripping over Mike, he stumbled, grabbing hold of the crystal to break his fall. Instantly, he felt the vibrating energy of the Earthkeeper coursing through his hands and up his arms.

The energy spread through his body, reminding him of the divine experience he had had during his grieving over Evan's death. "Please, help us," he cried.

A blast of brilliant white light suddenly exploded from the crystal, sending the demons crashing into the cave walls. They rebounded and scurried up the steep rock, escaping through the opening high above.

The large wolf was sprawled out, lying motionless on the ground. Eric rushed to it compassionately. As he reached out to touch the injured creature, it snapped at him. Snarling and growling, the wolf slowly struggled to its wobbly legs. Eric backed cautiously away from the bloody animal, returning to the safety of the circle with Mike and Tuwa. The wolf sniffed at the air and limped over to the lifeless skinwalker. Leaving a trail of blood, the wolf dragged the body out of the cavern and through the canyon.

Next morning, Truman and his son walked along the rocky lakeshore, bathing in the warmth of the sun as its rays streamed through the trees. To Truman, the gentle sloshing of the water lapping against the rocks and the songs of birds on the crisp morning air felt like heaven.

"Hey, Dad, how are we gonna fish without any equipment?"

Truman carefully scanned the ground as they walked. "Well, that's the thing. No matter where you are in the world, you'll always find the trash people have left behind."

He bent over and untangled a gnarly wad of fishing line from a piece of driftwood. "See? We have a hook and line; now, if we could just find something to use as a bobber…"

"Like this?" Aaron called out, holding up a dingy fragment from an old Styrofoam cooler.

"Perfect," Truman said proudly. "Now, we just need to dig for some worms or bugs."

The two sat quietly on a large rock, waiting patiently for a bite. With a crooked smile and watery eyes, Truman watched Aaron as he stared out over the water. Filled with a deep sense of satisfaction and pride, Truman put his arm around Aaron and squeezed him warmly, saying softly, "I love you, dude."

Smiling, Aaron said, "Dad?"

"Yeah, buddy," Truman answered.

"Are you and Mom gonna get back together?"

Truman was taken aback. "No, your mom is with Jerry now."

Aaron sat quietly for a moment, thinking. "But you're our Dad," he said. "Now that you're back, shouldn't you be together?"

"We are all together, for now," said Truman.

Concerned, Aaron asked, "What do you mean, for now?"

Truman spoke delicately. "I'm gonna take care of all of you. But once we get settled, you'll continue to live with your mom and Jerry. I'll be around though, and you and I will get to spend time together whenever we want."

"But Jerry can't take care of us out here."

Truman squeezed Aaron tighter, "Then, I guess, it'll be up to you, little man."

"What?" Aaron exclaimed, nervously.

"Don't worry," Truman smiled. "I'll teach you everything you need to know."

By midmorning, they had caught several small fish and were walking back to camp. Aaron bounced along happily with a huge grin on his face, incessantly chattering about this and that. Suddenly, the crackling reverberation of a thunderous explosion rumbled through the air, followed a moment later by a mighty shaking of the ground.

Frightened, Aaron asked, "What was that?"

"I don't know," Truman said, worriedly. "Stay calm." But a deep sense of foreboding was rising inside him. "You up for a run?" he asked.

Within minutes they had made it to the highway and, through the clearing of trees, were able to witness an enormous, bulging cloud of gray ash above the area several miles north of Flagstaff. The column of volcanic particles, three miles high, seemed to remain motionless in the air as if in a still photograph, while flashes of lightning flickered within the ominous cloud.

"What happened, Dad?" Aaron asked.

"It's a volcano."

Aaron was confused. "We have volcanoes here?"

"Didn't they teach you that in school?" Truman asked. "The whole area around Flag, something like two-thousand square miles, is a volcanic field with over six-hundred dormant and extinct volcanoes. You see that big mountain? How it's kinda scooped out like that?" he asked. He pointed at San Francisco Peaks, the large, multi-peaked mountain that loomed over the city. "It used to be twice that size, but it blasted out in a huge, side eruption about a million years ago, like Mt. Saint Helens. Sunset Crater was the last one to erupt, almost a thousand years ago."

Aaron stood still, thinking, soaking it all in. "Dad?"

"Yeah, buddy."

"What's a *square* mile?"

Truman laughed, "What *are* they teaching you in school, dude?"

Aaron shrugged his shoulders nonchalantly.

"Let's get back to camp, quick, so we can plan our next move," Truman suggested.

"What do you mean?" asked Aaron.

Truman explained, "Well, we were going to follow this highway through the town of Flagstaff, but for all we know, it might not be there anymore. There's gonna be a lot of ash falling. It can collapse roofs and even bury the town. It can turn to cement in your lungs. And there might be lava flows as well. We don't want to get anywhere near there."

Truman thought of Tabitha, hoping she had gotten out of town to safety. She had lingered in his mind since he'd met her. He was hoping to see her again. Hoping fate would once more cause their paths to cross. He turned his attention back to his son. Sensing Aaron's anxiety, Truman squeezed his shoulder, "We'll be alright, buddy. We'll go around north of it. We'll double back to Williams, up to the Grand Canyon country, then across the reservation from Tuba City. C'mon, let's go get the others and get moving."

# Chapter Twenty-nine

Having slept in short, rotating shifts, one resting while two stood guard against another possible attack, Eric awoke to a confusing view through the opening at the top of the cavern. The gloomy, crepuscular sky was a dull orange. "What time of day is it?" he asked.

"Midmorning," Mike answered. "We thought we'd let you sleep in a bit."

"No sign of the others?"

Mike shook his head. "I've been thinking, maybe we'd better go looking for them."

Eric asked, "Will the Earthkeeper be safe here?"

Tuwa nodded.

"Then, let's go."

They moved through the winding canyon, exiting awestruck at the sight of the towering plume of ash in the distance.

"Well, that explains the tremors we've been feeling," said Mike.

Having been solaced until now by the impression that the Colorado Plateau would be safe from any upheaval, Eric couldn't believe his eyes. His stomach was in knots. "Wow, it's really hitting close to home," he said softly.

Tuwa nodded, saying, "The spirits of the mountains are waking up."

Something clumped on the ground near the creek caught Eric's attention. Trotting over to investigate, he soon realized it was Ocho's sleeveless, light blue, denim shirt. Eric looked around for any other sign of Ocho. His eyes followed the blood trail from the canyon to the nearby mass of cottonwoods. Eric's heart sank, seeing Ocho sitting motionless on the ground, slumped over and covered in blood, his back against the Y-shaped tree. Wedged into the cleft, placed over the existing wolf skull, was the mangled head of the black-faced skinwalker.

Eric raced over to his friend. "Ocho! Ocho, are you alright?"

Ocho's tired eyes opened. "Hmm, what?" he grunted in confusion as his eyes came into focus. He smiled at the sight of Eric hovering over him. "Hey dude," he said in his gravelly voice. "What happened?"

"You don't know?" Eric asked. He glanced away to Mike, who looked back at him with an urgent expression.

Ocho skirted the question coyly with an inquiry of his own. "What do *you* know?"

Eric promptly answered, "We know a big white wolf came to our rescue last night when we were attacked by six skinwalkers."

"Really?" Ocho asked, seeming surprised.

"We know the wolf was you, Ocho," Eric announced confidently.

Ocho watched nervously for Tuwa's reaction, knowing that many Southwest Indian cultures are often very superstitious and view shapeshifting as witchcraft. Tuwa looked at the ground with no indication to be read anywhere on his face of what he was thinking. Ocho turned to Mike, who met his eyes with an apprehensive smile and nod.

"I am not a skinwalker," proclaimed Ocho.

There was a long, uneasy silence.

Ocho explained, "This power does not come from a dark place. When I couldn't fend for myself, Grandfather took pity on me and gave me this gift. It's a gift that I would never abuse."

The group stood quietly another moment, then Eric extended his hand, smiling. "I know, Ocho. You came to protect me—just like on my first night here, when I hit you with my truck."

"That was me, that night," Ocho admitted. "Grandfather brought me here to find you. To protect you."

Eric planted his feet firmly and leaned back, using all his weight to help his gigantic friend to his feet. Ocho staggered about

227

unsteadily, his back hunched over uncomfortably. Mike and Eric reached out to stabilize him. "You okay?" Eric asked.

Ocho nodded, wincing. "My back really hurts."

"Were you injured?"

"No," said Ocho, "not too bad. Just give me a minute. Merging just really takes a toll on me."

"Merging?" asked Eric.

"With the spirit of my power animal," Ocho replied.

Confused, Eric said, "I'm sorry, Ocho. Could you explain that a bit? Do you mean you become your animal spirit?"

Ocho shook his head, "Kind of. I really don't know how it works. First our spirits merge, then my body shifts. The instincts of millions of years of evolution are driving, and it's like I'm riding in the back seat, sometimes shouting out directions."

"Well, however it works, thank you, Ocho, for saving me last night," Mike said sincerely.

"Yeah, really," Eric added. "You did it again. But why did you growl and snap at me?"

"You did run me over," Ocho chuckled. "Really though—I mean, come on—it's a wolf, not a cuddly pet."

Concerned, Mike asked, "If instinct is in control when you are merged, are you a danger to us?"

Ocho, too, seemed concerned. "I don't know," he said. "That was the first time I've ever done it around other people. I've only ever done it to hunt. Usually, it's a long process of prayer and meditation, and dancing the movements of the wolf to call its spirit before I shift. But last night I sensed something wasn't right, and shifted without calling for it. The wolf came to protect you, so I can't imagine it would hurt you."

Handing Ocho his shirt, Eric asked, "So, is it like the movies? You wake up naked in a zoo, like in *An American Werewolf in London*? You obviously don't need a full moon."

Ocho snickered, shaking his head. "No, I left my shirt there when I dragged the body over here. I don't know how it works, but I never take off my clothes or jewelry or my knife. I just shift."

"The wolf spirit must manifest in this world by transforming every part of you at a molecular level—even your clothes and belongings," Mike suggested.

"Did you shift in front of the others?" Eric asked.

Ocho shook his head. "Could you imagine Charlie's reaction?" Ocho jested. "No, they don't know. I'd already left when it happened."

"Where were they?" Mike asked. "What was taking so long?"

Eric interrupted, anxious to get underway to find the others. "Can we talk and walk?" he suggested.

Ocho nodded and lumbered along while explaining, "It took a while to get everything together. We also had to modify the hoist for a longer cable. I had to take the winch off of your jeep, Mike."

"Sure," Mike nodded.

"We were having a hell of a time moving that hoist over the rocky ground," Ocho said. "It wasn't really that heavy, just awkward. We hit a big-time snag at the ravine, when Charlie slipped and said his ankle hurt too bad to keep going. I saw it happen, and it didn't look that bad to me. He was just being a wuss. I told him I could carry him back to the cavern so he wouldn't have to camp out in the open all night. But he kept crying about how much it hurt. So me and Kurt set up camp while Oliver went back to get some wrenches so we could take the hoist apart and move it in pieces. I wanted for us all to come back together, and we could just try again in the morning. But Charlie kept going on about the mysterious ways of God and how we needed to accept that we were right where God wanted us. That's when Grandfather told me something wasn't right. I ran back here as fast as I could, and by the time I got here, I had merged."

"Well, then, I guess God really does work in mysterious ways, because you sure saved Mike's arse," Eric joked lightheartedly.

"And the atheist sees the light," Mike quipped.

That comment touched a nerve in Eric. "Oh, *atheism*. I don't know anymore," he said. "I guess I just chose that ideology because I never understood why a loving god would sit back and allow so much suffering in the world."

Ocho interposed, "So people would learn to give a shit enough to put an end to suffering themselves."

"I've always thought the same thing about the extraterrestrials," Mike professed. "In all the years they have been observing our evolution—at least as far back as biblical times—it must have been really hard not to intervene with our earthly affairs and correct us. I mean, to leave us with our freewill so we can choose whether we continue to evolve or destroy ourselves. How godlike is that?"

"Where in the Bible does it say extraterrestrials were visiting back then?" Eric scoffed.

"Everywhere," Mike asserted, "On every page, depending on how you interpret it. Even to accept the traditional, dogmatic view of God is to accept the existence of a supernatural being not of this world, ergo extraterrestrial."

Eric had to hand it to him, the way he examined and tirelessly thought about things from so many angles. He really could make a solid argument for any of his unconventional ideas. "Good point," Eric said. "But, despite any argument anyone has ever made—and believe me, growing up in the Kingdom Hall with hundreds people like Charlie, I've been hammered by the best of 'em—nothing has ever convinced me of anything in a way that could forever shatter my being grounded in a mundane worldview. Even still, I don't think I've ever really been an atheist. I've never been undeniably certain of the absence of a god, anymore than anyone can really be certain of the existence of a god. How do you prove or disprove any of it? To deny or believe comes down to faith either way. How strange is it, that it's the same with your aliens?" He turned to Ocho, "Or with your Grandfather. Or with your belief in pervasive spirits," he said to Tuwa.

Tuwa laughed.

"What?" asked Eric.

"You fight so hard not to see yourself as what you have criticized for so long," Tuwa said. "It amuses me. You know what you have done and seen," he continued. "Why should you need to prove anything to anyone? Prove to the people of your mundane world that you were taken to the world of Spider Woman, or that she really helped you here in this world. Prove there have been flying triangles we all have seen. Or that Ocho shapeshifted into a wolf to fight the demon witches. Or that you commanded the

230

power of the Earthkeeper to save us all," Tuwa enumerated. "Is your mundane worldview really *not* shattered? What proof do you need to support your knowing what has happened? And what should stop you now from having faith in the possibility of things you might yet come to know?"

Eric stopped walking. After a few steps, the others paused and turned to face him.

"You're right," he confessed. "I'm doing it again. Rationalizing it all away because I'm too afraid to accept in myself what I've spurned for so long in others. Last night, when that light and energy shot out of the Earthkeeper, I was filled with a vibrating energy just like that time I told you about, when I was mourning for Evan, when I called out to God to let me feel Him."

For a long moment, Tuwa thought carefully for the words to speak, and debated on whether or not to even utter them. Finally, in a soft voice, he said, "I do not wish to criticize or offend anyone for their beliefs, but I have always found it curious how the white man's view of the Creator has always put a human face—a man's face—on the creative force. Maybe it helps you to understand such an abstract concept as an infinite, formless creative force, to give it a familiar face you can relate to. But to me, your god didn't make you in his image; you made him in yours. Please understand," implored Tuwa, "I am not saying this to take anything from the way you interpret your experience because, whatever it is to you, you felt the presence of the creative force behind all that exists. And it is a very special thing that happened. Special enough that your worldview *should* be shattered because of it."

Oliver and Kurt debated quietly about what to do with Charlie. It was already afternoon. The day was slipping away with nothing being done. Charlie had complained all morning that his ankle was hurt too badly to continue or go back.

"Look," Oliver announced happily, pointing at Ocho, Eric, Mike, and Tuwa hiking up the ravine, climbing toward them. Lying in the shade of a juniper, Charlie was unaware of their approach. "Charlie, here they come," Oliver said. "We'll get you out of here."

Upon seeing them, Charlie exclaimed, "You're okay?"

"Why do you seem so surprised?" Eric asked.

Shrugging it off, Charlie explained, "It's just that I thought we would have seen you a lot sooner. I thought something bad happened to you."

"Sorry to disappoint," said Eric.

Charlie scrambled nervously, "That's not what I meant. I was just..."

"Chill out, I'm just messin' with you," Eric said. "How's your ankle?"

"It hurts," Charlie said, "But it is a lot better."

Eric called Mike over to look at Charlie's ankle. "No, it's okay," Charlie said, climbing to his feet. He limped around, grunting, "Yeah, it's much better, I think I can make it."

Speaking in their native language, Tuwa spoke to Kurt who listened intently. He glanced around at the different people in the group. Finally his surprised eyes rested on Ocho, who had guessed that Tuwa had just told Kurt his secret.

Charlie called out, "I'm ready. Let's get this show on the road."

Ocho took suspicious note of Charlie walking lightly on his right foot. He searched the surrounding area, finding a stave for Charlie to use as a crutch. They gathered the pieces of the hoist and set off for the cavern.

# Chapter Thirty

Truman and his family pedaled their bicycles steadily up the center of the desolate highway from Williams toward the Grand Canyon. It had been nearly an hour since they had rolled past the last abandoned, weather-ravaged vehicle, back where the pine country gave way to an expanse of prairie. Separated from the roadway by miles of barbed wire, ranchland sprawled to the east and west of the highway.

"Oh my God, Dad," Allison shrieked, coasting to a stop. "What's wrong with all those cows?"

Scattered throughout the land, herds of cattle lay motionless on the ground. Their bodies were bloated and contorted, their eyes and mouths eerily agape. Truman immediately grew worried, scanning the skies and surrounding area for any sign of life. Finally, he spied a pair of ravens perched on a carcass pecking at the eyes and soft tissue.

"Phew, that's a relief," Truman sighed, spotting further life signs in several active gopher nests.

"What?" asked Jerry.

"I was worried for a minute that the air might be poisonous—maybe noxious gasses related to the nearby volcanism," Truman explained. "But I don't think that's the case, seeing other animals alive and well."

Nervously, Sheila asked, "Are you sure?"

"As sure as I can be," he responded.

"Then what killed all these cows?" Allison asked.

Truman shook his head. "I can only guess."

Several miles further up the highway on the left, another stretch of dead cows and their calves littered the ground. On the right, a small herd of bison roamed and grazed a modest tract of pasture. The barbed wire that ran parallel to the highway was adorned with eagle feathers, cloth streamers of red, black, white and yellow, and offerings of tobacco prayers bundled in small cloth pouches of the same colors. Bundles of sage and other herbs and dried flowers were placed reverently along the fence posts.

"What are those weird-looking cows, Dad?" Aaron asked.

"What are they teaching you guys in school? Those are buffalo," Truman explained. "Amazing, huh? About a hundred and fifty years ago these things used to roam in the tens of millions. By the 1900s, they were nearly extinct."

"Whoa, how'd they drop so fast?" Aaron asked. "Were they killed off by some kind of disease?"

"That's one way to put it, buddy. Human nature," Truman said. He knew Aaron didn't understand the metaphor, but continued without explanation, "They were slaughtered by the millions for their tongues and hides, and left to rot on the prairies. Between over-hunting and the land being fenced off with the introduction of cattle, they just didn't stand a chance."

"How could anyone do that?" Allison asked. "Why didn't anyone stop it?"

"There were some who wanted to protect them from extinction," Truman explained, "but Congress failed to act on it because they knew that the fastest way to subdue the last of the rogue Indian tribes would be to take away their primary food source. Didn't they teach you this in school? Anyway, there were thought to be as few as several hundred when independent ranchers took it upon themselves to preserve them and breed private herds from as many as twenty or thirty wild-caught bison."

"So, I guess ranchers aren't all bad," Allison said.

Truman pointed out several beasts from the herd. "See those white buffalo over there? It's weird there are so many. I read that white ones are really rare—something like one in ten million births. But that seems to be a whole family of them. I read about a white buffalo born on a ranch somewhere in Wisconsin back in the early nineties. Indians from all over the country made pilgrimages to see it because it tied in with some kind of prophesy—a return of the old ways, or something like that."

"Why do you think these buffalo aren't affected by whatever killed those cows?" Jerry asked.

"I don't know," Truman said, "but it's really interesting, given everything that's going on with the world." Truman motioned to Aaron. "You mentioned disease. I can't help but think of some recent cases we've been investigating: unusual die-offs and cattle mutilation."

"Cattle mutilation?" Jerry asked with some confusion.

Truman explained, "Since the seventies, ranchers have been finding cattle killed on their land. The authorities wrote it off, saying they were all killed by predators like wolves or coyotes. But there was absolutely no evidence of that. It was much more mysterious. All incidents were accompanied by sightings of strange flying orbs, and the cattle were all similarly, surgically dissected."

"Why?" asked Aaron.

"No one really knows," said Truman. "Some think the government is behind it. Others think aliens. But lately I've been wondering if the mutilations could be tied to the crop circle phenomena, which have also been linked to sightings of glowing, flying orbs."

Everyone looked confused. Sheila fidgeted anxiously, saying, "Come on everyone, let's keep moving."

"In a minute! I'm talking here!" Truman snapped impatiently. "Where was I? Oh, right," he continued. "For decades, all over the world, strange circles and huge geometric patterns have been mysteriously appearing overnight in wheat fields. Some were proven to be hoaxes. But in the authentic cases, the crops that were laid down and woven into these shapes all shared unusual characteristics: the plants were genetically altered in ways no one has been able to understand. Recently, some strange genetic disease has wiped out millions of acres of wheat and other crops around the world, similar to what we've been seeing lately in cattle populations. Like what we have right here. And when you put both of these unusual phenomena together, that is the scariest part. Something seems to be deliberately attacking the world's primary food supply."

Buried under several feet of thick volcanic ash, many of the rooftops of Flagstaff collapsed under the immense weight. From several eruptive vents northeast of the town, lava gushed from fissures in the earth, feeding rivers of the glowing molten matter that flowed over twenty miles. It wound through the easternmost part of town, covering roads and reducing everything it touched to embers. An ominous, red glow reflected against the haze of ash and smoke that hung in the skies above northern Arizona. This was compounded by an enormous forest fire, that had been triggered by the plane that crashed during the initial solar storm. The fire raged south of Flagstaff through Oak Creek Canyon, spreading into Sedona and sweeping across the Verde Valley.

The worldwide death toll was nearing three billion. Most of the casualties were the people trapped within dense populations of coastal cities and buried under the crumbling buildings. Massive earthquakes and tsunamis raged throughout the world's coastal areas, while dormant volcanoes around the globe awakened with a ferocity not seen for millions of years. Massive storms seemed as though they were consciously targeting and scouring populated areas. Just like the prophecies told to Oliver by his grandfather, droves of people flooded onto reservation lands. For days, survivalists and unorganized bands of refugees had been abandoning the cities and towns, fleeing into the canyon lands of the Colorado plateau.

Grunting as he set a heavy steel crossbeam onto the ground, Eric stood rubbing his aching lower back. Sweat ran down his forehead, stinging his eyes. The others in his group filed in one by one, each setting their piece of the hoist onto the ground and collapsing on the sandy cavern floor, exhausted and overheated.

"Honey, I'm home!" Eric's voice echoed throughout the cathedral-like vault as he laid his hand gently on the smooth face of the Earthkeeper. Instantly revitalized by the energetic properties of the crystal, he bustled about, taunting his bone-weary comrades. "C'mon, you old ladies, this isn't naptime."

Saying nothing, Ocho waved him off like a bug.

Eric sat quietly for a moment, but was restless. He fidgeted anxiously, finally saying, "Fine, then. Oliver, you got those wrenches? I'm gonna put the hoist back together."

Oliver tossed the wrenches to Eric and laid back, settling into the soft sand for a rest. Eric toiled with the hoist for nearly half an hour while the others napped. Once finished, he sat cross-legged on the ground facing the Earthkeeper. Sitting there he studied the web-like internal fractures and inclusions of the giant crystal and watched the illusory images they seemed to conjure as his eyes relaxed their focus. Dizzy and quivering inside, an unexplainable wooziness came over him, as though he were tumbling from an incredible height. The phantasmal images morphed into a flock of fluttering birds, wheeling and swooping in unison.

Charlie opened his eyes and looked around. The afternoon sun shone into the vault, causing warm hues of yellows and reds to reflect off the stratified, sandstone walls. He sat up and looked at the others sleeping soundly on the floor. Quietly he ambled across the cavern and sat next to Eric.

"So, I've been told you intend to stop the Armageddon."

"That's the plan," Eric said.

"How does Jehovah fit in to this plan?" Charlie asked.

"Don't know. He hasn't said anything about it," Eric smirked sarcastically.

"Well, actually, He has," Charlie argued. "You know what I'm talking about. Mike told me you were a Witness once. You know the truth."

Eric scoffed. "That was a long time ago. And let's just say I didn't agree with the teachings."

Charlie was appalled. "But we are the one, true church."

Eric became immediately frustrated and confrontational. "Do you have any idea how many religions say that? That kind of limited thinking about an infinite creator always seemed so contradictory to me. It just repulses me. Proclaiming to be the only truth—in a world of relative truths—just makes you seem false, you know? To me, anyway."

"Well you're wrong," Charlie insisted angrily. "And stopping Armageddon is wrong. There is only one way to the Kingdom, you goat. These tribulations *must* be carried out unhindered if evil is to be purged from the world. It's not too late, Eric. All you have to do is accept Him, and you will be saved with us."

Annoyed, Eric rasped, "I've had too many debates like this with too many people just like you. I know what my mission is here. I've never been more sure about anything in my life."

"God won't let you stop what is to come," Charlie insisted.

"Why are you even here?" Eric snapped. "Weren't you supposed to have been whisked away in a rapture of some sort before the shit started to hit the fan? Oh, that's right," Eric jeered. "Every prediction of the rapture your prophets have made since the 1850s have passed uneventfully."

Charlie stammered, "I—uh, I am right where God wants me to be."

Eric pondered Charlie's statement for a moment before responding. "Strangely, I would have to say the same goes for me. I am certain that I am exactly where I am meant to be, doing exactly what I am meant to do. But, you know, the funny thing about you hellfire types is how you encourage people to seek an experience to cement their testimony, but you reject the validity of any experience that differs from your dogmatic views." Eric stared piercingly into Charlie's eyes. "It's no secret that I've never been too sure about the existence of God—the concept of God that was forced down my throat all my life, anyway. But, I'm finally developing a picture of a creative force that resonates in harmony with what I know intrinsically. And if setting the Earthkeeper on Spider Rock goes against our Creator's plan, I'm sure I'll be stopped somehow."

"Oh, you will," Charlie sneered. "And I'll be there when it happens."

Aroused by the raised voices, Mike sat up and looked at Eric. "Is everything alright?"

Eric nodded. "We're just having a theological discussion."

Mike looked away at Charlie, then back at Eric. He gibed, "Yeah, that's a good idea."

Looking up at the gloomy sky through the opening in the ceiling, Eric said, "I'd really like to get a move on, so we're long gone before it gets dark. It's not safe to spend another night here."

Mike agreed. "I'll wake the others."

Within minutes they were stirring about, gathering their things. Ocho wandered over, inspecting the hoist.

"Making sure I didn't screw it up?" Eric asked.

"Yeah, actually," Ocho chuckled. "Looks alright. Did you get the bolts tight enough?"

"Check 'em if you want."

"Nah, I trust you."

"So, do we have any idea how this is going to work?" asked Mike.

Eric nodded. "Everybody, gather over here, around me." He placed a hand on the Earthkeeper and one on the hoist. "Okay, now we all need to focus on the image of Spider Rock there." He looked questioningly for Tuwa's approval.

Tuwa nodded, smiling.

Nervously, Eric waited for something to happen. Seconds seemed like minutes, but he maintained his focus, having faith it would work.

Charlie huffed impatiently. "This is just stupid," he mocked. "Whose predictions have *passed uneventfully* now?"

There was a quick flash of white light, and they found themselves perched high on a canyon wall. Eric glanced around the shallow cave and announced, "We're here."

Dumbfounded, Charlie looked carefully over the edge, down the sheer cliff face at the canyon floor far below. Startled by a canyon swift that swooped within inches of his head, he jumped away from the edge. "So unnatural," he muttered, mystified by the inexplicable teleportation.

"What'd you say?" Eric asked.

Charlie shook his head. "Nothing."

"Alright then, everyone, let's get this hoist anchored down somehow, and settle in for the night. We'll lower the Earthkeeper down first thing in the morning."

# Chapter Thirty-One

Leaving Sheila, Aaron, and Allison to set up camp a short ways off a dirt road lined with huge, steel power line towers, Truman and Jerry set off to search for firewood along the rocky scrubland several miles east of the Grand Canyon. The wind blew strongly from the east. A couple of large drops of rain smacked against Truman's face. Hearing distant, rumbling thunder, he glanced up, and noticed a bulging, gray cloud against a murky, eerily glowing sky. The strange cloud sagged and streaked downward as rain began to fall a couple of miles away. Each carrying a bundle of dry wood in his arms, Truman and Jerry talked as they walked.

"Truman, I want you to know," Jerry huffed, "I never thought you were cracked."

"What do you mean?" asked Truman.

"About your UFO encounter, and your belief in extraterrestrials," Jerry explained. "I've kept it secret from Sheila, but I've always been a believer. Ever since I was a kid. Remember what a Trekkie I was in school?"

Truman chuckled. "Yeah, I remember." His tone grew solemn. "I'm sorry about the way we all treated you back then."

"Well, that's just the way it is, I guess. Jocks ridicule nerds. Just like in any society. I'm sure you now know, you have the conventional accepted norm and the pariahs."

"I really am sorry. And believe me, karma is a bitch," Truman said. "I've learned too well how it feels to be the outcast."

"Yeah, I suppose you have," Jerry said. "It's a shame it has to be that way. I always looked forward to the day that all the people of the world would come together; equal in a common purpose. I really thought we might get there, too. It's sad, really. Until a few days ago, I always had such a hopeful outlook for the future." Jerry chuckled. "Ever the Trekkie, I was sure that the rapid technological advancements of the last hundred and fifty years were taking us toward our ultimate destiny. *Space, the final frontier,* you know? Now it seems we're doomed to revisit a frontier more like the old west."

"I always wondered if technological growth was accelerated by secret deals made with the E.T.s or, maybe, taken from crashed saucers," Truman suggested.

"Oh, no, no," Jerry argued. "Don't discount human ingenuity."

Having always known him as a pushover, Truman was taken aback by the conviction with which Jerry stood up for his opinion. Out of concern that his amused approval might be misconstrued as derision, Truman struggled to suppress his smile as Jerry continued to vent.

"To believe in extraterrestrial intelligence is one thing, but I've always been offended by the idea that they built the pyramids or laid the seeds of civilization and science. Personally, I always believed the UFOs were merely watching, waiting for us to mature to the point we could be included in some kind of galactic federation." Jerry concluded.

"I've often thought that, as well, actually," Truman said passionately. "Although, I've also had to entertain the possibility that their motives might not be benign. Based on the evidence found in ancient art and mythology, there is good reason to believe that they have been visiting us for thousands of years. I never understood what they were waiting for, if it were the case that they wanted us to join some cosmic society. But, then, if their motives were sinister, you figure with their technology, they could have taken us out at any time, and would have by now. I don't know, maybe they were just waiting for us to destroy ourselves. Whatever it is, good or bad," Truman exclaimed, vexed, "I just can't get my head around why there hasn't been undeniable, worldwide contact."

"Still needing that vindication, huh?" Jerry suggested.

"Yeah, I guess so," Truman admitted. Calming down, he continued, "Not that it should matter anymore."

There was a long silence. Jerry began to say something, but stopped. He fidgeted a bit and tried again, "You know, Truman, I know it's been a hard thing to do, to drag your former wife and her husband along on this exodus…"

"Not so bad," Truman assured him.

"No, I have read it on your face, how much it hurts when the kids call me dad."

Truman nodded, "I'm not gonna lie. It does hurt. But I understand. I was never there, and you were. You've been there for them, being the dad they needed. It only makes sense. It only hurts to hear them call you dad because it reminds me how much I've missed, and how I failed them, staying away for so long. But you, Jerry, you are a good man. I'm glad you've been there for them. And that you're still here for them."

"They're good kids, both of them," Jerry said. "Good like their father. I'm glad I've gotten this chance to know you better."

On their way back to camp, Truman and Jerry followed the edge of a long plateau that ran several miles parallel to the power line trail. As they moved along, they looked for an easy way down the steep, rippled hoodoos that formed the face of the plateau. It was near dark as they rounded a large, rocky formation. Startled, a small, armed group of woodsy men shot to their feet, training their guns on Truman and Jerry, who froze in surprise, dropping their firewood and surrendering their hands in the air.

"Are you armed?" one of the men asked in a gruff voice, his thick, gray mustache wriggling on his lip like a fuzzy caterpillar as he spoke.

"Just the knife on my belt," Truman said.

"At ease, boys," said the man to his company, one of whom was a skittish, apprehensive young man of perhaps seventeen or eighteen with rosy, flushed cheeks. They lowered their weapons, but maintained their intimidating demeanor. In a demanding tone, the leader asked, "What are you fellas doing out here?"

Having anticipated the question Truman had already crafted his response, immediately answering, "We came up here to get away from the storms that hit Williams."

"Is that where you're from?" the man asked.

Truman shook his head, "Los Angeles. I was driving home on I-40 from a trip to Santa Fe the day the northern lights started flashing in the sky. I've been hoofing it ever since my car died that day and was smashed to hell by a tornado."

The man turned his attention to Jerry, "What about you?"

Jerry trembled nervously, stammering, "I fled Kingman after an earthquake."

Appearing surprised, the men looked at one another. "And how did you two come to be together out here?"

"We actually went to school together," Truman said, "and, by luck, we happened to run into each other."

"Huh, what are the odds of that?" asked the man. "And there are others out here with you?"

"No, just us," Truman immediately answered. "We're just looking for a place to camp for the night."

The man conferred quietly with his companions. Huddled several feet away, they whispered, occasionally glancing back at Truman and Jerry. Finally, the man sauntered back and stood quietly looking the two over, taking special interest in the KA-BAR knife on Truman's hip. Truman took notice of the patch on the man's black cap, a wreath around a service ribbon. The words indicated that he was a Vietnam veteran.

He took his cap off briefly to scratch his shaggy, gray hair, and asked, "What do either of you know about what's going on here?"

"Something has knocked out the power," Truman said. "Best I can guess, an EMP of some kind. But I have no idea what could be causing the extreme weather or volcanic eruptions."

"Well, boys," the man warned intimidatingly, "we're staking claim to this area here. Go ahead and camp here tonight, but I want you long gone, first thing in the morning."

"No problem. We're only passing through," said Truman, "on our way to Utah."

"Why Utah?"

243

"My mother is there, all alone," Truman said. "I've got to get to her."

"Alright then," grunted the man. "Better get a move on, there's a storm coming."

With haste, Truman and Jerry gathered their wood and walked away, neither speaking a word. Fearing they were being followed, Truman frequently glanced over his shoulder.

One of the men in the group approached their leader asking, "Why'd you let them go?"

"They don't have anything we need, Kilgore," the man replied gruffly. "They'll be gone soon enough. Besides, the big guy's a vet. You gotta respect that."

Trying to keep up with Truman's quick pace, Jerry panted, glancing frantically over his shoulder. "Why did you lie to them?" he whispered.

"Just something about them sent up red flags. Other than their rifles and handguns, they didn't carry any supplies. They were on patrol, with a base nearby where there are more of them, I'm sure."

"They were awful paranoid, weren't they?"

"I know their type," said Truman. "They're better prepared for these times than anybody, and have been gearing up for this for twenty or thirty years or more. My guess is that they're operating under the assumption that we're under attack. That all this is some conspiracy, a calamity perpetrated by a shadow government bent on global domination."

Jerry asked nervously, "Do you think they knew we were lying about being alone out here? Maybe they know about Sheila and the kids."

"I don't know."

Arriving at camp, Truman immediately asked, "Sheila, have you seen anyone in the area?"

Sheila rose from spreading a large quilt neatly on the ground. "Not a soul," she said. "Why?"

"I'm sorry, kids. I need you to pack up and be ready to go in five minutes."

"Aww," the kids whined.

"No, we're tired," Sheila resisted. "We're not going anywhere."

"Dammit, Sheila!" Jerry shouted impatiently, "Listen for once, will you!"

Truman smirked.

"Don't you talk to me like that, you stupid jerk!" she hissed.

Truman rapidly snapped his fingers, the piercing sound catching everyone's attention. "Pack it up, kids. Let's go." He turned his attention to their angry mother. "It's not safe here. There are men out there with guns. Organized, militant, paranoid men. Load up."

Sheila opened her mouth to protest, but Truman cut her off before she could utter a word. "Now," he commanded sternly.

Sheila huffed, hastily snatching the blanket from the ground. She wadded it into a ball and shoved it angrily into the bike trailer.

Within minutes, they were back on the paved road, pedaling their bikes wearily through the darkness against the strong, dusty gusts brought in on the rapidly approaching storm. Bluish light flickered within the distant, black clouds as the low rumble of thunder rolled across the air.

They pressed on for twelve miles, the last forty minutes of their journey through torrential rain. Lightning bolts streaked and crackled across the sky, getting nearer with each strike.

"Head for that rocky outcropping over there!" Truman shouted.

They pedaled their bikes as far as they could across the rough terrain before running up a steep slope toward the shelter of the rock formations. An ear-splitting boom rang out instantly as a blinding, white arc of lightning hit the ground fifty yards away.

"Hurry!" roared Truman.

Huddled together under a large, protruding rock, Sheila cried, "Where is Aaron?"

Frantically scanning the area between them and the bikes, Jerry shouted, "There!"

Aaron cowered under a twisted, sparsely leaved mesquite tree, frozen with fear as blue and violet lightning strikes branched successively across the sky.

"Aaron!" Truman yelled, "Come on, hurry!"

Refusing to move, Aaron crouched under the tree, plugging his ears with his fingers. Truman raced as fast as he could, jerking his frightened son from the tree. Cradling Aaron in his arms, Truman raced back toward the shelter as fast as he could.

Stumbling on a loose rock, Truman and Aaron tumbled to the ground. Immediately, Jerry ran to their aid when, without warning, a white-hot flash of lightning knocked him down. The current surging though his body ruptured his eardrums and exited though his feet between his toes. The searing electricity instantly cauterized the flesh where his feet burst open. It shredded and melted his shoes before spreading across the ground. Jolted by the dissipating charge that flowed across the wet ground, Aaron and Truman writhed and contorted violently as the shock coursed through their bodies. Screaming, Shelia collapsed to the ground in tears.

From blackness, Truman's eyes came slowly into focus. He saw Sheila and Allie sobbing, but heard nothing but what sounded like a low rush of wind in his ears, coupled with a harmonic ringing. Truman picked himself up, grabbed Aaron and limped hurriedly to shelter. Without pause, he went back for Jerry and dragged the lifeless man to the safety of the rocky overhang as lightning continued to flash all around them.

Sheila cradled and rocked Aaron who was coherent but dazed. The pupil of his left eye was enormously dilated, and he was quite sore, but was otherwise fine. Jerry, on the other hand, was not breathing, nor was his heart beating. His shirt and pants were ripped open and singed, his skin blistered and burned.

Dropping to his knees at Jerry's side, Truman performed cardiopulmonary resuscitation, trying desperately to revive him. His heart racing, Truman frantically worked, compressing Jerry's chest and forcing air into his lungs. His hearing slowly returning, through a mechanical-like distortion he could hear Sheila and the kids crying and begging Jerry to please wake up and be okay. Truman paused and checked for a pulse and breathing.

The kids and their mother wailed, holding each other tightly. "It's all my fault," Aaron sobbed. Sheila squeezed him tighter. With no indication of revival, Truman went back to work on Jerry. He worked and worked, repeating the steps and checking for a pulse, over and over again. He struggled relentlessly for what seemed like hours, then collapsed from exhaustion.

"Where is everybody?" called Eric, as he glanced around the shallow cave. He was all alone, high up the canyon wall. Even the crystal and hoist were missing. Judging by the sun's position in the sky, he estimated that it was late morning. A panicked feeling came over him. Why did they leave him here? He felt horribly betrayed. Had they really turned against him?

Eric walked several feet to the edge and carefully leaned over, searching the canyon floor below for any sign of his companions. The water level of the stream flowing through the winding chasm was higher than when they had arrived, and was running swiftly. There was no sign of the others as far as could be seen in either direction. Wondering if they might have climbed out to the rim above, Eric twisted and looked up the steep wall when suddenly he slipped backwards and fell over the edge.

Eric's body tensed and his jaw tightened as he plummeted. The rush of air flapping through his clothes and hair gently lifted his arms as if perched comfortably on the armrests of a reclined chair. Dizzied by the blurring sienna and umber striations of the sandstone wall whizzing past, he fixed his eyes on a cloud in the sky and resolved to accept his fate. He relaxed his body, experiencing the state of freefall. A cliff swallow darted past him. Turning for another pass, it flew directly at Eric. The bird cocked his black, featureless eye at Eric and spoke, "Is this *really* happening, or another one of your dreams?"

This can't be happening, Eric thought, no longer aware of falling. I *am* dreaming. Instantly, he awoke and scanned the darkened hollow. Everyone was sound asleep. Eric was nearest to the wall, between Ocho and the Earthkeeper. He looked in disbelief at Kurt, soundly sleeping mere inches from the edge. It was early morning, still very dark. It was raining steadily. A stream of water ran down the cliff face and fell over the cave opening in a thin, shimmering, wet curtain. Emitting from deep within the web-like structure of the crystal, a subtle otherworldly glow faintly illuminated the natural alcove, oscillating between hues of green, blue, and violet.

Eric tossed and turned, trying to get comfortable on the uneven, rocky ground. Still rattled by the dream, he sat up, too antsy to sleep. He thought about their predicament, high on the canyon wall, and wondered why the wormhole couldn't have taken them directly to Spider Rock as it had done with the seer's temple. Looking at the heavy Earthkeeper, he dreaded the day to come and the arduous journey through the muddy canyon. As he gazed more deeply into the crystal, an image formed in his mind, revealing the team walking alongside the canyon stream. Resting their hands lightly on the crystal, which floated several feet above the ground, being pushed along as effortlessly as if it were a helium-filled balloon.

Confused, Eric shook off the vision and stared out to the dark abyss, thinking. The idea of levitating the half-ton gemstone was absurd. Eric pondered the vision for some time, wondering if it suggested a mundane solution presented through enigmatic symbolism. He knew it was physically impossible for such a heavy object to simply float on the air, but what about on water? If the overnight rain did in fact raise the water level of the stream, perhaps they could find materials nearby to build some kind of barge and float the Earthkeeper to their destination. Encouraged by the idea, Eric laid back relaxed, envisioning the group trudging waist-deep through the stream. Before them they pushed the giant stone on a floating barge crudely fashioned from the salvaged posts and planks of a crumbling wooden fence.

He was soon lightly asleep, his mind awash with flashing images and dreams. Fully aware that he was dreaming, most of the images were very abstract and symbolic. Making no sense at all, many contained flashing lights and geometric shapes, animals and birds. Once again, he had a brief vision of an enormous flock of fluttering birds, wheeling and swooping in unison—hundreds of individuals seemingly sharing a group mind. The visions streamed as one continuous thread, morphing one into another, but remained disparate, showing no apparent relationship. It was reminiscent to

Eric of his idiosyncratic method of rapidly blinking through the television channels, pausing briefly on interesting images and words.

One particular dream revealed a population of refugees growing so large on the reservation that, in an ironic twist, tribal leaders designated a reservation camp within their reservation for the droves of whites and other outside races flooding onto their lands.

Moments later, Eric had a horrible dream about a group of unscrupulous men that raided bands of refugees fleeing from the destruction of their towns and homes. They were well armed and well trained, and initially set out to rob people of whatever useful items they carried. All too soon, however, they took to kidnapping young women, with which they intended to build their tyrannical society. They were holed up along a dirt road that sliced through a transitional zone of desert and forest. A long plateau of rocky scrubland flanked the north side. A quarter of a mile or so away to the south, a large stand of ponderosa pines lined the steep, north-facing side of a mountain.

The fortified base from which they launched their raids was a multi-story fort constructed of split-log siding lashed over the existing steel, lattice structures of two parallel, overhead power line towers. As originally constructed by the utility company, the wide bases of the eighty-foot towers were anchored at four points to buried concrete pillars and connected sixty-five feet up by a forty-foot long triangular, steel framework, which the men had retrofitted to serve as a crawl-through catwalk to access the topmost points of the towers, now being used as armed lookout stations.

Eric felt uneasy, his stomach queasy as once again he felt as though he were falling. The sensation felt like a warning, but he couldn't explain it. He became nervous at the thought of the coming morning's descent down the cliff face. He briefly opened his eyes and looked at the crystal. Behind it, the rear wall of the cave seemed to ripple peculiarly. Blinking his tired eyes, he looked again more closely. The wall was still and quite normal. He laid back and closed his eyes. Exhausted and frustrated by not being able to get any restful sleep, he fidgeted and tossed and turned on the hard ground near the crystal as images flooded his mind. Finally, he visualized himself turning off the TV and exhaustedly tossing the remote on the couch. His mind went blank and he sank into a welcome deep sleep.

# Chapter Thirty-two

Huddled together under the rock overhang, Truman slept upright with his back against a large boulder. Sheila was next to him, still asleep, her head resting on his shoulder. Allison was slumped over, sleeping against her mother, while Aaron lay across them, sleeping comfortably with his head on Sheila's lap. She had fallen asleep stroking his hair, her hand still resting gently on his head.

The gravelly caw of a raven rang out. Truman opened his tired eyes and looked around, blinking at the morning light. Careful not to wake her, he pulled slowly away from Sheila at the sight of Jerry's lifeless body laid out under a blanket just feet away. The wind had blown a corner of the blanket back, revealing Jerry's pale, bloated face. His dulled eyes were rolled back and his jaw had dropped slack, leaving his mouth hanging eerily agape. He looked startlingly artificial, like a wax dummy, a resemblance exact in every detail, but lacking any spark of life or spirit within.

Truman gently pulled the blanket over Jerry's face and anchored it to the ground with a rock. He then set out in search of large, flat rocks, bringing them back and quietly placing them over the body until it was completely covered. His head throbbing and body aching—aftereffects of the indirect lightning strike—Truman eased himself to the ground in the shade of the overhang and watched his family sleep.

Sheila's eyes blinked open and looked at Jerry, entombed in rocks. Catching eyes with Truman, she looked away, saying softly, "Thank you, Tru."

Truman nodded.

She lightly stroked Aaron's head as he lay soundly asleep in her lap, her fingers gently twirling his hair. Her hand trembled. She drew in a fluttering breath and held it deep for a while before sighing heavily.

"You okay?" Truman asked softly.

"I wish I had been better to him," she said of Jerry. She looked lovingly down at Aaron. Softly, she said, quivering, "I was so scared I'd lost him too."

Truman sat quietly, saying nothing, just listening.

"I haven't been the best mother. I haven't been the nicest person," she added. "To him or you. There were times this sweet boy really needed me to just love him and let him know everything is okay, and I let him down. I wish I hadn't been so cold those times he wanted me to just hear him. But I resented him for bringing those things into our home. I resented both of you."

Confused, Truman raised his eyebrow. He soon realized she was referring to the otherworldly visitors she had described from her dream.

"I know," she said softly. "I've always rejected that they even exist. I don't know what they are. But even if it's only been happening in our minds, something has been happening...for years." She looked down at Aaron, pulling his hair back and lightly tracing his ear with her finger. "It scares the hell out of me," she said, smiling nervously. "There were times I would wake up in the middle of the night—not all the way—just enough to know something wasn't right. I wanted so bad to make sure he was okay, but I was too afraid to move. Besides, it seemed like there was always someone standing next to the bed keeping me from going. But then I would think it was Aaron standing there, too scared to go back to bed. It would make me so angry. I'd be short with him for days. I feel so bad about that. When I think about how scared he must have been, I wish I could go back and just hold him—instead of being so angry about it."

"Maybe all of it. Even my sightings. Maybe it was always about him," Truman suggested.

Sheila shrugged her shoulders. "All I know is that I can't stand the thought of losing him; or anything bad happening to these sweet kids. I don't even have a life aside from them. I just couldn't live anymore."

Having been listening, Aaron opened his eyes and reached up, caressing his mother's cheek with his hand. She gently grasped and kissed it.

"Mom?"

"Yeah, baby."

"I understand how afraid you are, but I never 'invited' anything into our home."

"I know, baby."


Mike and Eric leaned carefully over the edge, watching Tuwa descend as Kurt turned the hoist crank, slowly letting out more and more cable. Oliver was at the bottom looking up to encourage the old man. "That's it, Tuwa," Oliver said, "push off with your feet a bit—just like walking backwards. It's easy."

Tuwa worked his feet down the nearly vertical cliff face, over a rounded lip where the wall gradually inverted, becoming more than 90 degrees.

"That's it, Tuwa, just push off and hang," Oliver called up. "Let the guys do the rest with the hoist."

Kurt steadily lowered Tuwa ever closer to the ground. This section of the canyon was much wider at the bottom than at the top, with the gradually curving overhang above. Held by the thin, braided-steel cable, Tuwa dangled under the smooth, sandstone ceiling five to ten feet from the cliff wall. Built onto the sandstone walls under the overhang were the thousands of gourd-shaped, mud nests of an enormous colony of cliff swallows. Alarmed by Tuwa's presence, the birds rang out with a cacophony of fluttering wing beats and thin, squeaking twitters. Some birds darted swiftly around him.

Within moments, Tuwa was safely on the sandy ground. Oliver helped him unwrap the makeshift tow strap harness. "Fun, huh?" said Oliver.

Tuwa nodded, smiling. He patted his chest rapidly with wide eyes, his hand language indicating his accelerated heartbeat. Oliver trotted further out from the canyon wall. Waving his arms, he shouted up to his friends in the cave, "All clear! Bring her up!"

Kurt quickly wound up the hoist while the others decided who was to go next. "Alright, Charlie," Eric said, "Your turn."

Charlie shook his head nervously, insisting, "Not yet."

"It's alright," Eric said reassuringly. "There's nothing to be afraid of."

"What if that cable snaps?"

"Not gonna happen," Mike said. "That cable is rated up to forty-five hundred pounds."

Charlie glanced around at the others. Eric and Ocho looked rather impatient. "I'm not ready yet. Why don't you go, Mike?" Charlie suggested.

"I'll go," Mike nodded. "It's fine. You'll see."

Ocho and Eric helped harness Mike with the tow straps, wrapping them snugly around his waist, over his shoulders, and around his thighs. Connecting the ends above his center of gravity, just above his midsection, they carefully inspected their work and hooked him to the line.

"See ya later," said Eric.

"Yep," Mike answered. He walked to the edge and turned. His back to the abyss, he took several deep breaths, pulled the cable taut, leaned back, and carefully stepped over.

Mike was soon on the ground and the harness retrieved. "Okay Charlie," Eric said.

"What about Ocho?" Charlie suggested. "How 'bout he goes now and I help you get the crystal ready?"

Ocho shook his head defiantly. "No way, I'm with Eric."

"No matter who goes first, you or me. We're gonna be split up either way," Eric said. "Besides, if you go now, you can get a head start on building that barge. Take Mike and Oliver to tear down that fence down there."

Ocho reluctantly agreed and began suiting up for his descent. "Be careful," he said as he stepped over the edge.

"It's just Kurt and Charlie. What could happen?" Eric replied confidently. He stepped nearer to the edge, watching his friend sink further away. "You're nearly there," called Eric. "Almost to the overhang."

Ocho looked up at Eric, grinning nervously, and gave a thumbs-up. To Kurt's surprise, Charlie raced up behind Eric and shoved him over the edge.

"No!" shouted Kurt. "What did you do?"

The hoist surged, but remained securely anchored. Kurt quickly locked the winch and ran to peer over the edge. Ocho clung to the rock face with all his might, his heels locked firmly to their holds in the cliff. His right hand grasped the cable while his trembling three-fingered left hand clawed desperately into Eric's pant leg just above the ankle. Eric's loose-fitting jeans slowly peeled down his hips and left him dangling upside-down. Terrified and swinging lightly, Eric looked ahead at the vertiginous ground below as a swarming flock of birds flew out in droves from the cliff wall, swooping and wheeling.

"Hold on!" cried Kurt, racing to reel them up.

"He's slipping!" grunted Ocho. Unable to maintain his precarious grip, Eric slipped from Ocho's weakened fingers, hurtling toward the ground. Ocho cried out, "Eric!"

The fluttering black mass of hundreds of squeaking birds suddenly swooped in, completely enveloping Eric. Engulfed by their flapping feathery wings, the swarm carried him swiftly up to the cave. From within the tumultuous cloud of pounding wings and swirling downy feathers, Eric lunged angrily at Charlie. Grabbing him by the jacket, they tumbled into the rear wall of the cave and vanished. The wall rippled like a pebble on water for several seconds before returning to its solid state.

Astonished, Kurt ran to the edge and shouted to his friends below, "They're gone!"

"What?" called Ocho.

Kurt glanced around the cave, shouting, "Charlie, Eric, the crystal. Gone!"

"Pull me up, quick!" Ocho shouted.

255

# Chapter Thirty-three

Mike paced frantically, asking Tuwa, "What the hell just happened? Did I see that right? Was Eric really saved by those birds?"

Watching the wheeling swarm swooping and turning throughout the canyon and finally returning to their nests, Tuwa shook his head in amazement. "He truly is special, isn't he?"

"Apparently so," said Mike.

Nearly three-hundred feet above them, Ocho paced frantically around the shallow cave, asking, "What happened here?"

Shaking his head, Kurt stammered, bewildered, "Charlie just—from outta nowhere—pushed Eric over!"

"That son-of-a-bitch!" Ocho shouted angrily, slamming his fist into the cave's rear wall. "Where did they go?"

Kurt pointed at the sandstone wall, now spattered with blood from Ocho's hand. "Through there. To where, I don't know."

"Maybe back to the slot canyon?"

Baffled, Kurt just shrugged.

Ocho examined his bleeding knuckles. He turned his attention back to the rear wall of the cave and noticed the faint etching of Spider Rock. "There!" he exclaimed.

Just a few miles further up the canyon, Charlie and Eric tumbled across the uneven ground atop the lower of the two spires of Spider Rock. Six-hundred feet above the canyon floor, too involved in the fray to be aware of just where they were, the two fought and wrestled dangerously close to the edge of the narrow, subsidiary summit.

Falling backwards onto the hard ground, Charlie kicked with both legs and connected with Eric's chest, sending him reeling. Tumbling backwards several feet across the crest, Eric slammed forcefully into a large protrusion of rock, which, luckily, kept him from plummeting into the deep cleft that divided the two towers. Before he could recover, Charlie was on him, knocking him to the ground and pounding him with a flurry of fists. Blocking as many blows as he could with his left arm, Eric struggled to retrieve the war club Ocho had given him from his belt loop. Freeing the weapon, he swung awkwardly, smashing Charlie's left shoulder. Charlie shrieked as he fell off of him. Eric pounced, pinning Charlie to the ground. As Eric raised his club, his fiery eyes seemed to burn holes through Charlie's hardened front. Gritting his teeth angrily, he swung the club with all his strength at Charlie's twisted face.

"Please don't kill me!" Charlie cried.

Eric changed his aim mid-swing, striking the ground mere inches from Charlie's left ear. Flecks of stone pelted the side of his face with stinging force. Eric growled, "Are you afraid to die?"

Charlie squirmed, begging again, "Please, Eric. Please don't kill me."

Eric tightened his grip on Charlie's jacket and pulled him closer asking, "Why are *you* afraid to die? Everyone wants to go to heaven, huh? Just not today?"

Charlie began to sob. Tightly gripping the leather-bound handle, Eric brandished the club in Charlie's face, and through his clenched teeth warned him sternly, "Don't come after me again." His chest pounding, and body weakened and jittery by the receding waves of adrenaline, Eric climbed to his feet and staggered to the other edge of the peak. He dropped to the ground sitting with his back against the protruding rock, and composed himself. He was shocked at how close he had actually come to killing another human being—though he felt it would have been justified. He threw his head back and sighed. Recognizing the vertex of the nearby spire rising some two-hundred feet above them, he smiled, relieved. Pointing to the summit, he called out, "Charlie, we're nearly there."

Charlie looked up at the tower and grumbled, "Pagan steeple." He rose, surveying the distant, eroded ground below and sneered, "Babylon the Great." He carefully kneeled at the edge and leaned out, looking down the sheer side of the perpendicular tower.

"Oh, perfect. This is great. Just great. How are we going to get down from here? Eric, how do we get down?"

Eric smirked slyly, resting his hand on the giant crystal and pointing to the higher summit. "The real question is, how are going to get this up there?"

Cautiously Charlie approached, imploring, "Eric, you have to listen to me. We can't go any further. You must not stop Armageddon."

Irritated, Eric snapped impatiently, "Are you still on about that crap?"

"You really must stop," Charlie said. "Can't you see that you have been fooled by Ocho and Tuwa's pagan magic? Can't you see the unholy power being used all around you? It's just as I was told."

"Told? By who? What were you told?"

Charlie explained, "When you were all spirited away on the devil's errand, I was approached by a horrible, leperous Indian man, like the one that attacked Mike and Truman, and allegedly murdered Sean."

"*Allegedly? Devil's errand?*" Eric demanded, repudiating Charlie's choice of words.

Charlie continued unwaveringly, "He was a frightening creature. He raced toward me deliberately—menacingly, it seemed. I thought he was going to kill me. I begged him not to kill me."

"Really? You?" Eric jeered.

Unfazed, Charlie continued, "To my surprise, he pleaded with me to help end *his* suffering."

Eric gaped in shock at what he was hearing. "What the hell are you talking about?"

"He told me how he was driven by demons, cursed to wander in his crazed state, a slave to the will of a mind not his own. He told me the only way the demons could be cast out of him, and others like him, is to be cleansed by Jehovah's judgment—the judgment to come from the Armageddon that is upon us. He told me that you were bewitched and being tricked into using magic stones that will keep Armageddon from occurring here. That you have been fooled by a pagan deity into believing that by bringing her that crystal, you will help restore and preserve the land from the coming Armageddon."

"What the hell are you talking about?" Eric shouted angrily. "Can you hear yourself? I would totally expect to hear you spout some bullshit about an angel appearing to you, but you tried to kill me because a man 'driven by demons' told you to stop me?"

"It's not that strange if you think about it," Charlie said. "Death is evil's salvation just like the paradisiacal earth to come is ours. As strange as it may sound, people like him and Witnesses who obey the Truth have a shared interest."

"*It's not that strange if you think about it?*" Eric repeated in an agitated shriek. "You openly refer to yourself as a 'sheep' like it's a good thing. Blindly following an autocratic doctrine that condemns independent thought. Yet you always find a way to think in circles and twist logic to fit your narrow, theocratic views!"

"That's the black magic speaking through you!" Charlie shouted. "It's the same evil that pulled you from the Truth, you goat!"

"You want to talk about black magic? You've seen what those skinwalkers can do. What they did to Sean. I've seen one of those demons run hundreds of feet straight up the sheer side of this rock and fly away like a bird…"

Charlie interrupted, arguing, "And I've seen you defy gravity with the aid of spells that control the birds. You have clearly sided with the devil."

Angrily, Eric shot to his feet, pointing the club at Charlie, "You want to know the way down?" He backed him against the edge, growling, "I'm through talking to you."

"Ocho?" Kurt called. "Ocho, where'd you go?"

"Hmm? What?" Ocho said, blinking open his eyes and looking around in confusion.

"We were talking," Kurt said, "trying to figure out what to do from here, and you just sort of shut down."

"Spider Rock," Ocho said determinedly, pointing at the faded glyph. "I was trying to teleport us there, but it's not working. We're gonna have to hoof it." He hurried to suit up in the tow strap and clipped it to the cable. "Kurt, lower me down, okay?" Kurt nodded and raced to the hoist. Ocho stepped over the edge, saying, "Spider Rock. Get to Spider Rock."

From below, Mike, Oliver, and Tuwa watched Ocho descend against a darkening sky brewing with bulging clouds. The slow rumble of thunder rolled through the canyon. Blinking out the windblown sand, they struggled to keep their eyes fixed on their friend as he approached, nearing closer and closer to the ground. The second he landed, they ran to Ocho, helping him out of the strap.

"What's happening?" Mike asked excitedly.

Ocho stepped out of the harness, "We gotta get to Spider Rock as fast as we can. Kurt will catch up."

"Follow me," said Oliver, heading immediately for the confluence of Canyon de Chelly and Monument canyons.

Ocho followed briskly behind him, his bow and arrows jostling on his back. After several quick strides, he stopped abruptly. Frantically, almost in a panic, he removed his belt and large bowie knife, tossing them to the ground at his feet. He stood silently, swaying slightly with his fluttering eyelids loosely closed.

The others stopped and returned to him. Concerned, Mike asked, "Ocho, are you okay?"

Ocho heaved over, his hands scraping against the jagged rocks. In an instant he was completely transformed into the large, white wolf. Frightened and unsure of their safety, Mike scrambled to snatch up Ocho's belt and knife from the ground. With a scattering of small stones under its enormous paws, the animal tore away from the group, disappearing around a bend ahead of them. With Tuwa waving them on, Oliver and Mike chased after the wolf as swiftly as they could run.

From his perch atop the lower spire at Spider Rock, Eric sat quietly gazing into the crystal, thinking deeply about all that Charlie had said to him. The medicine pouch Tuwa had made for him hung from his neck by its long, braided cord. Eric lifted and examined it. Could it really be that he was bewitched, being manipulated to unwittingly thwart some divine plan? If so, he would heave the Earthkeeper over the edge right now. His stomach twisting, he shuddered at the thought of it.

His mind recalled the years of indoctrination and obtrusive preaching endured throughout his youth. The programming that he intrinsically rejected from the core of his existence seemed to be so fundamentally flawed. The idea that, aside from a very small congregation of righteous, enlightened followers, the rest of the world's peoples and cultures were led astray by a manipulative demonic force had always been difficult for Eric to accept. Even at a very young age, Eric had wondered if this was perhaps the devil's most successful deception. Could such an idea really make so many of the Creator's children unworthy of his love and acceptance?

But now, after years of staunch defiance, he doubted himself. Had the doggedly professed "Truth" that his mother and church had forced on him actually been true all along? Had he been blinded to it? Had he been led astray by an evil incarnate who, for reasons of jealousy and hate or some other ugly ambition, was intent on snatching sheep from God's flock as if a god would cease to exist without believers?

As Eric's mind reeled with such questions, the web of striations and inclusions within the crystal began to form rapidly morphing geometric shapes and fractal patterns similar to those that intrigued him so much as a child when he would lay in bed rubbing his eyes. He focused unblinkingly to the center of the unusual hypnotic display and within seconds his mind was flooded with sensory input. So realistically were his senses fed that, for a moment, he thought he had once again teleported. But he soon realized that he was simultaneously aware of his being seated in front of the crystal watching the patterns flashing within it. He wondered if he might actually be experiencing bilocation— existing in two places at the same time.

Acrid smoke permeated his sense of smell. His ears were filled with screams and cries and the clanging of steel. His split consciousness followed his senses to the maelstrom of a military raid on a small, burning village. Based on the clothing worn by the villagers and the armor and weaponry of the marauding soldiers, Eric quickly realized that the Earthkeeper was showing him scenes from medieval Europe. Every detail was exact to Eric's perception, giving the impression that he was really there. He flinched at an arrow fired in his direction. It passed through him. The villagers fled past him and soldiers advanced, but he remained unnoticed, an invisible, temporal tourist. He was shown the savage beheadings of thousands of people, executed by Christian armies for practicing their pagan religions. He witnessed the brutal torture and execution and burning of people across Europe accused of witchcraft. He was shown a sequence of images of inquisition and torture and forced conversion.

Next, he was transported to observe historical scenes in the Americas to attest to the conquistadors' arrogant judgment and denigration of the Mesoamerican and South American peoples' spiritual beliefs. To them, the native's veneration of the elements of nature was the unnatural worship of the devil. He saw the destruction of historical records spanning centuries, and the obliteration of scientific knowledge that far eclipsed the primitive astronomical understandings that the Church endeavored to squelch in their native European lands. He witnessed the enslavement and slaughter of millions killed in the name of God and greed. The Earthkeeper showed North America and its native inhabitants, forever transformed by the relentless spread of the barbarous West's interpretation and imposition of Judeo-Christian beliefs and values under the ideology of Manifest Destiny. He recalled the unusual vision of his mother among the roots of the ceiba tree, the dreamcatcher necklace hung around her neck.

The piercing cry of a hawk rang out over the canyon calling Eric's attention back to the present. He looked over at Charlie who was sulking at the far edge of the towering rock where he had been commanded to sit quietly.

"I've been thinking about all you've said about my being deceived and being under evil suggestions to serve the wrong side," Eric announced.

Charlie perked up, asking excitedly, "So you know, then?"

Eric nodded, "I do."

Charlie smiled.

"I know that it's not me who is deceived. It's you, and the people like you who have shaped the course of history. You think God wants you to impose an arrogant view that you are superior to anyone who believes differently than you do?"

Charlie became agitated and shot to his feet, arguing, "God had laid out a very specific set of laws and tenets through scripture. It's very clear—those who obey them are saved. Those who don't are damned."

Eric interrupted. "Oh, come on Charlie, there's something like 10,000 distinct religious faiths in the world, and 34,000 denominations of Christianity alone, and every one insists they are true. It's obviously not that clear. Look, you can quote scripture 'til you run out of breath, but it's just circular logic. You're only shaping your own truth by reinterpreting centuries of countless translations and reinterpretations, twisting them yet again to fit your point of view. And no imposed idea is truth. It goes against our free will. Like Ocho says, 'Spiritual understanding should come from within, understood by the spirit.' Truth is something intrinsically understood and felt, and it is as unique and personal as each individual's connection to the source of creation."

"Who's preaching now?" Charlie accused in his mordant voice. Eric had clearly wasted his breath. The whole time he had spoken, Charlie just stared blankly, his eyes showing no indication of registering even one of his words. Eric remembered how implicit and rigid Witnesses were in their belief. How well trained they were to tune out any other theological point of view as being the deceptions of the devil. It was a tactic necessary for one to return from the required door-to-door mission work with their faith intact, endeavoring to remain as closed to outside influence as their windowless worship halls.

Charlie and Eric continued to volley their beliefs at one another, neither successful in affecting the other's point of view,

263

and both completely unaware that five skinwalkers were steadily advancing on Spider Rock, stealthily maneuvering through Canyon de Chelly's off shoots: Monument and Bat canyons.

# Chapter Thirty-four

To pay their respects, Truman, Sheila, and the kids gathered reverently around Jerry's grave to share words of remembrance. Not knowing exactly how to get the ball rolling, they stood quietly for a long while, looking to each other for someone to make a move.

Finally Truman stepped forward. "Aside from what I knew of him back in school, I didn't really know Jerry that long, or as well as I would have liked to. But everything I did know about him really showed what a patient person he was. He was a good moral example, and a kind and encouraging father figure for these kids. But much more than that, I was very glad to learn—just yesterday—what a hopeful outlook he had for the future of humankind, even in these bleak and troubling times. He was a silent philosopher who never quite found his voice. Or, maybe, he just never wanted to press his opinions on anyone. Either way, it's a shame, because we all could've learned quite a bit about ourselves and our human potential through his insights."

"Jerry," Sheila said softly, "you were a good friend and a good provider—respectful, caring, easy going, good with the kids. You were everything I needed. I hope I was enough for you," she said with a faltering voice.

Truman winced as Allison said sweetly, "I'll miss you, Daddy," struggling to choke off the tears behind her puffy, red eyes. She fanned her face with her trembling hands as her tear ducts gave way and gushed forth, her voice breaking down to a quivering squeak as she sobbed, barely saying audibly, "I can't talk any more."

Aaron stepped forward, his left eye still enormously dilated, his body weak and achy from the jolt of lightning. He fidgeted awkwardly. Not knowing what to do with his hands, he dug his thumbnails deeply under the nails of each of his fingers as he murmured, "Jerry was always really nice." Nervously, he slid his hands into his pants pockets and continued, "He took me places and, like, asked how I was doing and stuff, and um, yeah..." He stepped back, looking at his father.

Truman laid his hand on Aaron's shoulder with a reassuring smile. Aaron whispered, "I thought I saw Jerry standing over there, but I don't know; the light is so bright in my eye."

Truman visually studied the area where Aaron said he had seen Jerry, then gently squeezed Aaron's shoulder, saying softly, "It's alright buddy, your eye is just letting in too much light. I'm sure it'll go down soon." He looked back to the pile of rocks that entombed the body and said, "Rest well, Jerry."

Together, the family worked to fold the blankets and break down their camp. Truman noticed Sheila's frequent and nervous glances, clearly wanting to say something but remaining quiet and unsure. "Hey kids, why don't you take all this stuff down the hill and load it into the bike trailer for me?" He watched the kids make their way down the trail out of earshot and quietly said, "Talk to me, Sheila."

"I'm just so scared," she gasped.

Truman's lips curved into a slight, reassuring smile. "It's gonna be alright," he said.

"Jerry was a really good friend," she said. "He took real good care of us." She looked away shyly, saying, "But I never stopped loving you."

"Oh, Sheila, no need for all that," Truman said dryly. "You'll be taken care of out here."

Embarrassed and offended, she looked Truman in the eyes, insisting, "I said it 'cause it's true."

Truman was taken aback. "I'm sorry," he stammered. "You're the mother of my kids, and you were once very special to me. There is a love I will always have for you. You can't just turn that kind of thing off, you know. So I understand what you're saying. But somewhere along the way, you made it very clear to me that the person I was becoming was not who you wanted to share your life with. I got it loud and clear."

Sheila opened her mouth to retort, but Truman talked over her. "But the person you rejected is who I really am," he continued. "And, you know, you're not the person you used to be either. If the people we are today were meeting for the first time, we wouldn't stand a chance of hitting it off. We can't change who we are. There's no point in living a life that's not our own, not being who we're meant to be."

Sheila turned away to hide her tears. Truman asserted, "Look, whatever happens, we have those two beautiful kids to love and take care of. I'm here to do that. And I'll take care of you too, so there's nothing to be afraid of."

"Except for being alone," she said sadly.

"Well, whatever," Truman said unemotionally. "We better get moving if we're gonna make any time." Within minutes, they were pedaling down the desolate highway.

They traveled for hours in complete silence. Late into the afternoon Truman veered off to the dirt shoulder and coasted to a stop, the others filing in behind him. "We'd best not push it, as tired and sore as everybody is," he said. Surveying the wide valley to the south of the road, he pointed far out saying, "You guys see those antelope down there?"

"No way! Where?" Aaron asked excitedly.

Truman leaned close to his son, allowing Aaron to look down the sight of his arm as he pointed. "You see 'em?"

"Yeah, cool."

"We'll park the bikes down there in that coulee," Truman said, dismounting his bike and readying his rifle. "I want you guys to set up camp around that bend out of sight. I'm gonna take this opportunity to stock up our food supply." Without another word, he was swiftly and stealthily making his way across the valley.

"Wait a minute, what's he doing?" Allison asked. "Is he going to shoot one of those poor creatures? Hasn't he seen enough death?"

Impatiently, Sheila griped, "Oh, Allie, give it a rest will you? We gotta eat something, don't we?"

Allison paced frantically. "I can't believe he's going to make me a part of this. Oh my God! This is not happening. I told him how I feel about this."

Ignoring her, Sheila walked her bike down the hill and into the coulee, calling back, "Come on kids, you heard your father." Aaron followed after her, carefully negotiating the slope. Reaching the bottom, his mother ordered, "Go and get Dad's bike, will you?"

Aaron nodded and started immediately back for the highway. He arrived at the road in time to see his sister racing her bike as fast as she could back in the direction they had come from. "Allie!" he shouted, just as she rounded a bend and disappeared from sight. Aaron scrambled down the hill, screaming, "Mom, Allie's leaving!"

Sheila bounded up the hill. Mounting Truman's bike, she struggled to maintain balance as she set off, her feet barely touching the pedals from its high seat. Aaron followed, struggling to drag his bike up the hill. By the time he reached the road to chase after them, he was far behind.

Several miles down the road, Sheila caught up with her sobbing daughter who had thrown her bike down and climbed onto a rocky ledge on the sheer side of a large hill that had been blasted and sliced through for the construction of the highway. Sheila nearly toppled over as she climbed down from Truman's oversized bicycle. She climbed up to Allison and wrapped her arms around her. "It's okay, baby," she said.

"I just want to go home," sobbed Allison. "I want everything to go back to the way it was."

"I know. I know," said her mother sweetly as she gently patted the girl's back.

"I was going to get to drive this year, and go to prom, and God only know what's happened to all of my friends," she cried.

"I know," Sheila said, trying to comfort her.

"And I *so* miss indoor plumbing," Allison said with a voice half laughing, half crying. "We girls just weren't meant to live this way."

"Believe me, I know," Sheila said emphatically, chuckling.

"Everything feels like such a horrible dream. I keep trying to wake up. Is this all really happening? Is Daddy really dead?"

Tears rolling down her cheeks, Sheila squeezed Allison tightly. "I'm afraid so, honey." She gently rocked her daughter for a while, then pulled back to look her in the eyes. "And if we're gonna survive this, you're gonna really need to cut your father some slack. He's the best chance we have."

"I know," said Allison, "but I can't figure out why he came back at all. Just to satisfy his conscience or something?"

Sheila shook her head insistently. "No. He came for you kids because he cares about you. He loves you very much."

"And because he still loves you too?"

Sheila hung her head sadly. "He cares about all of us."

Her emotions controlled, Allison sniffed and looked up at the late-afternoon sky. Cloud-splotched and set ablaze with rich hues of yellow, vermillion, and violet, the deep blue skies beyond were alive with multicolored ribbons dancing in the higher atmosphere. "It just blows my mind, how something so beautiful can cause such devastation."

Sheila looked up with teary eyes, sharing in Allison's awe of the dazzling firmament. "It's so beautiful..."

"Something good has to come of it," added Allison.

They both were suddenly jolted, startled by a deep, gravely voice booming down from above them. "Well, what do we have here?"

Standing at the top of the blasted hill looking down on them was McFarlane, the mustached war veteran that Truman and Jerry had encountered a day earlier. Across the highway, standing on the opposing hill, was another scruffy man, tall and barrel-chested with an assault rifle slung over his shoulder. Closing in on them from either side of the road below were the rest of the gang, six of them, their sartorial style favoring camouflage patterns and Mossy Oak hunter's apparel.

Among them was the skittish young man who had been present the day before. He looked nervous and hesitant as he approached, trying not to appear obvious in his struggle to keep from staring at Allison.

"Come on down, ladies," one of the men said. Unsure about what the men wanted, and whether or not they were in danger, Sheila and Allison held hands and timidly made their way down.

McFarlane quickly negotiated the steep hill, joining them on the road soon after. "Long way from home, huh, girls?" he said.

Sheila nodded.

"What are you doing out here?"

"Surviving, same as you," she said. "After Kingman was destroyed by an earthquake and fire, we came this way."

"Kingman, huh?" said McFarlane interestedly.

"You're the first people we've seen alive since we left," offered Allison.

"Where are the rest of your people?" he asked.

"Nearby."

"Oh yeah?"

Sheila nodded.

"We've gotten reports that all the nearby towns and cities have been either severely damaged or completely destroyed with heavy casualties. Unbelievable casualties," the man said matter-of-factly. "And it seems that Mother Nature doesn't plan to let up anytime soon."

"We're under that impression too," Sheila said.

His attention piqued, he asked, "Yeah? So what do you plan to do, then?"

"Hunker down in the high country and survive it."

McFarlane's wrinkly crow's feet stretched at the corners of his eyes as his leathery face formed a toothy grin that peeked out from under his bushy, gray mustache. "Really? Perfect."

Sheila's face screwed with a dubious expression.

Immediately sensing her skittish distrust, McFarlane hastily moved to put her at ease. Clearing his throat and using a smooth reassuring voice, he explained, "It's just that that's what we're doing out here too. We've been preparing for these times for quite a while, actually. We have a well-fortified complex not far from here, where we can ride this out for quite a time. Even use it as a secure base to rebuild a civilized society. We got adequate food stores and a garden. Does that sound interesting to you?"

Sheila and Allison smiled and nodded fervidly, like the glib people shown in cutaway audience shots on infomercials. Pleased by their reactions, McFarlane grinned widely.

From the hill above, a gruff voice called out, "Someone coming, sir! A kid on a bike."

"He's my son!" Sheila shouted.

"At ease, Benson," ordered McFarlane.

Aaron pedaled exhaustedly up the road. Huffing, he dropped his bike and latched his arms around his mother's waist, resting his head on her shoulder. "Everything okay, Mom?"

Sheila nodded, smiling, and squeezed him tightly. "These nice men have invited us to set up a permanent camp at their fort."

Aaron jerked his head to look at her sharply, asking, "But what about Dad's plan?"

"I'm sure your dad will agree that this is too good an opportunity to pass up." Sheila turned her attention to McFarlane, explaining, "Their father is a few miles further up the road right now, hunting."

"Ah, resourceful," said McFarlane. "Sounds like just the kind of man we could use."

"Oh, absolutely," said Sheila.

McFarlane removed his cap to scratch his head and looked up at the dimming sky. "I'll tell you what, it's gonna be dark soon. Why don't you ladies head back to the fort with us, so you can get set up and meet the others. I'll have a couple of my men take your son back to find and bring in your husband."

"Oh, he's not my…" Sheila stopped herself and nodded.

"Alright then," McFarlane smiled. "Rogers, Kilgore, take this boy to find his dad.

Aaron nervously pulled his mother close and whispered, "What if these are the people Dad and Jerry ran into last night?"

Shaking her head insistently, Sheila answered softly, "Your dad said the men they met were creepy. I don't get that vibe at all. These people are ordered and prepared. They're building a community, and without that, I don't know that I even want to survive out here."

Listening intently, McFarlane restrained his smirk, barely curling at the corner of his mouth.

271

Seeing peculiar dark and jagged halos around McFarlane and his men, Aaron squinted his dilated eye as he suspiciously looked them over. "Mom, I'm scared, I don't want to go with those men," he whispered.

Having overheard the boy, McFarlane called out, "Bobby."

The teenaged member of the outfit stepped forward, replying, "Yes sir?"

Allison smiled shyly at the young man and quickly looked away.

Aaron flinched as McFarlane extended his hand toward him to lay his hand on his head and muss his shaggy hair. McFarlane said, "Maybe you'll feel better if my son, Bobby, goes with you, huh? He's closer to your age."

"That's a great idea," Sheila said enthusiastically. "That'll work. Right, Aaron?"

Aaron shrugged his shoulders ambivalently.

"Great then," said McFarlane. "Bobby and Kilgore here will go with you to find your dad." He put his arm around Bobby and shepherded his son away from the group. "Get rid of him," he whispered gruffly.

Shocked and uncertain, the horrified Bobby looked at his father. "What?"

McFarlane pinched his son's shoulder tightly, answering sternly, "You heard me. Kilgore will take care of the dad."

# Chapter Thirty-five

Aaron pushed his bike along the highway with Bobby walking along beside him, the two seldom speaking. Following a short distance behind them was Kilgore, McFarlane's large, intensely focused and eerily silent right-hand man. His stomach bound in knots, Bobby was nervous and conflicted about his father's orders, but afraid of the consequences should he disappoint him.

His father had always been a hard man to please. Critical and demanding, he expected things of Bobby that were beyond his age and maturity, beyond his grasp of reason, and conflicting with his intrinsic sense of right and wrong. By five years of age, McFarlane had Bobby hunting, gutting and skinning game animals, and enduring extreme survival and combat training. By twelve, the home-schooled Bobby was taught to make pipe bombs and other improvised explosive devices.

Prone to longwinded and vehement conspiracy and anti-government rants, his expatriate father became involved with militia groups in response to the anti-gun movements of the eighties. Originally organizing and participating in public protests and demonstrations, he had taken to laying low by the early nineties, stockpiling weapons, explosives, and other supplies. For McFarlane, it had been a time for preparing for combat against the totalitarian regime he believed would soon clamp an iron lid on what he believed were God given freedoms.

Obsessively suspicious of the government in more recent years, McFarlane and his group had bought into rumors of the nationwide transport and stockpiling of millions of molded plastic coffins. They were convinced of what they called FEMA Trains: abundant stores of empty, vented rail cars stretching for miles on unused portions of railways throughout the United States. He and his group believed that the government, puppeteered by the elitist secret sect, the New World Order, planned to use the coffins and cars for the mass disposal of the millions of people who would be killed by the intentional release of deadly flu strains in an effort to better control a thinned world population. For the last few years, Bobby was made to stand for hours alongside the tracks, video camera in hand, to record the suspicious trains and post the footage on the internet, while his father's outfit trekked into the wilderness to plan and fortify their retreat from the blinded, bleating sheep of conformed society.

By thirteen, Bobby had begun to question his father's doctrines, and had misgivings about his mental soundness. In the days after the solar flares, Bobby was shocked to realize the horrific truth of what his father and the others were capable of.

Coming to an abrupt halt, Aaron dropped his bike on the pavement. His head pounding, and body aching, he bent over, bracing his weight with his hands on his knees. Cold beads of sweat appeared on his forehead, and his mouth flooded with salty saliva.

"You okay?" asked Bobby.

Spitting the excess fluid from his mouth, Aaron answered with a shaking of his head. Bobby and Kilgore watched as Aaron wrestled his urge to vomit. After several minutes, he rose, saying, "I'm alright." Bobby picked up the bike, and they continued on their way.

"You sure you're alright?" Bobby asked again.

Aaron nodded, "Just real achy, and kinda nauseous."

"Have you had enough water today?"

"I think so," said Aaron, "I'm just still kinda messed up from getting hit by lightning last night."

"What? Really?" asked Bobby.

"Yeah, I guess I'm lucky to be alive?"

Nervous and ashamed, Bobby looked away, his eyes darting anxiously across the darkening sky, spotted with high clouds and rolling waves of color. He glanced at the stone-faced Kilgore. "Yeah, I guess we all are," he said. "Wow, I've never known anyone who's been struck by lightning."

"Well, I wasn't hit directly. It hit my step dad first and killed him," Aaron said sadly. "Then it came through the wet ground and hit me and my dad."

"Your mom, your step dad, and your dad?" asked Bobby, surprised. "You're all out here together?"

Aaron nodded, "And my sister. We all came together from Kingman."

Bobby pieced together that Aaron's step dad and father must be the men they had encountered the evening of the previous day, but said nothing about it. He glanced back at Kilgore, who was again trailing several paces behind them, and wondered if the man had heard and put it together as well.

"Yeah, that's right, your sister," said Bobby. "I forgot about her."

"No you didn't," teased Aaron. "I saw the way you were looking at her."

Bobby's cheeks flushed and his lips curved into a slight, embarrassed smile which quickly faded upon remembering his orders. They walked another fifteen minutes in silence when Aaron stopped abruptly and looked strangely at Bobby.

"What?" Bobby asked. "What are you looking at?"

Aaron squinted. His eyes slightly crossed as he looked seemingly through Bobby. He scanned the area ahead and the area on the other side of him. Blinking several times, as if responding to a foreign particle in his eye, he mumbled, "Whoa, weird."

"What?" asked Bobby.

"It's just weird," said Aaron. "There was just a woman walking on the other side of you. When she saw me looking at her, she came toward me, trying to tell me something, and then started to fade. The more I looked at her, the harder she was to see, until she was...just... gone."

Bobby looked around in confusion. Seeing no sign of anyone having been there, he looked to Kilgore, who smirked smugly and shook his head. Bobby whirled back, inspecting the area once again. "I don't see anything," he said.

Frustrated, Aaron sighed, "Oh, I don't know. Maybe it's just my eye playing tricks on me again."

"What'dya mean, 'your eye?'" asked Bobby.

Aaron leaned in close, peeling his eyelids wide to give Bobby a better look at his dilated eye.

"Oh, okay," said Bobby softly. "I thought all this time you had two different colored eyes, but your left eye is just really dilated."

"Yeah, it's been like that since the lightning strike," said Aaron.

"No kidding."

"Yeah, it's weird. It's been really bright on that side. Gives me a really bad headache right behind my eye there, like, right behind my eyebrow bone. I've been seeing light around people too—like halos, almost, but different colors. And I've been seeing people that aren't there, too. I kept seeing my step dad standing there after we buried him. Now this lady."

Bobby started the group walking again. "What'd she look like?"

"I dunno, kinda heavy. But not really fat, just big," Aaron explained. He pulled the top of his shaggy hair back, away from his face, holding it in a loose ponytail in the back of his head, and continued, "She had long, reddish-brown hair with lots of gray streaks in it, pulled back kinda like this. White, freckly skin. Long, blue, denim skirt and a pink shirt with puffy sleeves. And she was wearing white tennie shoes. It was like she was trying to show me something. A bottle of pills or something."

Bobby became agitated. His cheeks flushed red, and his eyebrows furled downward.

"What's wrong?" asked Aaron.

"Sounds like my mom," Bobby said. "The way she was dressed, that's just how I remember her."

"You okay?" Aaron asked. "Now you look like you're gonna throw up."

"I'm okay," said Bobby calmly. "It's just that she died when I was twelve."

Aaron stammered, "Well, it's probably just my eye acting up. I've been seeing all kinds of strange stuff."

"I don't know," said Bobby. "It can't be a coincidence. What you described is much too specific to be a coincidence. No, there's more to it than that. That's my mom to a tee. All the way down to the bottle of pills."

Aaron was anxious and confused about what all this could mean. Was he seeing the ghosts of people who had passed? The thought of seeing ghosts was unnerving, but not frightening. After all, he had experienced stranger, more terrifying intrusions. He was actually quite intrigued. He asked, "Why would she show me a bottle of medicine? What's up with that?"

Bobby fidgeted. "Phew, this is really difficult. It was suicide. She swallowed a bottle of pills. I found her crumpled on the bathroom floor, wearing clothes like you described."

Aaron's eyes darted around nervously. "Whoa, I'm sorry," he said. "I didn't know."

"It's okay," said Bobby softly, looking at the ground as he walked. "What was she trying to tell you?"

"Aw, come on, Bobby, you're not really buying this crap, are you?" Kilgore grunted.

Bobby stopped and turned to face him. "Uh, yes, sir, I am. I mean, how could he just make all that up?" He continued walking. "What was she trying to say?" he asked Aaron softly.

"I'm not sure," Aaron said. "It was all so weird and broken up. Something about a boy. Saving a boy? Only the boy could save the boy or something like that."

Confounded, Bobby worked his mind to decipher the meaning of it.

"Bobby," grunted Kilgore, "Quit talking. We got a job to do, remember?"

Together, they walked in silence for another ten minutes or so, when Aaron recognized the way down to the coulee where they were to have made camp. Pointing across the rapidly darkening valley, Aaron explained, "My dad set off that way to hunt antelope."

Kilgore scanned the valley through a small pair of binoculars until he found Truman kneeling on the ground in the distance. He finished dressing out his kill and rose, heaving the limp animal up over his shoulder. He stooped to retrieve his rifle from its prop against a straggly, dead tree.

Kilgore readied his rifle. "Don't do it until you hear me fire," he told Bobby sternly then made his way to stalk Truman from the rocky formations that framed the south side of the valley.

"Don't do what?" Aaron asked nervously.

Bobby paced erratically, his cheeks flushed rosy red. He unslung the rifle from his shoulder and, with trembling hands, pointed it at Aaron's chest.

Aaron's heart raced and he felt faint. "Why?" he asked, fearfully. "What'd I do?"

Struggling to control his shaking, Bobby tensed his body and gritted his teeth. "Quick, down there," he ordered, motioning to the coulee. He trailed Aaron down the hill, careful not to slip on the loose rocks. "Against the wall, there," commanded Bobby, tears rolling quietly down his cheeks.

Frightened, Aaron walked as ordered into a level area surrounded on three sides by steeply sloping, fifteen-foot, rocky walls. Bobby trained his rifle on the center of Aaron's back, listening carefully for the sound of Kilgore's gunfire. Tears streamed from Aaron's eyes as he stood facing the bluff, his back to Bobby.

The apparition of Jerry inexplicably materialized before him. "Don't be afraid," Jerry said. "Turn and face him."

Hesitantly, Aaron turned.

"Hey! Don't move!" ordered Bobby.

"Do it. Face him," coached Jerry.

Through his tears, Bobby struggled to look down the sight of his rifle into Aaron's weary, fear-stricken eyes. The ghost of Bobby's mother again appeared between them. Her hand clenched in a tight fist, she bit her knuckle. She sobbed to Aaron, "Save my boy."

Jerry approached his stepson from behind and placed his hands on his shoulders, filling the boy with a calmness and fortitude he had never known.

Aaron looked directly into Bobby's eyes, pleading, "Bobby, don't do this. You're not a killer."

Bobby began to waver, but his fear of his father won out. He could almost hear the old man's usual shameful and derisive taunts, "Toughen up you little wuss, be a man." Keeping the rifle trained on Aaron, Bobby wrenched his neck and shoulder to wipe his tears with his sleeve. "I'm sorry. You seem like a cool kid, but I have my orders. Now turn around," demanded Bobby.

"Bobby…"

"Shut up!" he growled through clinched teeth. He wiped the last of his tears and snorted heavily, pointing the rifle at Aaron's face. "Turn around!"

"I won't turn around," Aaron said sternly. "If you're gonna shoot me, you're gonna have to look at me."

Truman traversed the barren valley back toward camp with the lifeless antelope slung over his shoulder, unaware that he was centered in the crosshairs of Kilgore's high-powered rifle scope. Positioned in a rocky outcropping nearly five-hundred yards away, Kilgore steadied his weapon, calculating all the variables, waiting for his moment. Stopping briefly to catch his breath, Truman admired the beautiful, fiery sunset blazing in the western sky.

"Gotcha," muttered Kilgore in a gravelly voice.

Suddenly, a crackling gunshot echoed through the air in the split second before Kilgore squeezed his trigger. Surprised, Truman jerked his head to locate the direction of the sound as Kilgore's rifle rang out.

"Dammit!" grunted Kilgore, the recoil tingling in his hands. His shot pierced the meaty hindquarter of the antelope carcass, grazing the fleshy muscle of Truman's upper arm as the bullet exited the animal.

Truman threw himself behind a small slope, the only cover nearby, and cast the animal aside. Panting heavily, he pressed himself low to the ground behind his inadequate cover and examined his stinging arm. Another shot rang out, hitting the berm and scattering dirt and flecks of stone over Truman's head. He spit the dirt from his mouth, the gritty particles crunching between his teeth, and scooted further down the slope. Carefully, he wrenched his neck upward to inspect the scattered earth to determine the angle and direction of the shooter. He scanned his rapidly

279

darkening surroundings for better cover, trying desperately to formulate a plan to turn the tables on his unidentified adversary.

Nearly a hundred miles to the east, bulging, gray thunderheads rumbled and heaved, coalescing into an enormous storm in the skies above Spider Rock. Howling winds whipped through the canyon, further darkening the skies with a haze of dust and sand. Squinting and blinking the dirt from his eyes, Mike shielded them with his arm and leaned into the wind, trudging exhaustedly through the thick sand banks that lined the canyon floor. "I've lost the tracks!" he shouted.

"I can't see a thing!" Oliver replied in frustration as he frantically searched the ground. "Not a damn thing!"

The skies grew darker. "How much further to Spider Rock?" called Mike.

"We could be there now for all I know," shouted Oliver.

"Dammit, Ocho, where are you?" Mike hissed.

As if in response to Mike's query, the resounding, haunting howl of a wolf called them on.

"This way," called Mike excitedly.

Lightning branched across the sky, intermittently illuminating the canyon with blue flashes. In the quick stroboscopic light, eerie, unnatural movement creeping up behind Oliver caught Mike's eye. With the next flash, Mike made out the image of the skinwalker with five red slashes painted on its face raising a bone dagger.

"Duck!" shouted Mike.

Oliver dropped to the ground and rolled away as Mike threw Ocho's knife, placing all his hope that whatever forces of good existed might guide the point to its target. The knife tumbled point over handle through the air. With a hollow thwump, the heavy blade sank deep into the center of the ghoul's forehead. The skinwalker fell backwards to the ground. Bones crunched as Mike stepped down on the painted face and used all his strength to jerk the giant knife from the skull.

"Like Arthur pulling the sword from the stone!" cheered Oliver.

Mike was suddenly sick. Feeling faint, he swayed on wobbly knees. "I've never killed anything before," he murmured in a stunned, monotone voice. "Not even a bug."

"But what you did—killing that witch—was the right thing. A good thing," explained Oliver. He stood over the body, surprised how little blood seeped from the mortal wound. "There's nothing to feel bad about," he said. "He's far from human, and he would've killed us both for sure."

"I'd better finish it," said Mike half-heartedly, "before the demon escapes through the top of the head." He reluctantly jabbed through the throat and began to saw the witch's head off, at first having difficulty guiding the blade between the vertebrae. His fingers wrapped tightly in the skinwalker's matted black hair, Mike held the severed head outstretched to keep the goopy blood from dripping on him as he carried it to a nearby juniper and wedged it into the gnarled branches.

"You all right?" asked Oliver.

Mike nodded. "I feel a lot better about it. I know I'd do it all again if I had to."

"Well, you just may," said Oliver, searching the ground for a branch thick and dry enough to be used as an effective weapon.

As Mike scanned the flickering darkness for further danger, the clouds burst opened and poured cold rain over them, instantly cleaning the dust from the air. Not too far away, looming above them, the flashing lightning revealed the dark, silhouetted shape of Spider Rock. The two towers rose from the canyon floor like unlit skyscrapers over a desolate avenue.

"Now we can see better without all the dirt in our eyes," Oliver said happily.

"But it's gonna be harder to hear anyone sneaking up on us," Mike complained. "Let's keep our wits about us. It seems like nature is against us."

As abruptly as it began, the rain ceased, leaving only the occasional sound of droplets splattering on the rocks as they fell from the tree limbs, and the musky smell of wet sage wafting on the humid breeze.

"Then again…," uttered Oliver.

The thick, gray clouds above them retreated, revealing a waning gibbous moon against a gap of clear, shimmering sky.

"Oh, thank God!" Mike rejoiced as the moonlight bathed their surroundings with a faint, bluish glow. Low to the ground, from the dark shadows within a cluster of junipers, two sets of gleaming eyes peered out at them. Nervously, Mike whispered to Oliver, "We're not alone."

Wide-eyed, they stared into the darkness, straining to make out the shapes of the bodies the eyes were attached to. The eyes crept toward them. Stepping slowly into the pale light, two coyotes stood rigid, looking menacingly at Oliver and Mike.

"Why do I have such a creepy feeling?" asked Mike, tightly gripping the bloody knife.

"Me too," said Oliver, standing at the ready with his heavy, wooden cudgel.

The coyotes' ears perked and twitched sharply, caught by a distant sound inaudible to the humans. They scampered away, disappearing into the darkness.

It was eerily silent. No crickets. No night birds. Just the soft susurration of the distant babbling creek, swelled with rainwater.

"Where do you suppose Eric even is?" asked Oliver.

Mike glanced around in the dark. "No idea. Ocho seemed pretty certain he'd be here somewhere. He could have made it to the tiptop of Spider Rock for all we know. After all, he did teleport from the canyon wall."

"Well, at the risk of drawing unwanted attention to ourselves, we could call out for him," suggested Oliver.

Mike nodded. Searching the area at the base of the monument, they called loudly, "Eric! Eric, where are you?"

# Chapter Thirty-six

Far behind the others, Tuwa made his way slowly in the dark through the wide canyon. The old man's body ached with each lumbering step. The moist air was still and quiet. Tuwa glanced up at the glimmering moon surrounded on all sides by ominous clouds that advanced slowly on invisible currents, threatening to once again squelch the dim light.

The shrill squeaking of a nighthawk rang out, startling Tuwa. The bent-winged bird flopped erratically, calling loudly as it circled the old man. He thought about the meaning of this unusual portent. Could it be a sentinel sounding an alarm, alerting his presence to dark forces? Could it be just the opposite? He looked up again to draw clues from the moon, encircled and threatened by clouds. He dug hastily through his satchel. Chanting prayers, he hurried to cast a protective circle of corn pollen and hunkered down, hoping Kurt wasn't too far behind.

From the shadows crept the two coyotes. They snarled and growled as they approached the old man. Tuwa stood firm, chanting his prayers. The coyotes circled the man, cautiously aware of the protective spirits Tuwa had summoned to defend him. The animals arose and stretched, morphing back to human form, and positioned themselves in an effort to surround him. Behind Tuwa and to the front now stood two skinwalkers with black-painted faces. Coyote skins draped from their heads and down their backs. Recognizing them from the assault in the cavern of glyphs,

Tuwa cautiously pivoted and maneuvered, trying to keep them both in view as they circled.

"Where is your seer?" one ghoul hissed in a legion of voices. "Where is the Earthkeeper?"

"Safe," replied Tuwa, constantly moving within his circle to maintain sight of both skinwalkers.

"Close your eyes and tell me where you see him, shaman," the witch hissed.

"No," insisted Tuwa.

The fiend sprang toward him, screeching, "Then I will take your eyes!"

At the boundary of Tuwa's circle, the skinwalker was thrown back forcibly, tumbling across the rocky ground. The lanky witch shot to his feet and roared, projecting on its waves of sound the massive specter of a frightful demon with a spiked exoskeleton, his whole being from head to toe, a piercing weapon. The discarnate wraith punched though Tuwa's defenses and grabbed him by the throat, choking him of air. Within Tuwa's protective sphere, his human and animal guardian spirits fought fiercely, hacking through the demon's armored limb. The severed appendage scattered and dissipated into the air like a black cloud of ash and smoke.

Weakened and gasping to recover his breath, Tuwa focused all his hope and prayer on his defenses. Rhythmically chanting and shaking his gourd rattle, he knew his guardian spirits of human ancestors and animal guides could harm only the incorporeal beings. But the temporal skinwalkers, housed in physical bodies, had the upper hand. It would be only a matter of time before they would wear him down and overcome his protective Medicine. The exhausted old man knew he was no match to fight off the demons in their host bodies.

The skinwalkers stood several feet from the cornmeal circle, their bodies contorted unnaturally as their earsplitting screeches continued to project their demonic overlords into a chaotic fracas with Tuwa's guardian spirits. The frantic battle raged at the boundary of the protective sphere, the demons and guardian spirits inflicting equal damage upon each other.

Running swiftly through the moonlit canyon, Kurt hurried to the sound of Tuwa's invocations. Recognizing the sacred incantations as a call to arms, Kurt snapped a dry limb from a lightning-struck ironwood tree, the branch splintering into a stiff jagged edge. At top speed, he burst from the shadows. With a mighty cry, he jabbed the splintered stave several inches into the back of one of the skinwalkers necks, wedging it under the base of his skull and prying upward, severing the nerves and spinal column. Propelled on its final scream, its connection to the crumpling, lifeless host-body cut, the demon—a dark, indistinct humanoid form—tumbled into the fray of Tuwa's sphere where it was overcome by the warring spirits and disappeared in an acrid cloud of dust.

The spike-shelled demon screeched and retreated back into its host body. Instantly morphing back to coyote form, it lunged wildly at Kurt, knocking him to the ground. The ravenous animal snarled as it clamped down on Kurt's upper leg and thrashed its head in a frenzy, its long canine teeth searching for the femoral artery as they shredded the soft tissue of his inner thigh. Tuwa paced nervously within his circle watching Kurt holler and squeal. Kurt determinedly fought the beast with one hand, pounding its hard head and digging for the eyes, while his other hand struggled desperately to dislodge the bloody ironwood stake from the skull of the skinwalker he had just dispatched.. The coyote's keen ears twitched and perked. The coyote inexplicably released its grip and scurried away, leaving Kurt writhing on the ground, his hands clutched tightly around his leg.

Climbing the ground that sloped steeply from the canyon wall to the base of Spider Rock, Mike cupped his hands around his mouth, calling, "Eric! Eric, where are you?"

"Here! I'm here!"

"Eric is that you?" Mike shouted happily, his resounding voice echoing through the canyon. "Where are you?"

"Up here!" Eric called, his voice bouncing faintly off the rocky walls.

Mike clawed at Oliver's shoulders, shaking him excitedly. "I knew it! I knew he had made it!" he cheered. He cupped his hands and hollered, "Are you at the top?"

"Not quite!"

"He must be there on the lower part," Oliver said, pointing up at the lesser of the two spires silhouetted against the stormy sky. "How in the world did he get up there?" he sighed, awed by the imposing, impossibly vertical formation.

Mike and Oliver were suddenly thrown to the ground, having been pushed apart as something blurred between them. Mike shook it off in time to see a figure fading into the darkness, running up the steep cliff face. "Oh no!" he cried. He called up, "Eric, there's somebody coming!"

Charlie rose excitedly from his rocky perch at the edge of the secondary peak. "Eric, did you hear that? Someone's coming. We're saved!"

Eric's heart sank as the crystal reflected the foreboding image of his ghost-faced adversary running swiftly and effortlessly up the side of the tower. He rose to mentally prepare himself. He breathed deeply as the leather-bound handle of his war club squeaked and crackled in his tightly gripped hand.

Nearly seven hundred feet below, Mike and Oliver paced helplessly when from the darkness sprang a dark figure with a skull-painted face. It flew several feet through the air and latched onto the sheer side of the spire, crouched like a frog. Mike recognized it immediately as the one that had nearly taken him down during their last encounter; the one who had lost his left hand to Ocho in wolf form. Clumsily bounding up the wall, the one-handed figure leapt from rock to rock.

Before the creature had climbed too far out of reach, Mike sprang into action. Climbing after him, he soon had a grip on the skinwalker's left heel. The witch kicked wildly, trying to shake him off as Mike slashed Ocho's blade several times through the calf muscles and Achilles tendons of both its legs. Mike spat out the blood as it dripped down onto his face and ran into his eyes and mouth.

Taking a firm toehold and grip on the rocky cliff face, he strained with all his might to rip the skinwalker from the wall. The two tumbled backward twelve feet to the rocks below. The impact knocked the knife from Mike's hand. It skittered across the ground and settled with a scattering of coarse sand several feet away.

Writhing with the wind knocked out of him, Mike felt around in the dark for the knife. Belly crawling after him, the skinwalker wrapped his incomplete limb around Mike's neck and locked it tight with his one hand.

The foes wrestled and squirmed around one another like snakes as the skinwalker struggled to maneuver into position to snap Mike's neck. Managing to get a firm grip on the skinwalker's pinky and ring fingers, Mike pried them back, snapping them at the knuckle. The skull-painted skinwalker hissed and growled, straining to maintain his grip. Mike lowered his head, wedging his chin between his throat and the skinwalker's arm to protect his vital breathing. Clawing at the witch's face and smearing the slippery grease paint with his left hand, Mike searched to gouge at the soft, vulnerable eyes.

Mike fought with all his might, but was no match for the ghoul's strength and stamina. He tired and slowed, no longer able to stay a step ahead of his opponent. The witch soon had him pinned facedown in the wet sand, adjusting his grip to break Mike's neck. Mike grunted through his nose, his vision and hearing fading and muscles relaxing as the skinwalker tightened his grip.

Warm blood sprayed over him and the ground when Oliver raced up behind them and jabbed Ocho's knife deep into the skinwalker's neck, slicing through the jugular. Oliver easily pulled the limp body off of Mike and began sawing through the neck when the coyote demon bolted from the shadows. Transforming as it leapt though the air, the gangly skinwalker, draped in a flapping coyote skin, slammed Oliver to the ground, ripping his arm awkwardly behind him with a loud pop. Oliver cried out in agony, his shoulder badly dislocated.

Suddenly the snarling white wolf streaked onto the scene and with a menacing growl knocked the skin-wearing witch to the ground. With blinding speed the wolf 's teeth ripped into the skinwalker's neck and shoulder.

Mike cheered happily, "Ocho!"

287

The wolf and the skinwalker tumbled violently across the rough ground as the lanky savage fought and bucked. Breaking free from the gleaming-white lycanthrope's toothy grip, the wounded witch jumped high onto the sheer side of Spider Rock, beyond the wolf's reach, and began to climb. The wolf scampered and paced back and forth along the base of the tower, ferociously barking and bouncing wildly off the rocky wall. It jumped higher and higher, its claws scratching at the coarse sandstone as it tried to gain footing on a protruding ledge. But each attempt failed and he tumbled back to the ground with a thud.

Still recovering from his bout with the skull-faced ghoul, Mike panted heavily as he raced to help Oliver pop his shoulder back into place.

"Go! Stop him!" Oliver shouted, handing Mike the large bowie knife.

Mike sheathed the knife in the fringed buckskin holster hung around his waist and sped away, slowly and steadily climbing up the sheer sandstone after the coyote-skinned witch.

As Mike scaled the rocky wall, the white wolf made one final leap against the stone tower and fell backwards, again hitting the ground hard. Shivering and contorting violently, the beast released Ocho's physical properties. The wolf's sparkling molecules swirled in a vortex of shimmering light. His transfiguration complete, Ocho stood straight and removed his bow from his back and an arrow from his quiver. Mightily he drew back the bowstring and squinted along the arrow shaft, searching the dark, lightning-flashed monolith above him for a target.

Finding the skinwalker high up the tower, Ocho loosed the arrow, sending it straight to its target. The shaft pierced the ghoul just below the left shoulder, pinning the coyote pelt tightly to his back. The skinwalker screamed out in pain. The pace of his climbing slowed. Dashing for the base of Spider Rock, Ocho tossed his bow and quiver of arrows to the ground and joined the chase, heaving himself upward ledge by ledge, handhold by handhold.

Retrieving the weapon from the ground, Oliver darted back away from the wall and scanned the cliff face above. Spotting the skinwalker a hundred feet up, he put the feathered shaft of the arrow to the string and pulled it back. The tension aggravated his sore shoulder, and his arm trembled painfully as he aimed and fired. The missile bounced off the rock several feet to the right of its target. Oliver drew another arrow back, sighted and released. This time the arrow sunk deep into the skinwalker's side.

Advancing cautiously up the spire, Mike glanced at the darkened ground nearly a hundred feet below and spotted Ocho further down the wall climbing toward him. The pinnacle loomed above him against a turbulent sky. Mike stretched to reach a narrow crag. Working his fingers into position, he lunged upward but lost his grip. His eyes as big as saucers and heart pounding in his chest, he slid down a flared, near-vertical slab of sandstone. Mike's face, arms, and knees scraped painfully against the gritty surface. His burning and bleeding fingers clawed at the rock as he slid downward.

Anxiously standing guard over the crystal at the center of the precipice, Eric scanned the dark void beyond the edges for any sign of his approaching enemy. His heart boomed in his chest, each throbbing pulse seeming to echo in his white-knuckled hand wrapped tightly around the handle of his war club. Concerned for Charlie who was resting flippantly near the edge at the far end of the peak, Eric barked, "Charlie, get over here!"

Charlie huffed, tossed a rock over the side, and rose grudgingly to stand with Eric and the Earthkeeper at the center of their island in the sky. Overhead, the bulging, gray clouds surged and flickered with electricity, the shattering boom resounding throughout the canyon. Eric continued watching the perimeter carefully. He yelled at Charlie, "Keep your eyes peeled."

"What for?" Charlie sneered.

Just then, the hideous white-faced ghoul launched over the lip of the secondary summit, landing crouched and ready to lunge from the protruding rock that rose above the ledge. Startled, Charlie and Eric sprang back. As his chest heaved, the sinuous cordage that bound the teddy bear tightly to the skinwalker's back gouged deeper into his blistered skin, and a rumbling growl rattled behind his clenched yellowed teeth.

Eric looked with disgust at the shriveled breast and baby's fingers as they swung on the braided cord hung around the necromancer's neck. He remembered the night the apparition of Oliver's grandfather appeared to exorcise the ghosts of Oliver's mother, grandmother, and twin brother—the way they dissipated into the air as shimmering white smoke when pulled from Oliver's chest. Glancing back at the bear tied to the skinwalker, he realized that the imprisoned spirits the witch derived much of his power from had been freed. Without questioning how he knew or by how much, Eric was aware that the skinwalker's power had been drastically weakened. Weapon in hand, he stood defiantly, taunting the witch, "Cute teddy bear."

The skinwalker cocked his head and scowled at Eric.

"You're not so tough now, are you? Not that you ever were," Eric mocked. "Killing women and a baby. Real tough guy, huh? You're weak and it shows. I know you're not so powerful now that your father has come to free the *chindi* you kept. The spirits of the family you murdered."

With a sinister grin, the witch brandished a claw-like weapon, crudely fashioned from a sharpened deer antler. For a brief moment, Eric's heart sank and he began to deflate. But he was intensely reinvigorated when he sensed his power animal, the sleek black jaguar, manifesting within him.

Equipped with vision able to simultaneously perceive the spirits of the elemental world and the beings residing in the material world, the skinwalker watched the glossy cat ferociously pacing the ground in front of Eric. The hideous wraith glanced at the higher summit that loomed above them, where he saw the spindly legs of the gigantic spider deity emerging from a rippling portal in the sky above the tower. Aware of the strength available to Eric, his fierce black eyes focused coldly on Charlie. He growled deeply, in a voice like a thousand screeching whispers, "You."

Eric held Charlie back safely behind the readied war club in his raised hand. Skirting around Eric, Charlie approached the demon explaining, "I'm sorry, he just won't listen to reason."

Frustrated, Eric shouted, "Get back here, you fool!"

"I tried to stop him but he was assisted by the pagans' black magic."

The witch laughed raucously. With blurring speed, it swooped down on Charlie and thrust the sharpened antler deeply into his belly. With a twist, the skinwalker yanked the weapon out. Charlie looked down at his open wound, stunned as his bowels bulged through the tattered opening sending a curtain of blood splattering on the rocky ground at his feet. The ghoul's empty black eyes stared coldly at Charlie as he crumpled to his knees and folded over, his face pressed into the ground.

With a roar, Eric lunged through the air at the fiend, swinging the club with both hands. The witch easily pivoted to dodge the blow. Slowing time to watch Eric's uncontrolled momentum pull him past, he slashed effortlessly, raking the sharpened claw down Eric's back. Eric screamed in pain as he turned swiftly. The smoky jaguar essence leaped from Eric's chest and dived into the skinwalker's lanky body. Stunned, the skinwalker staggered across the peak and nearly stepped over the edge.

The ghoul leaned back and roared forcibly. The jaguar and his demon overlord tumbled out of him, projected on the deafening sound waves. Eric blinked, confused and amazed by what he was seeing. The gruesome, insect-like demon stood nearly eight feet tall and blazed with fire. Eric was horrified by the specter before him: a preying mantis-like being with a large triangular head and bulbous compound eyes. It was one of the most frightening images of his nightmares. The demon sprang swiftly, seizing the jaguar spirit in its spiked, raptorial forelegs.

"Hang on!" Ocho shouted from below. He climbed as fast as he could to help Mike, who was dangling precariously from the sheer rock high above the canyon floor. Further above him, the coyote-clad skinwalker advanced unhindered toward Eric. Mike's weakening fingers quivered and his knuckles burned as he clawed desperately into the crag. Resolving himself to the thought that he had failed his friend, he looked to the summit far ahead and muttered, "Please help my brother."

Just then, a shimmering viscid cord dropped down from the top of the spire. Mike grunted as he hung from one hand, working feverishly to wrap the sticky strand around his waist. His fingers slipped from the rock and he hurtled toward the ground, working with both hands to secure the web as he fell. The lifeline stretched and sprang back launching him rapidly upward. Catching his breath, Mike looked down to see Ocho ascending swiftly as well, wrapped in a shimmering silken strand of his own.

Hoisted steadily toward the top, the two were soon caught up to the sluggish skinwalker. Determinedly scaling the cliff face, slowed by the arrows in its back, the ghoul struggled to maintain its pace, leaving a trail of blood to mark the path of its ascent. Ocho planted his feet into the wall. Pulling the cord taut, he ran with long bouncing strides across the sheer face until he reached the skinwalker. He gripped a handful of the witch's matted black hair with his left hand and the arrow shaft that stuck from its back with his right. Looking down from above, Mike cheered as Ocho lifted the ghoul from the wall and swung like a pendulum from the web, heaving the monster into the darkness below.

The ghost-faced skinwalker was distracted in frenzied combat with Eric's guardian jaguar spirit. Eric crept surreptitiously along the edge of the tower to flank him. With all his might he swung the war club at the skinwalker. He felt the large, rawhide-bound rock at the tip whip heavily forward in the split second before it collided forcefully with the fiend's head.

Severed from its host, the fiery mantis demon tumbled over the edge. Spreading its large wings, it circled gracefully, gliding back into the skinwalker's body as it collapsed to the ground. Eric pounced. Standing over the bleeding witch, he wound the club back for a killing blow.

Suddenly the faint crying of a baby rang out. Rattled, Eric refocused his eyes, surprised to see a baby lying on the ground at his feet. "Evan?" he asked in confusion. The baby squealed and cried, its hands with splayed, rigid fingers shaking and flailing as they reached to be picked up and held. Eric knew his son had long since passed. Intuitively he knew he was being deceived, but he could not bring himself to deliver the crushing blow that would end the fight.

Beyond the spectrum of his bewitched vision, the jaguar paced frantically, growling at the bloody, smirking skinwalker at Eric's feet. Clinging to the side of the tower that loomed above him, the giant spider watched, concerned as she reeled in her webs to haul Eric's companions closer to the top.

Conflicted, Eric backed away from the screaming baby, refusing to act. He began to weep. His vision became distorted with the flooding of tears. Club in hand, he dropped his guard to wipe his tears on his sleeve. Seizing the moment, the skinwalker shot to his feet and rushed at Eric.

From the ground where he had fallen, Charlie thrust out his hand, latching his fingers tightly around the skinwalker's rangy ankle. The charging ghoul slammed hard onto the rock.

Startled, Eric heaved back the heavy club and swung down to smash the skinwalker's head. In a flash, the witch reassumed the appearance of Eric's whimpering baby. Through tightly shut eyes, Eric sobbed as he delivered blow after blow, pulverizing the skinwalker's head into a gelatinous mass of sopping, black hair and fragments of bone. With each strike, the demon inside the witch was thrust deeper into the sacrosanct monument, imprisoning the neutralized specter within the sandstone of the subsidiary summit.

Charlie strained wobbly to his knees, calling, "Eric, stop! Eric! It's done."

Swinging the club wildly, the wooden handle snapped in his hands sending the stone-topped head flinging over the side. Sobbing uncontrollably, Eric collapsed to the ground, his strength exhausted. Charlie struggled over to Eric, wrapping his arms tightly around him and said compassionately, "God forgives you."

Eric nodded and opened his eyes to see the smoky apparition of his son escaping from his chest. The baby hung in the air, shimmering on the breeze above him. He remembered Ocho's words, "Don't keep him tied to you like that teddy bear, man. Let him go be at peace. Let yourself be at peace."

Eric wiped his tears and sniffed, "I forgive myself." The glowing spirit morphed before his eyes, rapidly aging through childhood and adolescence, growing into a handsome young man with calming, blue eyes. The vision revealed to Eric the true, eternal essence of his son. With a warm, loving smile, Evan disappeared on the wind.

Within moments Ocho and Mike were hoisted over the ledge to join their weary friend. The shimmering strands of web that had brought them dissolved the instant they landed on the lower summit. They looked around in confusion.

"Eric!" Mike rejoiced, running to embrace him.

Eric spoke curtly, "Forget about me, Mike. Charlie is hurt."

Having lost consciousness, Charlie was sprawled on the ground, bleeding from his belly wound. Mike hurriedly assessed him, saying frantically, "He's lost a lot of blood." He removed Charlie's jacket and wrapped it tightly around his waist, tying the sleeves into a knot to hold the innards from bulging further through the gaping hole in his stomach. "If we don't get him down from here and get some help soon, he's not gonna make it."

Ocho circled them nervously, scanning the blackness below the precipice as he paced the perimeter.

Eric inspected the lifeless body of the witch and asked him, "How many more are out there?"

Frustrated, Ocho shook his head, "I don't know."

"We need to finish this now," Eric said urgently. He looked to the top of the towering primary peak looming over them. "Why isn't she helping us now?" he complained.

Confused, Mike asked, "What do you mean?"

"Spider Woman," Eric explained. "She hauled you guys up here. Why can't she help us get the Earthkeeper the rest of the way? What's she waiting for?"

"Grandfather says divine beings won't do for us what we must do for ourselves," said Ocho.

Discouraged, Eric kicked the ground and roared. "We don't have time for this! What the hell are we supposed to do?"

Ocho placed his hands firmly on Eric's shoulders and said softly, "Settle down, dude."

Eric drew in a deep breath and slowly let it out.

"Now," Ocho said calmly, "ask again like you really want to hear the answer; and then listen."

Relaxing his stance, Eric shut his eyes and lowered his head.

"What is it you want?" Ocho asked softly. "Express gratitude, seeing it in your mind as though you already have it."

Eric's eyelids parted slightly, his eyes glancing around at the guys before settling on the Earthkeeper. Again he shut his eyes, holding the image of the crystal in his mind and asked internally, *how do we get up there*?

Moments later, he opened his eyes, frustrated. *Maybe you will tell me*, he thought, slowly approaching the Earthkeeper. Kneeling, he laid his hands gently on the smooth sides and gazed deeply into the large crystal. Scrying the Earthkeeper for information, an image formed in his mind of the four of them surrounding the crystal at the top of Spider Rock. He focused intently on the image until he assumed the point of view of his other self—the one in the vision. From the highest point of the spire, he looked down to the lower tower. The four of them and the crystal faded in and out of existence on the lower summit then inexplicably disappeared.

He looked around in wonder, focusing on the crystal before him. Mike and Ocho stood to the sides of the Earthkeeper with Charlie on the other side, unconscious on the ground. Eric looked down at the twisted body of the dead skinwalker on the secondary summit two hundred feet below. Speechless, Mike and Ocho looked around in disbelief. Laying his hand on the vibrating crystal, Eric met their wide, puzzled eyes. "Matter follows vision," he said with a coy grin.

The guys flinched and covered their heads as the bulging clouds above them crackled with brilliant white light, the shattering boom resonating in their chests. For miles in all directions, lightning streaked unremittingly through the sky. Bolt after bolt connected to the ground throughout the region surrounding the canyon.

Warm, tingling energy coursed from Spider Rock, through the Earthkeeper, and into Eric's hand, traveling throughout his body. The hair on his arms and head stood on end.

Laughing, Ocho pointed at Eric's hair, saying, "I love that crazy do."

"No! Eric…," shouted Mike as a white hot bolt of lightning shot down with a thunderous crack to connect with the leading energy that flowed up through Eric's body.

Some time later, Eric blinked open his enormously dilated eyes, frantically searching for the giant crystal. It was gone. The once murky-white stone that capped the tip of Spider Rock was now as clear as glass, fused with the properties of the Earthkeeper crystal, and gleaming with brilliant light. The billions upon billions of quartz flecks embedded within the sandstone that comprised the region were sparkling brilliantly, appearing like the stars that dotted the now clear skies above them. Eric looked out along the dark horizon, intrigued at how, with the twinkling stars in the sky above and the shimmering points of light in the ground below, the blackness beyond resembled the dark jagged swaths of galactic dust that divides the center of the Milky Way. It was as though the heavens were brought to Earth.

Materializing on a whirlwind of radiant light, a resplendent old Indian woman appeared before Eric and smiled. Her eyes beamed with adoration. She spoke directly into his mind, saying, "You did it, child. Thank you."

Confused, Eric asked, "What'd I do?"

Amused, the grandmotherly woman smiled. "Oh, *Hóya Mochni*, may you never lose your questioning nature."

"Really," Eric asked, "What'd I do?"

As she rapidly faded from sight, her voice echoed in his mind. "Most importantly, you took the first important step in becoming the man you were meant to be."

Eric intrinsically knew he had been shown the earthly face of Spider Woman. He understood that her appearing to him in human form was a result of his successfully bringing the Earthkeeper to Spider Rock. The crystal's energy had reestablished a permanent portal to allow the benevolent deity constant access between worlds. From her place in the material world, she could use her weaving power to influence the stability and fertility of the region. Those still blinded behind the veil that separated their world from hers could now learn to access the ability to weave their thoughts to transform the fabric of the material realm.

Sprawled across the luminous peak, Mike and Ocho were out cold, along with Charlie. Eric knelt between them, resting his hands gently on their shoulders. Immediately, they regained consciousness.

Ocho looked up at Eric, grinning. In a high voice, he squeaked, "My hero."

Eric laughed. "Guys, get up, you gotta see this," he said excitedly. Mike and Ocho rose vibrantly to their feet. "You alright?" Eric asked.

"Great," Mike replied, looking out awestruck by the glittering canyon.

"Never felt better," said Ocho, smiling widely.

Turning his attention to Charlie, who was lowly moaning as he drifted in and out of consciousness, Eric said urgently, "Let's get him some help."

# Chapter Thirty-seven

Staring over the edge of the pinnacle to the flickering ground far below, Mike and Ocho looked to Eric for some indication of what to do next. Eric jerked his head toward the edge to suggest that they jump over. They had learned over the last few days to expect miracles. They took several deep breaths and all together jumped into the dark abyss.

"This is awesome!" shouted Mike, as they fell. The forceful wind blasted through his mouth and filled his sinus cavities while tears rolled up his face from the corners of his eyes.

The sheer face of Spider Rock, just feet away, blurred past as they plummeted, rapidly free-falling for nearly ten seconds, though it felt much longer.

Watching the ground race up to meet him, Ocho grimaced nervously. Inexplicably, he and the others rapidly came to a near-stop, just feet above the Earth. Silken strands connected to them set them gently on their feet. The webs dissolved from their waists as Mike and Eric roared and cheered. They chest-bumped and high-fived like rowdy teenagers at a theme park. Ocho dropped to his knees, bending over to kiss the earth. He looked to the peak high above and said reverently, "Thank you."

Oliver scrambled over excitedly to greet his companions. "That looked like so much fun! What an amazing night!" he said.

"The people will be so happy to know that Spider Woman still cares for her children."

Noticing Eric's bloody shredded shirt, Oliver examined his back for injury. Finding no wound, he asked with much surprise, "You're not hurt?"

Eric wrenched his neck to look over his shoulder and inspect his back. He answered happily, "I guess not."

"You and Ocho are okay too?" he asked.

Ocho nodded in agreement as Mike answered enthusiastically, "I feel great! Really charged!"

The four of them looked skyward to watch Charlie's slow, controlled descent. Wrapped in a cocoon woven from Spider Woman's shimmering thread, the unconscious Charlie was soon set gently on the ground. Ocho gingerly lifted the cocoon and cradled Charlie's limp body in his arms. They each quietly expressed thoughts of gratitude to Spider Woman and set off toward the town of Chinle.

Shortly into their journey, they rounded a bend in the wide canyon and saw two figures moving slowly through the darkness toward them. Mike jerked the large bowie knife from the sheath. In the pale moonlight they soon made out Tuwa and Kurt. The old Hopi lumbered through the sand, supporting Kurt as best he could as he limped along on his painfully bitten leg.

"Oh no, Kurt. Your leg!" Oliver exclaimed. "God, I hope that doesn't slow you down too long."

"Me too," Kurt said sadly, looking down at his mangled upper thigh, bandaged tightly with the blood-soaked nylon pant leg from his breakaway track pants. "I don't know what I would do if I couldn't run."

The men cheerfully greeted their Hopi friends. Tuwa dug through his satchel, retrieving a dried sprig of a fragrant velvety-leafed plant and a fan made of feathers. Striking a match, he set fire to the cluster of leaves and blew it out. A rich, pleasant smoke wafted from the sprig. Tuwa approached Eric with the smoldering herb.

Eric stepped back hesitantly, asking with a twisted face, "What is that?"

"Sage," Tuwa answered confidently. "It is a cleansing ritual, similar to what you saw when Oliver was blessed by his grandfather."

One by one, Tuwa smudged the crew with the purifying smoke. They then rested briefly to share stories of what they had been through and accomplished during the night. Tuwa beamed proudly as Eric explained how he had moved the Earthkeeper to the highest point of Spider Rock. His spiritual guide showed particular pleasure and interest in hearing Eric's account of meeting the grandmotherly Spider Woman deity.

"She was just so beautiful and loving," said Eric adoringly. "She said something strange though, in some other language. Something like, um, *Hóya Mochni?*"

"She was speaking Hopi," said Tuwa. Interestedly, he asked, "How did she use it?"

"She said something like, 'Oh, *Hóya Mochni*, don't ever stop asking questions,' or something like that." Eric smiled. "She was so loving. I got the sense she was just really amused by me, like how adults get when kids say cute stuff."

"Spider Woman gave you a Medicine name," Tuwa explained excitedly. "Hopi words can have different meanings, depending on how they are used. *Hóya* comes from a traditional dance about leaving the nest. The way she used it, she called you 'Free'. She acknowledges the same freedom in you that has impressed me so much—the way you are open to seeing things in new ways because you are not restricted by any set dogmas, and your willingness to question the nature of greater mysteries."

Eric grinned pretentiously, saying, "And the maverick finally gets his due." Then he asked, "What does *Mochni* mean?"

"Bird."

Mike, Ocho, Oliver, and Kurt roared with laughter while Eric pouted his lip and furled his eyebrows in a scowl.

Amidst the snickers from the younger men, Tuwa asked in confusion, "Why is that funny?"

Mike snorted and wiped tears from his eyes, barely able to speak through his laughter. "Free Bird? She named him Free Bird? It's a classic rock song! There's not a bar band in the world that hasn't had some belligerent drunk request 'Free Bird!'"

Feigning inebriation, Ocho cupped his hands and hollered in a deep, slurred voice, "Free Bird."

Eric blushed with embarrassment.

Not amused, Tuwa spoke seriously. "Well, I think it fits."

"Whatever. Screw all ya'll," Eric said in a disappointed voice. "We better hurry and get Charlie to the medical clinic in Chinle."

"I'm on it, Free Bird," said Ocho emphatically as he lifted Charlie.

Mike rose, razzing Eric by obnoxiously vocalizing the distinctive guitar riff.

"Yeah, you're real funny," Eric huffed.

Walking ahead of Ocho, Eric moped along sullenly following the group as they blazed through the winding canyons. Tuwa fell back and approached him as they walked. "You don't like the Medicine name you were given?" he asked.

With a long face, Eric shook his head, upset about being fodder for laughs. "It makes sense, I guess. I've always loved birds, and they apparently love me back. I just hate that stupid song," he said crossly.

"It's not about the song," said Tuwa.

"Well what it is then? Why would she give me a name that would open me up to potshots like that?"

"You are growing and learning very quickly," said Tuwa, "opening to understand visions and concepts that most people will never begin to glimpse. The most important aspect of spiritual enlightenment is knowing to never take yourself too seriously. Forget the song. Remember the meaning behind your new name."

Shaking it off, Eric nodded.

Tuwa carefully looked Eric over, inspecting the air around him. "Are you feeling okay?"

"I'll get over it."

"I mean, are you sick or hurt after being struck by lightning like that?"

"My ears have been buzzing with a lot of noise since then. It's like being in a crowded place. And stuff looks different," Eric admitted.

"How so?" asked Tuwa

301

"I don't know—different. Strange."

Tuwa's eyes asked for more information.

"Everything seems pixilated, I guess, like a bunch of little pinwheels spinning. In the static, I see a persistent overlapping image: a tall, wide-based shape, a latticed structure of some kind. I don't know, almost like a radio tower or something. It seems familiar. No biggie, it's easy enough to look past and ignore." Eric glanced around the moonlit canyon at the different trees and shrubs. "Also everything has a faint halo around it. I don't know, maybe I've got a migraine coming on or something."

Tuwa nodded. "Maybe."

"One weird thing, though. When we were resting back there? Before you blessed us all with that sage smoke? In the halos around the guys, there were dark, jagged patterns interrupting the glow around them. And there were all these, like, weird little faces outlined by the smoke, and they scurried away real fast when you waved the feathers over them. Who knows? I am really tired. Maybe my eyes are just playing tricks on me."

"They'll get clearer," Tuwa assured him.

Although Eric was not yet ready to accept it, Tuwa had gathered from their earlier conversations that the young man had always been blessed with a form of divination, being presented with messages that were embedded within the fragments of audio that streamed together as he scrolled obsessively through the radio and television stations. Watching how Eric had been experiencing visions more frequently throughout their journey, Tuwa was happy to see that Eric was rapidly opening to continuously see two worlds simultaneously: the world of spirit and the temporal realm grafted onto it. It was a common trait among Native American Medicine men and other shamans of the varying cultures of the world, past and present, and one that Tuwa also shared. Looking Eric over, Tuwa wondered what other abilities were yet to manifest as a result of the energy exchange that took place at the moment of the lightning strike, when elements of the powerful Earthkeeper and the sacred site merged with him.

The night grew eerily darker and silent as the group traversed a narrow passage between a thick grove of cottonwoods and shrubs. Eric's senses were heightened. His ears twitched tightly, searching for any sound as his keen eyes scanned the darkness.

Unaware of the shift in energy, Mike and Oliver chattered happily as they outpaced the others. Taken by surprise, the coyote-clad skinwalker sprang at them from the darkness, knocking Mike to the ground. His weakened shoulder popping loudly, Oliver cried out in pain as the ghoul took him by the arm and flung him through the air into a large tree trunk. The fiend was on top of him before he could recover. Mike raced up from behind to grab the witch around the neck. Kurt sprinted over as fast as his injured leg would allow, joining the struggle to pull the enemy off of Oliver.

The snarling skinwalker thrashed and bucked wildly, digging his clawed hand into Kurt's wound. With a mighty surge of power, he threw Mike and Kurt like rag dolls across the ground as Eric joined the melee. The witch jerked a small bone dagger from his knotted hair and leaped at Eric. With lightning fast reflexes, Eric raised his hands, freezing the witch midair.

Confused, Eric looked to the others for an explanation. Their faces awash with astonishment, Mike and Oliver approached the suspended skinwalker for a closer look. Kurt limped over and glowered bitterly. "It's the one that mauled my leg."

Ocho hurried to catch up. Setting Charlie's silken cocoon gently on the ground, he circled the suspended skinwalker. Noting the arrow wounds in its back, he grumbled, "I was worried we might see this one again." He set off to investigate the surrounding area and found a moth floating motionless in the air as well. Upon closer examination of the sinister witch, he was able to detect extremely slow movement. He turned to Eric, saying excitedly, "You slowed time!"

Eric was astounded. "Really? How?"

"Who cares?" replied Ocho. "Think of how easy it'll be to kill this one."

Mike removed the belt from his waist, returning the sheathed knife to Ocho, who yanked out the blood-crusted blade and clutched a mass of hair and coyote skin in his enormous hand.

"Wait!" said Kurt angrily. "This one's mine."

Standing down, Ocho flipped the knife, presenting it to Kurt handle first. Kurt eagerly took the enormous knife and limped toward his nemesis. Eric watched him approach the skinwalker and noticed an unusual mass slithering within Kurt's aura. He recognized the reptilian beast. It was like the inherent evil he had encountered rising from within himself at the seer's temple. Visible only to Eric, the multiple-headed creature swelled beyond the boundaries of Kurt's energy field, wrapping its venom-barbed tentacles around both the frozen skinwalker and Kurt as he determinedly raised the blade.

"Stop!" shouted Eric.

Resentfully, Kurt lowered the blade and scowled at Eric, his expression demanding to know why.

Channeling words from somewhere beyond himself, Eric pointed to the skinwalker and admonished, "When we lust for killing or kill for revenge, we lose ourselves to the same evil that overtook him."

Disappointed and angry, Kurt looked to his mentor. Tuwa nodded in agreement with Eric. "So, what, we're just gonna leave him there?" he asked scornfully.

"Oh, we're gonna kill him." Eric immediately replied. "He has to be put down. But for the safety of the people of this world and the protection of what is right, not revenge."

Kurt clenched his teeth and gripped the knife tightly, scowling at Eric. Behind his fiery visage, the evil inside him swelled menacingly, the sinuous snake heads writhing and striking, snapping their fang-filled jaws inches from Eric's unflinching face. Eric stared down the beast, saying calmly to Kurt, "You can still choose. Just let it go. You know what is right."

With a hesitant nod, Kurt handed the knife back to Ocho. Instantly the beast deflated and retreated within him. "You're right, Eric. Thank you."

Ocho drew in a calming breath and plunged the knife into the immobilized skinwalker's throat. No blood escaped as Ocho easily sliced off the head and handed it to Eric. Hearing the demon thrashing around inside it, he walked purposefully into the grove and wedged the head deeply within the tangled knot of branches in a nearby tree.

Rejoining the group, Eric said, "Let's roll," as if nothing had happened.

Without warning, the skinwalker's lifeless body dropped to the ground, sending forth a wide, spreading pool of blood.

Playing cat and mouse for the better part of the night, Truman and Kilgore had exhausted nearly all of their training and cunning to stalk and outsmart the other. Truman crept along the boulder-strewn ridge that framed the valley, pushing his opponent closer to the coulee below the highway. Unaware that his family was not where he had instructed them to camp, he was anxious to neutralize his enemy before he would stumble upon them.

As Truman peeked around a large rock face, the moonlight revealed the shape of a man lying on his belly. He was positioned behind a row of rocks further down the ridge below him, sighting down the length of a rifle aimed toward the valley beyond. Truman was relieved to have the drop on him. He crept up cautiously behind the man, keeping his rifle trained on the center of his rival's broad back as he approached.

Wanting to confirm the target as his enemy, he held his fire until he could be sure. Drawing closer, Truman's heart sank as he realized he had been duped. The figure he had worked so painstakingly to draw a bead on was nothing more than a pair of pants and a shirt stuffed with scrub brush. The dummy was cleverly positioned behind the rocks to appear to sight down the length of a weapon, which was nothing more than a dried stick of wood.

"You were good," a voice rang out deeply from the cover of a large boulder behind him.

Truman whipped around to face the one who had bested him, seeing only part of the man and his trained weapon silhouetted against the moonlight as he peeked out from behind his well-strategized position. In a dry, deep voice, the man taunted, "Don't worry; we'll take real good care of your wife and daughter."

Truman flinched as a booming gunshot echoed throughout the valley. He frantically searched his body for injury. Confused he looked back at his foe in time to see his limp body slide from the boulder and slump to the ground.

Behind a smoking rifle barrel further up the ridge, beyond the dead antagonist, stood Bobby.

"Dad!" shouted Aaron, jumping from his hiding place behind a boulder. He raced down the hill to Truman, knocking him back slightly as he collided and wrapped his arms tightly around his father's waist.

"I can't stop thinking about Truman all of a sudden," said Eric, blinking compulsively to ignore the persistent image of the large tower that nagged his vision.

"He's probably back at the slot canyon by now, wondering what the hell happened to us," suggested Mike.

"No, I don't think so," answered Eric. "I've got an unsettling feeling about him."

"I've been worried about him too," added Kurt. "I'd better run ahead and look for him."

"Not on that leg," Mike insisted. "Besides, where would you begin to look? You've seen those volcanic plumes from the direction of Flagstaff. There's no way he could have made it back that way."

"Yeah, you're right," Kurt agreed. "That's probably what held him up."

"I sure hope he and his family are alright, though," Mike sighed.

Eric stopped abruptly. His ears strained to listen intently while his eyes searched to locate the sound he was hearing. "Someone's coming," he warned.

They hurried to hide within the darkened grove as the steadily plodding sound of hooves grew nearer. Following the sparkling canyon trail toward them, rode a middle-aged Navajo man leading six horses.

"Who is he, Oliver?" whispered Eric.

"I don't know him."

"Then, maybe we should just let him pass and be on our way," suggested Mike.

"We sure could use those horses, though," said Ocho.

306

"Well, we're not just going to take them," Mike insisted.

"That's right," Eric agreed. "We'll wait for him to pass."

Moments later the mysterious Navajo rode slowly through the grove, looking carefully through the trees on each side. Tightly pulling the reins to stop his horse, the man glanced around cautiously, seemingly waiting for someone—or something. His dirty white horse's ears twitched and his head bobbed nervously. The rider shifted his feet to wedge the heels of his boots tighter against the stirrups. He wore faded black jeans and a blue denim jacket. Pulled low on his head, concealing full view of his face, was a dusty, black cowboy hat with a large, mottled eagle feather in the band.

Counting the horses, Mike whispered nervously, "How many skinwalkers were there? Could he be with them?"

"Skinwalkers don't need horses," insisted Ocho.

They waited nearly ten minutes for the man to leave before Ocho decided he and Oliver would walk out to greet him.

"*Ya'at' eeh*," Ocho called out.

The man kept a cautious eye on Ocho and Oliver as they approached. He asked, "Where is the *belagana*, Free Bird?"

Oliver and Ocho looked at each other smirking, trying to contain their amusement at hearing the name. Listening from their hiding place behind the trees, Mike grinned and slapped Eric on the back.

"*Belagana?*" asked Eric.

"Means white man," explained Tuwa.

Curious how anyone else could be in on the joke of his new nickname, he emerged from the trees. "You found me," he said.

The horseman seemed to recognize him. He smiled saying, "I was told I would find you here."

"Who are you?" demanded Eric, as Tuwa, Mike, and Kurt walked out behind him.

The man answered, "I am Bernard Yazzie of the Cliff Dwellers People, born for the Bitter Water Clan."

"Who told you to look for me? How do you know my name?"

Bernard explained, "Spider Woman came to me in a dream. She showed me what you did here tonight, and asked me to bring horses to help you on your journey."

"Thank you," said Eric welcomingly. "We have an injured friend we're trying to get to medical help."

"By horse, we can be there in under an hour," said Bernard assuredly. Handing Eric a stack of warm frybread bundled in a cotton cloth, he said, "My wife made this for you guys."

After hastily devouring the delicious bread, they were mounted up and on their way. The group couldn't stop laughing at the sight of Ocho sitting so tall that his horse looked like a small pony under him. Eric sat forward in his saddle, sharing his pinto horse with the unconscious Charlie who was slung over the animal's back.

The early morning air was crisp and filled with the pulsing chirps of crickets. The sky above shimmered with bands of violet and green. The steep walls sparkled brilliantly with billions of points of twinkling light as they followed the stream that wound through the canyon floor. Traveling effortlessly by horseback, Eric took advantage of the opportunity to use his energy sensitive eyes to take in the darkened canyon in a new way. The trees radiated shimmering light in a dazzling synchronous display, seemingly to acknowledge Eric as he rode past.

"I have lived here my entire life and never seen it so beautiful," said Bernard.

Within forty minutes they had exited the canyon, emerging onto the road that would take them through the small town of Chinle.

Immediately after crossing the border of the national park, Eric's eyes honed in on a large microwave radio relay tower built onto a small, rundown building. The wide-based tower rose nearly a hundred feet and was covered with parabolic reflectors and large shell antennae. He was troubled to understand why the image pestered his mind, and again thought of Truman. Staring obsessively at the tower, he wrenched his neck and twisted his body sharply in the saddle as he rode past, struggling to understand its significance.

Tuwa maneuvered his horse alongside Eric's and asked, "What is it?"

"I don't know. It's the shape of that tower."

"Is that the one? Is there something important here to be done?"

Frustrated and discouraged, Eric shook his head and set his puzzlement aside. "No, the most important thing right now is getting some help for Charlie here."

The horses' hooves clopped sharply on the heavily eroded asphalt as they rode through town. Although it was early morning—the sun not due to rise for another two hours—many local people had gathered curiously on the sidewalks to watch the procession. Mystified by the brilliantly twinkling landscape, the superstitious Navajos debated on how to interpret the extraordinary omens. They whispered secretively to one another, pointing at the shimmering, silken cocoon and glancing skittishly at Eric.

Coming to a halt in the parking lot, washed out and dotted with potholes, Mike dismounted and dashed around the corner of the building to find the entrance of the small clinic. Hysterically, he ran back to the group, rambling excessively, "It's okay guys, they're open. It's twenty-four hour. I told them we have a critically injured patient coming. They're getting ready for him. Quick, let's get him down from there…"

Irritated, Eric shouted, "Michael!"

Embarrassed, Mike stepped back trying to calm himself.

Eric razzed, "Jeez, you busy body! Even in a small town without power—ten minutes back into civilization, and you're overwhelmed by the buzz."

The group chuckled at how easily the enormous Ocho stepped down from his horse. He walked over and lifted Charlie's cocoon off of Eric's horse.

Climbing down from the saddle, Eric suggested, "Why don't you all wait here? I'll take him in."

With a raised eyebrow, Ocho flashed Eric a dubious look.

"Whatdya think I'm stupid?" Eric quipped. "Of course I was gonna let you lug him in there for me first. Kurt, you'd better come too and get your leg looked at." He turned to their new friend, saying warmly, "Bernard, I can't thank you enough."

With a tip of his hat, he said, "Call me Bernie."

The doctor and his staff were stupefied by the glimmering shroud that was woven tightly around Charlie's limp body. The sticky substance stretched from the white doctor's hands as he searched for some kind of seam or easy way into the cocoon. "What is this?" he asked squeamishly.

Plainly, Eric replied, "Spider's silk."

"What happened?"

"He was stabbed in the belly by a skinwalker," Eric said matter-of-factly. "It's pretty bad. Lost a lot of blood. Spider Woman wrapped him up this way to preserve him until we could get here."

The skeptical doctor stared blankly at Eric as if waiting for him to laugh it off and tell the real story.

Eric snapped impatiently, "You want me to lie?"

Not knowing what to think, the doctor fumbled through the drawers for a pair of shears. The otherworldly veil dissolved the instant the gleaming stainless steel instrument touched it. Charlie sat up with a panicked gasp for air and looked around in confusion.

"It's okay, Charlie," Eric said reassuringly as he eased Charlie back onto the bed.

Exhausted, Charlie struggled to stay alert, his eyes rolling back into his head as he drifted in and out of consciousness.

"Charlie, stay with me. Stay with me," coaxed Eric, slapping his cheek and sharply squeezing his face as the doctor assessed his condition. "Charlie, tell me about your family. You have kids?"

Charlie gasped tiredly, "All dead. Drunk driver. Catholic priest, of all people." On faltering breath he murmured with disdain, "Abominable church."

Eric was empathetic, finally able to understand and forgive why Charlie had been so insistent on preventing him from achieving what he perceived to be the stopping of Armageddon. He remembered the strict doctrines of the faith they once shared in common, particularly the adamant rejection of the notion of an immortal spirit. Charlie had been operating on the belief that at the moment his family was killed in the accident, they were simply extinguished. His only hope in ever being with them again was in the resurrection to come after the Armageddon of his belief.

"He's lost a lot of blood," said the doctor. "Without a transfusion, he's not going to make it. But we don't have a large enough supply here." Frustrated, the doctor paced anxiously, thinking. "Ordinarily we would rush patients to the hospital in Shiprock for an injury of this nature. But without power or functioning vehicles…"

"Use my blood," Eric urged.

Shocked, the doctor looked at him strangely.

"I'm a universal donor."

Charlie clutched Eric's arm with his weakened hand. In a quiet, gravelly voice he whispered, "No. Let me go."

"What? No," Eric insisted. "You saved me back there, Charlie. Now I'm going to save you."

"I am saved."

Frustrated, Eric argued, "It's because the church forbids transfusions, isn't it?"

Charlie nodded. Short of breath, he mumbled tiredly, "If I break that law, I can't be resurrected to share eternity with my family."

Unable to contain his contempt for the rigid dogma, Eric rolled his eyes and scoffed.

"You know the Truth," Charlie whispered exhaustedly.

"I do," Eric contended angrily, unable to let go of the impression that he somehow had to repay him for tripping up the skinwalker. "I know that deep inside you are afraid to die. I know you have at least a shred of doubt, but you are too afraid to question it—afraid that if you go against the doctrines to save yourself, you will damn your self."

Charlie's eyes confirmed what Eric had said.

"So what's it gonna be then?" Eric asked sharply. "What is it that guides you, here in the end? Faith or fear?"

"Fear," Charlie gasped, a tear rolling down his cheek. "All my life, fear. Fear of this moment." He squeezed Eric's hand and looked him in the eye. "But, here in the end? Faith."

311

Eric smiled acceptingly and whispered in his ear, "It's not the end." He pulled back and looked Charlie in the eyes. "I'm glad you were here. You helped me more than you could know."

Charlie closed his eyes and settled back into his pillow. Minutes later, his hand went limp and slid from Eric's as he let out a deep, final breath. Eric watched Charlie's smoky apparition escape from the body and float to the ceiling. Looking down at Eric and his body, Charlie's eyes grew wide with surprise.

Eric looked up at the spirit and smiled. "You just go someplace else," he explained encouragingly. "Go and find your family. Just follow your thoughts of them."

Charlie smiled and faded quickly from sight.

Eric sank into the soft chair beside Charlie's body and rested comfortably for several minutes, thinking. Then he rose to share the news with the rest of the gang. He emerged from the clinic to a clear, sunlit morning. A small crowd of curious Navajos had gathered outside the medical center. Oliver stood surrounded by the crowd, recounting the story of their quest. Upon seeing Eric, the crowd glanced over whispering, their eyes not landing directly on him. Many timidly scampered off, unable to see past their superstitious fear of contact with lightning-struck objects.

Looking up and down the desolate street, Eric took notice of the many different churches and businesses crammed into the half-mile stretch of road: the Catholics, Baptists, Lutherans, Seventh Day Adventists, Mormons, the closed Burger King and Chevron fueling station, and directly across the street, the Kingdom Hall of the Jehovah's Witness all competing for the patronage of the town's meager population of people.

Ocho and Mike hurried over. "How is he? Can we see him?" Mike asked.

Eric shook his head, saying delicately, "He's not there."

Mike understood the meaning of Eric's esoteric answer and looked at the ground sadly. With a brief nod, he laid his hand gently on Eric's shoulder. "I figured his chances were slim."

Eric pointed at Bernard waiting patiently with the horses and asked, "What's he still doing here?"

"He said he'd wait to see if we might still need him," Ocho explained.

Mike asked, "So, what do we do now? What's next?"

Eric leaned wearily against the wall. "Oh, I don't know. Settle in. Get some rest. Wait for a sign, I guess."

Just then, from the direction of Canyon de Chelly, a large, familiar, boomerang-shaped craft gleaming as bright as the sun glided overhead. Mike and Ocho giggled excitedly while Eric rolled his eyes. The object stopped and hovered beyond a row of tall power line towers in the distance. Eric's thoughts were inexplicably called back to Truman. Overcome with nagging worry, Eric finally made the connection between the image that lingered in his mind and his strange dream about the armed men who launched their raids from the fortified power line tower.

"Tuwa! Oliver!" Mike called, pointing at the strange object.

Silently, the anomalous triangle drifted north, northwest in the direction of the slot canyon, soon disappearing from view.

Ocho smirked slyly. "Follow the signs, dude." He slapped Eric on the back and whooped, "Let's fly, Free Bird."

# About the Author

Ethan Foxx holds a Bachelors degree in History and English, with a concentration of study in Southwest cultures. Ethan conducts tours of the Grand Canyon, Sedona, and places throughout the reservation lands of Northern Arizona. He is an accomplished artist in many expressive mediums. As a painter, Ethan uses airbrush, acrylics and oils to paint handmade drums, as well as traditional surface mediums. Ethan is also a vocalist and multi-instrumentalist musician, known for his work in several musical styles. Ethan maintains the website www.EthanFoxx.com to display and promote his works. Ethan lives with his children in Glendale, Arizona.

www.ingramcontent.com/pod-product-compliance
Lightning Source LLC
Chambersburg PA
CBHW051238260626
47162CB00002B/502